TO KILL A CONSUL

THE HISTORIES OF SPHAX SERIES

BOOK FOUR

ROBERT M. KIDD

While some of the events and character are based on historical events and figures, this novel is entirely a work of fiction.

978-1-8382720-8-1 Kindle/e-book
978-1-8382720-9-8 Paperback

The Histories of Sphax series

~ book four ~

Dedicated to Margaret Clarkson

Insubres
Podonus river
Placentia
Boii
N
W
E
S
Adriatic
Sea
Bona
Mutina
Ariminum
Pisae
Arnus
river
Faesulae
Arretium
Etrusia
Cortona
Perusia
Lake
Trasimene
Umbria
Cosa
Rome
Campaign
Map
Tyrrhenian
Sea

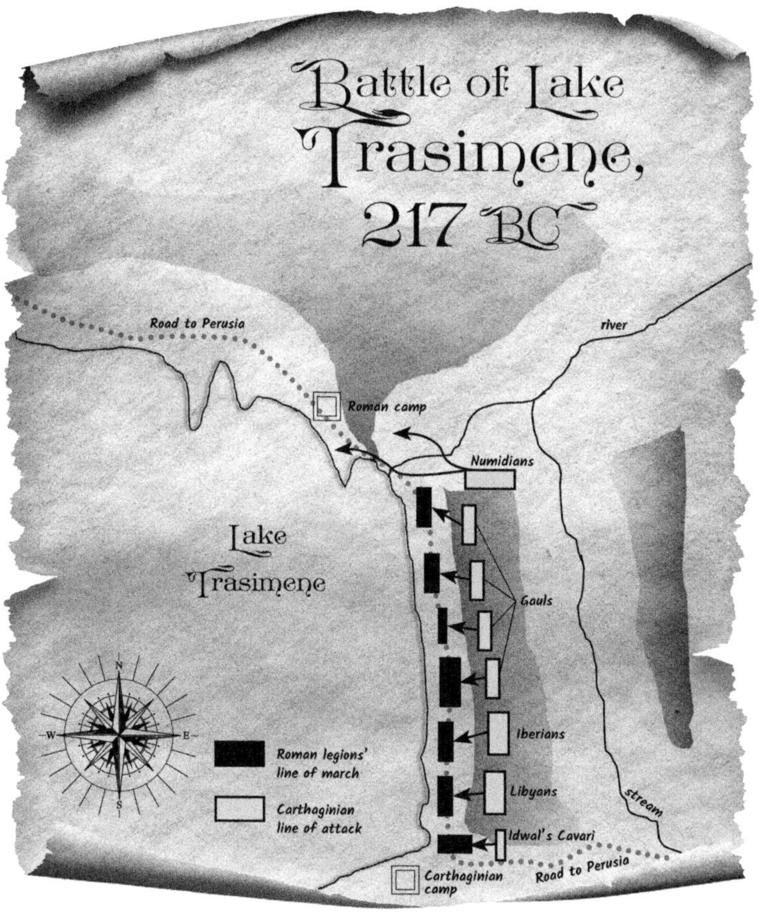
Battle of Lake Trasimene, 217 BC
Road to Perusia
river
Roman camp
Numidians
Lake Trasimene
Gauls
Iberians
Libyans
Roman legions' line of march
Carthaginian line of attack
Idwal's Cavari
stream
Carthaginian camp
Road to Perusia
N
S
E
W

LIST OF PRINCIPAL CHARACTERS

characters marked with an asterisk are real historical figures. The rest might well have been.

Adherbal	veteran Numidian eshrin captain and Maharbal's second in command
Agbal	Numidian. One of the youngest members of Sphax's eshrin, with keen eyesight
Aribal	Numidian eshrin captain
Artula	Daughter of the Anamares elder, Garos. Wife of Meilyr, Anamares chieftain
Betua	Daughter of Boii chieftain, Carmo, and wife of Insubres chief, Ducarius
Cleon	Corinna's two-year-old son
Corinna	Daughter of Queen Teuta of Illyria* and Sphax's lover
Drust	Cavari warrior and trusted lieutenant of Idwal
Ducarius*	Insubres chieftain and husband of Betua

Gaius Flaminius Nepos* Elected Consul of Rome, 217 BC. High-handed hothead, responsible for ordering the deaths of Sphax's parents.

Gala Veteran Numidian eshrin captain

Hannibal Barca* Born 247 BC, Carthage. Renowned Carthaginian general who invades Italia in 218 BC

Hannon Trusted Numidian veteran in Sphax's eshrin

Hiempsal Numidian eshrin commander

Himilco Numidian eshrin captain and Sphax's trusted lieutenant

Idwal Son of Lord Cenno, chief of the Cavari Gauls. Idwal is the leader of the Cavari contingent in Hannibal's army and Sphax's closest friend

Jubal Numidian. The youngest member of Sphax's eshrin

Jugurtha Trusted Numidian veteran and chief scout in Sphax's eshrin

Mago Barca* Younger brother of Hannibal

Maharbal* Numidian, and the son of Himilco. Hannibal's second in command in charge of his cavalry

Manissa Veteran Numidian eshrin captain

Meilyr, father and son Anamares chieftain and husband of Artula. His twelve year old son (also called Meilyr) is a notable musician

Queen Teuta* Wife of King Agron,* who gains the throne after his death in 231 BC. Defeated by Rome in the First Illyrian War (229 BC), she sues for peace and is banished to Rhizon in the north of Illyria. History remembers her as the Pirate Queen

Sosylus of Lacedaemon* Greek historian in the 3rd century BC. Campaigned alongside Hannibal throughout the Second Punic War, recording the events of his campaign

Sphax Born in Numidia, January, 235 BC. Son of Prince Navaras of Numidia* and Similce Barca,* sister of Hannibal Barca*

PART ONE

The Many Faces of Hannibal

ONE

To all the world he looked like an elderly Greek merchant. It was a bitterly cold April morning, yet, unlike Sphax, the old man had spurned a riding cloak in favour of a plain woollen himation, and his venerable silver locks and full grey beard belied his upright bearing and powerful physique.

But in the name of the gods, why was a Greek merchant riding Hannibal's stallion, Arion?

As their paths crossed the merchant croaked, 'Greetings, young man,' in a quavering voice reflecting his years. 'A plain day, is it not?'

Sphax could not take his eyes off the man's mount, barely managing a cursory nod in greeting. Could he be mistaken about Arion? Certainly the Greek's saddle and reins were plain and workmanlike, as you would expect of a merchant, whereas Hannibal always arrayed Arion in a magnificent saddle cloth.

Could he be wrong? Surely not. Sphax had trained the stallion for chariot racing at the circus, and when Arion became the most celebrated horse in Rome,

Sphax had determined to spirit him away and present him as a gift to Hannibal.

With ever stride of his mare, Sphax's suspicions and doubts grew to a pitch where he could bear it no longer. Nudging Dido around he trotted back down the track and fell in step beside the Greek. 'Would it be impertinent, Sir, to enquire how you acquired the stallion you are riding?'

'Not at all, young man,' replied the merchant without a sideways glance. 'I bought him as a foal from a horse trader in Perusia. May I also enquire as to why a Numidian is interested in a stallion, when your people never ride them?'

Though perfectly correct, Sphax noticed the man's Greek was laced with a strange accent he couldn't quite place, which only added to his suspicions that all was not as it appeared.

Ignoring the question Sphax ploughed on. 'Do you have business in the Carthaginian camp, Sir?'

'Grain is my business,' he replied, staring resolutely ahead. 'I hear Hannibal's army is in dire need of it … such a dreadful winter.'

Again, that strange accent grated on his ears. This man was no Greek! 'And who have you been given leave to approach in our camp?' Sphax asked innocently.

For the first time the man turned to face him. 'For a Numidian captain you are full of questions, young man.'

Numidians carried no marks of rank. How could he possibly know? Sphax had been paying so much attention to the stallion he'd overlooked the glaringly obvious: the milky cast in the man's right eye.

He suddenly sat stock still and stared. 'Uncle … is it really you?'

Slowly the corners of the man's mouth twitched, then broadened to become a leering grin of triumph. 'Good morning, Nephew. I trust you are well,' beamed Hannibal in Punic.

'But … but …' Sphax could only splutter, 'you're in disguise! And alone! Where is your escort, Sir? Why are you dressed—?'

'—As a Greek merchant,' his uncle laughed. 'As I almost deceived you I suppose I do owe you an explanation.'

'I would be most grateful, Sir. But where is your escort — your bodyguards? Have you ridden all the way from Bona alone?'

'Of course not,' his uncle replied dismissively, 'I left my guards in our encampment not an hour ago. Your concern is touching,' he added with a hint of sarcasm, 'but there are sound reasons why a disguise is necessary in the present circumstances.'

'What are these circumstances, Sir? Why would you need to disguise yourself?'

Hannibal gazed around at the vast emptiness of the grasslands south of the great Padus river. 'My informants tell me that assassination plots abound amongst the Gauls.'

Sphax was horrified. 'Surely not, Sir! Without you we would be lost … leaderless.'

'That is not how our allies see me, Sphax,' his uncle sighed. 'To them our army is nothing more than a burden to be fed and quartered. Where is the plunder I promised them? The wealth ... the lands? No, Nephew, we are as welcome here as a plague of locusts.'

Sphax's curiosity got the better of him. 'Is that a wig, Sir? It's quite remarkable ... I would never have guessed.'

'I've had four of them made, and different outfits to complete the disguise. I intend to rotate them. That way I keep assassins guessing.'

'Then for all our sakes, I would prefer you put your faith in your Adrymachid bodyguards rather than wigs and false beards. They at least will defend you to the last—'

'Bodyguards would give the game away. I would be recognised! Better to perfect my disguises and fool the assassins; that way I can move around freely, undetected.'

'Who are these plotters and conspirators, Uncle?' Sphax found himself anxiously fingering his ivory image of Artemis. 'Confide your suspicions and I swear by the goddess, Idwal and I will hunt them down.'

'Where to begin?' Hannibal laughed. But it was a hollow laugh. 'As soon as a plot is hatched, a rival chieftain hastens to inform me of his neighbour's treachery. The Cisalpine Gauls have fought one another for so long they've forgotten how to stand together in common purpose.'

Edgily, his uncle's eyes flicked over the empty grassland. 'Years ago in Iberia, my brother-in-law, Hasdrubal the Fair, was murdered by such treachery amongst Gauls. It was a lesson I've never forgotten. But I must confess I'm a little disappointed that you were able to see through my subterfuge.'

'By all the gods, Sir, your disguise is perfect. Your own mother wouldn't know you! Even your voice fooled me! But I would recognise Arion on a starless night in Hades. I implore you, Sir, until this threat to your life is removed, please do not ride Arion.' Frowning, Sphax added, 'Your disguise is perfect. But Arion is universally acknowledged as your warhorse.'

'I will do as you say, Nephew. You're right, it was Arion that aroused your suspicions.'

'But why are you riding to our camp alone at this hour, Sir?'

'Three days ago I summoned every chieftain in Cisalpine Gaul to a council of war in my brother's pavilion to take place this morning. What better way to test my disguise and flush out assassins?'

'Then one of those attending may be a traitor, Uncle.'

'Possibly,' agreed Hannibal, almost with indifference. 'If it eases your fears for my safety then ride with me, Nephew, and attend my council of war. Your eshrin can await their recall — I assume that's where you're heading at this hour. I have much news for you, and would welcome your insights in my counsel with Maharbal and Hanno.'

This was unheard of! Only once before had Hannibal invited him to a council of war, and Sphax had never been allowed the indulgence of *insights.* His eshrin would relish the prospect of an extra day of idleness, so it wasn't a difficult decision to make.

The southerly gate of the camp came into view on the horizon. It was mostly empty now, save for a few eshrins of Numidian cavalry that were keeping a close watch on Placentia and its riverborne trade. Orison, chief of the Iberian Oretani, had generously gifted his grand pavilion to Sphax and Corinna, and this is where they'd set up home upon their return from Illyria.

'There is news, Nephew, which may interest you, though you may not like it.' It seemed ominous that Hannibal's smile deserted him. 'You are already aware of my extensive network of informants throughout Italia, but it may still surprise you to learn that I have agents in Rome itself.'

It didn't just surprise him, it astounded him. He knew his uncle's network was vast … but in Rome! Sphax shook his head in sheer admiration.

'Judging from your expression, I see you would be more than interested to know that this year's Consuls will be Gnaeus Servilius Geminus, and Gaius Flaminius Nepos.'

At the name Flaminius, Sphax froze. For him the name opened a Pandora's box of hatred he'd barely been able to keep locked. Flaminius had ordered the murder of his parents, and condemned Sphax to ten years of slavery before he'd freed himself and joined his uncle's army at the Rhodanus.

Before he'd left Rome for that last time, his plans for escape well advanced, he'd stolen out from his filthy quarters by the stables to the little shrine of the goddess Artemis. There were far grander shrines to Diana in Rome, including a temple dedicated to the goddess. But Diana was *not* Artemis! Her little shrine had been erected by Greeks to their beloved goddess. Sphax was a devotee. That evening, prostrate before her ivory image he'd sworn a solemn oath to seek revenge and justice on Gaius Flaminius, sealing it with his own blood.

Sphax was aware his uncle was speaking to him earnestly, imploringly. But it was of little use. Pandora's box had been violently flung open at the mention of Flaminius, and now the red mist of hatred had descended that words could barely penetrate. He heard his uncle say; 'We need to channel our anger and hatred into a resolve for justice and retribution,' and later, 'My dearest sister Similce was murdered on the orders of this man!'

At last Sphax got a grip of himself. 'You're right, Sir. I appreciate your advice,' — the little of it he'd heard — 'I must not be mastered by hatred. Justice and revenge are best served cold.'

'Well said, Nephew. Now, tell me everything you know about this new consul of Rome.'

Sphax tried to clear his head and gather his thoughts. 'Firstly, Sir, bear in mind that Flaminius is a new man, not from a noble family. He's no Julii or Fabii, but of humble origin. To reach such heady heights of power in Rome, new men have to possess insatiable ambition, overweening confidence in their importance, and the ability to rabble-rouse the plebeians in order to challenge the authority of the patricians. Flaminius is such a man.'

Sphax went on to document Flaminius' contentious career, beginning with his election to tribune, fifteen years ago. His law to re-settle thousands of ex-legionaries on the lands of the Boii had led to insurrection, Illyrian piracy and a multitude of unforeseen consequences. Having wormed his way onto the Roman fleet as a self-appointed military tribune during the war with Illyria, he'd wielded a power and influence far greater than any of the consuls. It was he who'd been astute enough to recognise the propaganda value of exposing an alliance between Carthage and Illyria, and ruthless enough to demand that Carthage's embassies be exterminated.

When he finally ascended to the consulship, Sphax reminded his uncle, Flaminius' hatred of Gauls meant he immediately marched his legions north to strike against the Anamares and Insubres, a campaign that was nothing short of slaughter and butchery. Sphax described having to witness his triumph outside the temple of Jupiter, watching as columns of chained Gauls were led to the slave markets.

'At the time, Sir, rumour was rife that his military tribunes won him his victories, and that his own leadership in the campaign had been inept. Naturally, I had more than a passing interest in this, so I made extensive enquiries. This low opinion of his military leadership seemed to have been universally held. There were even rumours that the senate were reluctant to grant him a triumph, and it was only passed because of threats from Flaminius to stir up the common people.'

'Then to sum up,' Hannibal began, deep in thought. 'We are dealing with a man with a misplaced sense of his own importance, self-righteously arrogant, yet with a ruthless streak; totally devoid of moral principle or honour, and furthermore, with questionable skills in military leadership.'

Sphax laughed. 'I believe you've got the measure of him, Uncle. That is indeed a perfect description of Gaius Flaminius Nepos.'

'Then let us plan his destruction with cold-blooded reason. Justice will prevail. Flaminius will answer with his life for the calamities he's inflicted on both our families. Believe me, Sphax, from what you've told me, Melqart himself could not have gifted me a more predictable adversary.'

They were about to cross the waterlogged ditch that marked the entrance to the southern gate of the Carthaginian camp. Two sleepy-eyed Numidians grabbed a spear each and tried to look alert.

It was obvious from his uncle's expression he was regarding this challenge as a final test of his disguise.

Puzzled, the two sentries were eyeing the old man suspiciously. 'Who's he, Sphax?' they chorused.

'Don't worry, lads,' Sphax grinned, winking at his uncle. 'I can vouch for him. He's quite harmless.'

And so it was that the celebrated leader of the Carthaginian armies rode into his own camp under the noses of two sentries, completely unrecognised.

TWO

Wig and false beard removed, his uncle's face had returned to its familiar brooding severity. 'We march south and invade Etruria in two weeks' time,' he announced to the gathering.

There was sudden consternation at Hannibal's words, then all was uproar inside Mago's crowded pavilion amidst shouts of, 'Impossible! We cannot round up our cattle in time …' and, 'Our granaries are empty!'

Hannibal, seated on a large chair at the front of the gathering, closed his eyes, appearing to be lost in deep thought whilst waiting patiently for the commotion to subside. Beside him sat his younger brother, Mago, and both were flanked by their trusted generals, Hanno and Maharbal.

'Your Gauls are a little restive this morning,' whispered Sphax to his friend Idwal, sitting beside him on a bench at the back.

'They're not *my* Gauls!' Idwal replied with his habitual frown. 'And nobody likes surprises—

'More of a thunderbolt than a surprise, wouldn't you say?'

Looking around, Sphax recognised few faces. Most of them were Cisalpine Gauls from the tribes of the Insubres and Boii, dressed in their finest war gear, hair braided and perfumed in the peculiar style of the Ligurian Keltoi and favouring tunics and plaid braccae in rich autumnal colours. Some even wore the tight-fitting, knee length trousers Rome had insultingly named femenalia. Unlike Idwal and the western Gauls, the Ligurians didn't sport luxuriant mustachios and were mostly bearded, but like their cousins beyond the Alps, they were not shy about flaunting their considerable wealth. Soft Greek lanterns in Mago's resplendent pavilion glittered on helmets inlaid with silver and gold, priceless coats of chain mail, gold torques and long Gallic blades.

The faces he did recognise were Magol, chief of the Boii, who'd crossed the Alps to speak at Hannibal's Council of the Gauls held beside the Rhodanus back in August; the handsome, battle-scarred face of the Iberian chieftain, Orison, and Meilyr, Sphax's faithful friend and chief of what was left of the noble Anamares tribe after Flaminius' butchery had driven them from their lands.

It was disquieting, thought Sphax, that some amongst them might be plotting the downfall of the leader they'd all chosen to follow. The object of this treachery suddenly opened his eyes and rose imperiously to his feet. Raising a hand to silence what remained of the muttering he cast his brooding gaze around the room. With Hannibal's uncanny knack of riveting attention upon himself by his sheer presence, a hush descended on the pavilion as his listeners hung on his every word. Hannibal's opening remarks surprised them.

'You are perfectly right,' he conceded. 'We could not possibly prepare our baggage trains, mules and strings of pack-horses, fill our wagons with grain and drive our herds before us in time for an invasion on such a scale. It would be a labour even beyond Herakles! So we must turn our thinking on its head and find a novel way to surprise and confound our enemies.'

Sphax hadn't noticed the venerable figure of Sosylos, Hannibal's historian and philosopher, sitting amongst the crowded front bench. Now the silver-haired Greek rose and translated his uncle's Punic into Gallic.

'Etruria is the garden of Italia!' continued Hannibal. 'It produces two harvests a year. Its pasture provides more beef and pork than Rome can eat. It grows everything from olives to onions, and its wine is the finest in the land.'

Conjuring a theatrical smile he continued, 'It would be a foolish merchant who tried to sell his grain in a land where fields were ripening with wheat and whose granaries were bursting with spring harvest. What fool would drive cattle to sell in a land already overgrazed by such beasts? And what merchant would be foolish enough to sell his wines in the finest vineyards in the land?' His uncle allowed the Greek to translate.

'Are we not thinking like these foolish merchants? Driving cattle before us to butcher on the hoof, hauling wagons of wheat to provide bread on the march, not to mention the miles of pack trains to supply us with everything from cabbages to wine! The sooner we reach Etruria, the sooner our men can fill their bellies with what it has to offer. Once there we will live off the fat of the land and have no need of wagons of grain or herds of cattle.

'We take only what we need to get us over the mountains and through the marshes of the Arnus. A little hunger will put fire in the men's bellies and ensure they march swiftly. We strike hard and fast.'

After Sosylos translated, these last revelations met with some disquiet. Sphax guessed it was because Gauls had no love of marching, let alone *swift* marching … Before the disquiet was allowed to grow to a murmur, Hannibal silenced it with a dismissive wave.

'We have but two choices. One path lies south-east, over the mountain passes to Ariminum and then down the Adriatic coast. But we would have to re-cross the mountains to threaten Rome. Magol informs me that Consul Gnaeus Servilius has already taken up residence in Ariminum, and his legions guard the mountain passes north and west of that city. Servilius is cautious and wily. To prise him out of Ariminum would be slow and costly. We have no siege equipment to storm its walls, and delay would allow Rome to concentrate its forces against us. For these reasons I consider the south-eastern road barred.'

Nodding at Sosylos, he allowed the Greek to translate and the facts to sink in. 'Which leaves us with little alternative but to strike south-west, into Etruria. But with Melqart's guidance, this is the route I've long favoured. Not only is it the shortest, it places us in the heart of Italia, within striking distance of its wealthiest cities and two bounds from Rome itself.'

Like the messenger Hermes, saving the best for last, as Sosylos fell silent Hannibal smiled broadly at the gathering. 'It may please you to know that Servilius' fellow consul has already set up camp outside the gates of Arretium with his legions. And it pleases me even more to reveal that Servilius' fellow consul is none other than Gaius Flaminius Nepos.'

This met with much chest thumping and raucous approval. Flaminius was the most hated figure in Liguria after his barbarous campaign six years ago. Driven from their lands, with thousands of their children and womenfolk sold into slavery; the name Flaminius was seared into the memory of the Insubres with a hatred that was beyond loathing. Now their blood was up and they wanted revenge.

Raising his voice above the jubilant rumpus, Hannibal cried, 'I intend to bait him like a chained bear, prodding and poking until he makes a fatal error. Then we will strike him a mortal blow and grind his legions into dust, just as we routed Sempronius' legions not a mile from this very pavilion. I swear by the sacred axe of Melqart, you will be revenged for the calamities Flaminius has inflicted on you. No legion of Rome dare stand against Ligurians when their cause is just.'

At this point his uncle's tone changed from triumph to urgency. 'But we must do this swiftly, before Servilius can come to his aid. That's why I plead for haste. We march in two weeks. Make all preparations.'

As Hannibal sat down the murmuring resumed. But now Sphax sensed the mood had changed from one of doubt and unease, to one of confidence and enthusiasm for what lay ahead.

Sosylos invited questions from the assembly, and to Sphax's surprise, his friend Meilyr immediately rose to his feet. Tall and fair-haired, with mustachios to rival even Idwal's, Meilyr cut a handsome and imposing figure amongst the gathering.

'I welcome the opportunity,' he began, 'for the Anamares to regain its lands. Lands stolen from us by Flaminius. Once, my people dwelt on the land bordering the marshes of the Arnus. I know the place well. At this season it's a wilderness, a watery deathtrap fit only for serpents and waterfowl. I've seen horses drown, sucked down into its oozing mud, and wagons disappear in its quicksands. It is no place for an army, let alone our camp followers! Which means our women and children will only be able to join us after the midsummer festival of Epona, when the waters recede sufficiently to make its passage safe. There are other roads to Arretium. I urge you, Hannibal, look to another way!'

Sosylos translated the Gallic so quietly, it was only after Idwal told him what Meilyr had said that Sphax realised the gravity of the Anamares' misgivings … and its consequences. He would never risk Corinna and her son, or their servants for that matter, in such a treacherous place. Which meant that in two weeks' time he would be setting out alone. Knowing Corinna would insist on joining him whatever the risk, he would have to prepare his arguments carefully!

Hannibal rose to his feet once more and eyed the Anamares' chief gravely. 'What I have to say in answer to Meilyr concerns you all. For once we step into that watery wilderness there can be no turning back, or avoiding its undoubted perils.' His uncle hesitated, nodding at Sosylos to translate so as to give him time to gather his thoughts.

This was uncharacteristic, thought Sphax: his uncle's quicksilver mind was always two steps ahead of an argument. Perhaps it reflected his own lingering doubts about the path he'd chosen. But he began confidently enough when Sosylos fell silent.

'Long have I weighed in my mind the risks and rewards of a march that would take us through the swamps. I would never undertake such a perilous journey lightly, so to begin with I questioned merchants and travelers who crossed the marsh regularly. "In what season is it passable?" I asked. "How deep is the water? Is there higher ground to rest and sleep? What is the shortest path?" I asked a hundred questions and formed a picture in my mind of what we would have to face if we took this path.' Closing his eyes, his uncle paused to allow the Greek to translate.

'Then, with the enticement of a little silver, I came upon two Etrurians who claimed to guide merchants safely through the swamps in all seasons, even after the autumn rains. Naturally I was suspicious. I questioned them at length and tried to corroborate their claims with merchants who'd used them as guides. Their descriptions tallied with what the merchants told me. They were speaking the truth. I've now paid them handsomely. They are to be our guides through the swamps.

'Be under no illusion. The passage of the marshes will be a perilous trial: its waters are not fit to drink and harbour pestilence and disease, there will be quicksands and deep water to navigate, and precious little chance to rest and sleep. But the rewards far outweigh a little discomfort.

'Avoiding the marsh will add an entire week to our march. I am certain Flaminius will come to the conclusion that our army would never risk its passage, so the place will not be watched. For three days our army will simply disappear from sight, and when we emerge from its waters we will take the Consul's legions by surprise.

'Conscience impels me to say something more, but I speak reluctantly, for I fear what I have to say will be unwelcome to your ears and make me even more unpopular than I am at present.' Again, Sphax noted the hesitation. 'I have never approved of taking wives and children on campaign. By its very nature war is fraught with uncertainty and risk. As your leader I willingly shoulder that responsibility, and with every waking thought I look to our men's safety and welfare. To burden me with the safety of your wives and children is not only unreasonable, I believe it to be unfair. And I will not base military decisions on the comfort and convenience of your wives.' Tell that to Corinna, thought Sphax!

'With good reason I left my own wife in the safety of our home in Cartagena. There she will remain until this war is won and we have peace.'

As Sosylos began to speak, the muttering began again. Sphax sensed the doubt and unease. So did his uncle. When the Greek finished, Hannibal raised a hand commanding silence. 'To ease your fears,' he said, 'I ask that Meilyr himself questions my guides. And only when he is satisfied will we undertake the passage of the marshes. Are we agreed?'

This did indeed meet with universal approval. Meilyr nodded and resumed his seat on the bench as quiet descended on the assembly. 'Then the council is closed,' declared Hannibal. 'I wish you all good fortune with your preparations for war.'

With the clink of iron and polished metal as thirty chieftains got to their feet, Sphax realised his first council of war was at an end. Now all he had to do was keep his uncle alive for the next two weeks and brace himself for an almighty argument with Corinna.

'Hannibal won't like it,' growled Maharbal, who was not in the sweetest of tempers after being given less than an hour's notice that the twelve thousand cavalry under his command were to march in two weeks' time! They were sitting on their usual stools in the general's workmanlike pavilion, cluttered with weapons and amour.

'He doesn't have to like it, Sir,' argued Sphax.

'The last thing I need at this moment is to find nursemaids for your uncle. I've seen his disguises before. They make him look rather fetching … get him to show you the one with the golden curls — he looks like a Sicilian whore. Only the beard lets him down—'

'—You're not taking this seriously, Sir.'

'Look lad, he rides back to Bona this afternoon with Orison and fifty of his Iberians. Your friends Idwal and Meilyr will also be accompanying him with even more warriors. I pity the assassin bold enough to take on that lot!'

Maharbal cradled his cup and took a swig. 'Now that our Gauls' greed is set on plundering Etruria, once back in camp Hannibal will be perfectly safe.

Believe me, there will be no more plotting or talk of assassination. But if it eases your conscience, have a word with Orison. For reasons that escape me, he's taken a shine to you and listens to your nonsense. You can be assured his Iberians would lay down their lives for your uncle.'

Sphax made a mental note to do just that. 'And what do you require of me, General?'

Maharbal glared at his young protégé. 'Instead of sailing off to visit the wonders of the Adriatic, I want you to do some work for a change!' Sphax couldn't help but smile. If it had only been like that!

'And you can wipe that smile off your face,' his general snapped. 'Over the next two weeks you'll be run ragged and become a stranger to sleep. Our cavalry is strung out and quartered across Liguria. We need to concentrate our forces at Bona, where our march begins. I'll be mustering the Iberian heavy cavalry. They will need the largest share of supplies, and as your uncle has forbidden wagons, everything will have to be carried by our pack trains. Bear this in mind.'

'Without wagons our trains will just grow longer to compensate,' observed Sphax. 'Which rather defeats the object.'

'Dog's twat, lad, I know!' grumbled Maharbal. 'But your uncle's mind is fixed on that accursed swamp. He thinks of nothing else—'

'Why, Sir?' asked Sphax, totally bemused. 'What's so special about a swamp?'

'For any general it's a gift from the gods. Imagine being able to disappear from the sight of your enemies for three whole days! Doesn't one of your Greek goddesses have some kind of cap?'

'Yes of course,' cried Sphax. 'Athena's cap of invisibility—'

'Well, there you are then … what general would refuse such a gift to confound his enemies? That slackhead Flaminius will have a nasty surprise when we emerge from that swamp. That is, if it doesn't prove to be the death of us all.' Sphax nodded, understanding at last the significance of the place.

'I ride to Bona at first light. I'm leaving the muster of the Numidian eshrins to you, lad. I need them in Bona in two weeks. You're in charge.'

'Me, Sir!' bleated Sphax, too shocked to say more.

'Yes. You, Sir,' laughed Maharbal. 'Your first duty will be to round up all the captains and summon them to a meeting this evening. Appoint Himilco as your lieutenant — he's a promising young man, that one — but don't forget about those old rogues Manissa and Gala. They've done this before. You haven't.

'Start bringing the eshrins quartered north of the Padus over the river as soon as possible. Use this camp as your base. Three days of wading through a filthy swamp will not do much for our ladies' hooves. I'm afraid many of them will go lame, so we'll need replacements. I want you to scour the grasslands north and south of the river; if it has four legs and a mane, press it into service.'

For the next hour the general talked of nothing but fodder, javelins, tents and blankets, ropes and drill. By this time Sphax's head was swimming, and he worried he would not be able to remember the half of it. But as he took his leave of Maharbal to do the rounds of the camp and summon his captains, an excitement began to kindle in his belly.

This was his destiny. Just as it had been for his father and his father before him. He was a Prince of Numidia, born to lead his people into battle. Maharbal had recognised his qualities and nurtured them, and at the Trebia he'd proved himself. He was eighteen years old, the same age as his uncle when he'd led his first campaign. Sphax felt ready.

THREE

Maharbal had been right. For the next four days Sphax was lucky if he managed to snatch a few hours sleep each night beneath the stars on the grasslands beside the Padus. As the late April mists dispersed and spring blossomed, the warmth of the sun brought these rich and fertile grasslands to life. Dawn would see him rising with the call of the lark, cantering though carpets of orchids and cuckooflowers, flushing all manner of waterfowl before him. For the first time since that winter of winters, he came to see the beauty of the place, with its endless horizons and the harmony of its seasonal rhythms.

And, for the first time, he also began to fully appreciate what it took to keep a Numidian eshrin on campaign. Like a Roman eques' turmae, Numidians divided their cavalry into squadrons thirty men strong, but instead of three decurions, eshrins were led by a single Numidian captain. Only Numidians commanded Numidians.

Goatskin tents were his first concern. Eshrins were allotted five, each sleeping six men. But after their journey through the Alps and the ravages of that terrible winter, many had been lost or were unserviceable. Next on the list were grindstones. There was a shortage. Grindstones milled the men's daily corn allowance, roasted over campfires every morning to bake flatbreads. Nothing was guaranteed to inflame the ire of Numidians more than ruining their breakfast!

His people were inveterate bellyachers. Sphax remembered a story his father once told him about a Numidian waiting amongst the crowds at a temple, moaning to the gods about the heat of the day: 'I'm sick of this,' he'd grumbled to a friend, 'I'll take my complaint to Ba 'al Hamūn, himself.'

'How did you get on? his friend asked when he returned. 'I gave up. The queue was too long!'

Sphax asked his seasoned veterans, Manissa and Gala, to commission repairs and replacement tents. 'And for the love of Ba 'al Hamūn, find more grindstones!'

By the second day he'd realised there was little point in allotting these two separate jobs. Ordered to set out in completely opposite directions with different tasks, they simply trailed one another, so that everything took twice as long as it should have done. Manissa and Gala were inseparable. Where one went, the other followed. Yet they were such odd bedfellows.

The surfeit of Manissa's dark curls would have provided more than enough hair to cover his friend's bald head and bare chin, and Gala's stooping, wiry frame was hardly reflected in his companion's barrel chest and over-ripe belly. In terms of speech, it would be fair to say that Manissa spoke and Gala nodded.

Maharbal had insisted he listen to their advice. But what that amounted to usually descended into oaths and dire warnings of calamity should archaic Numidian law be ignored. What Sphax relished was Manissa's esoteric titbits about Roman soldiery. 'Did you know that the cost of an eques' tent is deducted from his pay?' He did not. But gems like this amused him.

His lieutenant, appointed by Maharbal himself, was of a different metal. With his searching blue eyes — unusual in a Numidian — and the serious look of a scholar, Himilco was two years Sphax's senior and quickly became his rock. Over the next two weeks, Sphax came to rely on his quick mind and clarity of thinking.

In camp, except for a water ration — another archaic tradition — the men paid for their own food. But on a march, rations were allotted and doled out. Which meant that calculations had to be made, supplies requisitioned and merchants or sutlers paid in silver. For the first time in his life, Sphax had to think about lentils, beans, peas, salted pork, cheese, sample olive oil and judge the quality of wheat. The worst of it was that sleep offered little respite; he was beginning to dream about food!

Often his servants were more useful than Himilco. Cesti and Lulin turned their noses up at unripe corn — green they called it — and they could sniff out a dishonest merchant at ten paces. Neither was his lieutenant versed in the discipline of mathematics. Sphax had to dredge from memory childhood lessons in the art of multiplication and division. His Greek tutor Elpis, with his wife Airla, had lived for years under the threat of dire punishment for secretly educating a slave boy. Of necessity, these days Sphax was never far away from his wax tablet and his calculations.

But by far his biggest concern was that accursed swamp. It loomed in his mind like a recurring nightmare. Hannibal had reckoned on three days to complete its passage. Horses had to graze regularly: even a day without grass or fodder would upset their delicate digestion, and judging from the descriptions of Meilyr and his uncle, that watery Hades would offer little in the way of luscious water meadows! Which meant they would have to supply three days of fodder for over three thousand mares, not to mention the hundreds of pack animals they were taking.

And it wasn't just fodder. Maharbal had impressed on him that they would need scores of torches to light the way in the darkness. To stray off the track at night would mean certain death.

Then there was the foul water through which they would have to trudge. Horses were not fussy about what they drank. But his uncle had mentioned pestilence and disease! How bad could it get?

After four relentless days of cantering over the grasslands beside the great river, Sphax was exhausted, and it was time to give his weary mare a rest. Sixty eshrins and wagonloads of supplies were now back in camp, south of the river. He and Himilco had made a good start.

As he rode back to camp in the gathering twilight, Sphax realised he couldn't put off any longer something he'd been dreading since Hannibal's council of war. Tomorrow he would have to tell Corinna that she and their household would not be allowed to join him when they began their great adventure.

He would rather face the massed ranks of a Roman legion than his lover's fiery temper, but there was nothing for it, he would have to steel himself and weather the storm.

* * *

'I will not miss this place when we're gone,' Corinna confessed, gazing listlessly around at the endless vistas of grassland. 'My spirit yearns for mountains or a rising sea. Anything but this!' She was astride her beloved stallion Alastor, in company with Aethon, a Seleucid mare Sphax had won in a wager with Corinna's mother, Queen Teuta of Illyria. At considerable cost, they'd managed to transport both horses down the Padus to their camp beside the great river.

Aethon was the most beautiful horse Sphax had ever set eyes on. Her luminous golden coat reminded him of the fables about the blazing steeds that pulled the chariot of Helios, and so he'd named her. Two hands taller than Dido, she was the swiftest mare he'd ever ridden, and though he'd won her trust, she was wild and wilful, and didn't always obey his commands.

After his first good night's sleep in days, Sphax had suggested to Corinna they ride together that morning, giving him the perfect opportunity to broach the dreaded announcement he had to make. But his mare had other ideas. To his annoyance, Aethon had decided this was the morning to pit her will against her would-be master. Within a mile of leaving the camp, Sphax found himself in a battle of wills, a head-to-head showdown for who was in control. This was the last thing Sphax needed that morning.

Nudged to the right, Aethon trod left. Encouraged to trot, Aethon came to a halt. In desperation, Sphax slid from her flank, turned his back on her and strode away, pretending to be indifferent to her whinnying and calls of distress. To his relief, she followed him, nuzzling his back and demanding to be petted. He ignored her and strode on. As her pleas for attention and nuzzling became more clamorous, he would stop and stride out in a different direction. Only when her demands for attention became frantic, did he finally stop and turn around to face her, staring into her eyes. Patiently Sphax waited for her head-bobbing and nickering to cease, all the while staring gently into her eyes. Only when she was calm and perfectly still did he mount her.

Commanding her to walk, he first nudged her to the right, then to the left, finally bringing her to an abrupt halt. In each case she obeyed. Instantly.

All the while Corinna had been watching, fascinated. Now she smiled, shaking her head in admiration. 'That was extraordinary, my love. I've never seen anything like it.'

'I was only telling her that she needs me more than I need her.'

'Well, she seems to have got the message.'

Sphax laughed. 'I've got a sinking feeling I'm going to have to repeat this lesson many times before Aethon will do what I ask of her.' Stealing a glance at Corinna he added, 'Like someone else I know, this mare is wilful and has a mind of her own.'

'Meaning me, I suppose,' pouting and arching her generous eyebrows. 'You should be grateful your lovely mare knows her own mind.' Suddenly distracted by something that had caught her eye, she pointed, 'See that ditch. The last person to jump it is a slackheaded Scythian!' Then she was off.

Fast as she was, Aethon didn't stand a chance. Alastor was like a bolt of lightning. But that was the nature of stallions: over short distances they were fast and furious, but over the leagues of an exhausting march they simply didn't possess the stamina. Jennets like Dido and Aethon would outpace their brothers within ten miles

Aethon didn't even come a close second. Corinna was waiting for them as they leapt the ditch. 'What kept you?' she smirked.

Sphax laughed. 'There is no honour in a man besting his lady in a horserace. Your goddess, Hera, would frown on me, and at the moment I need her on my side.'

'She *is* on your side, my darling, as are all the gods of Greece and Illyria. The barbarous Romans must be taught a lesson they'll never forget.'

'Talking of which,' Sphax began hesitantly, realising the dreaded moment had arrived. 'I have an announcement to make.'

'I too have an announcement to make,' revealed Corinna, beaming from ear to ear.

'You go first.'

'No! I insist that you—'

'It would be unwise for a man to ignore his mistress's announcements,' bluffed Sphax, relishing the temporary delay. 'Please, my darling, what is your news?'

'I am with child,' she declared, bequeathing a seraphic smile on him. 'You are to become a father.'

At which point, either through shock or astonishment, he found his legs involuntarily gripping Aethon's withers and she bolted at high speed, leaving Corinna helpless with laughter. She was still laughing when he returned, having brought the mare under control.

'If I believed in the auguries,' she spluttered, 'I would swear that was a sign that you are about to desert me in my hour of need!'

'No!' he blurted out, flushing. 'I would *never* desert you … it just … came as a shock.'

'Trust a man to gallop off at the first whiff of responsibility.' Sphax realised she was enjoying herself, relishing his discomfort.

'To be perfectly honest with you, my darling,' he began solemnly, 'I had never thought of myself as a father until we rescued Cleon and I realised the responsibilities a child brings. What young man of eighteen thinks about fatherhood? Now I hardly recognise the slave who fled to his uncle's army and crossed the Alps. That boy's head was full of nonsense. Honour and glory. There is little of either in war, just necessity. But I hope you've seen with your own eyes that I've changed.'

'Indeed, my love, you have changed,' Corinna replied gently, laughter forgotten. 'Over these past weeks I've watched you with Cleon. You are patient and gentle; he couldn't wish for a more loving father.'

'How long have you known about your pregnancy?'

'These past three months.'

Sphax was shocked by this revelation. 'Three months! Why did you not tell me?'

'Because I needed time to think, and decide what's best for our son—'

'Then it's a son you carry?' Sphax was finding it difficult to control the emotions that were crowding in on him.

'As far as a mother's intuitions can be believed, I'm about to bear you an heir. But you are not listening to me, Sphax,' shaking her head. 'Don't you see? This changes everything!'

'Yes … I see that now,' his mind lost in a fog of ignorance. 'But I don't know anything about pregnancy and childbirth, only that it is perilous and women risk their lives bearing children.'

'Of course you don't,' Corinna laughed, 'you're a man! Over the coming months my belly will swell like a leather wineskin filled to the brim, I will be plagued by women's sickness, grow irritable and develop a passion for melons. In a month or so I will be unable to ride, and towards the end, barely walk. These are but some of the ills that will afflict me over the coming months. As you see, there is much to look forward to!'

It finally dawned on Sphax — a little guiltily — that he'd been let off the hook. 'Then it will be quite impossible for you to join me when we descend upon Italia. In fact, I need to get you and our household to a place of safety with all speed.' To ease his conscience he added, 'I was beginning to have misgivings about risking you on this march, my darling. Our passage through this swamp already fills me with dread, and there are bound to be countless dangers and alarms along the way. Besides, this campaign will last for months. I have no wish for our child to be born in the land of our sworn enemy.'

'Then I'm pleased to see you've come around to your uncle's view that women and children have no business on campaign.'

'So you knew all along what Hannibal had decreed,' muttered Sphax, sheepishly.

'Of course I did, Sphax. It's all around the camp … everyone knows! But when were you going to tell me?'

Now he felt truly foolish. 'I was afraid to,' he confessed, 'I thought you were eager to take part in our great adventure.'

It was Corinna's turn to look downcast. 'I too have dreaded telling you how I feel. It was only when we returned from Rhizon I realised a pavilion is not a place to raise a two year old child. You know that I would follow you to the ends of the earth, and relish the hardships and dangers. But to risk Cleon on such an adventure? That would be rash and irresponsible. Besides Cleon, now I have to think about our unborn child. Should I miscarry on the march, without a physician or midwives, you may lose both of us, Sphax. Surely you see this?'

'Of course I do,' he assured her. 'But now I'm beginning to question whether I should go on this wild adventure. After all, my first duty is to protect you, Cleon, and our unborn son. Perhaps that is my true path—'

'That is *not* your true path, my love. You are a Numidian warrior, born and bred, sworn by solemn oath to your uncle and Maharbal. Your first duty is to the men under your command. Duty and honour mean that Cleon and I come in a poor second. And that's how it *should* be! That's how it *must* be in times of raging war. The surest way to protect me and your unborn son is to drive Rome from the face of the earth. You are one of Rome's deadliest enemies. Hannibal will have need of you.'

'You're right,' he said, sighing deeply. For the first time he acknowledged the desperate emptiness he would feel when at last they parted. So much was uncertain. When would he see her again? When would he be able to look upon his child? Absently he began to finger his ivory image of the goddess. What fate had Artemis in mind for them both? he wondered. Along with Eileithyia, the goddess was also the patron of childbirth. He would pray to them both, every day. At last he asked, 'Have you given much thought to where you will go?'

'I've thought of little else.' As if by unspoken consent, they both started riding back to camp. 'In the end I decided I should return to Rhizon. Relations have always been strained with my mother, but my father, Demetrius, will always protect me from her excesses.'

'I'm anxious about Cesti and Lulin. Will you be able to take them?'

'Don't worry, Sphax, I've already asked them and they've agreed to come, along with our servant boys.'

'Then your plans seem more advanced than mine. Himilco and I have so much still to do.'

'I've had more time to plan and prepare,' she smiled, reaching out a hand to rest on his shoulder. Alastor and Aethon were matching each other, stride for stride. 'Believe me, my love, this is for the best. Parting will be torture, like tearing a soul asunder, but I must think about Cleon and our unborn son. If Cleon is to ascend the throne of Illyria, he will need a loyal kingdom and to be taught the customs of his peoples.' Corinna paused, then added, 'And there is a further complication.'

'What's that?'

'Artula has asked if she can come with me.'

'Why?' puzzled Sphax. Artula was the wife of Meilyr, chief of the Anamares Gauls. Sphax and Corinna had once saved her life, along with her son, also called Meilyr. Her village had been attacked by a party of rampaging Roman equites. Her own father, Garos, had not been so lucky, cut down by the pitiless enemy. Sphax and Corinna had been invited to cast their blazing torches on his funeral pyre, three days later. Since then, Corinna and Artula had become close friends.

'Her son, Meilyr, wants to join his father on campaign.'

'But he's just a boy!' protested Sphax. 'Ten at the most—'

'Twelve in fact … but nevertheless, still a boy. His father made the mistake of gifting him a carnyx — you know how fond the boy is of blowing that hunting horn of his — well, now he has a more warlike instrument to awaken Morrigu. Day and night he begs and pleads with Artula to be allowed to follow his father. She just wants to get him as far from this place as possible.'

'I don't blame her,' he agreed. 'In Rhizon he would have the Adria between him and the arms of Morrigu.' The war goddess of the Gauls decided who would live and die on the battlefield. 'But his father would never risk such a thing.'

'She's not taking any chances, Sphax. Meilyr is a persuasive lad, and the carnyx trumpeters are not in the front ranks.'

Sphax recalled the last time he'd heard the unearthly wailing of the instrument at the Trebia, not a mile from where they were riding. It was true that the carnyx trumpeters had not been at the sharp end of those ranks of Gauls, but it hadn't stopped Rome's legions butchering them by the score. Wisely he said nothing.

* * *

Before the fateful council of war, time had dragged for Sphax, the world seemingly half suspended, waiting for that first breath of wind that would fill its sails and impel it to turn once more. Hannibal, it seemed, had conjured not a breeze but a tempest. The world was not turning, it was spinning. And now there were simply not enough hours in the day.

Crisis followed crisis. Their camp, set amidst a sea of grassland, meant that feeding two thousand horses was not a problem. But feeding two thousand extra Numidian mouths was a different proposition. Rather than breaking into their freshly garnered food stocks, he and Himilco decided to send scores of eshrins south to Bona. Exporting the problem seemed easier than solving it.

Then there was the four-legged problem. They simply didn't have the numbers of pack animals needed to carry their baggage, food and fodder. That winter of winters had not only decimated their own animals, it had also taken its toll on all the lands north and south of the great river. What had made a bad situation infinitely worse was that the Insubres had sensed an opportunity. Rather, their womenfolk and elders had, for in every village the men had left for Hannibal's army. Sphax could hardly blame these poor folk, but the price they were demanding for a flea-bitten donkey had doubled, and the war chest Maharbal had left him was emptying at an alarming rate.

Whilst he and Himilco agonised and debated, Manissa's solution was brutally simple: 'Why don't we just take'em, and toss them a few coins. They plow with oxen and have no need of donkeys or mules.' Conscience demanded Sphax find an alternative solution. Numidians were not pirates, and the Insubres were their allies. On the other hand, his Numidians were risking their lives to defend these people.

Finally they hammered out a compromise. Payment for pack animals was fixed: otherwise, creatures were to be confiscated. Instead of sending out a captain and lieutenant to barter, Sphax ordered entire eshrins turn out to impose their will. Such an intimidating show of strength worked wonders.

At the end of the first week, the vessel Corinna had hired rowed upriver and beached on a sandbar within sight of their pavilion. For Sphax, it came to represent an ever-present symbol of their imminent separation.

After she'd been made fast, Sphax and Corinna looked her over, admiring her sleek yet sturdy lines. Forty paces long, undecked, with sixteen oars and a great mainsail, she was not dissimilar to the keles in which they'd crossed the Adria to reach Brundisium. Her captain, a fair-haired Boii tribesman named Brennos was surprisingly young. The captains Sphax had come across had been old salts in late middle age, and few had been blessed with sweet tempers. On both counts Brennos appeared to be the exception.

Corinna had met him not a month before when he'd delivered a shipment of grain upriver to their camp. What had impressed her was that the cargo of wheat had come from Pharos. Sphax knew Pharos. It was a tiny island set in the northern Adria, out of sight of land and miles from anywhere. It must have taken a considerable feat of navigation to sail from its shores, cross the Adria and find the single channel that led directly to the great Padus river.

Reassured though he was that Corinna and their household would be in safe hands, as he slid off the vessel to the sandbar, he did so with a heavy heart as the prospect of absence drew ever closer.

Over the next few days a thousand things were spoken of, yet so much was left unsaid as they clung to one another in their sleeping couch every night. Then on the eve of her departure, in the second watch of the night, Artula tore into their pavilion and woke them. One glance at her distraught expression told them something dreadful had happened.

FOUR

'Meilyr's gone!' Artula wailed.

'When?' asked Sphax, rubbing the sleep from his eyes and reaching for his tunic.

'I don't know,' she cried, wringing her hands in agitation. 'He must have waited until I fell asleep, then crept out of our pavilion.'

'He can't have got far,' Corinna reassured her, slipping on her chiton.

Sphax wasn't so sure. If the lad had taken a horse he could be miles away by now. 'Has he taken that pony of his, Artula?'

'May the goddess Epona curse me! That's the first place I should have looked,' rushing for the vestibule and almost overturning an oil lamp in her haste.

By now the commotion had awakened Zwalia, Cesti and Lulin in their sleeping quarters at the far end of the pavilion. Now dressed, Corinna was staring into Cleon's crib to check he was still sound asleep.

Wrestling with the buckles of his sandals, Sphax shouted across to the servants, 'Find torches. Do the rounds of the camp. Ask the sentries if they've seen the boy, or a horse riding out of camp.' With that he reached for the flap of the vestibule and followed Artula into the night.

* * *

They'd given up the search at first light, gathering in Artula's pavilion to decide what to do next. Sphax had ordered a thorough search of the camp by all the sentries on duty that night. But Meilyr had not been found. Neither had his pony.

It remained unspoken — for Artula was inconsolable — but Sphax's worst fear seemed confirmed when a sentry on watch by the southern gate told him someone had crept out through the gate at midnight. Sentries only challenged those trying to get in! It was a dark moonless night, and the Numidian could not be certain, but he thought they may have been leading a horse. The southerly gate led to the road to Bona, and Meilyr's father.

'He's ridden off to Bona to persuade his father to take him on campaign,' stated Artula with resignation, facing the inescapable truth at last.

'Your husband will never allow that to happen,' insisted Corinna, 'you must know that, Artula.'

'You don't know my son,' she said, 'he will plead and beg until he's flayed my husband to the bone. Eventually he'll relent. He always does. He's never been strong enough to deny his son.'

With brooding dark shadows encircling her eyes and her fair hair matted and uncombed, it pained Sphax to see Artula in this state. She'd always been such a steadfast friend and comfort for him. Now it was his turn to return the service. 'Besides his carnyx, what else has the lad taken?'

Artula took a deep breath to compose herself. 'His cloak, a blanket, some bread, a water flask, oh … and a grindstone for corn is missing from our kitchen.'

'Everything a warrior would need on campaign,' Sphax noted. Corinna shot him a disapproving glance. He ignored it. 'I'm afraid you're probably right, Artula. The lad is heading for Bona and the Anamares camp. Juba's eshrin is due to head south later today. I'll wake him immediately and get them on the road. Your son's pony is no match for Juba's jennets. They should catch up with him.'

'I'll join them,' Artula insisted. Sphax nodded.

They were about to leave when Corinna intervened. 'Wait, you two! Meilyr is never going to allow his son to accompany him on campaign. He will send the boy back, under escort if need be. I'm sure—'

'No, Corinna, he won't. I've never seen my son so determined. His mind is made up. It's as if he's been possessed by Morrigu herself.' Artula's gaze flashed between Corinna and Sphax. 'Yesterday he told me he'd sworn a sacred oath to Morrigu to avenge the death of his grandfather. The blood was still wet on his hand.'

Sphax recalled the events of that bleak winter's day last December. As Artula had grabbed the hand of her son and raced towards the safety of Sphax's javelins, a desperate cry had rung out and both had turned to witness Roman equites cutting down a blind, defenceless old man, the wise chieftain of all that was left of the Anamares. That man was Garos, Artula's father, the boy's grandfather.

'Then I will go with you,' declared Corinna, facing the inevitable truth at last.

'No, Corinna. Your plans are set, there is a fair wind from the west and your vessel is ready.' Shaking her head, Artula added, 'I fear this might not be as simple as it would appear. Suppose Meilyr doesn't approach his father immediately. He may go into hiding and wait for the march to begin, in which case there would be no turning back. His father would have little choice but to take him. I know my son; he's clever and resourceful, especially when his mind is made up. Finding him may take weeks, not days.'

'Then let us embrace and say our farewells. For you must go,' and with that Corinna reached out with both arms and drew her dear friend to her bosom.

Within the hour it had all been arranged. Artula had strapped a few essential possessions to a pack horse and ridden out of the southerly gate with Juba and his eshrin. After waving them off, Sphax walked heavy-legged through camp towards the distant sandbar and another embrace and tearful farewell.

'When will our son be born?' Sphax whispered in Corinna's ear. He was clinging to her, dreading the moment when he would have to release his arms and finally let her go.

'In the autumn, my love,' she whispered tenderly. 'I will ripen with the season's fruit and pluck him in September.'

'So, as our army goes into winter quarters, I will cross the Adria and look upon his face. Then we will marry. This I swear to you, as long as I live.'

'You *must* live!' she sobbed. 'I could not bear to live without you. You must survive the coming storms, for my sake … and your son's.' He kissed her fiercely, full on the lips, and when the kiss came to an end he gently released her. For the last time.

'Farewell,' he cried, reaching for the gunnels and leaping into the shallow water beside the sandbar. Walking at pace, he neither turned around to wave, or stole a last look as the vessel caught the great river's current and was swept downstream out of sight.

Sphax was desperate to immerse himself in activity. Anything to fill the void of emptiness that now engulfed him. What saved him from despair was work, hard, unrelenting work. Luckily, there was still much to do.

He found the nights almost unbearable. His now empty pavilion, devoid of everything but their sleeping couch, his few clothes scattered around and a rack of javelins, seemed to mock him. On the first night he slumped on the couch dog-tired, yet sleep still evaded him. After tossing and turning for a couple of hours he got up and walked the rounds of his sentries until dawn provided relief in work.

On the second day of their parting, Sphax ordered the camp stewards to take down his pavilion and store it. In the meantime he found his small goatskin tent and erected it himself, close to his eshrin's encampment. That evening he shared their campfires and banter before managing a few hours of sleep.

He also missed Idwal. His dear friend's wise counsel and good sense had always got him through the darker moments of his life. But Idwal was seventy miles away in the army's encampment outside Bona. He would not see him for another week.

And so it was with immense relief that on the third morning after Corinna's departure, he led his eshrin through the southerly gate at the head of a thousand Numidians. A new chapter in his life was about to begin, and Sphax was eager to turn the page.

FIVE

It had been so long since Sphax had ridden with an army on the march he had to recall the lessons his mentor, Maharbal, had taught him. And indeed, there was much to remember. After several alterations to his march plan, by the afternoon of the first day he thought he'd got the measure of it.

His all-consuming nightmare was the strings of pack animals. They almost outnumbered his Numidians. Even riding in three parallel lines abreast the column straggled back for more than half a mile. If they were attacked — and Maharbal had drilled it into him that he *must* expect to be attacked — the plunder to be ransacked from their pack trains would be the target.

Sphax finally solved this conundrum by placing the trains directly behind the Numidian van and surrounding them with ten eshrins. This solid phalanx of horses was made possible by the nature of the terrain. Other than a few Boii settlements dotted here and there, the track lay as straight as an arrow, south east, through mile after monotonous mile of flat grassland with barely a tree in the way.

With two eshrins scouting on each flank and Himilco a mile out front with three, by the second day Sphax felt reasonably confident they were invulnerable to any sudden assault. But he was watchful. Doing the rounds of the campfires every night he reminded his captains to stay alert.

On the afternoon of the third day, Sphax realised with a kind of grim satisfaction that he hadn't thought about Corinna all morning. It was progress of sorts he thought, but it offered as little consolation as the good-natured teasing and banter he suffered around his men's campfires in the evenings. He was growing tired of being referred to as 'the lovesick captain'. Most of the time Sphax gave as good as he got, and if the barbs came too thick and fast for a riposte, he would take himself off to check on Aethon. He'd assigned a trusted groom to look after her, leading her by a guide-rope, but all this was new to the mare.

In the far distance to the south west, Sphax suddenly noticed clouds of black smoke rising in the cold dank air. Turning to Agbal, who had the keenest sight in his eshrin, he asked, 'You've travelled this road before: is that smoke coming from our camp at Bona?'

'No, captain,' Agbal answered, squinting anxiously into the distance. 'We won't catch sight of the place 'til late tomorrow morning. That smoke's coming from the south west, away from our track.'

Smoke from an unexpected quarter was never a welcome sight, and sometimes meant trouble.

Making up his mind, he yelled over to Manissa, 'I'm taking my men to investigate that smoke on the horizon. I'm leaving you in charge. For the love of Ba 'al Hamūn, stay in formation!'

Looking down the length of his thirty-man line, Sphax raised a javelin.

To a man his men rode Iberian or African jennets. With their easy lope they could canter effortlessly for hours. As he nudged Dido into this stride the entire eshrin took their cue from him and surged forward. After half a mile he was surprised to see Himilco's three eshrins ahead. They should have been at least two miles ahead, not here. Something was wrong.

Himilco had drawn them up in a solid line. Waiting. A faintly acrid smell drifted on the air. From the fires, he guessed, though he couldn't see flames or anything that would produce so much smoke. It was only when he rode up to Himilco that he understood.

Half a mile ahead was a gentle ridge, hardly high ground, but enough to obscure the view of the shallow valley beyond, and that's where the smoke was coming from.

Himilco was grinning. 'I see the smoke has aroused your curiosity, as well. I've sent out scouts.' Aribal and Hanno, Himilco's other captains, rode over to within earshot. Sphax nodded in greeting. At that moment two men came galloping down the ridge at high speed, drawing in their mares in front of Himilco.

'There's at least one Roman turma in that Boii settlement over yonder,' growled one the scouts, eyes flashing between Sphax and his captain. 'The bastards have fired some roundhouses.'

'What's the ground like?' Sphax asked.

'Flat as an elephant's arse! Just rolling grassland … few trees. Fields of corn far side of the settlement. We could ride ten eshrins abreast in that valley.'

'One single turma of thirty equites!' crowed Himilco gleefully. 'I fancy those odds, Sphax.'

Sphax smiled ruefully to himself. For three days these men had ridden without incident or a care in the world, yet in the next breath their hearts were pounding and they were reaching for javelins, spoiling for a fight. Such was a soldier's life.

Sphax's heart might not be pounding, but his thoughts were racing: what was a single turma doing in these parts, miles from their base in Ariminum? A legion's equites numbered three hundred. Where were the other nine turmae?

Still scowling, the other scout gazed imploringly at Sphax. 'There's bodies everywhere, Sir. We could hear screaming. It's not a pretty sight.'

His partner nodded, spat, and repeated, 'Roman bastards.'

'How big is this Boii settlement?' asked Sphax. 'A village? Town?'

Shrugging, the guides stared at one another before suggesting it was the size of a small town.

That decided it for Sphax. Turning to Jugurtha astride his mare beside him, 'Gallop back to Manissa' he ordered, 'tell him to bring up four fresh eshrins with all speed. They're to head for this Boii settlement. He's to leave Gala in charge of the trains.'

'Wise thinking, lad,' said Jugurtha, nudging his mare to the rear. 'A reserve might come in handy,' and with that he was off.

By now the men from eshrins on either flank had broken ranks to hear what was being said, so he hardly had to raise his voice. 'Timing and surprise are key. We must attack the settlement as one. Upon my signal, Aribal will peel away and attack from the north, Hanno from the east and Himilco from the west. I will delay my charge to allow you all to get into place before I attack from the south.'

An afterthought occurred. 'I need prisoners. Spare any that throw away weapons and look to surrender. Now get into line and let's give Rome a nasty surprise.'

Before he nudged Dido into place he glanced at Himilco. For the past two weeks he'd worked with a thoughtful, blue-eyed scholar. Now he met the gaze of a savage warrior. Sphax suddenly recalled the grim-faced lieutenant he'd fought alongside at the Trebia.

Clutching javelins threaded with a throwing thong in their right hands and spare javelins and a small hide shield in their left, eshrins rode in silence and rarely needed orders. Cheering was considered unseemly, even unmanly. There was no roar of triumph as a storm of javelins were hurled. Numidians dealt out death in silence. Every man knew his place in the line and what was expected of him, and unlike Roman legions, Numidians didn't give a fig about straight lines or rigid formations. Captains rode in the centre of each eshrin so their men could see them clearly.

Usually a wave of a captain's javelin was sufficient to set them in motion, and that's exactly what Sphax did next.

As the wave of horsemen approached the top of the ridge he kept the pace at a trot. The slope was deceptively steep and there was little point in tiring their mares uphill. At the crest the landscape revealed itself as if the shutters of a window had suddenly been flung open. For the first time since the march had begun, Sphax was looking at a horizon perhaps fifteen miles distant. But his gaze was not seeking out horizons.

What caught his eye were two blazing roundhouses in the middle of a settlement not half a mile distant. Figures on horseback seemed to be dashing and weaving through the dirt tracks. He guessed the equites were chasing villagers, but at this distance he couldn't be certain. What was certain was that some figures lay still and motionless in the dirt. Himilco's scouts had been right. It was not a pretty sight. Sphax nudged Dido into a canter.

Ahead of them was a cavalryman's dream: lush grassland dotted with low-growing shrubs and bushes, hardly an impediment to a jennet's stride. Leaving the separation of his eshrins until the last moment, Sphax raised his javelin three hundred paces from the settlement.

Because they'd achieved complete surprise, what followed next was the most chaotic and bewildering fight Sphax had ever experienced. After it was all over, Sphax cursed his rashness in ordering it in the first place, and swore never to risk such an encounter again. If they'd met a turma of equites on the grasslands, odds of four to one in their favour would have been decided the outcome in a single charge. But in the confines of a crowded settlement, numbers counted for little, swords and spears proved to be far more effective than ranged weapons like javelins, and their hide shields were useless. Sphax never bothered with them anyway.

Boii settlements were not laid out in regular, grid-like streets. Numidians met startled equites on narrow dirt tracks, hemmed in by roundhouses, dead and wounded strewn on the ground, screaming women shepherding children to safety and old men wielding weapons they'd not used for twenty years. Adding to the confusion was the fact that the villagers had never set eyes on Numidians in their lives. With no way of distinguishing friend from foe, all they had to go on was that these dark-skinned cavalrymen seemed to be skewering Romans.

Flanked by Hannon and Agbal, Sphax soon found himself surrounded by a mob of hysterical villagers, desperate to escape Roman spears. 'Run past us to the fields,' he screamed in Latin, hoping some of the Boii would understand. Most did. But his words also attracted the unwelcome attention of several equites who'd been shepherding the fugitives.

Hannon's javelin accounted for one of them, but spears were now flying their way. Screaming, a young girl who'd been clinging to his leg took a grazing blow to her arm. Slumping to the ground, a bloody stain began gathering on her tunic.

'Fly! Fly!' he screamed again. 'Run for your lives. To the fields … flee to the fields!'

Leaping from Dido, he gently dabbed the blood from her arm and carried the child into a roundhouse. He had little choice but to leave her sobbing in pain, but he knew the wound was not deep. She would live.

At last the crowds had begun to thin, allowing his men the space to hurl javelins. Two more equites slumped in their saddles. As more of his eshrin joined him the wary enemy began to back away.

On horseback the narrowness of the street — it was hardly that, just a dirt track between roundhouses — would only permit five Numidians to ride abreast. If they met a similar number of equites in a charge, it would hardly be to their advantage. This was madness, he realised.

'Dismount,' he shouted to his men. 'Our mares only hinder us here. Dismount and fight on foot.' Even on foot, with a throwing thong Numidians could hurl their javelins twice the distance equites could throw a spear.

Now they could stalk their enemies shoulder to shoulder in lines of ten, javelins raised, ready to fly in an instant.

Now dismounted, Sphax formed his eshrin in three lines of ten. He was about to signal his men forward when he thought better of it; the enemy could just as easily be inside!

'Search every roundhouse!' he yelled, pointing to the open doorways either side of him. After all six houses had been declared abandoned, he was about to order his men cautiously forward when three horsemen appeared out of nowhere, spears held aloft. His Numidians met them with a hail of javelins. Once more three saddles were emptied and riderless horses trotted aimlessly through their ranks.

Sphax waited for his men to thread fresh javelins before he shouted, 'Forward, lads. Slowly!' He could now hear the screams and cries of battle all around him. His front rank reached the fallen equites. Agbal put one of them out of his misery to recover his javelin. From here the track turned southwards, widening to a circular area lined by roundhouses.

'Wait here,' he commanded, drawing his dragon sword from its sheath strapped to his back. 'Search the other houses,' he added, before slashing aside a leather drape acting as a door and entering the house.

Even though there was a small fire burning in a brazier and an oil lamp near the entrance, it took his eyes several heartbeats to adjust to the gloom. It was then he realised he was not alone.

On a mattress lay a half-naked woman, her tunic ripped and tattered. Kneeling over her was a decurion, left hand wrestling the woman's wrist whilst his right hand was jammed over her mouth to prevent her crying out. A tasselled helmet, spear and crimson cloak had been cast aside for other pleasures. Sphax had no time to decide who was the most surprised by this unexpected encounter.

As the Roman made a grab for his spear the woman screamed. Sphax leapt forward, scything his long Gaulish blade through the air. It took most of the man's neck with it.

Choking and gurgling he slumped over his tasselled helmet in a quickening pool of blood. Sphax was left staring at a voluptuous pair of breasts.

'Do you like what you see?' the woman hissed, her voice shaking with a mixture of fear and rage.

It was as if he'd been slapped across the face. Hastily turning his back to respect her modesty he croaked, 'No, madam … I mean, I'm here to defend you … not dishonour you.'

'I'm glad to hear it!' She replied in Latin laced with a thick accent. After much shuffling she eventually stood beside him, pale and trembling from her ordeal, her face red and bruised. What was left of her tattered plaid tunic she'd covered with a henna-dyed shawl to hide her nakedness. Lowering her eyes she mumbled, 'I'm in your debt for saving me from that animal.'

'I'm Sphax, commanding Numidians marching to join Hannibal's army.' He too lowered his eyes. 'And you are not in my debt.'

'I am Betua, daughter of Carmo, chief of the Boii in these parts. My husband, Ducarius, is already with your army at Bona.' Anxiously she pleaded, 'I must find my father, he will be in grave danger.'

'Of course,' he agreed, glancing at the decurion to make certain he'd breathed his last. Once outside he checked his men were still holding their formation and asked if all the houses had been searched. The nodding abruptly changed to smirking and lewd whispering as Betua walked through the doorway. But Sphax's thunderous expression instantly put a stop to it.

'This is Betua,' he said sternly, 'daughter of the chief. Unlike you laggards, her husband is already serving with the army at Bona.' Rounding on them he raised his voice. 'You will address her as mistress, and be courteous at all times. Understood?' There was a muttering of agreement.

But in broad daylight, even their lovesick captain could see she was quite a beauty. He made no mention of the *animal* he'd left half-decapitated in the roundhouse. Turning to Betua he asked, 'Where might your father be?'

'His feasting hall or the stables. Both have doors that can be bolted and barred.' Lowering her voice to a whisper she added, 'That's where I was going when that bastard grabbed me and forced me into the house. This street leads there.'

'How far?'

'Half a mile.'

Sphax groaned. The place was much bigger than he'd imagined. Hearing hoofbeats once more he yelled, 'Javelins!'

This time there were five of them. Forty paces from their lines they reined in abruptly, took one look at the ranks of raised javelins and thought better of it, hastily backing away.

'Let's get this over with,' he snapped, finally losing all patience. Giving up the idea of searching all the houses — it would have taken all day — it was time for a new plan.

'I want those in the second rank to thread javelins and have them at the ready. If the first rank can't kill everyone we meet, the second rank will dash forward and finish them off. Now forward … and keep marching!

'Stay beside me,' he told Betua, sheathing his sword and fingering his iron saunion.

Striding down that track soon became a sickening nightmare, a stroll through a corpse-ridden Hades that would long be etched in his memory. Every twenty paces or so they would come upon the bloodstained pile of rags that marked the body of an old man or woman, left where they'd fallen like way markers on a Roman road. Not all were old. Whilst every step added to the rage he was feeling, Betua was beside herself; weeping silent tears as she bent over each body in turn, hoping for signs of life. Sphax's only thought was that someone would pay for this senseless slaughter.

To his immense relief, after two hundred paces he caught sight of Himilco and his eshrin, guarding what appeared to be a crossroads, fifty paces ahead. He'd also had the good sense to order his men to fight on foot.

Himilco strode over. 'Dog's twat, Sphax! I hadn't bargained on this.'

'None of us did. Any wounded?'

'Two,' Himilco sighed. 'One badly. I've left them in a house over yonder,' nodding in the direction of the track leading off to the right.

'Any sign of Hanno?'

Himilco shook his head. 'I've heard his eshrin fighting though … and Aribal?'

'The same. Sounds of battle, but no sign of him. This place is like a labyrinth … you could hide an army here, let alone a turma of equites.'

Sphax had an idea. Selecting a javelin he laid the rest on the ground and called to Betua. With the iron point he scratched a cross in the dirt and asked, 'If we are standing at this crossroad,' pointing to the place on his dirt map, 'could you draw for me the streets that lead to the feasting hall and stables? I'll find something to mark their position.'

Handing her the javelin, he entered the nearest house and started rummaging around. After a few moments he found what he was looking for and by the time he returned, Betua's map had grown considerably.

After standing back to take in her creation, she added a couple of final marks before nodding at Sphax. Reaching for the pair of wooden bowls he'd collected she placed them carefully.

He and Himilco stared at them. 'It looks as if the hall and stables lie outside the town. What lies beyond them, Betua?' Sphax asked.

'The town's market place, and beyond that more roundhouses, granaries, warehouses—'

'Could you draw these houses?' Handing her back the javelin.

'But there are no streets there. You asked me to draw streets.'

'I know. But it will help me visualise the place.' Dutifully she drew a large semicircle surrounding the wooden bowls. 'So, your market place is completely enclosed by roundhouses and warehouses, and you're sure these three streets are the only ones that lead there?'

Betua nodded. 'Our market is renowned in these parts, in my language it's called the *magos loer*, the field of the moon, because it takes the form of a crescent. That's where we hold the festival of Rigantona, our goddess of the moon. You may know her as Epona.'

Sphax knew all about Epona, but goddesses would not help him plan an attack. Pointing to features with his javelin he explained all this to Himilco, who had no Latin. 'What do you think?' he asked, when he'd finished.

'Well, that market place would provide space for cavalry,' Himilco agreed. 'So it's quite likely that's where they are. But think about it, Sphax. Your eshrin alone has accounted for five of the bastards, including a decurion. Mine has killed three. If Hanno and Aribal have done the same, there can't be many of them left … no more than eighteen … if—'

In that instant Himilco's voice was drowned by the gathering thunder of galloping hooves. 'Javelins!' they both yelled. Hastily they formed their men into two lines to defend the left hand track at the crossroads. There they waited anxiously.

To everyone's relief it turned out to be another false alarm. Aribal's eshrin had arrived, galloping at speed along the narrow track in a column four abreast. Leaping from his mare, the captain strode over to greet them. Not much older than Sphax, Aribal was a likeable hothead, with a permanent grin, luxuriant raven braids threaded with silver beads, and a fearless swagger his men worshipped.

'Where's the enemy?' he asked eagerly.

'You tell me,' Sphax laughed.

'We had a run in with a few of them early on, sticking a couple of them before they turned tail and fled. Since then … nothing. Butchering old men and women seems to be more to their taste,' Aribal observed with a rare scowl.

'Have you any wounded? asked Sphax.

Aribal shrugged, his grin returning. 'Masinissa has a scratch.'

'Come and take a look at this map we've drawn,' suggested Himilco. Using a javelin he pointed to the tracks and indicated the position of the market place. 'We think that's where they've gathered.'

Sphax could see Betua restlessly pacing, impatient to set off for the feasting hall and discover the fate of her father. With the arrival of Aribal's eshrin the last part of his plan neatly slotted into place. The problem had always been timing. Now Aribal's mares provided the solution. 'Everyone gather round,' he bawled. 'This is what we're going to do.'

Waiting until everyone was in earshot, Sphax pointed his javelin straight ahead. 'Moving silently, my eshrin will take this track. Once we come in sight of the market place my men will hide in the nearest roundhouse.' Turning to Himilco he continued, 'Take your eshrin back down this track to where it meets the one leading to the market place. Once you sight the market place stay hidden.'

Next he turned to Aribal. 'Walk your mares — take your time — back to the track that carries straight on to the market place.'

'We saw that track,' Aribal said, nodding.

'Wait a little before you show your face, that way you'll give Himilco time to get in place; he's got the farthest distance to walk. It might be wise to get your eshrin into single file, so when you do ride out into the open you can quickly get into line. If what's left of the turma is at the market, your eshrin will provide the bait to flush them out. Do not charge! Just form line and wait. Once the enemy's eyes are fixed on you, Himilco and I will fall on them. When you join the fight we should have them hemmed in from three sides. It's high time we avenged the slaughter of old men and women.'

Instead of marching in a solid phalanx, this time the eshrin crept forward in two files, either side of the track, staying as close to the houses as possible for cover. They were in a highly vulnerable formation in the event of a sudden cavalry attack, but Sphax thought it worth the risk. It was more important they weren't spotted. Betua was not pleased to be placed at the back of one of the files with Agbal keeping an eye on her. But he was worried that if she saw her father in real danger, she might do something foolish and wreck his plans.

After eighty paces he thought he could faintly hear the sound of voices. Ten paces ahead the track turned to the south east. Raising a hand to signal his eshrin to halt, Sphax crept gingerly around the back of the next roundhouse until he could see what lay ahead.

The enemy were much closer than he'd anticipated, no more than forty paces away. He counted at least ten equites, most on foot, but three were mounted, one of whom was barking a stream of orders. Another decurion, Sphax guessed. With satisfaction he noticed that none were carrying their heavy oval shields. Shields offered the best protection against javelins. Their thigh-length coats of mail could be pierced by a javelin flung with venom.

Although his view was restricted to what could be seen between the last two roundhouses either side of the track, it was enough. He could clearly see the feasting hall Betua had described. Shaped like a tortoise, its great thatched roof was supported by huge oaken piles, sunk into the ground. Either side of the hall and beyond was the field of the moon, beloved of Rigantona.

As he watched, crouched low on his haunches, a sickening feeling gathered in the pit of his belly. Sphax realised his carefully laid plans were now in ruins. Aribal would hardly be in place, let alone Himilco. But something had to be done now, before it was too late!

Equites were collecting firewood and stacking it before the great oaken doors of the feasting hall. Two of them were pouring a golden liquid over the pile from clay jars. He was certain it was oil. They were about to fire the building. And its thatch and timbers would go up in flames like a tinderbox.

If he was to save Betua's father and the town's elders, his eshrin alone would have to strike fast. He made up his mind. Too many old men had died that day.

SIX

Racing back to his eshrin Sphax gathered them around him. Whilst threading his saunion he spoke quietly but resolutely. 'Thread javelins and form lines. We charge now. The bastards are about to fire the feasting hall.' Glancing at Betua he caught the look of horror on her face. 'The chief and all the town's elders are inside. If we act swiftly we can save them. We haven't time to wait for Himilco and Aribal. By my reckoning, we still have twice their numbers.'

Taking his place in the middle of the front rank he urged them forward. By the luck of the gods they were only spotted when they spilled from the track onto the field of the moon. By now they were all breathing hard, but javelins were already flying, spinning their deadly courses. Screams and cries of pain filled the air.

Sphax was saving his saunion for the mounted decurion, now staring at them with a mixture of surprise and contempt as he drew his sword and tightened reins. As the man nudged his stallion forward,

Sphax raised his saunion, tightened the leather around his fingers and raced forward to hurl.

But his aim was poor. If, in that fateful moment, the decurion hadn't raised his sword, the saunion would have sailed harmlessly over his right shoulder. As it was it pierced his upper arm, the leaf-shaped barb going clean through flesh and bone. Flung with such force it propelled the man sprawling from his saddle, shrieking in pain as the blade fell from his grasp.

Seeking revenge for their wounded decurion, the last of the mounted equites headed straight for them, spears raised. Sphax's next javelin met the throat of one of them, whilst Vermina's accounted for the other.

'Glad to see your aim's improving,' grunted Hannon. Why was it that whenever a fight grew hot and vicious, he would find Hannon beside him? Had the veteran taken on the role of bodyguard, he wondered? It had happened so many times before, Sphax found it difficult to dismiss this conclusion. He could hardly object. Hannon's javelins never missed.

On foot, Numidians always fought in small groups, taking it in turn to hurl javelins. That way there was always a weapon at the ready in case of a sudden rush or nasty surprise. It was Hannon's turn to throw, but as Sphax looked anxiously around him, checking his men were still standing, all he could see of the enemy were dead, or groaning wounded.

'It's over, Sir,' said Vermina, almost disappointed. 'I've counted fifteen, including that decurion you stuck.'

Suddenly he burst into laughter, 'The bastard's trying to crawl away with it stuck in his arm. Shall I put him out of his misery, Captain? You'll be wanting your saunion back.'

How easily Numidians deal out death, Sphax thought for the hundredth time. 'No. Keep the fellow alive. I need to question him. He's much to answer for!'

Before the brief fight had begun, Sphax had ordered Agbal to restrain Betua and keep her out of danger. Now she managed to wriggle free. Racing past him, leaping the dead and wounded she ran up to the oaken doors of the feasting hall and began pounding with her fists, yelling something in her own tongue. She must have got a response from inside, for suddenly she stopped pounding and fell silent.

Slowly the doors swung open and Betua flung herself into the embrace of someone hidden in the darkness of the doorway. Moments later, Carmo, chief of the Boii, emerged with an arm around his daughter. In late middle age, yet still retaining something of the vigour of his youth, Carmo had the bearing of a soldier, a beak of a nose and keen, pale blue eyes. But the procession of village elders following on behind presented one of the most comical sights Sphax had seen for a long time.

There were nine of them. The sprightliest among them must have seen over sixty summers. But he looked youthful by comparison. It was not their age that amused his men — Numidians venerate age and wisdom — but their extraordinary motley collection of ancient armour. What might have fitted forty years ago now looked faintly ridiculous: ill-fitting helmets covering eyes, chain mail swirling about ankles and breast plates resting on oversized bellies.

For the second time that afternoon, Sphax had to silence his men's sniggering with stern glances.

Carmo approached, his arm still around his daughter's waist. 'We owe you a debt of gratitude, Sir,' his Latin more fluent than his daughter's. 'Not only for saving my old bones and those of my elders, but my daughter informs me you've spared the town much slaughter.'

There was no mention of Sphax sparing his daughter from violation, but then he realised this was a delicate matter of honour, not to be spoken of. 'The Boii owe no debt of gratitude to Numidians or Hannibal, Sir. Your people have always remained our staunchest allies. Victory at the Trebia would not have been possible without the bravery of your warriors.'

'Eloquently spoken.' Carmo was effusive, yet his eyes continually darted amongst the dead and wounded equites littering the ground. 'So you are Hannibal's nephew?' Sphax nodded. 'You have quite a reputation, young man. I've heard of the skill and courage of Numidians, but to see the results of it! Is it true that your only weapon is the javelin?'

'It is, Sir.'

'Had I not seen this with my own eyes, I would not have believed such a weapon capable of execution on this scale.'

As if from nowhere, the market place suddenly teemed with Numidians coming from every direction, some on horseback, others, like Himilco's eshrin, on foot. Even Hanno's eshrin made a belated appearance with five prisoners in tow and a string of stallions. But what caught Sphax's eye was a single Numidian, galloping at high speed towards him. It was his veteran scout, Jugurtha. Sphax knew instantly there was trouble.

Bowing to Carmo, he said, 'Forgive me, Sir. I must take my leave. My scout approaches.' At least he was spared another discussion of javelins.

With his grizzled beard shot through with silver, and eyes that seemingly saw round corners. Jugurtha was not much younger than Betua's father, yet he leapt nimbly from his mare. 'You'd better join Manissa's eshrins outside the town,' he insisted, adding cryptically. 'There's something you must see.'

'What is it?' Sphax asked.

'I think you should see it for yourself, then you can best judge.'

Jugurtha was *never* evasive. What was going on? Turning to Hannon he ordered, 'Bring one of the equites' stallions over for me to ride.'

'If I were you, lad, I'd take Aribal's and Hanno's eshrins with us, and round up our own mares fast.'

Sphax saw that Jugurtha was giving him what amounted to a tacit set of orders. Jugurtha was a veteran of countless campaigns; as a boy he'd even fought alongside Sphax's father, Navaras, in the Truceless War. Sphax trusted Jugurtha with his life.

When Hannon handed him the reins of a fine grey stallion, Sphax told him to round up their mares and meet him on the grasslands outside the town, adding, 'And make it quick, Hannon.'

Himilco, Aribal and Hanno were deep in conversation with Betua and her father. 'Get over here, you three, I have new orders for you all,' he shouted.

As two of the captains got their eshrins into columns of four as he'd instructed, Sphax turned to Himilco. 'You're in charge here. See to the wounded if you can and keep that decurion alive — I'm anxious to question him.'

Jumping into the saddle, he tried once more with his tight-lipped scout. 'Now, what's this all about, Jugurtha?'

'This turma,' the scout began, nodding at the dead, 'weren't firing the settlement, they were lighting a beacon.'

Beacons could only mean one thing. This was worse than he'd imagined.

Sphax found himself staring at a legion's entire contingent of cavalry, drawn up in line with rigid

Roman precision. With their crimson cloaks and dyed horsehair plumes stirring in the breeze, they looked like some blood-red rampart, spiked with spears. They were no more than a mile away, atop the shallow ridge they themselves had descended to come to the aid of the town. But from where they'd ridden down its slope, the ridge veered to the south, and that's where the equites had positioned themselves, blocking the road to Bona and the south east. They looked wary and watchful. Waiting.

He was also waiting. His own eshrin would arrive soon with his mare. Then he would attack, trampling this crimson rampart into the dust.

When Manissa had first pointed them out, Sphax had been astonished. 'Why haven't they attacked? They have twice your numbers!'

'Those arsewits weren't sure how many eshrins we might be hiding in the town.'

'Well, they know now. Have you seen any of their alae?' he'd asked next. Roman cavalry rarely operated on their own. Beside their own equites, each Roman legion was allotted an allied cavalry squadron.

'Not a Campanian cocksucker in sight, lad,' Manissa had told him. 'Pity though ... the Iberians pay good silver for their breastplates!' Sphax had laughed. As different as a Samnite was from a Lucanian, they were all Campanians to Manissa.

'I want you to find me a messenger,' he'd told Manissa earlier, 'someone who can ride fast and understand clear instructions.' Sphax would have preferred to send Jugurtha, but the scout's mare was blown and badly needed a rest.

Manissa had brought over a young lad riding a dun-coloured Egyptian mare. Stressing the urgency of the situation, Sphax had instructed him to find Gala and order the four scouting eshrins on the flanks to form up and attack south along the ridge, striking the equites' right flank. Hiempsal — the most impetuous of the four captains — was to command. Gala was to stay put and guard the pack trains until he received further orders. When he'd finished, Sphax had asked the lad to repeat the message to be sure he'd understood.

He'd calculated the risks. The last thing he wanted was Gala blundering into those equites, that's why he'd ordered him to stay put. But if the equites' *real* objective was their supply columns, Gala's six eshrins would be enough to give Rome an unpleasant surprise.

At long last Hannon appeared with the rest of his men. Mounting Dido, Sphax formed his eshrin in the center of the Numidian line and nudged his mare into a walk. He was soon urging her to canter, and with each successive stride he could feel the mounting exhilaration coursing through his veins like a heady wine. These were the moments he lived for. The thunder of hooves became deafening. His saunion had already accounted for one decurion, now another would suffer the same fate. Sphax fingered his leather thong and tightened his grip. They were closing fast now.

Glancing to the north he caught sight of Hiempsal's four eshrins thundering along the crest of the ridge. Now they outnumbered the enemy. If Hiempsal was timely and grasped the opportunity to fall on the equites' rear, two irresistible waves of horsemen were about to deliver fatal blows. Caught in the coming firestorm of javelins, the enemy would be annihilated and scattered to the four winds.

In that instant the same inevitable conclusion must have entered the head of a tribune or a decurion. Rome turned tail and fled! One hoofbeat they were there, in the next they'd vanished. It must have been a case of every man for himself. Almost three hundred equites disappeared the way they'd come; back down the slope. Chasing would have been pointless. And so it was over before it had begun.

As they brought their sweating mares to a halt, laughter and jeering broke out all along the Numidian line. But it was no laughing matter for Sphax. All he felt at that moment was anger and desperate frustration. He'd won a pointless moral victory. So what? The bitter truth was that he'd let a golden opportunity to destroy a legion's cavalry slip through his fingers.

'You will tell me everything I want to know,' demanded Sphax, barely able to hide the contempt he felt for the decurion trussed like a sacrificial pig in the chair opposite him. They were sitting in a corner of the feasting hall beside a brazier to ward off the evening chill. One of Himilco's men had removed his saunion and bound the decurion's upper arm, probably saving the man's miserable skin. Earlier, Sphax had handed the other prisoners over to Carmo. Recruited from wealthier citizens and the merchant classes, equites fetched high ransoms. Meagre recompense for the misery they'd inflicted, but the chief was grateful. 'In truth,' Sphax continued, 'you'll tell me things I would never have guessed or even dreamt of asking. You'll become a fount of information, a veritable oracle—'

'—I wouldn't count on it, you black savage.'

Sphax slowly unsheathed his dragon sword; appearing to examine its exquisite workmanship he fingered the guard and pommel, which had been shaped in the form of an elephant's tusks. With an agile flick of his wrist he suddenly rested the point of the blade against the man's unwounded upper arm. The man flinched. 'This blade pierces more easily than my saunion. I'm sure you don't want to lose both arms …'

'What do you want to know?' the man muttered, eyes never leaving Sphax's blade.

'How many legions and alae has Servilius gathered at Ariminum?'

Sphax responded to the decurion's silence by prodding the blade so it pierced the man's woollen tunic, pricking his skin and drawing blood.

'Two,' the decurion said quickly. 'With Samnites and Lucanians on the way.'

'Which legion are you from?' Sphax asked casually.

'The third.'

'So …' taking a logical guess, 'the fourth legion's equites are in Ariminum?' Sphax's mind was racing. This was vital information. Their pack trains were still half a day from Bona. Whereas ten turmae could be attacked, twenty presented more of a problem.

'I don't know. But they weren't with us.'

Hiding his relief, Sphax continued, 'Did you have any alae with you?'

'No,' grunted the decurion. 'I've already told you, we're still awaiting our Samnites and Lucanians.'

The man was getting positively cooperative, thought Sphax. But this was another golden nugget of information. 'What were your orders when you set out from Ariminum?'

'How should I know! Ask that cocksucker of a tribune, Titus Collina.'

'And you were doing so well,' observed Sphax with mock sympathy, jabbing his blade a little deeper. This time the man cried out.

'We were to search for Hannibal's army north-west of Bona …. raid Boii villages … burn their crops … the usual.' Words were now spilling from his mouth faster than water from a Roman fountain. Sphax didn't like the sound of *the usual.*

'What were your orders concerning this town?'

'It was supposed to be empty. We were told the Gauls had fled the place weeks ago.' For the first time the decurion met his gaze levelly. 'We were to light beacons so the other turmae could find it, even after dark. But as soon as Marcus saw all those women and children, he had other ideas—'

'Who's Marcus, and what do you mean by *other ideas*?'

'Marcus is the primus decurion, I'm just a lackey … a tertius. When he saw all those young women and children he told us there was a fortune to be made. His father runs the biggest slave market in Rome. He told us to round them—'

'You slaughtered defenceless old men and women!' Sphax had to fight the urge to ram the sword down the bastard's throat. 'Why?'

'I … I swear that was not me. Marcus said no one would pay silver for old men.'

'So you butchered them!'

'No … no! I swear! Once he caught sight of that woman and dragged her off it all stopped. I swear to you.'

Sphax could now put a face to this Marcus, or at least a half-decapitated head. 'Marcus has already paid with his life for that'.

The man's jaw dropped. 'Dead?'

'Very!' Sphax suddenly felt weary of the conversation. Had he expected answers? An explanation? A confession of guilt? Sphax knew from the tales he'd heard of the sacking of Saguntum what happened when soldiers were let loose on a town. Without glancing at the tertius decurion, Sphax sheathed his sword and walked away.

At dawn the next day, all the folk from the town he now knew to be Mutina, turned out to say their farewells. His little army and pack trains had camped on the grassland outside the town. Luckily for many of his captains, who hadn't far to stagger back from the feasting hall late that night. Carmo had been generous with his mead, which most of his men had never tasted before. There were many sore heads that morning. Sphax did warn them!

He was touched when Betua presented him with a beautiful drinking horn, its base and lip decorated with bands of silver. 'I shall treasure it,' he'd told her as he'd mounted Dido.

'I hope to meet you again in Bona. I travel there later this afternoon to say farewell to my husband, Ducarius, a chief of Insubres.'

'Until then, madam, farewell.' But in truth, Sphax was not sorry when the town faded into the distance, hoping his memories would do the same.

The rest of the morning was uneventful. In the sultry heat, Sphax rode with Himilco, a mile ahead of the Numidian van and pack trains, passing the time pleasantly enough. But what pleased him most was the sight of a range of hills, rising up from the monotony of the flat grasslands. As these uplands drew closer, his spirits rose with them.

Shortly after midday the town itself came within sight. Bona proved to be much bigger and grander than Sphax had imagined, with as many stone buildings as traditional Boii wood and thatch roundhouses. Sturdy wooden walls with watchtowers enclosed a central area. But to the east of the town lay an even more populous city of almost sixty thousand martial inhabitants, whose vast sea of tents and pavilions stretched as far as the eye could see.

Less than a mile from the Carthaginian encampment, he could see they were about to be greeted by a welcoming party of three horsemen, two of whom he recognised.

'As usual, you're late, young man,' growled Maharbal with his habitual friendliness. At least his standard bearer Bartho was grinning, pleased to see him. Sphax nodded a greeting to the third member of the party, whom he didn't recognise. With shoulder length blond curls and full beard, he had the look of the northern Gauls Idwal had told him about.

'Yesterday we had a run in with the equites of the third legion. This may have delayed us, Sir.'

'The third legion!' laughed Maharbal. 'Not the first or the fourth? How can you be certain?'

'Because I asked them,' explained Sphax, trying not to laugh.

'Had a good chat, eh? Share jests and tell each other stories …' Now Sphax did burst out laughing. There was no dealing with Maharbal when he was in a mood like this.

'We took six prisoners from a turma attacking Mutina, a town twenty miles north-east of here.

I interrogated a decurion we captured.' Now Sphax had his general's full attention. 'Consul Servilius has legions three and four with him at Ariminum, but his alae — Lucanians and Samnites — have not yet joined him. They're still on the road. Which means the first and second legions are with Flaminius at Arretium, awaiting Campanians.'

'This is useful, Sphax,' Maharbal conceded. 'Where are these prisoners?'

'I felt honour-bound to hand them over to the Boii chieftain, Carmo. The equites had needlessly butchered many of his townsfolk, so I left him to deal out justice.'

'What were equites doing in those parts, far from Ariminum?'

'Their orders were to find our army, which implies they were unaware we've already moved south,' reasoned Sphax. 'Besides, they would expect to see Numidians scouting ahead of our army, not in the rear. When tribune Titus Collina reports back to Servilius in Ariminum, I'm convinced he'll tell the consul our army is only now in the process of moving south. I think my uncle has stolen a march on Rome.'

'You may be right, lad,' agreed the general. 'But tell me, what happened to the rest of the equites?'

'I was about to encircle them when they turned tail and fled, Sir.'

Maharbal laughed. At which point the blond-haired Gaul smiled and winked blatantly at him. Only then did Sphax notice the cast in the man's right eye.

PART TWO

THE LAND OF FLOOD AND FLAME

SEVEN

Sphax's stay in Bona was short-lived. Hannibal was desperate to move south and keep the initiative. Sooner or later Servilius would send his scouts northwest, and an encampment of sixty thousand men was impossible to hide. Better to disappear into the wilderness of the mountains and keep the consul guessing as to the whereabouts of the army.

He spent the second day in the company of Idwal, Meilyr and an increasingly desperate Artula, searching the town and camp for their missing son. Sphax thought he glimpsed the lad in the marketplace, but it was a fleeting sighting and he couldn't be sure. For the next hour the four of them searched every street and alleyway around the marketplace. But there was no sign of him.

So on the third day after the Numidians had entered camp, Sphax said farewell to a tearful Artula, leading his eshrin into the thickly wooded hills to the south west of the city, ahead of an endless drumbeat of marching feet.

Even in this high country the weather was warm and pleasant. After the sultry heat of the plains, Sphax found the mountain air fresh and invigorating. Few people lived in these mountains. Over the course of their seven day journey he could count on the fingers of one hand the number of settlements they passed through.

After a day or so Sphax slipped into the easy rhythm of a march. Maharbal had given him four eshrins to scout ahead of the marching columns — the footsloggers. Not all these were soldiers. An army on campaign needed blacksmiths, grooms, saddlers, fletchers and wheelwrights, carpenters, cooks and bakers; a great host of skilled tradesmen to service and feed the men wielding the swords and spears. The absence of women was most noticeable in camp. It felt strange to Sphax's ears not to encounter the laughter of children at play or mothers scolding disobedient sons, not to mention the gaggles of gossiping whores, parading down tent lines in search of trade.

Every night the camp stewards laid out the ground for tents and the endless lines of rope to which horses were tethered. Fires were lit and sentries posted as the smoke from a thousand campfires wafted the aroma of baking flatbreads, cured pork and smoked fish across the camp.

Libyans set the pace of the footsloggers. They were the most trusted, highly trained and disciplined infantry in the army. Their prowess at marching was legendary.

It was said that a Libyan could march twenty miles by day and ten in his sleep. Despite being weighed down by armour, an oval shield and a heavy wooden pike, half-again the height of a man, marches of twenty-five miles in a single day — an average for cavalry on horseback — were by no means unknown. Yet Sphax reckoned that over the course of the seven days the most they managed in a single day was a paltry twelve miles. The problem could be laid fairly and squarely at the feet of the Insubres and Boii.

Somehow the Gallic temperament was not amenable to the discipline of a march. A column of Libyans in step gained strength and collective purpose from their common stride. Such a stride lends a rhythm and motion which fosters a resolute spirit and stamina.

Gauls had no such ethos. They were individuals, who fought and marched for themselves. After a few miles they began to straggle and drift behind. After seven they began to fall by the wayside and drop out. Most evenings saw the laggards limp into camp, but some never returned.

Sphax's constant companion was the guide Marcus, a swarthy, tousled-haired Pisani, who'd spent most of his life piloting cargoes down the Arnus river. Sphax had sailed from Pisae to Massilia and knew the town well, but as a topic of conversation he'd exhausted it in less than a mile. Marcus spoke Latin and a little Gallic, but the only language he warmed to was the jingling of gold and silver. As the mountains grew more rugged and the forests denser, the old salt fell into a stupor of silence and began to look increasingly out of his watery element.

But men, like life itself as it turned out, were full of surprises. It was rumoured that Marcus and his fellow guide, Julius, were to be paid a talent of silver for guiding Hannibal through the marshes. A princely sum indeed for humble sailors. Late one morning after six dreary miles of silence, he asked, almost indifferently; 'And what are you going to do with all your newfound wealth, Marcus?'

'Julius and I will build the sturdiest double-planked corbita that has ever tasted salt. We intend to sail her through the pillars of Hercules and set course for the lands of the north.' There was a glint in the old rogue's eyes Sphax had never seen before. 'They say that in the far north there are fire-breathing dragons, fountains of boiling water that appear miraculously out of snow and ice, men with only one eye in the centre of their foreheads … they even say that on a winter's night you can see the gods dancing in the sky on pillars of shimmering light! All my life I've listened to such tales — Julius and I speak of nothing else — now I intend to see them for myself.'

Sphax laughed. Marcus' words had come as a torrent of wide-eyed revelation. Except for the acquisition of wealth, he'd never before heard the man speak about anything with much enthusiasm, let alone with such passion and wonder. Because of the unusual length of his dragon sword, he kept it strapped behind his back so he could reach over his shoulder for the hilt. Quickly unbuckling the belt, Sphax handed the sheathed blade to Marcus.

Inlaid in pure silver along the length of the bronze sheath was a depiction of a slender dragon, wings unfurled, clawed legs trailing behind, its mouth spewing forth tendrils of silvery fire.

Marcus stared at it in wonder. 'Where did you get this? It must be from the north! Only one who'd seen such creatures could depict them so clearly.'

Sphax knew the craftsmanship to be exquisite, almost without equal. 'It was a gift from my dear friend Idwal,' he replied with pride, 'chief of the Cavari Gauls. The smith who fashioned it had never seen a dragon in his life, but in Gaul, so common are the tales of these fearsome creatures he could easily conjure the beast in his mind's eye. I too have a longing to see such creatures … from a fair distance,' he added with a grin. 'Turn it over.'

'Elephants!' Marcus exclaimed. 'Like the giant Surus that Hannibal sometimes rides.'

'It depicts the crossing of the great Rhodanus river by our elephants last summer.'

'I've heard tell of this feat. Were you there, master Sphax?'

'I played my part,' he replied levelly, recalling with a shudder being tossed like a rag by thrashing tusks. Flung overboard into the river's swift current, he'd clung for dear life to the side of the raft that was being towed to the eastern bank. He'd been lucky. Several mahouts had drowned that day.

'The sheath alone must be worth more than a talent of silver,' Marcus had crooned in the familiar tone he reserved for discussions of wealth.

'It's not for sale. This will be my son's sword, when he comes of age.'

That evening Marcus and Julius turned up at his campfire, swapping tales late into the night of dragons and the one-eyed cyclops. From that day onwards, the journey across the high mountains of northern Italia passed pleasantly enough.

* * *

Dawn broke on the seventh day to reveal a cloudless azure sky with not a breath of wind. Helios' chariot would be pitiless today, decided Sphax, and sure enough by mid-morning his men were mopping their brows with the sleeves of their tunics. For the past two days they'd descended valleys only to climb the next ridge and begin the procedure all over again. But it seemed to Sphax that each ridge was gentler and lower than the last, as if the mountains were tumbling down to the plain, somewhere below them, unseen.

That morning he and Marcus had been joined by his fellow guide Julius, and a boisterous party of Numidian captains. It seemed harsh to order Hanno, Aribal and Himilco back to their eshrins, when all their men had to fear were a few mountain goats. Besides, he was glad of their company and high spirits. The guides had fallen into a sullen reverie, knowing they were fast approaching the floodplain of the Arnus river and the momentous task Hannibal had set them.

After halting briefly at midday for bread and cheese, they refilled clay flasks from a stream and begun the ascent of what, Marcus assured him, was the last spur of the mountain range they had just crossed.

When at last they reached the crest of the ridge all conversation and banter was snuffed out in an instant. It was as if the gods had struck them all dumb.

Sphax slid from Dido and shielding his eyes from the sun, stared to the south. Ahead of him lay not a marsh, but a vast inland lake that stretched as far as the eye could see, its only feature a faint ridge on the distant horizon some thirty miles away. Looking to the south west he could clearly trace where the sparkling waters of the Tyrrhenian sea met the murky brown waters of the swamp. Gazing to the south east he saw how the ridges and spurs of the mountains formed narrow peninsulas that disappeared into the flood. Even if they kept to the high ground, it would take days, if not weeks, to circumnavigate this watery wilderness.

'Wait here,' he commanded his captains. 'Marcus, Julius … you're with me.' Mounting Dido he nudged her forward, allowing her to pick her own way down the half-mile of steep track to the water's edge.

He saw immediately that the view from the ridge had been deceptive. It was indeed a flood, not a sea, its waters bubbling and swirling with hidden currents that were driving it ever westwards towards the sea. What met his gaze was not the inland lake he'd seen from the ridge, but a drowned landscape of half-sunken trees, copses and woodland, whose spring flush of newly formed leaves were beginning to wilt and turn yellow under the deluge. On withered stumps rising from the murky depths sat cormorants, like ravenous harpies, drying their sinister black wings in the hot sun. Only the shrill calls of geese and waterfowl disturbed the dead calm of the foetid air.

He'd been in such a place before. Where the waters of the great Podanus river met the Adria lay a drowned wilderness fit only for wild beasts and birds of tooth and claw. Even with a sturdy river craft it had taken them three desperate days to escape its watery grip. If they had been on foot there would have been no escape.

'I've never seen it this bad,' observed Marcus, grimly.

'Me neither,' agreed Julius, shaking his head. 'But after the winter we've had, I'm not surprised. I can't recall a winter with so many tempests and snowstorms. It was as if the gods were trying to drown us!'

This offered Sphax little comfort. 'In the name of Hades,' he stormed, 'how do you intend to guide sixty thousand men through this stinking shit-hole? I wouldn't send Herakles himself into this cesspit. It's worse than Tartarus!'

'Your eyes deceive you.' Sphax was astonished how calmly Julius had uttered this ridiculous statement. 'Tell me what you see.'

'Miles of rank, stinking swamps! We haven't a hope in Hades of crossing it!'

'Then you are a fool, master Sphax,' growled Marcus. 'Look again,' he insisted.

'Trees!' snapped Sphax. 'I'll grant you there are trees and stumps. But what good are trees and stumps in a swamp … do you expect us to climb them? Anyway, most of them look as if they're dying from this foul-smelling sludge.'

'When we were standing on the spur, do you recall seeing a ridge on the horizon?' Sphax nodded. 'The track we're standing on,' Julius continued in a measured calm guaranteed to infuriate the Numidian, 'leads directly to that ridge. Once we gain that ridge you'll not see another drop of water for miles, and our work as guides will be done.'

'Now look more closely,' encouraged Marcus. 'Not with a mariner's eye, but with those of a landlubber, the eyes of a travelling merchant. From here the track follows the line of poplars to the edge of that birch wood over there,' pointing to the middle distance. 'Do you see?'

'Yes,' said Sphax, grudgingly.

'Julius and I know every stunted oak and alder from here to that ridge. We've travelled it more times than I care to remember. Wet or dry it makes no difference, the trees are our signposts, our way-markers.'

'What about the depth of this cesspit? How do you know where it's deepest? And where do we sleep? Like birds? In trees?' railed Sphax, unconvinced.

'The deepest waters are where the track fords rivers or streams. But they're not that deep. What fool of a traveller would ford a river at its deepest!' cried Marcus, exasperated.

'We carry poles to test the depth, Sphax,' added Julius more calmly. 'That way we avoid the deeper pools.'

Sphax had once seen two Iberian shepherds wade into the icy waters of the swollen Druentia high in the Alps. Using poles in the way that Julius had described they'd found the shallowest way to cross a river thought to be impassable. Within days their entire army had crossed safely with few mishaps. He had to admit that it could be done.

'Can horses drink this water? It smells rank!'

'Of course,' hissed Marcus. 'It won't do them any harm for a few days.'

'But I wouldn't advise any of your men drinking it,' tempered Julius, cautiously.

Sphax sighed. There was nothing for it. Hannibal's mind had been decided weeks ago. The die was cast. It was either the swamp or turn back.

'I'm going to ride back to Hannibal and Maharbal and inform them we've arrived at the marshes. As best you can, tell my Numidians what lies in store for them over the coming days.'

With that he nudged Dido away from the water's edge and started up the spur. At the top, four eshrins of Numidians had dismounted and were staring in disbelief at what would appear to them as a great inland sea.

'I'm going to ride back and find Maharbal and my uncle,' he told Himilco. 'I want our four eshrins to form a guard along the length of this ridge. Let no soldier from our army pass through and see for themselves what's in store for them tomorrow. If they do they'll start deserting in droves. I'll insist that Hannibal makes camp in the valley bottom, well away from this ridge and prying eyes.' An afterthought occurred to Sphax: 'Think about ways we can store extra drinking water. The stuff you can see down there is worse than drains from our latrines. Also, check the torches are to hand. I wouldn't like to lose my way in that place at night.'

'In the name of Ba 'al Hamūn, Sphax, can we make it across that … lake?'

Sphax shrugged. 'Ask Marcus and Julius. They seem to think so.'

'You've seen that swamp, lad?' asked Maharbal. Sphax simply rolled his eyes. 'As bad as that, eh?'

'Our guides think it's passable,' he said evenly, adjusting Dido's walk to that of the general's Egyptian mare.

'It better be. We're paying them enough for their trouble.' Maharbal's keen grey eyes fixed him with that familiar sardonic expression. 'But you haven't ridden back four miles to tell me how bad it's going to be. What's on your mind, lad?'

'Has my uncle Hannibal fixed the order of march through the marshes?'

Turning about on his mare, to all appearances Maharbal seemed to be intently studying the four columns of Iberian cavalry riding abreast in the shallow valley. But Sphax knew better. Instinctively he knew that the general was avoiding his eyes, knowing he wouldn't like what he was about to hear.

'More or less what it is now,' answered Maharbal, in a tone that gave nothing away. 'Libyans out in front followed by our Iberian foot and all the baggage. Iberian and Gallic cavalry next, followed by the Ligurian Gauls, Insubres and Boii—'

'And our Numidians?' interrupted Sphax, in alarm.

'Rearguard. With your uncle Mago in command.' For an instant the general met his eyes. 'Oh, I almost forgot. Your uncle will have his companion cavalry with him … you know, those *gentlemen* from good families in Carthage. So you will have nothing to fear.'

It was worse than he'd imagined. It took him some time to take in the implications of Hannibal's order of march, and its dire consequences.

Gathering his thoughts he said at last, 'Once we set foot in that marsh the Insubres and Boii will straggle. Within a day or so they'll drift miles behind. Every mile they fall behind will take them further from our baggage trains, fresh water and food. I realise Hannibal has placed the baggage in front of them as a carrot, but they'll still fall behind. The food and water in those trains is their only lifeline, their only chance of surviving, but at the end of each day's march they will not have the strength left to reach those trains. Don't you see, many will just give up and turn back!

'So,' he continued, glaring at Maharbal, 'my Numidians are to be nursemaids? We are to goad and exhort our allies to march, or does my uncle have something more sinister in mind? Indeed, I know how his mind works. I've seen how cold and ruthless he can be. We are expected to be executioners, aren't we? Stick a few Boii with javelins … teach them a lesson … set an example!' Sphax realised he was shouting and fell silent.

'You forget, boy, that they are also *my* Numidians!' Maharbal snapped with undisguised anger. 'Whatever Hannibal has in mind, I would never give such an order. You are neither nursemaids nor executioners, but I expect you to do your duty.' With a dismissive wave of the hand he added, 'Besides, Mago's in command, not you.'

'With respect, Sir, you know full well that will not be the case.' Maharbal grunted but said nothing.

He was fond of his uncle, who was only four years older than Sphax himself. But Mago possessed neither his elder brother's quicksilver mind, nor his resolute, decisive temperament. Although he'd been in nominal charge of the ambush forces that fell on the legions' rear and decided the battle of the Trebia, it had been the sheer force of will of his dear friends Adherbal and Idwal that had kept their men disciplined and alert, shivering through that interminable night in a sodden ditch. And it was Adherbal who'd taken the fateful decision to strike. Unlike Mago, the venerable Numidian had paid for it with his life.

'You don't have to remind me of my duty, Sir,' continued Sphax, now calm and in control of his temper. 'But I do have a request to make.'

'What is it, lad?' asked the general, anger forgotten.

'That the pack trains we assembled in camp and brought to Bona be returned to us. If the Insubres and Boii fall behind, our own men will find themselves even further behind if we are to provide a rearguard. I'll place them between our Numidians and the Gauls. That way at least we'll have fodder for our mares.'

'Agreed,' said Maharbal without hesitation, 'I'll make the necessary arrangements.'

'There's something else.' Sphax needed to warn the general. 'Tonight we must camp in the valley some distance away from that last ridge. I've placed four eshrins in line to guard and seal it off. On no account must our men be allowed to view the marsh from that ridge. If they see what lies in store for them there may well be a clamour to turn back! Believe me, Sir, it will do little for morale if they see what I've just seen.'

Maharbal nodded grimly, but made no comment.

EIGHT

It was past midday when Sphax finally nudged Dido into the swamp's lukewarm waters at the head of three thousand Numidians. And calamity struck almost before his journey began: were not the sinister webs of the Moirai ever thus?

So narrow and restricted was the submerged track, Marcus and Julius had insisted the army march as a single column no more than six men abreast. For cavalry this meant columns of three, and so since dawn he and Mago had watched the interminable lines step warily into the marsh's murky waters in the order that Hannibal had laid down.

Sphax had slept badly, and the little sleep he'd managed had been fitful and laden with portentous dreams. At one point he'd woken suddenly in a cold sweat, gripped by an unknown fear. It was only after he'd stumbled out of his tent into the moonlight he realised what he must do.

Fingering his ivory image, he was certain the goddess had spoken to him. Quickly he strode up the valley to where their pack trains were tethered in roped lines. There was no sign of any of the grooms, but glancing down the line he picked out Aethon immediately. The instant his hands reached out to her his fears left him. From now on he wouldn't let her out of his sight. First thing tomorrow he would order the groom to ride with his eshrin. Sphax knew the lad would be delighted, seeing it as a promotion.

Shortly after dawn he raised his javelin and signaled the Numidian column into the murky waters of the swamp. Instead of gazing at the men under his command he should have been paying attention to the silvery, diamond-backed shape that was ominously gliding towards him on the surface of the water. But Dido saw it. Without warning she frantically reared up in terror, catching her rider off balance and throwing him into the water with an almighty splash. Too late, Sphax saw the cursed viper and made a lunge for it. Gripping it halfway down its length he flung it as far as he could, but not before it had sunk its fangs into his forearm.

Seeing what had happened, Jugurtha quickly dismounted and bent over him. Grabbing Sphax's arm he located the puncture marks, squeezed until it hurt and began sucking out the poison, spitting the contents into the swamp. Sphax was too shocked to object.

After several more mouthfuls and bouts of spitting, Jugurtha stared at him, concerned. 'I think I've sucked out most of the poison, lad, but your arm will likely swell and you'll feel as sick as a dog later. Nasty things, serpent bites.'

By now quite a crowd had gathered. Looking around at their concerned faces, Sphax handed his clay water flask to Jugurtha. 'I'm truly grateful for your skills, my friend. Drink and cleanse your mouth.' At last his heart had stopped pounding and he felt in possession of his senses.

He would have to say something to his men. Otherwise, they might see this as an evil omen, a harbinger of disaster. His men were superstitious, simple folk. Old beliefs die hard and linger on.

Raising his voice he began, 'If I were a Roman, I would take this to be a sign from the gods, an augury of doom and calamity. But I am not a Roman. I am a Numidian. Our people are made of sterner stuff! Our gods Ba 'al Hamūn laugh at such pitiful ignorance and superstition.

'Only slackheads believe that a battle is decided by the flight of birds or a journey must not be undertaken because a dog pisses in the road. Romans can't even take a shit unless a cock crows!' Sphax was reassured by the laughter. 'As an augur it foretells only that my arm may swell and my belly ache, but no worse than yours after drinking that foul vinegar you call wine.'

Sphax managed a grin. 'Now get on your horses and think no more on this.' Mounting Dido he raised a javelin and nudged her into a walk, this time paying more attention to the murky surface of the slime.

His arm did swell up and he did feel nauseous. But that was by no means the worst of it that afternoon. Swarms of biting insects seemed to rise up out of nowhere, attracted by horseflesh and any exposed limb. Bites on the face were the worst, and his men were forever flailing arms in the air to ward off what looked to others like an invisible enemy. Jugurtha and Hannon, riding beside him, both agreed they would leave the swarms behind as they rode deeper into the marshes and away from dry land. Sphax prayed this would be the case.

What he'd dreaded most turned out to be the least of his anxieties. When he'd first seen the marsh from the ridge he'd been struck by how characterless it appeared; just a vast inland lake as featureless as the sea itself. He now knew better, having heard Marcus and Julius describing its hidden rivers, woods and copses. But Sphax didn't possess their knowledge. He had no map or chart.

If, as he suspected, the Insubres and Boii fell behind and lost contact with the Libyans at the head of the column, they would be cast adrift in its emptiness. How would they find their way in this wilderness? His worst fear was losing the track and leading his men into quicksands or deep water.

As it happened, he needn't have worried. Ahead of them almost sixty thousand hooves and feet had churned up the mud, turning it a sticky dark brown. All he had to do was follow the river of brown sludge and he couldn't go wrong.

In the blistering heat of that endless afternoon, he found himself nodding asleep to the monotonous splash of Dido's hooves. It was disconcerting, as if his senses had closed down, deprived of stimulation and numbed by the uniformity of this vast emptiness. As one place looked more or less the same as the next, it became difficult to measure progress; it was if they were treading water, standing still.

Sphax had undertaken long journeys at sea where the horizons gave the illusion of never appearing to change. But this was different. At sea, waves were constantly in flux with an ever changing motion of sparkling colour and depth. Here nothing changed. The opaque, mud-choked water hardly threw a shadow, let alone reflecting the clear blue skies above. Except for the disturbance created by horse's hooves, the marsh lay as flat and unruffled as a marble counter in a butcher's shop.

With an effort of will he forced himself to think and prepare for what lay ahead. Dusk was approaching. They would need fresh water, food and fodder for their mares. Torches would have to be readied and fire strikers checked. There would be a hundred things to do, and Sphax was grateful for it.

That morning he'd told the men guiding his pack trains to halt on the track at night and light torches. At the time he hadn't realised how important this would be: in daylight it was easy to follow the brown stain marking the track, but at night …

And as night fell a chilling wind arose with the gathering darkness. After the unbearable heat of the day the air suddenly grew cold as the breeze whistled and moaned over the unseen waters, drying sweat on faces and forearms. Soon he found himself shivering.

Raising his clutch of javelins and half turning he yelled, 'Halt and light torches. Once we can see our way forward we'll close up with our trains and rest for the night. See to your mares first.' Sphax could hear the command being echoed and relayed down the length of the column.

Other than a faint crimson glow in the west, all was now in darkness. The moon had been fulling every night and the ides of May were only two nights away, but this evening Selene's long-maned horses would not stir for another hour. He sensed Hannon fumbling in one of the sacks straddling his mare for a flint fire starter and sheep's wool kindling. Soon the veteran was holding a flaming torch aloft as others flickered into life ahead and behind them, illuminating the night in a river of torchlight.

Torches were for them, not their mounts. Horses could see much better than their riders in the dark. Flanked by Hannon and Jugurtha bearing torches, Sphax was confident their mares would not stumble as they rode the short distance to the head of Mago's column of cavalry.

'Dog's twat, Sphax, this is the foulest cesspit I've ever set foot in!' grumbled his uncle between swigs from a wineskin. 'What possessed my brother to come this way?'

Ignoring the question that only his uncle could answer, Sphax said tartly, 'I hope that's water and not what I think it is.'

'Water!' Mago spluttered. 'This, my dear Sphax, is the finest passum that ever passed the lips of a humble soldier. Believe me, after the day I've just endured I'm in need of every drop. Do you want a swig?'

Sphax declined. His guts had been gripped by a maelstrom of nausea since the snakebite, and in any case, he was not fond of the sweet raisin wine reserved for Roman senators and the like. From what he could see in the torchlight, over the course of the afternoon his uncle had shed the burden of breastplate, helmet and shield to his flag bearer and companions. Even the expensive linen cape he'd been wearing that morning had disappeared in favour of a simple white tunic, but unlike Sphax's, his was made from the finest Egyptian cotton.

'We should close up with our trains, Sir. They have gained some distance and my mares are desperate for fodder—'

'And my belly for food, Nephew,' Mago rejoined, taking another swig from his wineskin. 'Let's go,' he commanded at last.

Peering into the darkness, it was just as Sphax had feared. He could just make out the twinkling lights of their pack trains' torches, but he guessed they were nearly a mile ahead. Mago and his Carthaginians had been careless, allowing a yawning gap to open up between themselves and the trains. Throughout the afternoon, Sphax had been careful to halt frequently, closing any gaps that developed between his eshrins. Now their fate was in the lap of the gods.

In the dark they would have to ride in a straight line, heading for the torches at the back of the pack trains. Unfortunately, the submerged track rarely followed a straight line!

'Leave me your torch, Hannon, and ride back to our eshrin,' Sphax ordered. 'Make sure our Numidian columns ride directly behind Mago's men. But be prepared to halt if you hear shouting.'

Despite his misgivings he managed a wry smile. 'The shouting will be coming from me and Jugurtha if we stray from the path into deep water … or worse.' Ignoring Jugurtha's grimace he continued, 'If this happens you must find a way *around* us. Only risk one man at time to locate the track and stay in shallow water. In the name of Ba 'al Hamūn, don't just blunder ahead blindly. That way lies disaster!'

Before he nudged his mare around, Hannon placed a hand on Sphax' and Jugurtha's shoulders. Something he'd never done before.

Catching up with Mago, Sphax advised, 'It might be wise if Jugurtha and I scout some way ahead of you. We may have lost the track, Uncle. At least we can warn your column before it gets into difficulties.'

'You're right, Sphax,' he sighed ruefully, at last appreciating the predicament his tardiness had placed them all in. 'Go ahead.'

Cursing the darkness, Sphax nudged Dido forward. Even Marcus' vague waymarkers of trees and copses might at least have given them a hint as to the direction the track had taken, but their torches cast such a pitiful light it was impossible to see much beyond their noses.

For the best part of an hour they stepped cautiously forward and their luck held out. Wearily staring into the night he could now see their trains illuminated in torchlight, only a few hundred paces ahead. But then disaster struck.

Without warning, Dido suddenly plunged into a deep trough. As the waters reached her withers she instinctively came to a dead stop, standing stock still, water swilling around Sphax's waist, a hidden current tugging at the hem of his tunic. 'Riverbed!' he screamed, heart pounding. Jugurtha had not been so fortunate.

Stepping into an even deeper pool his mare had begun swimming, lowering her head and kicking out with both pairs of legs, the action flinging Jugurtha headlong into the water. For a heart-stopping moment Sphax lost sight of him as he disappeared under the surface. After an eternity in which Sphax was sure his comrade had drowned, a violent thrashing arose from beneath the water and a hand suddenly appeared clutching a dripping torch.

Dropping his own torch Sphax made a grab for it, and gripping Dido's flanks pulled it slowly towards him, praying that Jugurtha was clinging to the other end. Slowly the man's head emerged from the water, coughing and fighting for breath.

'Step back, Dido. Step back,' he repeated as calmly as his rising panic would allow. To his immense relief the mare obeyed. In this way Dido was able to bring both of them back to shallower water.

For a moment they simply stared at one another, Sphax panting, heart racing, Jugurtha racked by coughing and spluttering. But at least they were both alive. When Jugurtha's breathing eased to a rasping wheeze, Sphax began to look around. Mago's men had formed a semicircle of torchlight some thirty paces away. He saw that the moon had risen at last, unnoticed, casting her silvered glow that was worth more than a thousand torches. He thanked the gods. At last they could see!

'Are you unharmed, Sphax?' somebody shouted.

Recognising Mago's voice he answered, 'Yes, Uncle.'

'And your man?'

'He looks like a drowned rat, but he'll live. Listen, Uncle,' he continued more urgently, 'we stumbled into a riverbed that crosses the track. I'm sure of it. I could even feel the river's current. But our pack trains and everyone else have crossed, so there must be a ford nearby. Until we find that ford it's not safe for you or your men to approach. Do you understand?'

Ignoring him, one foolish rider began to ride boldly towards them. 'Be careful,' Sphax yelled, 'It's not safe here!'

'Don't you worry, Captain, I know what I'm doing, unlike that useless old fool standing beside you!' It was Hannon. 'I might have known the slackhead would get you into deep water! I shouldn't have let you out of my sight.'

Jugurtha began laughing, which started another coughing fit. Even Sphax found himself grinning.

When he drew close enough, Hannon took one look at the sodden figure of Jugurtha and burst out laughing. 'You look as if you've pissed yourself, old man!'

'Ha! *You* would have shat yourself, you senile old goat.'

Amusing as this exchange of endearments was, Sphax had had enough of this banter. 'I see you've brought cavalry lances with you, Hannon. Are you thinking what I'm thinking?'

'Probably, lad. D'you remember them shepherd boys wading into that river whatsitsname in the mountains?'

'The Druentia, I believe is the river you have in mind. And as I recall, the Iberians used poles. But lances will do equally well.'

'See, you old bastard!' Hannon crowed. 'Me and the captain see eye to eye. We plan ahead and think straight. We don't end up like a drowned rat, tossed into the nearest pisspot.'

This wasn't strictly true, thought Sphax. Only Dido's keen instincts had saved him from suffering the same fate. He was about to put a stop to Hannon's gloating when Jugurtha intervened.

What followed next was astonishing. Putting two fingers from each hand to his lips, Jugurtha began a shrill whistle, as piercing as a shepherd's pipe. In the silvery moonlight Sphax could clearly see Jugurtha's sleek black jennet responding, ears pricked, alert, preparing to swim back across the river.

'Look upon my arts, and despair!' Jugurtha announced imperiously, as if he was about to reveal a great mystery. With this enigmatic statement he turned his back on them and started splashing back to the deeper water where a moment before he'd almost drowned. Sphax and Hannon stared at one another.

'What's the old fool up to?' asked a bewildered Hannon.

'Come back, Jugurtha,' Sphax yelled, 'that's an *order*!'

For the first time his veteran scout disobeyed, completely ignoring him. Instead, putting fingers to his lips he began whistling once more. This time the mare responded by swimming strongly towards him. After she'd covered no more than twenty paces, Jugurtha altered the tone of his whistling to a sudden, high pitched squeal. Instantly the mare stopped, ears still pricked, eyes fixed on her master. Sphax guessed she must be treading water in the middle of the riverbed, where the water was at its deepest. If only men could swim as well as horses, thought Sphax.

'Good girl, Sophonisba,' they heard Jugurtha cry out in soft, reverent tones. 'That's it, my lovely … now follow me. Swim, Sophonisba. Swim!' he cried, splashing through the water to his right as fast as he could.

Hannon snorted in derision. 'I knew it! The old goat's gone soft in the head!'

Sphax suddenly realised Jugurtha was almost certainly wading parallel to the probable course of the river, whilst his mare was following him like a shadow, swimming from its hidden depths, midstream. For the first time Sphax had an inkling of what his scout was up to.

Above the splatter of spray, Sphax heard Jugurtha continually lending encouragement. 'Not much further, my lovely … keep going … that's it.'

Once again, Jugurtha's high pitched squeal pierced the night, and once again his mare stood stock still. In amazement Sphax realised she was no longer swimming, but standing in water that barely reached her knees.

With Jugurtha's supreme mastery of horsemanship, Sophonisba had found the ford all by herself, saving the three of them hours of laborious work prodding and poking the submerged riverbed with lances: an ordeal that would have put their lives in continual jeopardy. Sphax was full of admiration.

To demonstrate his triumph, Jugurtha waded boldly towards his mare and once mounted, signaled both to join him, as if surprised at what the fuss had been about.

Hannon greeted his old friend warmly. 'Dog's twat, Jugurtha, you've really gone soft in the head. Sophonisba! My lovely! What a sentimental old fool you've become in your dotage.'

Sphax was more generous. 'Indeed your arts are to be admired and celebrated, Jugurtha.'

But he had no intention of entering the contentious debate about the naming of horses. Numidians felt strongly about this. Some, like Sphax and now Jugurtha, apparently, considered their mares to have personalities, a character and spirit that was unique to them, and them alone. So just like people, a personal name seemed appropriate, no more than their due. But most Numidians felt otherwise. A name, they argued, conferred ownership and possession, a sentimental projection of human feelings, not the creature's feelings. Horses were not slaves to be owned and commanded.

Both Jugurtha and Hannon lavished the same love and care on their mares. This was more a question of perception and the nature of the human and animal soul. As Idwal was always keen to point out, amongst the greatest minds of the age, this debate was as yet unresolved.

After posting sentinels with torches to mark the ford, it took an interminable two hours to bring the endless weary columns of Numidians safely across to where the pack trains had camped for the night. Worried about straying too far from the track, Sphax ordered his men to set up station either side of the pack teams. By the time this had been arranged to his satisfaction, their mares were famished. After all they'd endured that day he ordered a double ration of fodder.

For the second watch of the night he'd insisted the men dismount to give their mares a complete rest, but after filling their bellies with cold rations and refilling water flasks, all his men could do was slop around in the mud, water up to their knees.

Dismounting from Dido had given him another disagreeable shock. All afternoon the water had remained lukewarm, but at night it became unpleasantly cold. Himilco blamed it on the chill breeze, wafting over the water's surface. But whatever the explanation, it only added to their misery.

Fixing a permanent grin on his face and drawing on his reserves of resolve, Sphax waded from eshrin to eshrin, slapping backs and retelling jokes and old stories. It was the least he could do. Perhaps the *only* thing he could do to lighten their present predicament.

In those dark nights of despair when the army reached the high Alps, he remembered watching Hannibal doing the rounds of the campfires, exuding confidence and enthusiasm, breathing life and hope into the desperate, half-starved men shivering in the firelight. For Sphax it had come as a revelation that leadership was needed most when things were going badly. But what would he give for a campfire this evening!

After midnight he remounted Dido and resting his head against her mane and neck, tried to sleep. For an hour or so he tried this way and that, resting a cheek on her mane, his folded arms or cupped hands. But it was hopeless, and only added to his frustration. At times he must have drifted into sleep, waking with an awkward jerk to prevent himself sliding down her shoulder. But such sleep was so fleeting it offered no relief from the aching tiredness that bore down on his eyelids like leaden weights.

Old hands like Jugurtha and Hannon claimed it was easy to sleep on the back of a horse. Tomorrow he would demand to know how! In fact, falling asleep on the back of a horse had its own perils. All night he heard the frequent sound of an almighty splash followed by a string of curses as Numidians came to a rude awakening falling from their mares into the swamp.

In the end he gave up and dismounted, finding the most comfortable position leaning against Dido's rump with his arms resting on her croup. At least from here he could gaze up at the stars.

During his voyages at sea and his attempts to steer, Corinna had taught him a little about navigation and the stars. It had been a revelation. Now he lost himself for a while tracing the three stars of Orion's belt and the bright star below it named Orion's sword. Sphax reminded himself that this star, flanked by two dimmer stars, pointed due south, the direction of their march.

Sure enough, the star confirmed their direction of travel. Sphax couldn't decide why he found this arcane knowledge so satisfying, but he did.

Even this innocent distraction turned out to be short-lived. All too soon heavy clouds rolled in from the west, drawing a curtain across the heavens that hid both moon and stars, plunging them into pitch-black night. To complete his misery, rain began to fall.

The fourth watch of the night was sheer torment. Fingering his ivory image, he prayed to Artemis to speed Eos' winged horse, and the dawn.

NINE

Next morning Sphax found it almost impossible *not* to fall asleep to the steady rhythm of Dido's hoofbeats sloshing through the marsh. Despite last night's frustration, he found it all too easy to sleep on the back of a horse, as long as it was moving!

There was just one problem. Unless he was flanked by Jugurtha and Hannon to keep him in check, he had a tendency to veer off into the marsh. Later, the two of them confessed that on one occasion that morning they'd let him wander off. Just to see what would happen! Apparently, he'd headed off in a south easterly direction, much to the amusement of the entire eshrin, before captains further down the column also headed in that direction, spoiling the men's fun. Only then had Jugurtha come to his rescue and led him back to the straight and narrow, still sound asleep.

By mid-morning he felt refreshed, his spirits restored. The rain had ceased falling before the day had dawned cloudless and warm, burning off the mists that hung like wraiths above the surface of the marsh. His men's bellies were full, their mares had plenty of fodder, and with every passing hour the hard miles receded into the distance.

Three days Hannibal had promised them. It would take no more than three days. That meant

enduring just one more night of misery and they would be free of this accursed place forever. Sometime tomorrow they would cross the last of the five rivers of Hades and reach the land of plenty.

The dusk was gathering when they came upon the first of the dead animals. To begin with it was an occasional scrawny mule or pack horse. None was from their pack trains. Judging from their terrible condition, they were already half-starved and exhausted before they'd even set foot in the marsh. Its cloying, churned-up mud had done the rest.

It was distressing for his men. Numidians were sickened by such cruelty. Who could be so barbarous as to abandon innocent creatures to die where they had fallen? they asked. But worse was to come.

In the last hour before making camp they came upon entire teams of pack animals lying in the mud, still roped and harnessed together and bearing jars and sacks strapped to their flanks. Sphax was horrified when he realised that some of the creatures were still alive.

His men did what they could, releasing any that still had strength, allowing them to drink from their flasks and sparing fodder meant for their own mares. Rather than abandoning any

that were too far gone to a slow, miserable death, Sphax ordered their throats to be cut, something that grieved his Numidians. Better a swift death than a lingering one, he argued.

When he came upon an entire team of eight horses, sprawled in the mud from bearing an excessive burden of wine jars, his horror turned to fury. The creatures were in a pitiable state, but some still lived … just. In a rage, Sphax was about to smash the jars and free them when a thought stayed his hand. Why shouldn't his men enjoy what had clearly been intended for the table of some pampered Carthaginian?

Telling his men to gather every flask or jar they could lay their hands on, he invited them to come and fill up, amazed how inventive Numidians could be when it came to finding novel receptacles for wine, even if some of them looked quite unsanitary! Sixteen amphora hardly provided a feast, but it cheered his men through another interminable night in the swamp, where dawn couldn't come soon enough.

If they had only known what dawn would bring they would have slept on in innocence rather than wake to a living nightmare. That day they witnessed sights so gruesome and horrifying they would be etched forever in the memory of Numidians. It was as if a great running battle had taken place, and they had stumbled on its aftermath. The river of brown sludge was littered with the bloated carcasses of dead mules and pack horses that had perished in the night.

They should have been grateful for the shallower water they were wading through, which barely reached halfway to their mares' knees, but this shallower depth and the burning heat of the day seemed only to distil and concentrate the rank stench of death and putrefaction that met their nostrils. Now every stump and tree that rose from the swamp was thronged with squabbling, black-feathered vultures, fighting to keep a seat at the banquet to come.

Anxiously studying the exhausted, careworn faces of his men, Sphax could see the toll this terrible journey was exacting. A sombre silence had descended like a pall on the column. After threading their way through mile upon mile of carcasses, his men rarely looked down, but stared dully into the distance, praying their ordeal would come to an end.

Sphax was also staring into the distance, searching for that ridge of high ground that marked the limits of the marsh, but it was nowhere to be seen. In his present disoriented state he would sometimes mistake a distant line of trees for this promised land, his spirits suddenly soaring, only to be dashed as he drew closer and realised his eyes had deceived him.

At one point he'd insisted Agbal join him at the head of the column to look for the ridge. With his keen eyes, Agbal would surely see it. After squinting for an age at the horizon, he slowly turned towards Sphax, grimly shaking his head. 'I can't see it, captain. There's nothing there.'

'But it must be there, Agbal … it *must* be!' Growing ever more desperate, 'Look again!'

Shoulders slumped, Agbal wearily turned to squint once more into the distance, struggling to see what was not there, to please his captain.

In the end Jugurtha had to intervene. 'Leave the lad alone, captain,' he pleaded, 'if Agbal can't see that ridge, nobody can. Can't you see the lad's done in?'

Shortly after midday they came upon a party of Gauls, the first trickle of what would become a tide of broken, desperate men. What his Numidians would come to call the *walking dead*, though few were left on their feet.

Some sat motionless in the mud, heads buried in hands, whilst others lay sprawled, heads propped on an elbow above the water. Beneath the water's murky surface, many stared heavenwards with unseeing eyes, mouths ajar. But mostly they lay face down, long since embraced by the arms of Morrigu.

Miraculously, they even came upon a few that were sound asleep, lying precariously on carcasses of mules whose bloated bellies had risen above the flood.

All were unrecognisable as men, let alone Gauls. Caked from head to foot in oozing brown mud, most of their clothing had long since been discarded, along with every weapon of war, giving them the appearance of grotesque beasts that had given up the will to live, and would soon become one with the swamp that had engulfed them.

Leaping from their mares, the men of his eshrin splashed through the mud to do what they could. As other eshrins joined them they searched for the living, handing out flasks of water and whatever bread or cheese they carried in sacks strung over their mares.

But these men were beyond aid or sustenance, beyond rescue or even hope.

Many waved his men away or stared blankly at them. All had understood Sphax's pleas in Latin to rise and be helped onto horses, yet most remained dumb, inert, as if they'd entered some shadow-world beyond the reach of the living. Four Insubres and a young Boii were all they managed to save.

It came as a terrible shock to realise how deep the mud was underfoot. Sphax guessed the shallower the water, the deeper the mire. After a few laborious steps, he understood why this catastrophe had been inevitable. The mud reached well above his ankles. Every step had taken an effort, as if the mud was resisting, sucking him down and sapping his strength. Walking became exhausting, as if lead weights had been attached to his sandals. Hannibal had been right all along, wagons would have become stuck in this quagmire within half a mile.

When the Libyans at the head of the army had marched this stretch, Sphax guessed that the mud beneath the water had been solid and firm. But that was not the case after sixty thousand boots and hooves had churned and ploughed. Now it was nothing less than a death-trap.

It must be exacting the same toll on his mares, Sphax reasoned, or perhaps hooves offered less resistance and four legs helped to spread the weight. Whatever the case, unless he took decisive action, sooner or later their mares would suffer the same fate as the Gauls and pack animals.

Once the Gauls they'd rescued were helped on to spare pack horses he decided to test his theory. Nudging Dido off the track he headed east until he reached ground that was not stained dark brown. Dismounting, he tested the submerged ground underfoot. To his enormous relief, although his sandals still squelched, the undisturbed mud was much firmer.

Leaving the track was not without its risks, he realised. On that first night it had almost cost Jugurtha his life! But the alternative was no longer an option. If his Numidians stayed on the track, eventually their mares would almost certainly suffer the same fate as the Insubres and Boii.

Himilco's eshrin was next in line. Taking Jugurtha and Hannon with him, Sphax rode through his eshrin to where the young captain was handing fresh water flasks to Insubres they'd rescued.

'We've got to get our Numidians off this track, Himilco. You've been sloshing around in this mud, so you must have realised that every step is agony. I don't know about you, but it feels to me as if my legs are made of lead!'

'Me too,' agreed Himilco, wearily. Sphax had never seen his friend looking so pale and drawn.

'The track we're following has been churned by the boots of our army, and it will only get worse. I fear for the Gauls. But unless we take drastic action we will suffer the same fate.'

'What do you suggest, Sphax, we turn back?'

Sphax was shocked. There was something bordering on despair in Himilco's tone. 'No! Of course not,' he said firmly. 'All we have to do is stay on firmer ground either side of the track.'

Forcing a smile he continued, 'I've just tried it, and the ground *is* much firmer. It will make the going so much easier for our mares and save their strength for what lies ahead. When we reach our pack trains tonight we'll advise the teams to do the same.'

'Won't that put us in even more danger?' objected Himilco. 'We were told that leaving the track would put us in peril. There may be quicksands, or hidden riverbeds like you and your scout here almost drowned in the other night!'

'I'm not suggesting we *leave* the track, Himilco, just *follow* it, as closely as we can, but from firmer ground.

Quite frankly, I would rather take my chances with quicksands and riverbeds than get bogged down in this stinking mire. You've seen what it's doing to the Gauls, not to mention the pack animals. That way lies despair!'

Himilco sighed. 'I suppose you are right. How do you propose to go about it?'

'Behind us are over three thousand Numidians stretching back in a single column for over two miles. If we march as a single column we'll churn up the ground as badly as the army has done, making the going as difficult for our rearmost columns as this filthy track. So we must march in two columns; one to the east of the track and one to the west of it. That way we do less damage to the ground.'

'But that will take the rest of the afternoon to sort out,' Himilco argued, wearily shaking his head.

'Not if I give the task to my new lieutenants,' Sphax responded, grinning genuinely at Hannon and Jugurtha. 'As each new eshrin approaches, you Hannon, will point them east of the track. When the next approaches, Jugurtha will signal them west. And so on, until you reach the last eshrin. Do you understand?'

Both nodded, before it dawned on Hannon what the implications meant for the two of them. 'But captain,' he growled, 'that means me and this slackhead here will be at the back of the queue when it comes to rations time.'

Trust Hannon's first consideration to be his belly, thought Sphax. 'Don't worry, Hannon, I'll save you a morsel or two!' Returning his gaze to Himilco he added, 'I shall lead the eastern column, you are to lead the western column, agreed?'

'Agreed, Sphax,' at last sounding less doubtful about the new plan.

'Which leaves us with the problem of what to do about the Insubres and Boii.'

'They are such a proud, pig-headed people,' grumbled Jugurtha. 'Most of 'em refused to be helped! What can you do with such folk, captain?'

'Any that can be saved, *must* be saved!' Sphax demanded. 'At the very least they should be warned about the track and encouraged to leave it, just as we are doing. I want every eshrin captain to tell his men to keep a sharp look out for stragglers. Even if the Gauls object, I want our men to drag them off that track. By force if necessary!' Eyeing his newly appointed lieutenants he pressed the matter. 'You two will explain this to every single captain down the line. This is not an instruction … it's a command!'

Within a few strides it was evident to everyone that the going had become easier. Immediately Sphax sensed Dido's stride was freer and less laboured. Staying clear of the brown-stained track and parallel with Himilco's column to the west was easy enough, but progress was painfully slow. In the heat of the afternoon, every passing mile saw the numbers of straggling Gauls slumped in the mud grow at an alarming rate.

Every few hundred paces his men would stop and do what they could. He soon became hoarse from yelling, 'Save yourself! Get off the track!' Some merely asked for water, determined to struggle on. Others had to be dragged from the quagmire and carried to firmer ground, drained and exhausted. Even after they'd recovered, Sphax doubted they would have the strength to continue the march. Some, mostly young men and elderly veterans lay cold and lifeless, beyond salvation.

As the unrelenting afternoon dragged on, Sphax could see a dilemma looming. A mile or so ahead he could see that the track followed the edge of an extensive forest of birch trees, their silver-grey trunks emerging like scrawny herons' legs from the flood. At first sight it looked impenetrable, but as they drew closer it became evident the trees were not as dense as he'd feared. Concerned they would have to re-join the river of mud, something he was loth to do, he decided to take a risk.

Bringing his men to a halt at the forest's edge, he raised a javelin and yelled, 'Single file from here. Stay close together.' The last thing he did before plunging under the canopy of wilting yellow leaves was to take a careful bearing of the sun's direction in the sky. This would be his beacon to chart a southerly course.

Sphax sensed the forest's undergrowth was soft and spongy under Dido's hooves. Mosses and ferns, he guessed, long since decayed in the floodwaters. Beneath the trees the air was cool and pleasant, and other than the occasional fallen tree blocking his path, progress was steady. Whenever the trees grew sparser, he would check his position against the sun and correct his direction of travel, but this was rarely necessary.

Sooner than he'd anticipated, Sphax suddenly emerged from the trees into a landscape that was unsettlingly different from anything he'd seen over the course of the last three days. Halting his men, he shouted for Agbal to join him.

Less than two hundred paces to the west, he could make out the endless throng of Gauls, snaking their way along the track. Beyond them should have been Himilco's column. But it was nowhere to be seen.

His pace through the forest had not been much slower than walking a mare over unobstructed ground. If anything, Himilco should have been ahead of him, not behind him. What could have delayed them?

Due south, directly ahead of him, all he could see was an uninterrupted pool of water that appeared to stretch for half a mile before it met a line of scrubby willows and thickets of alder.

'What do you make of this place, Agbal?'

'I don't like the look of that water. It looks deep to me. But have you noticed the Libyans, captain?' Agbal asked, pointing to the south west.

He had not. But now Sphax squinted with interest. Shielding the sun from his eyes, he could just make out two figures holding what appeared to be pikes, standing perhaps thirty paces apart. Sentries, he wondered?

Guards? But in the name of the gods, what was worth *guarding* in this shit hole?

'Two more have been posted opposite them, do you see?' observed Agbal, equally puzzled.

Sphax didn't see, unless he counted two blurred shapes as seeing. 'Are you sure they're Libyans?'

'Only our Libyans wear Thracian helmets and carry pikes. Wait a moment, Sir … there's some Gauls trudging between 'em!'

Then it dawned on him. Cursing himself for being such a dull-witted Scythian, Sphax explained, 'Those Libyans aren't there to guard anything, Agbal. They've been posted to mark something, that's why two more have been placed opposite. They're sentinels, not guards! They are marking the ford across the Arnus river.'

Now this strange landscape made perfect sense to him. 'Do you see that line of willows and alders in the distance?' Agbal nodded. 'When the floods recede in a few months, those trees will once again sit atop the river's bank.'

Sphax's attention turned to a more pressing problem. 'Can you see anything of Himilco's eshrin, Agbal?'

'They're on foot over there,' he shrugged, jutting his chin westwards. 'Seeing to those Gauls.'

Feeling rather foolish, Sphax wondered for the hundredth time what it would be like to see with Agbal's eyes. 'Then let's go and do what we can for them.' Raising a javelin, he pointed towards the river of mud and nudged Dido into a walk.

Himilco wasn't hard to find. He was sitting motionless on his mare in the middle of the track, with a look that Sphax could only describe as resigned despair. It was easy to see why.

It had become a sickeningly familiar sight that day, but this time it was on a scale that could not be imagined. In either direction as far as the eye could see, the river of mud was choked with the half-naked bodies of the dead and dying, sprawled amidst the discarded paraphernalia of war.

Hundreds of his Numidians were carrying the living to the relative safety of firmer ground. But there were so many, and it was exhausting work. Allowing Dido to gingerly pick her way through the human debris he continued south, towards the ford across the Arnus river, searching faces for signs of life.

Sphax didn't recognise the boy at first. Only after a second glance was he certain. It was Meilyr, lying flat on the arched back of someone lying prone in the mud, the boy's arms still locked around the neck of the person who'd been carrying him.

'*No!*' cried Sphax despairingly, leaping from Dido, certain he would find the body of the boy's father beneath the son.

Moaning softly, the boy could hardly lift his eyelids, but he was alive. Freeing his arms from the body's neck, Sphax lifted him up and carried him over to Dido, placing him gently on the mare's back.

Kneeling in the mud and shallow water, Sphax turned then raised the limp body out of the water, cradling it against his chest. And once more he cried out in despair, railing against the injustice of the gods.

It was not his father that had lifted the exhausted child onto their back, but his mother.

Artula had found her son at last. Only her undying love for her child would have sustained her through those agonising miles before her strength finally failed and she sank into the mud, utterly spent. Was it with her dying breath that Artula had arched her back? A final act of sacrifice that had saved her son from drowning. Sphax would never know. Only the gods had witnessed such selfless courage. And only the Moirai had decreed it.

He could not leave her here, abandoned to the flood and this accursed wilderness. It was unthinkable! Aethon would bear her noble body to her husband, so she could be mourned and the last rites of the Anamares dead observed. She deserved nothing less.

Tenderly he closed her eyes and began wiping the mud from her face with the hem of his tunic. For the first time he noticed her long golden curls had been shorn. Crudely and in haste, it would appear. To hide her sex, Artula must have taken a knife to her lovely hair.

When he was satisfied with her appearance, Sphax lifted her slender body over his shoulder and whistled for Dido to follow. In this way they carried their burdens to where the groom was holding Aethon's lead rope, and there he carefully placed Artula across the flanks of his golden mare.

Sphax and Himilco combined their columns once more, riding as a single column towards the Libyan sentinels and the ford across the Arnus river. The floodwaters were much deeper here, rising above their mares' hocks, but once they were safely over, Sphax again split them into two columns and bade them stay off the track.

With Meilyr seated in front of him on Dido, Sphax stopped regularly to dribble water on the boy's lips. Behind him Agbal and Juba rode either side of Aethon to make sure her precious burden did not slip or slide from her back.

On this, the longest and darkest of days, it was by torchlight that their exhausted columns at last came in sight of the pack trains and the prospect of rest and relief.

But the Moirai never slept or ceased their weaving. And that night Sphax's threads passed between their bony fingers.

In the third watch of the night, just as Meilyr was beginning to stir from his troubled sleep, three riders approached their camp. It was the guide Marcus, flanked by two horsemen bearing torches aloft.

'You must come with me, my friend. Your uncle has summoned you.'

'What's wrong, Marcus?' Sphax demanded. 'What's happened?'

'Your uncle has a sickness common in these parts. He may not last the night.'

TEN

'I wanted to look upon you for the last time, Nephew,' murmured Hannibal, in a voice that Sphax barely recognised. 'It is fitting those passing from this world into darkness are attended by their kin. You and Mago are dear to me … that is why I have summoned you both;' offering his hand, which Sphax reached up and clasped with both of his.

'I am here, Uncle. I swear I will stay by your side until Hades gives up his dead.'

'I hope that will not be necessary,' he muttered, withdrawing his hand. 'My right eye has lost the power of sight, but it was a feeble organ at the best of times. Now this half-wit of a physician tells me the sickness has spread to my left eye, yet he offers me neither potion nor medicine for the ailment, or relief from its agonies.'

Sphax exchanged sceptical glances with Mago, standing beside him. Except for his disembodied voice and presentiments of dark foreboding, Hannibal didn't look like a man destined for the next world.

Staring heavenwards he lamented, 'Would that my dearest friends Silenos and Sosylos were here! Sosylos would faithfully record the fateful passing of Hannibal for all history to judge. Silenos would have a soothing balm …' suddenly breaking off, the recollection of his friends too painful to bear.

'Why has Melqart deserted me?' he began again. 'Before my great task has been accomplished? A task that I alone am destined to fulfil.' Falling into a reproachful silence his uncle stared at the faces around him, as if seeking an answer to this unanswerable question.

Gazing at those faces and the vast throng gathered around their leader, it struck Sphax that the finest poets of the age could not have conceived of a scene more dramatic and poignant. Hannibal himself was mounted on the giant Surus, the only elephant to survive the snowbound peaks of the high Alps and that terrible winter of winters, beside the Padus. Even the beast itself seemed to sense the somberness of the occasion, standing motionless, his noble head and fearsome tusks erect.

Gathered in a great circle of phalanxes stood hundreds of Libyans in silent vigil, each holding a flaming torch aloft that lit the scene more brilliantly than any actor's stage, torchlight dancing off helmets and breastplates, turning the floodwaters the colour of molten gold.

Besides Mago, every officer of rank and Carthaginian of noble birth were gathered around Surus, standing knee-deep in unpleasantly cold water.

Maharbal and the Libyan general, Hanno, stood to his left, whilst to his right he recognised the Iberian chieftains Gárgoris, Orison and Balkar. Many familiar faces he failed to put a name to, but judging from the amount of gold and silver on display, they were men of power and rank. The only chiefs noticeable by their absence were those of the Insubres and Boii. No doubt delayed by the oversized boots of ten thousand marching Libyans, he thought sourly.

It had taken Sphax and the guide Marcus three gruelling hours to reach Hannibal's Libyans at the head of the march. In the moonlight he'd passed camp after miserable camp of Gauls, huddled together in the darkness with not a pack animal or supply team in sight. Gauls were not only drowning that day, they were starving.

But if he was honest, his worst fear was catching sight of Meilyr and having to break the tragic news to him. So far he'd been spared this onerous duty, but it weighed heavily on him.

After describing — in more detail than he'd care to remember — the affliction that had struck down his uncle, Marcus had passed on the only good news Sphax had heard all night: that the ridge leading to the promise of dry land could be clearly seen from the Libyan camp. But not in the dark, so instead he examined the face of his uncle.

His right eye, the one with the cast, looked painfully swollen and inflamed, but it could be just a trick of the light, he reasoned; everything looked inflamed in that blood-red torchlight. As for his left eye. Sphax could see it was weeping an unhealthy yellow pus which his uncle wiped with a rag from time to time. Otherwise, Hannibal sat astride Surus like a marble statue, immovable and resolute as ever.

According to Marcus, this sickness rarely proved fatal. Borne by the pestilence in the water and carried on the vaporous cold night airs of the swamp, it preyed on weakness and frailty, conditions to which the mind was as susceptible as the body. It was his uncle's invocation of the god Melqart that had stirred the memory.

It was almost a year ago when Maharbal had told him. 'The bane of Melqart,' he'd explained, 'is how your uncle describes the black despair that descends on him from time to time. When in the grip of this stupor he shuns all company and becomes dead to the world, incapable of action, let alone of making a momentous decision. He swears it's because of the oath he made to his own father, your grandfather, Hamilcar Barca.'

Maharbal had gone on to describe how his uncle, a boy of nine, had been taken by Hamilcar to the great temple of Ba'al in Carthage. On that sacred altar, his grandfather had sacrificed a lamb and bade his son kneel and wash his hands in the blood of the animal. Then, in the presence of priests, he'd made him swear a solemn oath that to his dying day he would remain an enemy of Rome.

'This, your uncle claims, is the origin of his curse,' Maharbal had explained. 'The blessing, Hannibal has always told us, is that his life has a higher purpose rarely bestowed on mortals. He has been touched by fate and must follow the star of his destiny. But if he ever falters in this divine purpose through doubt or indecision, the wrath of Melqart will descend upon him as punishment. This is his curse, Sphax, and because of it he is deserving of our pity and compassion.'

Melqart was one of the old gods Queen Dido had reclaimed from the Phoenician city of Tyre. Sphax knew little of these old gods. To him they seemed from a different time, a different age, like worshipping Cronus and the Titans, ignoring the fact that they'd been overthrown by Zeus and the Olympians.

Even if this archaic god had the power to inflict Hannibal with blindness, why would any god seek such a punishment? Vengeance? Retribution? Disobedience? For what?

Not for one moment had his uncle wavered, doubted, or strayed from his star of destiny. That they were here, in this terrible wilderness shunned by gods and men, was testimony to the fact that Hannibal had steered the swiftest and most direct course towards his enemies, never questioning his star, or faltering in his purpose.

Perhaps therein lay the problem.

Had his uncle been blinded to the possibilities of calamity, disaster? With the fate of his army in the balance, marooned in the flood, was he now racked by doubts and indecision? Maharbal had told him the bane of Melqart preyed on such thoughts. Gods can only send signs. Was the blindness a sign?

Marcus had said the disease sought out weakness and frailty. Sphax knew that sickness afflicted the soul as well as the body.

With the promised land within sight, within touching distance, this was not the time to waver or falter. Even if they could, there was no turning back. Sighted or not, tomorrow the army would follow their leader out of the flood onto dry land. Only then would they lick their wounds and count the cost. Fate had so decreed, and only the Moirai decided our destiny. Sometimes, even the gods must be denied.

Sphax reached for his ivory image and bowing his head, prayed fervently to the goddess to spare the sight of his uncle's remaining eye. When he was satisfied Artemis had heard him, he gazed up at Hannibal and said, 'I have prayed to the goddess to spare you. But now I must take my leave, Sir. Our Numidians will need me before dawn brings the trials of a new day. The rearguard is in a pitiable state, and that is where my duty lies.'

'Has Hades yet given up his dead?' was all his uncle said.

'Hundreds, if not thousands have already drowned this day or died from fatigue. Hades has been kept busy! Meilyr, chief of the Anamares, begged you to find another way, yet you refused. Now Meilyr will pay a terrible price for your stubbornness.'

All around him Sphax could hear mutterings of unease. He ignored them. 'If Melqart has deserted you, Sir, I think it's high time you turned your back on him.'

Wading through the water to where a groom was feeding fodder to Dido, he mounted and snatching a torch from a Libyan soldier, wearily nudged her north. He'd passed so much unforgettable misery on the way to the Libyan's camp he could hardly lose his way.

* * *

They had made the funeral pyre in a beautiful glade on the south side of the wooded ridge, so that even in death, as Artula's soul soared into the afterworld, freed from the shackles of the flesh, she would not have to look upon the wilderness of floodwater that had decided her fate.

Many gathered that day to honour and say farewell to Artula, who was loved by all who met her. The forty or so Anamares warriors that had survived the ordeal of the floodwaters were joined by Idwal's Gauls from the Cavari tribe and every Numidian from Sphax's and Himilco's eshrins.

Meilyr and his son had been there all afternoon, either with heads bowed in silent prayer, or placing precious items on the pyre that Artula would need in her life to come. Meilyr had raised a questioning eyebrow as Sphax placed the drinking horn Betua had given him amongst the piles of cups of wine and salt, saddles, bridles and reins. Precious as it was, Sphax had wanted to gift Artula something crafted by Gauls alone.

Late in the afternoon Sphax's attention was drawn to a striking Gaul who strode up to Meilyr and after solemn greeting, embraced him in warm friendship. Dressed in plaid tunic, braccae and cape rich in autumnal browns, the two seemed deep in conversation when to his surprise, Meilyr pointed towards him and the man walked over to where Sphax stood in silent vigil.

'I will be forever in your debt, Sphax, Prince of Numidians.' Unsurprisingly, Sphax was taken aback. Even more so when the man suddenly bowed low before embracing him in a grip of iron.

'I see you are at a loss, lad,' chuckled the Gaul after he'd released Sphax from the embrace. 'I am Ducarius, chief of the Acerrae Insubres, and …' he paused to grin broadly, 'husband of Betua, daughter of the Boii chieftain, Carmo.'

With fair hair worn loose and unbraided, winter-blue eyes and mustachios to rival Idwal's, Ducarius' handsome face reflected the ancient lineage of the Insubres, issuing from the forests of the north, beyond the Alps.

'I was sorry not to meet you in Bona — Betua was keen to introduce you — but it seems Numidians appear and disappear at will. By the time I asked your general, Maharbal, to direct me to your pavilion, you were already in the mountains, twenty miles due east! But thank the gods you appeared before Mutina in time to save Betua and her people. That's why I shall forever be in your debt.'

'You are not in my debt, Sir. My men simply did their duty, and my only regret is that we didn't come to the town's aid sooner. We might have spared your wife's people much bloodshed.' Sphax grimaced at the memory. 'Our enemies behaved like animals that day.'

'Make no mistake, Numidian, we will have our revenge!' Sphax was alarmed at the sudden transformation of the Insubres' expression. 'Especially on that butcher, Flaminius. Long have I sworn to Morrigu that his rotting head will adorn my hall for generations to come.'

At the mention of Flaminius' name Sphax winced, yet this was not a time to inflame passions and call for vengeance; they were here for Artula's passing from this world. For the first time Sphax noticed Ducarius was holding a small cup in his right hand, delicately wrought in gold. He guessed its purpose.

'Betua's courage astounded me on that day in Mutina. You are blessed, Sir, she is a remarkable woman, just as strong as the lady we have come in grief to honour this day.'

Instantly the savagery left the Insubre's face. 'Morrigu tells me our paths are destined to cross once more, Sphax. Until then, I bid you farewell.' With that he stepped forward and delicately placed the golden cup on Artula's pyre, leaving Sphax wishing the Keltoi would give up speaking in riddles.

Just as Ducarius had left his helmet, chain-mail and blade behind before entering Artula's sacred glade, no weapon of war or wailing carnyx was worn or carried that day. As a woman of peace, Artula would not be met in the next world by Morrigu, but by the loving arms of the goddess Epona, who would greet her with the gift of a white stallion with which to roam the rich grasslands of Albios in eternal peace and joy.

As the sun set and the evening star began to rise, Meilyr spoke to the assembled company. 'It is time to say our last farewells.'

With that, Sphax's eshrin rode forward in torch-lighted procession. At the head of the column, Aethon was still lightly bearing the body of Artula, covered by a linen sheet and flanked by her faithful guardians, Jugurtha and Hannon. When the procession drew alongside her last resting place, it was her own people who lifted her gently from the mare and placed her tenderly on top of her pyre.

Forming a broad half-circle around their chief and his son, the Anamares began a slow, rhythmical chant that echoed around the glade. Sphax was standing beside Idwal, who was doing his best to translate the proceedings, but the Anamares dialect often defeated him.

The Anamares had taken none of their wise men on this desperate march, so Meilyr himself conducted the ceremonies with a solemn dignity empty of tears, in a voice beyond loss and grief.

Rarely was Sphax touched by music, but he found the most moving and haunting moment of the evening was when Meilyr picked up a lyre and sang a lament to his mother. His ethereal, melodious boy's voice was not unlike his mother's, whom Sphax had heard sing on many occasions. There were several verses, but Idwal gave him a fair translation of the last verse.

Then, *Páistín Fionn,* come back, come back —
A homebound bird o'er the glancing track.
The door is open — the hearth is red —
And our love is calling you, Dear Fair Head.

Somehow, Sphax felt it was a sign of true nobility that feared Anamares warriors, the bravest of the brave, could be reduced to weeping by the voice of a child.

As he stood blinded by tears, a torch was suddenly thrust into his hands and Sphax stumbled forward to set a flame into the heart of Artula's pyre. The last thing he remembered as the flames illuminated the earthbound glade, was the cascade of sparks that shot heavenwards like a shower of shooting stars, emblazoning Artula's ascent to Epona.

* * *

'You look half-starved, lad,' said Maharbal, making him sound like some street urchin, invited to a feast. Grinning from ear to ear he added, 'Fill your belly from the table and rest your bones on that couch over yonder,' wafting a hand towards a divan. 'The salted pork is particularly good.'

Striding over the elaborate mosaic of nymphs and satires to reach the table, Sphax poured himself a generous cup of wine and helped himself to the pork, slowly taking in the unaccustomed luxury of his surroundings.

Maharbal had made himself at home in the atrium, the family room in which the previous owners had spent their days and received guests and clients. Judging from the empty plinths, niches and sparse furnishings, they'd left in a hurry, but not before rolling up carpets and removing family busts and statues of their household gods. Luckily for Maharbal, it seemed they'd had neither time nor space to cart away the luxurious divan he was lounging on, or, by the sounds of it, most of the contents of their kitchens and cellar.

It was indeed a lovely room. At its centre, a small square in the roof opened to the skies, ensuring the room was always light and airy and in the hottest months, comfortably cool. Directly beneath it sat a pool to collect rainwater, elaborately inscribed with images of shells and the goddess Venus. Even the wood-panelled walls had been painted to represent scenes of Pan's pursuit of the nymph Syrinx, a theme taken up in the elaborately tiled mosaic floor that bordered the impluvium.

Maharbal clapped his hands. As if from nowhere, three young girls appeared, and in the most comical

Latin, he asked, 'Bring more wine … and while you're at it, more food.'

As the girls disappeared, giggling and shaking their heads, Sphax had to smile. Why was he not surprised? Given a day in Hades, Maharbal would have found servants willing to cook and clean for him and a pretty woman to share his bed. If Maharbal had fallen from the skies like Icarus, he would have landed safely in a warm lagoon and been greeted by the loving arms of sirens. The man was proof against fire, flood and earthquake. Indestructible!

Given the exodus of nobles, merchants and rich farmers when the army emerged from the swamp, it was hardly surprising they'd left behind a compliant workforce of cooks, bakers and bottle-washers, not to mention a harvest of pretty women. But Sphax hadn't been summoned to admire the furnishings of the general's new residence, or his household arrangements.

'Has my uncle forgiven me at last?' asked Sphax, loading his words with an indifference he didn't feel.

'On that score I bring tidings both good and ill.' There was something mischievous in the general's tone. He was enjoying this. 'On the one hand he feels you have been insubordinate, unfaithful and disloyal.'

'And the good tidings?'

'That *was* the good tidings, lad.'

Sphax groaned. It was worse than he'd imagined. After taking a deep draught of wine he asked, 'Has the sickness taken his left eye?'

'No, lad, Melqart be praised. The sickness has abated and his left eye has been spared, though physicians have removed the diseased right eye.' Without a trace of a smile, he added, 'Giving him a somewhat unsightly appearance.'

'That is welcome news, at least. Blind generals don't make good leaders.'

'That's not the case, Sphax!' Maharbal erupted. 'Do you really believe blindness would have prevented Hannibal from continuing the campaign, fulfilling his destiny … following that star of his? He would have called for a litter and asked *us* to be his eyes. Not even Melqart himself will deflect him from his course!'

The general was staring at him. 'Blind or not, his men would have followed him! To the ends of the earth if it was necessary. As would all who love him … me included.'

Sphax knew what to say — he'd had time to think about it — but he didn't know *how* to say it. At least not without making things worse. So he held his tongue.

That is, until his mounting exasperation got the better of him. 'But don't you see, Sir, that's the crux of the problem. His men did follow him. Into a disease-ridden swamp where they dropped like flies. In their thousands! Along with our pack animals and where he himself lost the sight of an eye. That is too high a price to pay for blind loyalty. What good is a leader who never listens to reason? To sound advice? He may as well be blind—'

'Calm down, lad.'

'Calm down!' stormed Sphax, rising to his feet. 'You can tell my uncle that I have not forgiven *him*! And I can assure you that my list of accusations against him is far longer than his against me. What use is blind loyalty? For someone who prides himself on his logical thinking, why does he sometimes choose to ignore what it is telling him? Are we not to question? To use our reason? Or are we to be driven to the slaughtering pens like dumb beasts?'

'Sit down, lad,' Maharbal pleaded. 'This is not the time for accusations and recriminations. Disaster has been averted. Even your uncle acknowledges this was largely due to your advice to the rearguard to march beside the track.'

'By then it was almost too late. We lost so many, Sir,' slumping wearily into the divan. 'The Insubres and Boii have lost at least a thousand apiece, and the Anamares have been decimated. These men are irreplaceable. At least for this campaign.'

For a moment Sphax gazed through the compluvium at a patch of blue sky emerging from the cloud. 'Do you recall, Sir, the night I asked you why Hannibal had not turned on the legions of Scipio at the Rhodanus and destroyed them? Considering the question was posed by an ignorant boy who knew little of war, your openness and candour made a deep impression on me.

'You told me that every officer in the army had pleaded with Hannibal not to march north, but to wait and face the enemy from a position of strength. Yet, he refused to listen to any of you. If my uncle had followed your advice, Roman legions would not now be threatening Hasdrubal in Iberia, and we would have retained enough strength to march directly on Rome.'

Sphax turned his eyes from the patch of widening blue and stared at his general. 'All too often I'm afraid, Hannibal's star leads him off course. It is our duty to remind him of this.'

Other than an occasional grunt of reluctant agreement, Maharbal had remained silent during Sphax's tirade. Nervously, a young servant boy appeared, gingerly placing a jug of wine on the table, extending the awkward silence that had descended and giving the two protagonists time to reflect.

Maharbal said at last, 'Hannibal will listen to reason, Sphax. It's a matter of finding the right time and place. When he's … receptive.'

Sphax knew exactly what the general was getting at. 'You mean when he's not acting out some theatrical death scene from the back of an elephant!'

'That's not what I meant,' Maharbal protested. 'You accused him in front of hundreds of his own men, his most loyal men, our Libyans. That was certainly *not* the right time and place to tell him he'd made a bad mistake.'

'I'm sorry, Sir,' Sphax sighed, 'you're right of course. But by the time I reached his camp late that night, I was in despair. My men and I had spent the day dragging what was left of the living out of that filthy mud. Wading through a river of corpses doesn't put one in an amenable frame of mind. And when I came upon the body of Artula ... It's just that ... sometimes I despair of his *theatricals.* He has neither the wit nor wisdom of a Sophocles. What begins as a stirring tragedy soon descends into comedy unworthy of even Plautus!'

'Hannibal's audience isn't high-minded Greeks! It's the common soldier, Sphax, who wouldn't know one end of a petteia board from the other. I'll grant you he likes to put on a show and play to the crowd, but I've never seen him fail to get his message across.'

Sphax could see that Maharbal had a point. But on the subject of theatricals they would have to beg to differ. It was time to change the subject. Rising, he poured himself more wine and speared more of the delicious pork into his bowl.

'What news of the army, Sir?' he asked casually. 'Our Numidians have spent the week snoring their heads off and caring for our ladies. They're not in good condition, their hooves have softened and they took a beating in that swamp.'

'Whilst you've been idle, lad, I've been busy. Patrols report that our hot-headed consul is encamped beneath the walls of Arretium. Now the business of prodding and poking is to begin in earnest. Tomorrow the army marches east to put the town of Faesulae to the torch.'

'Are our Numidians to lead this march, Sir?' he asked eagerly.

'Yes … at least some of them. But not you, Sphax. You will be marching west.'

'Why?' he asked, unable to hide his disappointment.

'Because your uncle has received some momentous news that demands immediate action.' Now Maharbal had Sphax's attention. 'There are reports that a Carthaginian fleet has been sighted off Pisae.'

'But this could change everything!' Sphax cried excitedly. 'They could be carrying reinforcements, siege equipment, elephants … it could change the course of the war!'

'Exactly,' Maharbal agreed, smiling at Sphax's revived enthusiasm. 'That's why you're heading west, to Pisae. It all made perfect sense when I put it to Hannibal. After the events at Brundisium, you have more knowledge of ships and fighting at sea than any of us. You're also familiar with the town and its harbour. But above all, I need to keep you and your uncle out of each other's sight for a while, at least until tempers have cooled. What better way than to send you in opposite directions!'

Sphax's mind was already racing. 'I think I may need more than a single eshrin, Sir.'

'How about ten, lad? Will that be enough?' Maharbal was enjoying watching Sphax's reaction to these thunderbolts. 'If the vessels are carrying siege equipment or a troop of elephants, they will need a strong escort. Besides, it wouldn't hurt to put the wind up the good citizens of Pisae and remind them there's a new power in the land. It's on the supply route to Scipio's army in Iberia, and I'm told Roman vessels anchor there regularly. The sight of three hundred Numidians might persuade them that trade with Rome is not in their interests.'

'Pisae has a city wall and strong gates—'

'You'll find a way in. You usually do.'

'How long have I got, Sir?'

'Two weeks. But ten days would be better. After we've dealt with Faesulae, your uncle will be eager to march south to taunt Flaminius. Whatever that fleet is carrying, we will need it. Urgently.'

'Understood.'

'Choose your eshrin captains wisely. Oh,' grinned Maharbal, appearing to have overlooked a minor detail, 'Hannibal suggested that Idwal and that lieutenant of his join you. Just to keep an eye on you, of course.'

That was the second piece of news Sphax had heard that day.

ELEVEN

Other than the occasional observation on the beauty of the rugged countryside to the south or the vistas of the flooded Arnus valley to the north, Sphax and Idwal spent the morning doing what they always did when they had the pleasure of one another's company: arguing.

For the past few months, Idwal had been expounding the ideas of the Stoics, Zeno and Chrysippus, with Sphax doing his level best to demolish them, or at least point out the flaws. Unfortunately, Sphax's only grounding in ethics was the treatise Aristotle had written for his son, Nicomachus, a work he'd studied in secret with his Greek tutor, Elpis, when a slave in Rome. But even the incomparable barbs Aristotle had provided him with were proving insufficient to pierce the chain-mail armour of Stoic logic.

'I grant you that health is not in itself a virtue like justice, but dog's twat, Idwal, it would be difficult to live a happy life without it!'

'Are you saying the ill or infirm are incapable of happiness?'

'No, of course not! But you must concede that ill health makes life difficult and more of a struggle? Just as wealth paves the way to an easier life.'

'Stoic thought classes wealth, just like health, as an *indifferent*; something that has no bearing on virtue or happiness. Wealth corrupts as much as it brings benefits and ease of living. Only the four cardinal virtues confer true happiness.'

And so it had gone on throughout the morning. Cut and thrust had been met with shield and sword, ground had been yielded and recovered, advances risked in the face of threatened flanks, ambuscades had been laid and sprung, yet by mid-morning neither combatant felt he could claim outright victory or was willing to concede defeat. So the two of them acknowledged a temporary stalemate, agreeing a convivial truce.

Himilco and Idwal's lieutenant, Drust, had long since left them to it, preferring to scout ahead and swap jokes and gossip in their mangled Latin. Trailing behind, three hundred Numidians were simply grateful not to be trudging through the misery of knee-deep sludge. Besides, Sphax's eshrin at the head of the column had heard it all before. For them, health, virtue and happiness were more a matter of filling their bellies and finding a comfortable bed for the night.

Sphax glanced ahead to see Himilco and Drust galloping towards them at high speed. Raising the clutch of javelins he was carrying in his left hand he halted the column.

Breathing hard, Himilco gasped, 'There's a couple of farmsteads ahead with grain stores and a stables.' Catching his breath he added, 'We didn't see anybody around, they must be working in the fields. They've left a few wagons scattered about the place.'

Wrenching his thoughts from the contemplation of Stoic indifferents, Sphax glanced at Drust. 'What did you make of it?' he asked in Greek.

With raised eyebrows and his infectious grin, Drust reminded, 'Remember getting in and out of Brundisium, Sphax? I reckon those wagons might get us through the gates of Pisae.'

Idwal fixed his familiar frown and turned to Sphax. 'How far are we from the city? And if we do what I think Drust has in mind, are we to attempt it in daylight, or wait for nightfall?'

For Himilco's benefit, before Sphax thought fit to reply he translated what had been said and hinted at, into the Numidian tongue of Tassynt.

Turning his gaze to Idwal he switched to Greek. 'Do you see that hill?' pointing to a saddle-shaped ridge a couple of miles ahead. 'From there you have a clear sight of the city and the sea beyond. But what's more important is that once we ascend that hill, every guard on the city's walls and gates will also have a clear sight of us!'

Sphax recalled the painful memories of standing on that very hill with Fionn, not a year ago. 'From what I remember, the eastern gate of Pisae lies three miles distant.'

'So,' Idwal summarised, 'if we take the eastern gate in daylight, could we hold off the guards long enough for your Numidians to gallop to our rescue? Three miles is a long way!'

'Even so, daylight would be best,' argued Drust; 'with every hour of darkness, sentries grow more suspicious of folk wanting to enter their city … and farmers don't ship grain at night.'

After a heated debate between the three of them in Greek, Sphax translating the shifting arguments so Himilco could enter the fray, they finally came to a decision.

Three long, deep-bellied grain carts were standing outside the stables. Inside were stalled six stallions, docile and past their prime, but they would have to do. In an empty storehouse they found rolls of hemp sackcloth, stored for bagging the spring harvest. Mercifully, none of the owners and masters of this property showed their faces, sparing him the problem of what to do with them. Nevertheless, as Sphax anxiously watched the harnessing of the horses, he was certain the residents were in hiding, watching their every move. Would they have time to alert the authorities in Pisae?

Standing on that grassy knoll, staring down at the clay-red roofs of Pisae and the glittering expanse of blue sea beyond, evoked a succession of painful and poignant memories for Sphax. It was here that his beloved Fionn had declared, "My home lies somewhere over that sea. Never again will I return to this accursed land." How prophetic she'd been. But instead of returning home, she'd followed him. To her death. The fates had conspired, and now she lay cold and abandoned beneath her cairn of stones in the high Alps, beyond all remembrance of home and kin.

'From Faesulae, you say,' sniffed the captain outside the Lucca gate. 'That's two days' journey. Why Pisae? Arretium is but a day away from Faesulae.'

Sphax glanced up at the twin towers either side of the gatehouse bristling with levelled spears and suspicion. Idwal, seated beside Drust in the lead wagon, was playing his part well, but none of this was going exactly to plan.

'I've already told you, captain, this shipment is bound for Massilia. I have a contract with Tarbo, one of your ship's captains here in Pisae.' It was always better to spice lies with a smattering of truth. Tarbo was the captain who'd borne Sphax and Fionn to Massilia a year ago.

Unsheathing a short stubby sword, the captain of the guard pointed in turn to the wagons driven by Sphax and Himilco. 'And who are these shit-faced bastards?'

'My slaves,' replied Idwal, wincing at the uncouth language.

Sphax knew the type. The captain's shaven head and god-given arrogance gave him away. This man was no Pisani. He was an ex-legionary from Rome. As far as Sphax was concerned, this sealed his fate.

Pointing the tip of his blade at Drust's throat the captain bawled, 'You! Get down from the wagon and untie these ropes. A contract, eh ... let's see what you cocksuckers are offering.'

Sphax's first thought was this might work to their advantage. If they seized the moment, one of his Numidians hiding beneath the sackcloth could stick a javelin in the bastard's guts. But it was too risky. On the walls above, spears were still levelled, and although the bar had been removed, the gates showed only a sliver of an opening.

Viciously, Sphax yanked back on both reins. Squealing in sudden pain, both stallions reared up alarmingly, kicking out with their hooves as their ears shot rigidly backwards. The ex-legionary captain nearly jumped out of his skin, flattening himself against the gatehouse wall. Promising, thought Sphax. So the bastard felt uncomfortable around horses. At least he wouldn't start poking around the harnesses, where Idwal had secreted a sword and spear alongside the wagon shaft.

'Get that ... beast under control,' the man snarled, a tremor evident in his voice.

Leaping on to the back of the left hand stallion, Sphax cried, 'Whoa boy! Whoa ... easy there ... easy,' and glancing in mock sympathy at the captain, 'Sorry, Sir, these two are skittish. They almost killed a groom last week,' he added for good measure, all the while searching for that sensitive spot on the stallion's withers where the shoulder joint met the backbone. To produce a knee-jerk reaction in a horse that would make it rear up, all Sphax had to do was find the right tendon and give it a sharp squeeze. Dutifully the creature rose up on its hind legs.

Reaching for the right hand stallion he found the same tendon and squeezed. Soon Sphax had the two stallions bucking and rearing like dancing puppets.

The ex-legionary was terrified. In the confined space of the gatehouse archway, it was becoming increasingly difficult to avoid the wild flailing hooves of the stallions. Sphax watched as the terror on the man's face grew to the point where he could bear it no longer.

In that instant two things happened at once. The great oaken doors of the Lucca gate opened wide enough for Drust to wedge his spear between them, and a scything stroke of Idwal's blade parted the captain's head from his wretched body. At last they were in.

'Rise up, Numidians!' Sphax commanded, leaping from the stallion and tearing at the ropes securing the sackcloth. From the walls above he could hear the pounding of running feet and the frantic shouts of men unsure of what to do next. His only thought was to get Himilco's wagon into the relative safety of the archway, away from those levelled spears on the battlements.

Pressing his shoulder against the left hand gate Sphax shoved with all his strength, but it hardly budged. Guessing the mechanism was controlled by chains and lead counterweights he yelled, 'I need help, men!'

Cursing and sweating, it took six of them to force open the gates wide enough to drive Idwal's wagon through and Sphax's wagon into a position where it wedged them open. By then at least, Himilco's men had manhandled their own wagon into the safety of the archway, but not before two of them had been wounded by spears.

Either side of the gates were the massive ramparts of the gatehouse towers, linked by a battlement taller than the city's walls. Whoever commanded those towers controlled not only the Lucca gate, but this stretch of the city's walls. From above, Sphax could hear the clamour of iron on iron. Idwal and Drust had joined battle, and they would need help.

Commanding Himilco to defend the gates from any attack from within the city, he led his six men through the open door of the right hand tower. Racing up a wooden spiral staircase through two floors, they arrived on the battlements not a moment too soon.

Flailing their long Gaulish blades before them, Idwal and Drust were barely keeping their enemies at bay. At any moment it seemed they would be overwhelmed by a cursing mob of guards wielding spears and shields, baying for their blood. But other than helmets, the guardians of the Lucca gate wore little in the way of armour, and that was their undoing.

Within a heartbeat six javelins were spinning towards bare necks and exposed shoulders. Cries of triumph were suddenly replaced by screams of pain as Idwal and Drust rushed forward to ease the passage of the dying, tossing their bodies over the battlements.

It was over. Three survivors managed to flee back down the steps to the city wall, six paces below, nervously backing away to make certain they stayed out of range of Numidian javelins, whilst ten pierced and broken bodies lay inert at the foot of the gatehouse ramparts.

'Where are Jugurtha and Hannon?' asked Sphax, looking around.

Stooping to pick up a discarded shield, Idwal shot him an anxious glance. 'I sent them to storm the other gatehouse.'

Now concerned for his men, Sphax unsheathed his dragon sword and helped himself to an oval shield. 'Juba, Vermina, Gauda,' he commanded. 'You're with me.'

Sphax had never liked shields. Only recently had Idwal been training him to use one. But he had a healthy respect for the spears the guards were carrying. Forcing his left arm through the first strap he clenched his fist on the wooden bow and began clattering down the stairway.

Before the gates, Himilco had not been idle. Two wagons had been swivelled around parallel with the gate arch to form a barrier, and after unhitching some of the horses, four of his men were now mounted.

'Where are your wounded?' Sphax enquired of his lieutenant.

'In the cart blocking the gates. We've done what we could … one is in a bad way.'

'Jugurtha would be able to do more for them. Have you seen him, or the rest of my men?'

'No, but I've heard the sound of fighting coming from that gatehouse,' answered Himilco lamely, pointing to the gatehouse Idwal had ordered Sphax's men to storm.

Then why didn't you do something about it? he almost scolded, but managed to bite his lip.

At first sight Sphax's concerns seemed justified. Reaching the first floor the sight that met him was Hiempsal, slumped against a wall, hands pressed against his blood-soaked tunic.

'It's not deep, captain — I'll live.' But the next sight allayed his fears.

From the safety of the inner wall, Hannon and Jugurtha were playing a dangerous form of bear baiting with the Pisani sentries blocking the stairs from the floor above. Taking it in turn, and beginning with a flurry of insults to fire them up for the challenge, each would nimbly dance into view of the staircase, briefly offering themselves as a target for a spear, before beating a hasty retreat. At the same time, as each dancer stepped up to the challenge, Gala, Cirta and Syphax would steal forward, javelins threaded, hoping for a glimpse of an exposed limb to target. Judging from the body spread-eagled over the staircase and the scattering spears on the floor, this lethal game had reached a wary standoff.

'Hannon, Jugurtha, Syphax … keep them occupied! The rest of you follow me.' With that he bounded down the staircase to the street where Himilco had placed his barriers.

'Hold your position, Himilco,' Sphax yelled breathlessly, racing for the open door of the right-hand gatehouse. By the time they'd ascended three flights of the spiral staircase to the battlements, they were all gasping for breath.

'It's a standoff in the other gatehouse,' wheezed Sphax. 'The Pisani have made a stand on the second floor to block my men climbing the stairs.'

'Then it's simple,' grinned Idwal. 'All we have to do is cross the battlement above the gate and we'll have them trapped like rats!'

'My thoughts exactly,' smiled Sphax, his breathing easing at last. 'I told Jugurtha to keep them occupied.'

Leaving Drust and three Numidians behind, Sphax, Idwal and five men from his eshrin tiptoed across the battlements above the gates and took up positions above the gatehouse stairway. Although Sphax couldn't see the guards from where he was crouching behind his shield, he could clearly hear them cursing the javelins coming their way. It was time to end the killing.

'Brave Pisani,' he shouted down to them, 'duty and honour have been served. Long will this city celebrate the heroes who defended this gatehouse against fifty Numidians and the mighty chieftain of the Cavari. If you live, you will hear these stories for yourselves and receive the gratitude of the good citizens of Pisae. But I must confess, noble Pisani, that prospect is unlikely. You are outnumbered, surrounded, and without a hope of relief.

'Surely valour should be rewarded with life and honour, not pain and death! When you fall, who will tell of your heroism? Do you expect your enemies, already shamefaced at failing to overcome such a pitifully small company, to speak of your gallantry? No, brave warriors, our shame and humiliation would never permit us to speak of such things. So alas, brave souls, your valour will remain forever untold.

'But if you were to lay down your weapons and surrender, I swear by Juno that you would be free to march into the city with heads held high … free to tell your families and neighbours of your deeds this day.' Sphax paused to let all this sink in. 'What say you? Do you choose—?'

The rest of his speech was drowned by the deafening clatter of helmets, spears and shields being tossed to the floor. As Idwal, Sphax and his men descended the staircase to collect the weaponry, they were joined by the three Numidians from the floor below. Ten heads, preparing to be held high, were somewhat crestfallen when the Pisani realised they'd just surrendered their weapons to eight ragged-looking Numidians, and a Gaul armed only with a sword.

If only war was always as easy as this, mused Sphax.

Drust appeared at the top of the staircase. 'Agbal must have given his signal. The rest of your Numidians are approaching the gates. They make a grand sight, Sphax!'

'What about the walls? Any sign of men approaching from the southerly gate?' he asked.

'No. It's so hot today they're probably snoozing … it is the sexta hora, after all. If it wasn't for that bastard ex-legionary at the gate, we would have walked into this place. Militia aren't real soldiers, just townsfolk handed a shield and spear.'

Sphax wasn't so sure. 'Three of my men have already been wounded, and there is another gate,' he reminded everyone, 'just as formidable as this one.'

'Storming a gate from the *inside* is hardly a strategic challenge, Sphax,' noted Idwal with a sardonic grin. 'I'll wager my scroll of Chrysippus that when we turn up at the southern gate with three hundred Numidians, the sentries will throw down their weapons.'

'Agreed,' laughed Sphax. 'And if I lose, I swear my men will turn this place upside down to find you and Drust the finest jar of mead Pisae has to offer.'

Sphax lost the wager. Eighteen sentries simply handed over their weapons. Like the ten that had already surrendered, Sphax let them melt away, back to their homes and families. As with all militias, they were, after all, just bakers and shopkeepers, not soldiers.

Years later, Sphax would proudly tell the tale — far too often, his friends teased — of how Pisae became the first city in Italia to fall: not to a great Carthaginian host, but to three hundred Numidians, a Cavari chieftain and his faithful lieutenant.

TWELVE

When at last Sphax reached the southern quays of the harbour, the news that greeted him was the last thing he wanted to hear. They were too late. The Carthaginian fleet had sailed on the tide, early that morning.

Wandering along the quaysides with Idwal, talking to sea captains and merchants, they soon pieced together everything that was known about the Carthaginian's week-long stay. And like the squadron's sudden departure that morning, nothing made any sense. According to all the accounts, seven days ago a quinquereme and eight triremes ghosted silently into the lagoon east of the northern quays, where the broader Arnus meets the Auser river. It was the old sea dogs, veterans of the first war with Carthage who recognised the emblem of the sun's disc topped by the moon, emblazoned on their sails.

All had seemed clear: Hannibal was invading by land and now Carthage by sea. Expecting the city to be stormed at any moment, alarm bells were rung and the militia summoned to defend the city's walls and gates. Messengers were hastily dispatched to Lucca, Faesulae and Consul Flaminius in Arretium, begging them to send relief.

As they'd watched the invaders drop anchor and take down sails, the citizens of Pisae had held their breath, gathering in the forum outside the temple of Juno, praying to the goddess for salvation.

Pisae had feared that dawn would reveal a great host drawn up outside the city's walls, ready to storm the city and put them all to the sword. But to everyone's astonishment, not a single siege tower, catapult, ladder or ram was to be seen, let alone the expected ranks of Carthaginians. Rumours circulated that it was just a bluff: the invaders were biding their time, waiting for them to lower their guard.

Yet days passed. Uneventful days, days without incident. The squadron bobbed at anchor in the lagoon whilst the militia wearily patrolled the walls, keeping a watchful eye on their visitors.

Then, on the seventh day: jubilation. That morning the Carthaginian squadron left just as unexpectedly as it had arrived a week ago. Bleary-eyed militiamen returned to their homes to catch up on sleep whilst the steps of the temple of Juno burgeoned with offerings.

At least for Sphax, the postscript to these accounts brought some wry amusement. Usually, they went something like: 'And then you black devils turned up at our gates! How long are you planning to stay?'

'No longer than the Carthaginian fleet,' Sphax invariably replied, before adding, 'then we'll leave you in peace.'

Dusk was falling and the lingering heat of the day was being quenched by a gentle shower of rain as clouds rolled in from the north. Himilco, Drust and his eshrin were waiting for them by the row of shops and popinas on the far side of the quay. Mounting Dido he turned to Himilco. 'Is the city secured?'

'An eshrin has been assigned to every gate and two eshrins are patrolling the city. But I don't think they'll give us any trouble … there isn't a soul on the streets. It seems the Pisani have taken to their homes and barred their doors.'

'Then it is well done, my friend. Follow me to where Idwal and I will set up quarters. I want you to pass the word to all our captains; they should meet me there for a council of war on the stroke of the fifth watch.'

'Why so late? Our men are tired—'

'So am I … so are we all, Himilco! But there is much to decide *before* we meet.'

In light of the disappearance of the Carthaginian squadron, Sphax desperately needed to discuss their next moves with Idwal and Drust. How to pacify the city his Numidians had just taken would have to wait. It was going to be a long night.

Because it held such fond memories for him, Sphax set up headquarters in the faded grandeur of the old hospitia by the Lucca gate. It was where he'd stayed with Fionn, almost a year ago, in a spacious room with a balcony overlooking the street.

Bursting into the place that evening at the head of thirty javelin-wielding Numidians and a Gallic chieftain, he was offered a suite of rooms on the ground floor that boasted access to the atrium, a library, and the hospitia's peristyle gardens. Greasing the plump palm of the proprietor with an indecent amount of silver, he was assured that he and his guests would be treated like kings. After the tribulations of the past weeks, Sphax believed his men deserved nothing less.

Within the hour, Sphax and his two companions were seated on couches in the cavernous tablinum beside a table groaning with luxurious dishes and delicacies. Lobster, oysters and turbot were served in delicate sauces seasoned with dill and turmeric, followed by courses of hare and pigeon in a rich broth of onions, eggs and spinach. True to his boast, the proprietor had found a jar of mead fit for a Cavari chieftain and wine that would not shame an emperor's table. Sphax was loth to dilute it with water, but tonight he had to keep a clear head.

'What are we to do now?' he groaned, sinking back into the couch to ease the unfamiliar eruptions in his belly from overindulgence. 'Our mission was to contact the Carthaginian fleet and escort whatever they were carrying back to Hannibal. As the bird has flown, or in this case, sailed, it must be concluded our mission is over.'

Idwal was shaking his head, his familiar frown already fixed in position. 'I think we should first evaluate the accounts the merchants and captains have given us this afternoon. Only then can we come to a clear decision about the status of our mission.'

'From everything you've told me,' began Drust, tentatively, 'what puzzles me most is why the fleet didn't come ashore for supplies and fresh water? If you recall, when we sailed from Epidamnos to Brundisium, the first thing the *Hera* had to do was take on supplies, especially of fresh water. And ours was only a two day voyage. The journey from Carthage would take days — perhaps even a week. Have quinqueremes and triremes the capacity to stow more supplies?'

'No, Drust,' explained Sphax. 'Idwal and I can testify to the fact that a quinquereme has no more cargo space than the *Hera* had, and far more mouths to feed. Which leads us to only one conclusion: the fleet must have put into harbours along the way, perhaps in Sicily or Corsica?'

'Or the vessels had been stripped of everything but the rowing benches,' Idwal suggested. 'In which case they could travel light and fast, with far more space for stowage. They would also be able to outrun a superior Roman fleet, should they have encountered one. Anyway, what makes you think they came from Carthage? I think it far more likely they sailed from Iberia.'

Sphax was shaking his head and grinning at his friend. 'Why do I get the sinking feeling you're about to elucidate a hundred reasons to substantiate this theory?'

Chuckling, Idwal ignored this good-natured barb. Spearing an oyster with the sharp end of his spoon he swallowed it whole. Winking at Sphax, Drust was also grinning. Idwal's timing was always impeccable — they would have to be patient.

But it seemed their patience was to be tested a little longer. Suddenly Hannon burst into the room, irritated and flustered in equal measure. 'There's a man outside, demanding—'

He never got to finish the sentence. Hot on Hannon's heels a giant of a man dragged two Numidian sentries into the room as if they were no more of a hindrance than wayward children.

'Who is in command here?' the stranger barked, voice muffled beneath a black cloak that swaddled him from head to foot.

Springing to his feet Sphax confronted the stranger. 'I demand you tell me your name—'

'And I demand to know why you're late!' roared the stranger with equal venom. 'My son delivered a message to Hannibal's camp a week ago. Now it's too late … the fleet has sailed.'

These last revelations brought Idwal and Drust to their feet.

'Hannon,' Sphax spoke calmly, 'take Juba and Syphax back to your sentry duties outside the hospitium. I believe Agbal is shortly to relieve you. Say nothing of this to the men.'

Worried about the safety of his captain, Hannon was reluctant to leave, but Sphax waved him away. A servant boy entered and began removing the empty plates from the table.

'Leave them,' ordered Sphax. 'Bring a chair and cup for our new guest.' He noticed the stranger draw the cape closer around his face and turn away so as not to be recognised. Evidently he was playing a dangerous game. Now Sphax was intensely curious.

He'd heard so much about Hannibal's extensive network of spies and informants, a web whose invisible threads reached inside the very walls of Rome, but no one had ever met these men, or could tell him anything about their character or motivation for risking their lives. Even Maharbal, his uncle's trusted friend, could tell him little, other than that Hannibal had cultivated them over many years through prodigious letter writing and the hospitality of guest friendship.

Then there was the question of payment. He knew that much of Hannibal's information was bought, sold and paid for in silver, a simple transaction that profited both buyer and seller. But this was different. Judging from the stranger's anger that his message had not been heeded, and the risks he'd taken coming here this evening, this man was not risking his life for silver. Sphax sensed he would be deeply offended at the suggestion. Something else was at stake here.

After the boy returned to place a stool and silver goblet by the table, Sphax said, 'Under no circumstances are we to be disturbed. Go back to the kitchens. We will summon you if needed.'

Once the lad had left, Sphax turned to their uninvited guest. 'I am Sphax, nephew of Hannibal and commander of the three hundred Numidians that have taken this city.' Gesturing towards his companions he added, 'May I introduce Idwal, chief of the Cavari Gauls, and his lieutenant, Drust.'

For an instant the stranger stared at them all before throwing back his hood to reveal a shock of silver-grey curls that fell to his shoulders, solemn grey eyes and an aquiline nose sunk in a face so deeply furrowed it spoke of a lifetime of tribulation. Unfastening the brooch that clasped the cloak tight around his throat, he let the garment fall to the floor and took up his seat on the stool.

'I am a Carthaginian. My name is Malchus, but when I escaped the siege of Lilybaeum and fled to this city, that name was not safe here, so the Pisani know me as Mentor, a poor Greek who fled the ravages of Carthage in Sicily to save his wife and young child. Though my allegiances lie elsewhere, Pisae has been good to me, and I've made my fortune here.'

Sphax poured a generous cup of wine and handed it to the man.

'I've heard the name, Sphax — you seem to have gained something of a reputation amongst our enemies — but I had no idea you were Hannibal's nephew … I didn't think your uncle had any relatives, other than two brothers and a sister.'

'Neither did my uncles until I escaped slavery in Rome a year ago to join them at the Rhodanus. I am the son of his sister, Similce—'

'Then you are the son of Navaras, a Prince of Numidia in your own right.' Wide-eyed, Malchus sighed heavily. 'I see that tragedy has stalked your young life. At the time it was understood that the child perished with his parents when pirates fired their ship.'

'That's a lie! Illyrian pirates had nothing to do with their deaths. Our ship was captured by a Roman fleet. Blaming my parents' deaths on pirates ensured Queen Teuta's name would be forever blackened in the eyes of her allies, and sent a clear warning to Carthage not to meddle in Rome's war with Illyria. I myself was spared death for a life of slavery. The tribune who ordered the cold-blooded murder of my parents is now consul, encamped with his legions outside the gates of Arretium, not a hundred miles from here.'

For a moment a reverent silence descended on the company before Malchus spat the cursed name of Gaius Flaminius Nepos. 'Now it all makes perfect sense!'

Knowing how much distress this was causing his friend, Idwal was desperate to move the conversation on. 'We are eager to hear of your life on Sicily, Sir, and of your escape. If I could trouble you to speak in Greek, my lieutenant will be able to understand.'

If anything, the mood of their guest appeared to darken at the prospect. 'I was born into a world of war, young man,' lamented Malchus, speaking Greek like a native. 'Men of my years tasted the bitterness of strife with our mother's milk.'

Sphax recalled that Carthage's first war with Rome lasted twenty-three years … half a lifetime. He shuddered at the thought.

'My father was governor of Drepana,' Malchus continued, 'a city on the west coast of Sicily with safe anchorage and strong walls. When I came of age, I raised a company in my city and marched to join Hamilcar in the field.' Pausing suddenly, he stared at Sphax as if understanding something for the first time. 'Believe me, young man, the noble blood that flows in your veins has been forged in the flames of war. All who knew your grandfather, Hamilcar Barca, loved him. If he'd so commanded, we would have followed him into Hades itself.

'By the mercy of Ba 'al Hamūn, these days I only recall those six years of war in dreams from which I wake in cold terror. Every season we defeated Rome's legions, but like the spawn of dragons' teeth, a fresh harvest of warriors sprang up every spring to spill their blood and sow a new crop. With each passing year we were ground down and grew weary beyond measure. In the last days we retired to fortresses such as Lilybaeum and Drepana.

'Even then we were not without hope. We watched as the legions foundered on our walls like waves on a rocky shore. Carthage supplied us well by sea. All we had to do was stand firm, and the tide would surely turn. But then that arsewit, Hanno, blundered into the enemy off the Aegates Islands and led our great fleet to utter destruction. He was our last hope …' Malchus trailed off, drifting into uneasy silence.

With a deep sigh he stiffened, appearing to cast off the shadow of his past. 'But I didn't come here this evening to bring up this foul bile, these tales of woe from an old man, an old soldier who should know better than to fill young heads with despair! I came to find out why Hannibal has left it too late to contact our squadron. There may be a price to pay for such tardiness.'

The three of them looked at one another, wondering who was to deliver the bad news. In the end it was Idwal who spoke up. 'I'm afraid your son would not have been allowed to deliver his message to Hannibal in person. At the time he was suffering from a fever that blighted his eyes. In the Arnus marshes he lost the sight of his right eye, and when at last we reached ground where he could rest and recover, the sickness spread to his left. Our entire army feared not only for his sight, but indeed, for his life. By the mercy of the gods he was spared, retaining the sight in his left eye. Since then he's made a full recovery.'

'Thank the gods he was spared!' murmured Malchus, shocked by the news. 'Blindness would have been an unthinkable calamity. But my son was told nothing of this. His message was delivered to a general named Hanno — must I be forever dogged by that name — who swore his master would learn of it as a matter of urgency.'

Sphax groaned. Of all the generals it would have to be Hanno! Brave, steadfast Hanno, the first into battle but the last to recognise a strategic opportunity when it stared him in the face. 'I agree that a great opportunity has been lost, Sir, but what can you tell us about this mysterious squadron?'

'Very little,' admitted Malchus, shaking his head. 'I believe this was arranged between Hannibal and his brother before he set out for the Alps and the invasion of Italia. May is the beginning of the campaigning season. I believe that Hasdrubal had been ordered to send ships from New Carthage in Iberia to assist Hannibal's army in any way it could. Pisae or Genua would have been the likeliest harbours to make contact with the army.'

Was this one of the reasons for Hannibal's undue haste in beginning the march and choosing the shortest path, Sphax wondered? Even the guides he'd chosen were Pisani, and the city was only a day's ride from their camp. 'When did you last have contact with Hasdrubal, Sir?'

'Two weeks ago I sent a ship to warn him to expect trouble. A Roman fleet had been sighted off Pisae heading north-west, no doubt carrying reinforcements for Scipio's army in Iberia. I'm still awaiting the vessel's return.'

'What we in the army are most anxious to learn,' explained Idwal, 'is what this squadron might have been carrying, and its usefulness in our campaign against Flaminius. For instance, we are in desperate need of siege equipment, or as my friend here would prefer, a troop of elephants. Either way, our orders were to escort the cargo safely back to camp.

I think it safe to assume they were not carrying substantial reinforcements of men, otherwise they would have taken the city for themselves. If their cargo was indeed siege equipment or elephants, surely they would have beached the vessels, unloaded everything, and gone in search of our army. Which leaves us with the probability they were not carrying anything of value for our present campaign.'

'Nevertheless,' Sphax objected, 'a fleet of this size operating off Pisae could make it difficult for Rome to re-supply and reinforce Scipio's armies in Iberia.'

'I agree, Sphax, but—'

'*And*,' Drust argued, sitting bolt upright on his couch, 'such a squadron could transport two thousand men hundreds of miles south in a matter of days!' Turning to Malchus he asked, 'How long does it take one of your vessels to reach Ostia, Sir?'

'With a fair wind, less than three days.'

'Warships are faster,' beamed Drust. 'Which means we could have two thousand Numidians blockading the mouth of the Tiber, even Rome itself, in two days!'

'Until Rome's Sicilian fleet was ordered to drive them off,' Idwal counted sourly. 'By which time our Numidians would be stranded and cut off.'

'Numidians are always stranded and cut off. That's how they like to fight!' parried Drust. 'Besides, they could live off the land.'

'He's right, Idwal,' Sphax waded in, 'it wouldn't be like a traditional siege, but our Numidians could stop every wagonload of wheat from reaching Rome's markets. We could starve the city just as effectively as ranks of infantry and siege engines.'

'And when Rome sallies out of the Servian Gate with ten thousand legionaries, what then?'

'We scatter to the four winds of course!' laughed Sphax. 'Then our Numidians would surround the lot of them and pick'em off like lice, company by company.'

As much as Malchus was enjoying the cut and thrust of these young strategoi, time was pressing and decisions had to be taken. 'Gentlemen, gentlemen … it's clear you all understand how useful this fleet could be in your campaign. But it's not here, it has sailed. What are you going to do about it?'

Sphax was now clear what they should do. 'Tomorrow the three of us will take ship and sail south in search of them. Within the week I swear that squadron will be back on station off Pisae.'

'I would offer you one of my own vessels, but if I was seen to be aiding you in any way it would look suspicious and put at risk my position in the city.'

'I fully understand, Sir. Fear not,' he smiled, conjuring a face from his past, 'I already have a captain and a ship in mind.'

THIRTEEN

'You!' The manner in which the word was flung at him seemed to capture the very essence of fear and loathing and still embody every known curse in the Latin language.

'And a fair morning to you too, Captain Tarbo,' Sphax greeted him jauntily. Other than a few more missing teeth and a thinning of his wispy grey hair, the old goat was much as he remembered him when he and Fionn had sailed to Massilia on his vessel a year ago. Clearly his disposition showed no signs of improvement. 'How flattering of you to remember me!'

Tarbo hawked and spat noisily. 'What are you doing here?'

'If you haven't already noticed, my men and I captured this city yesterday. But today I need your vessel. I suggest you provision her immediately and prepare to cast off.'

Before Tarbo had time to object, Sphax, Idwal and Drust strode up the ramp onto the deck of the deep-bellied grain ship, taking up position at the foot of the steps that led to the steering platform. Standing above them incandescent with rage, Tarbo let out a stream of obscenities, scattering sibilants and spittle to the wind. His crew of six slave boys, all in their early teens stood rooted to the spot, eyes shifting anxiously between their captain and the three warriors, armed to the teeth.

'Get a move on, you three,' yelled Sphax at Jugurtha, Hannon and Agbal, struggling up the ramps from the stone quay, laden with sacks of supplies and spare javelins. Turning to stare up at Tarbo on the steering platform he growled, 'Has she sufficient provisions for a five day voyage?' The man glared back without answering.

Sphax's patience was wearing thin that morning. After Malchus left, the council of war with his captains dragged on long into the night and he'd barely managed an hour's sleep. Drawing his dragon sword he marched up the steps, ducked under the tiller bar and pointed it at Tarbo's throat. 'Once before I seem to remember threatening to part that ugly head of yours from its body. This time it's not an idle threat!'

Tarbo knew it. Flinching, he stepped backwards, tripping over an oar cable and landing clumsily on his backside, only to find Sphax standing over him with the blade still pricking his throat. 'We have fresh water and supplies for a week,' he croaked, wondering what had happened to the foolish lad who'd spent the entire voyage to Massilia spewing up his guts in the hold, not a year ago. Sheathing his sword, Sphax helped Tarbo to his feet. 'Cast off immediately and take advantage of the tide and this north-easterly. We sail south to Cosa.' All he got in return was a grunt, but that was enough.

Idwal, Drust and the Numidians had already made themselves at home in the deck cabin at the foot of the steering platform steps. There was no seating or benches, so all five sat on the floor with legs outstretched, backs resting against the planked walls of the cabin. In a corner lay a filthy straw-filled mattress surrounded by a clutter of plates, bowls and the remains of a half-eaten breakfast. It would be cramped and uncomfortable, thought Sphax, but at least the roof would keep the weather out.

Nodding at the half-eaten breakfast he grinned at Idwal, 'No wonder the captain's in such a filthy mood. Anyone volunteer to take him the remains of his puls?' There was a resounding silence at this suggestion. 'No? Well, I suppose the old goat will have to go hungry. I'm going to watch the vessel cast off,' and with that Sphax ducked out of the cabin's open doorway on to the deck.

Once all the mooring ropes had been unwound from the iron bollards on the quay, the vessel drifted steadily on the tide towards the stronger currents of the Arnus river where it met the sea. Racing around him the young crew were now calling to one another to gather the sheets and cables that would raise the great square mainsail.

Idwal joined him as they watched Tarbo haul on the tiller bar to bring the lumbering corbita around to the south-west. In teams of three to starboard and larboard, the boys gathered ready to haul on the sheets, and to the accompaniment of a rhythmic chant, the great sail rose and steadily filled. Instantly he felt the timbers surge forward beneath the heavy swell of the Tyrrhenian sea.

When the crew turned their attention to raising the supparum sail on the bowsprit, Sphax would have to intervene, knowing full well Tarbo would be furious — the supparum aided steerage — but they would only be borrowing it for a little while.

The boys were puzzled by his request, nevertheless they did exactly as he ordered, stretching out the linen sail flat on the deck and placing empty clay jars on the four corners to stop it flapping around in the breeze. Puzzled as the crew were by Sphax's instructions, this was nothing in comparison to the astonishment he'd met with when requesting the staff of the hospitium find him six jars of liquid oak gall ink and paint brushes … all before dawn!

Soon Sphax's painting team went into action, carrying horse-hair brushes and jars of ink onto the deck. On his knees he dipped his iron stylus into the ink and began to draw the outline of a staff down the centre of the sail. When he was satisfied with this he formed a crescent shape above the staff and finally a circular disc below it. At last he stood back to inspect his work.

His Numidians were critical. 'The sun disc isn't big enough,' observed Hannon. 'And the moon needs to be pointier, captain,' suggested Agbal. Jugurtha thought it would do, but even he didn't sound convinced. Idwal and Drust observed strict neutrality.

'Well,' he said in his own defence, 'you lot can make it bigger or pointier when you fill it in with the ink. Get started.'

When they'd filled in his outline with the brushes and added their own little flourishes, the Numidians got to their feet and stood back to take a look at their handiwork. Already the oak gall was beginning to dry, turning from an opaque grey to an ever deepening black.

Sphax had to smile, it did look like a child's attempt to paint a Carthaginian standard, but seen from five hundred yards away in a rolling sea, the smudges and imperfections would be overlooked. It might just save them from a trireme's ram, and that was the only thing that mattered.

'It will pass muster,' was Sphax's final verdict. 'Leave it to dry for a little while, then we'll let the boys raise it on the bowsprit.' Gazing up at Tarbo's scowling face he added, 'Perhaps our captain will stop grumbling then.'

An hour later, Sphax climbed up to the steering platform with a basket of bread and cheese as a peace offering for Tarbo. Without a word of gratitude the captain wolfed it down in silence, taking generous swigs from the jug of water Sphax had placed at his feet.

'Do you want me to take over the bar for a while …?' Tarbo suddenly roared with laughter at this suggestion. Sphax was astonished. Never before had he seen the old goat crack his face with a smile, let alone laugh!

'At least you could eat your meal in peace,' he persisted. Tarbo said nothing, eyes fixed on his next course heading, somewhere on the distant shoreline.

If anything, Sphax felt slightly resentful at the captain's mocking laughter. 'Your tiller bar and the cables that attach it to the steering oars are so easy to handle a child could use it to follow a course. It doesn't even require much strength! I grant you it's a clever arrangement, but if I was to put two heavy steering oars in your hands and ask you to navigate the seas of the Adria, I doubt you would have the strength or skill to get very far.'

Now he had Tarbo's full attention. 'You have done this?' he growled, incredulous.

'Three months ago, in the storm season,' Sphax exaggerated. 'From Ariminum to Rhizon in the bay of Kotor, though I shared the task with the ship's master, who was teaching me the art of navigation.'

'The Adria is but a fish tank in comparison to the storms and heavy seas we endure in the Tyrrhenian.'

Images of the mountainous foaming seas and raging tempest the night they'd been shipwrecked flashed into Sphax's mind. 'Is that so?' he muttered, distractedly.

'It is, boy, and you would have us foundered on those rocks below that headland before I'd finished this cheese!'

Sphax glanced up at the flapping mainsail. 'At least I wouldn't be spilling wind as wastefully as you appear to be doing,' he taunted, descending the steps in the wake of a spray of spittle and instruction for the crew to loosen sheets.

As the afternoon dragged on the Numidians slept. Sphax had always envied their ability to sleep; whatever the hour, day or night, they simply curled up and began snoring their heads off. For the three of them still wide awake, in the confines of the little deck cabin it felt as though they'd been penned up with a sounder of grunting swine, making conversation all but impossible.

So he, Idwal and Drust had taken to strolling the deck, talking to the slave boys, asking their names and what their lives were like aboard Tarbo's trading ship. It came as something of a surprise to find they all spoke well of their captain, and were proud to show them their quarters below deck where he'd supplied them with benches, decent mattresses and warm blankets. Sphax had to admit it looked more ship-shape and comfortable than the squalid corner of the deck cabin Tarbo had claimed as his own quarters. For the first time he noticed that none of the boys went barefoot, and all had clean tunics and tidy hair.

If anything, the north-easterly had stiffened throughout the afternoon and they were now making excellent progress, but as dusk approached, Sphax grew uneasy.

All day Tarbo had kept the coast of Italia on the distant horizon, a few miles off the larboard bow. But as darkness descended he seemed to be making no move to change course and look for a safe anchorage on the coast. As they approached the solstice, Sphax knew the days were lengthening. Was Tarbo simply cutting it fine?

Nights at sea were unavoidable, nevertheless always fraught with some risk. Wherever possible captains preferred the safer option of seeing out the hours of darkness in a safe anchorage, ashore.

That evening the sunset was spectacular. When the sun's flame-red disc began to slip beneath the waves, he and Drust exchanged anxious glances. Drust had also received lessons in navigation from Corinna and was all too aware of the dangers of a night at sea. It was high time to tackle Tarbo. If it wasn't already too late.

As moral reinforcements, Idwal and Drust followed him onto the steering platform. 'Are we not to seek safe anchorage tonight, Captain?' he asked politely. 'Surely we're not in such haste that we need to risk a night at sea?'

'For you, maybe,' shrugged Tarbo, 'but the sooner we get there, the sooner we get back. I have a cargo of wine for Massilia back in Pisae.'

'Which will still be there upon our return,' pointed out Idwal, not unreasonably.

'Curse the lot of you!' exploded Tarbo. 'You board my ship like pirates, force me to sail to Cosa then question my judgement. You're worse than pirates … nothing more than thieving bastards, lower than a serpent's belly! Cutthroats! Robbers! Get off my—'

'Calm down, Tarbo!' roared Sphax, with a force that stopped his tirade in its tracks. 'All we're asking you to consider is whether arriving half a day earlier at Cosa is worth risking the lives of your crew and your vessel.'

'Don't tell me you're worried about my crew. Liars! It's your own skin you're worried about.'

Sphax saw it was hopeless. Tarbo was unmovable. Besides, darkness was falling so fast that heading for the coast would put them in greater danger than staying out at sea. But for the first time, Sphax wondered about the captain's state of mind.

The question of the captain's state of mind did arise in their discussions in the deck cabin. Idwal had woken the Numidians with a none too gentle prod of his laced boots so they understood what was going on, but Hannon and Jugurtha seemed more concerned whether the salted pork and flatbreads would last another day.

When Sphax suggested Tarbo did have a point, despite his ravings, and that what he'd accused them of was factually correct, this thunderbolt met with stony silence.

'We're not pirates, Sphax,' Drust said at last.

'In Tarbo's eyes, we are exactly that, I'm afraid.'

'Then we must convince him otherwise,' Idwal argued. 'Once our mission is accomplished he will have his vessel back and be paid generously for his services.'

But that was not Sphax's chief concern. Even though the first watch of the night had barely begun, Tarbo had been standing at the tiller bar for twelve hours. What had struck him most about that last fractious encounter was how weary and haggard the man looked. And there had been something desperate and futile about the insults he'd flung at them: as if he was out to prove someone wrong.

Sphax guessed that *someone* was him. He hadn't exactly covered himself in glory since he'd come aboard! From the outset he'd been arrogant and boastful. Largely lying about navigating the Adria and accusing Tarbo of being too old to wield a steering oar. He'd behaved shamefully, without a shred of virtue. But why? Why had he felt the need to … humiliate the captain?

The answer was painful to acknowledge. During that last voyage with Tarbo he'd spent most of the time groaning and spewing up his guts amongst the rats in the cargo hold. But it wasn't just the sea sickness: he'd been haunted by memories too horrific to confront. Sleep had offered no respite. His dreams had been filled with images of taunting legionaries and the brutal murder of his mother. For his former self, the young man that had set out from Pisae on that May morning, the sea had held far more terrors than he cared to admit at the time.

Before he'd set foot on the vessel, Sphax had boasted to Fionn how he would protect and defend her. Yet it was she who'd cared for him, forcing him to drink, feeding him morsels he managed to stomach and cleaning up his vomit. When on the third day they'd sighted the Roman fleet of Consul Scipio, it had been Fionn who'd shamed him into action, insisting he stop wallowing in self-pity and come up on deck to take a look for himself. By then, he was certain that Tarbo and his crew despised him.

When the ship had run into a sudden squall off Massilia and the waves had risen like foam-tipped mountains he'd cringed, white and terror-stricken in the deck cabin, paralysed with fear. Sphax remembered gazing up at Tarbo on the steering platform, face set like marble in the teeth of the tempest, a rock, steadfast and resolute, everything he himself aspired to be. At that moment he'd never felt more ashamed of himself. Even now he shuddered at the memory.

He had Corinna to thank for exorcising the shades that haunted his troubled past and with it his fear of the sea. But it was now time to redeem himself, and make peace with Tarbo. Gathering up the basket, he filled it with flatbreads, salted pork and what remained of the cheese before filling a jug with water.

'Where are you going?' asked Idwal.

'Where I should have been all along,' sighed Sphax. 'Standing beside our captain on the steering platform. If he's to get through this night, he will need my support.'

'Do you want me to join you?'

'Thank you, my friend, but no. This is something I must do alone.'

Above the larboard bow the moon had risen in the starlit heavens, casting her silvery glow over the shimmering seas and the outline of the vessel as she dipped and crested each successive wave. Though the moon was on the wane, once Sphax's eyes had adjusted to the darkness there was enough light to move around the platform safely. The breeze had dropped to a murmur, causing the mainsail and supparum to flap occasionally, but it was of no consequence in these light seas. He guessed Tarbo had ordered the crew to tie off the sheets before they'd retired to their quarters below deck.

Beneath the hood of his cloak, all Sphax could make out of the captain was the silhouette of his jutting chin and beak of a nose. Other than a cursory glance in his direction, the man barely acknowledged his presence, but when he proffered the basket, Tarbo fished out a flatbread and began chewing, afterwards reaching for the water jug to slake his thirst.

'Since I commandeered your vessel and ordered you to sail to Cosa,' Sphax began, keen to get this over with, 'I've acted in a high-handed, arrogant manner, for which I'm profoundly sorry. You're quite right, we have behaved like pirates, showing you none of the courtesy and respect you deserve, or gratitude for what you're doing for us. All I can offer to make amends, is to swear a solemn oath that when we return to Pisae, I will pay you handsomely in silver for your inconvenience and any expense you've incurred.'

Throughout this monologue, Tarbo neither glanced in his direction nor issued one of his cursory grunts to acknowledge what was being said. Sphax judged he may as well have spoken to the swan's neck carving over the stern for all the good it had done. Nevertheless, he felt better.

Other than the faint murmur of conversation from the deck cabin below them, time passed in an uncomfortable silence. From time to time he offered the basket to Tarbo who selected whatever he fancied. So light was the sea that night the captain could safely eat and drink with both hands, leaving the steering oars to plough their own course southwards.

'What happened to that girl of yours?' asked Tarbo, softly.

The question was so unexpected it caught Sphax off guard. Gathering together thoughts that were still raw and painful he was slow to reply. 'Fionn was killed,' he said finally. 'Our army was attacked by Gauls in the high Alps … she fell …' His voice trailed into silence.

'Those whom the gods love ….' Tarbo quoted the old proverb. 'She was quite a beauty.'

Turning slowly around, Sphax searched the heavens for her star. Finding the square quartet of stars Illyrians call the Great Wagon, his eyes flickered to the east, and there she was: what the Greeks call Kynosoura, but what from ancient times his own people had named Phoenice, the star of the north. Somehow, since her death he'd come to associate her memory with Phoenice, the brightest star in the northern heavens. If she had not followed him to her death, Fionn would have followed that star to find her kin in the far north. Would that she had.

Often he searched it out. For some unfathomable reason it offered consolation and the blessing of memory. 'Her star shines brightly this evening,' he said gently, awakening from his reverie.

'Which star would that be?'

Sphax turned and smiled at Tarbo. 'Phoenice. But you may know her by another name.'

'Ah … Stella Polaris.'

'Yes, the northern star. If only Fionn had followed her star, and not me.' For a while the two of them gazed at the southern heavens, locked in the silence of their own thoughts.

At last Tarbo broke the silence. 'You seem to know something of stars?'

'Very little, Sir' — careful to answer truthfully this time. 'A brief lesson one evening whilst at sea in the Adria.'

'What star am I following on my present course?'

Sphax stepped behind the captain and squinted over his shoulder. Lining up the vessel's bowsprit gently rising and falling in the swell, he allowed his gaze to rise until it met what he'd guessed he would find: Orion's sword, glinting between two lesser stars.

'I have only a novice's knowledge of navigation, Captain, but I think you're aiming the bowsprit at Orion's sword, which would give you a bearing of due south. Above it I can see the three stars of Orion's belt. I was taught that these stars give navigators the bearings for east and west.'

'Then you were taught well,' grunted Tarbo, not unkindly. Stepping back from the tiller bar he spoke the last words Sphax had ever expected to hear from his lips. 'Take hold of the bar and get a feel for her.'

Shocked, he hesitated, staring incredulously at the captain. With both hands Tarbo gestured again towards the bar. Gingerly, Sphax reached forward and gripped the wooden bar. Instantly he felt it alive with tremors and subtle movement, almost imperceptible, yet tangible, like running a hand over skin and sensing the muscles and tendons beneath. He'd thought of it as a dead thing, a lump of wood that would only respond to brute force. How wrong he'd been.

'Think of it as a farmer ploughing a furrow,' explained Tarbo between swigs from the jug. 'His oxen are yoked together as a team. Pull on the reins to starboard or larboard and the oxen will respond in tandem … as one. In the same way the tiller bar is connected by cables to both steering oars to ensure they too work together in tandem.'

Placing the empty jug on the deck he suggested, 'Try it. Take her to larboard a little and steer south-east.'

Gripping hard he heaved the bar to his right. Suddenly the deck swayed and yawed alarmingly. It felt as though he was wrestling with the entire power of the Tyrrhenian sea.

'Fool of a boy,' stormed Tarbo. 'Don't rip her head off! Gently, boy! Gently!'

Easing it slowly back to its original position, Sphax felt the vessel steadying and righting itself. He tried again, this time by degree, sensing the tremors of resistance as the blades of the oars carved through the water.

'Straighten her up,' grunted the captain. With little resistance on the oar blades, Sphax found the bar moved easily back to its central position, and this time the deck hardly swayed. 'Now set her back on course. Due south. Keep half an eye on the bowsprit and this time treat her like a lady, not some popina whore.'

Sphax stared down at his hands and braced himself to ease the tiller bar to the left. 'Look up, you slackhead!' snapped Tarbo. 'Your hands don't know where south is.'

Sphax did as he was told, fixing his gaze on the tip of the bowsprit, but the flapping supparum didn't make this easy. Slowly he felt the vessel coming round to starboard. Tarbo was now standing directly behind him, breathing down his neck.

When he'd lined the tip of the bowsprit directly below the triple stars of Orion's sword he eased the bar back to its resting position and heaved a sigh of relief.

'That will do. Hold this course,' was all Tarbo said before he sat down at the back of the platform, propped his back against the neck of the swan carving, and began stuffing the last of the cheese in his mouth.

When some time later, Sphax turned to ask if he could tighten the flapping supparum, he saw that Tarbo's chin was lolling on his chest. The captain was sound asleep.

FOURTEEN

When Sphax's initial panic diminished to a mild terror, he realised he could always wake the captain in an emergency, even if it meant letting go of the tiller bar for a few moments. He'd seen Tarbo do this, and the worst that could happen was the vessel might drift off course a little. The old goat was obviously exhausted, what harm would it do to let him have a few hours' sleep? They were far out to sea. Even with Sphax's woefully inadequate knowledge of geography, he reasoned a southerly course would steer them miles away from any treacherous rocks and reefs off the coast, and the islands of Corsica and Sardinia were far to the west.

Sphax's only worries were that dawn seemed like a lifetime away, the flapping supparum was obscuring the bowsprit and beginning to annoy him, and in a couple of hours the moon would sink beneath the waves leaving him blind, navigating by starlight alone. Nevertheless, he made up his mind to let captain Tarbo sleep on.

'In the name of the gods, what's going on? Where's Tarbo?' Recognising the urgency in Drust's voice Sphax's head jerked upwards and he opened his eyes. He'd fallen asleep with his forehead resting on the tiller bar. Again! It was almost pitch black, the moon had set and the only light left in the world was starlight.

With his dark plaid cloak wrapped around his head and shoulders he could barely see Drust standing at the foot of the steps leading to the steering platform. 'I'm navigating at the tiller bar, Drust. Tarbo fell asleep. I'm following the course he set me.'

Except he wasn't! Desperately Sphax searched the southern heavens for Orion's stars. This time he'd allowed the vessel to drift badly off course. With dawning horror Sphax realised they were heading east, back to the coast of Italia with all its reefs and headlands. How long had he slept?

Below him he could hear Drust in fits of laughter. 'A fine jest, Captain Sphax. And what course would that be? Up the Tiber to Rome? Or the reef off Hades?'

He didn't have time for this. Easing the bar gently to his right, he sensed her slowly come about to starboard. In the darkness he couldn't even make out the mainsail, let alone the supparum on the bowsprit. All he could do was imagine a line pointing down the centre of the ship and trust his instincts. When he judged he was directly beneath Orion's sword he allowed her to swing further starboard, setting her on a south-westerly bearing. As far as he was concerned, the more sea he put between himself and that coastline the better.

Drust was still chuckling. 'Has Tarbo lost his tongue, or have you thrown him overboard?'

'Listen to me carefully, Drust,' struggling to keep the desperation out of his voice. 'You need to get up here. But be careful! Feel your way up the steps and onto the platform. Be sure to duck under the bar. Find a place to sit beside me.'

Moments later Sphax felt a hand grasp his ankle. Reaching down he grabbed the hand and yanked Drust to his feet so they were standing shoulder to shoulder.

'By the gods, it's dark,' Drust exclaimed. 'Where's Tarbo?'

'I told you, he's fast asleep—'

'Tell me that's a jest, Sphax. You can't be serious.'

'Never more so, my friend. I've been navigating this vessel for the last … what time is it?'

'Epona preserve us!'

'And every other goddess! But how long before dawn?'

'I don't know, Sphax. I woke up, saw you still hadn't returned, and came in search of you. At a guess I would say we've just begun the fourth watch, which means dawn is still hours away. Where's Tarbo?' he repeated, looking around — a rather pointless exercise in the inky darkness.

'Last time I looked he was flat out, sprawled against the swan's neck.'

'Well it's high time we wake him so he can resume his duties.'

'Why?' Sphax argued, not without a touch of irritation. 'The old goat will simply tell me to stay on our present course.' As their present course was south-west, this wasn't strictly true, but the last thing he wanted was an awakened Tarbo pointing this out, at least not before he'd corrected his own mistakes. He did have some pride!

'But you don't know how to sail this vessel!' Drust shouted, exasperated.

'Yes I do!' trying to keep his voice down so as not to wake the captain. 'Tarbo gave me a lesson in navigation before he lay down. All we have to do is keep her on a steady course. Before they turned in, the crew set the sails to take advantage of this northerly. It hasn't changed direction.'

Sphax judged he'd soon correct his course errors and could then head south again. It was time to give Drust a lesson in navigation. 'Take my place,' he said. 'I'll show you how easy it is.'

'No, Sphax. Wake Tarbo!'

'Just try it …' pleaded Sphax, releasing his hands from the bar and taking a step backwards, leaving Drust with little choice but to take his place.

'I don't know what I'm doing,' groaned Drust. 'I beg you, Sphax … wake Tarbo.'

'I don't want you to *do* anything at the moment. Just hold the bar and listen to me,' Sphax begged. 'You can do this, Drust. I know you can.'

Drust groaned again. 'The bar is juddering.'

'No, that's just you shaking.' Pointing at Orion's sword he said, 'Do you see the bright star I'm pointing at?'

'The one with the fainter stars above and below it?'

'Exactly,' beamed Sphax. 'Those stars make up Orion's sword, and the brightest of them points due south—'

'Where did you learn all this stuff, Sphax?'

'From Corinna,' he said simply. 'Now concentrate. You're standing dead centre in the stern. In your mind's eye, I want you to trace a line running down the middle of the ship to the tip of the bowsprit. Got it?' Drust eventually nodded. 'What you're going to do is swing the vessel to larboard until that imaginary bowsprit is pointing directly beneath that bright star. Do this by easing the bar gently to the right … don't be heavy handed … just a light movement. Are you ready?'

'As I'll ever be,' sighed Drust.

'Now,' he whispered, holding his breath. With relief he felt the timbers gently sway to larboard as she came around. 'When you're directly below the star, ease the bar back to its starting position. You'll know when you've reached this by sensing the sideways pressure on the bar, there should be no movement to right or left, as if it's in a resting position.'

It had only taken a few moments. But Drust had set her on a southerly course far more smoothly than Sphax had on his first attempt. 'Perfect, Captain Drust, but try and avoid that enormous rock, dead ahead—'

'Where?' yelled Drust, horrified.

'In your imagination! I've been seeing them all night until I realised there aren't any rocks in the middle of the Tyrrhenian sea, just islands, and we're miles away from any of them. Just hold this course and wake me if there's an emergency.' And with that Sphax curled up on the deck as best he could and closed his eyes.

Sphax felt a boot repeatedly prodding him in the ribs. With an effort of will he struggled to a sitting position and began rubbing the sleep from his eyes. His body felt as stiff as the deck he'd been sleeping on.

'The crew are beginning to stir,' warned Drust, 'so I thought I'd better wake you.'

Wearily, Sphax got to his feet and stretched his arms wide, yawning all the while. 'When this is over, I'm going to find the softest bed in Pisae and sleep for a week.'

Squinting up at the sky he saw that the stars had dimmed, as if the pre-dawn greyness had put out their fire. Orion's sword was still visible, but was no longer the shining beacon it had once been. 'Did you find working the tiller bar as dull an occupation as I did?'

'Not at all,' Drust disagreed. 'After a while I found it strangely compelling to be able to sense every breath of wind and change of tide and current. The tiller bar is a remarkably sensitive organ.'

Sphax laughed. 'You're a poet, not a warrior, Drust. Your eloquence never fails to delight me. But even poets need to fill their bellies. I'm going to raid Dubal's food hoard. I'll be back with breakfast shortly, then we can wake our captain from the arms of Morpheus. The old goat's had more sleep than either of us!'

When Sphax returned with a hurriedly collected sack of leftover food and jugs of water, Drust was surrounded by three older boys from the crew, demanding they be allowed to wake captain Tarbo.

Drust was frowning, exasperated, 'Help me out, Sphax! This is beyond my Latin.'

One of the boys, who the others called Naso, was cursing Drust for taking over the duties of their captain, whilst the other two chipped in with choice insults about their lack of skill and seamanship. Sphax had to agree with their overall assessment!

Even in the short interval it had taken to gather breakfast, the light had improved. Sphax glanced at the stern. Tarbo was still stretched out beneath the swan's neck, sleeping like a baby.

'By all means waken your captain, Naso,' Sphax grinned at the lad. 'Right now we are in desperate need of his skills and have no intention of usurping his command. He simply needed his sleep.'

Handing the sack and jug to Drust, he watched as the boys crowded around their captain. 'I'll take over whilst you breakfast.' Drust didn't need a second invitation and gratefully sank to the deck, swigging from the jug.

'Murderers!' the boys suddenly chorused. Naso glared at Sphax and spat the words, 'He's dead! You've killed him!'

For a heartbeat Sphax and Drust just stared at one another, dumbstruck, before rushing to the stern and pushing the boys aside. Sphax rolled Tarbo on to his back. His body felt stiff, and there could be no doubting the lifeless, staring eyes that would see nothing more of this world. Just to be certain, Sphax slid his hand under the captain's tunic and rested his hand on Tarbo's chest, the seat of breath and pumping blood, of life itself. But the skin felt cold to the touch and any breath had long since departed this body.

Sphax stared at Drust and slowly shook his head before withdrawing his hand. 'His heart must have failed,' he said to the boys kneeling beside him. Naso was still suspicious, glowering.

'As you boys were retiring to your quarters I brought him food and water. After he'd eaten he gave me a lesson in navigation then lay down to rest at the stern. He was tired and worn out, so it came as no surprise that when I next looked he seemed fast asleep.'

Locking his eyes on Naso, Sphax added, 'I swear to you by all the gods that I was not the cause of your captain's death. Only the Moirai decide our fate, and last night Atropos cut his thread, not me.'

By now tears were streaming down the cheeks of two of the boys. In view of Tarbo's irascible temperament, Sphax was again struck by the evident affection the young crew had for their captain.

But he was still staring into the dry eyes of the eldest of them. 'Look closely, Naso, and you will see that Captain Tarbo hasn't a mark or scratch on him. Drust and I had nothing to do with his death, and only a fool would suspect us of such a crime. Don't you see? Now we are all in grave danger! Captain Tarbo was the only man aboard who could safely sail this vessel into the harbour at Cosa. What are we to do now?'

Naso nodded, the awful truth finally dawning on the lad. 'I must tell the rest of the crew, Sir.'

'Yes you must,' agreed Sphax, resting a comforting hand on the lad's shoulder. 'We should all meet up on the deck and decide together what is to be done.'

In the time it had taken to decide that captain Tarbo had left this world for the darkness of Hades, the sun had risen, suffusing the world of the living in the golden light of dawn and a new day. With not a coastline or headland in sight, as Sphax and Drust looked about them they both realised they were truly lost at sea.

Idwal had the good sense to treat the body of the captain with dignified reverence, which further won over the young crew. Supervising the Numidians, Idwal made sure the body was borne respectfully in a funeral-like procession to a bench that had been secured to the deck cabin and there the boys carefully wrapped their captain in a shroud of sailcloth.

After these solemn proceedings Drust agreed to man the tiller bar whilst Sphax and Idwal gathered the six slave boys around them to discuss how best to reach the safety of the harbour at Cosa. It turned out that Naso was a natural leader who had the trust of the other boys, but a young lad called Sabinus, who'd served with the Tarbo the longest, claimed to know the coastline from Pisae to Tarantum like the back of his hand. Sphax and Idwal were sceptical, but Naso and the other lads were adamant: Sabinus knew more about the tides and harbours than any of them.

So it was decided. Naso would be put in charge of the sails, whilst Sphax and Drust manned

the tiller bar under the guidance of Sabinus. The sharp-eyed Agbal would act as lookout on the prow, leaving Idwal, Jugurtha and Hannon to help with hauling sheets and ropes.

Sphax was still haunted by memories of that terrible shipwreck months ago off the Illyrian coast, when two boys not much older than Tarbo's crew had drowned. When he told Sabinus they'd kept the vessel far out to sea last night the lad's jaw had dropped. 'But there's scores of small islands out to sea.' It came as a chilling discovery that the Tyrrhenian was not as empty as he'd supposed, and from the list of islands the lad reeled off, it was nothing short of a miracle they hadn't been wrecked on one of them.

For the next few hours the vessel laboriously wallowed in heavy seas, pitching this way and that at the mercy of the waves. The wind was still at their backs, but no more than a whisper; then, without any warning it suddenly freshened to a blustery north-easterly.

Sabinus clapped his hands in joy. 'The gods favour us this morning.' With the wind now filling the mainsail and the supparum, to Sphax's surprise it became easier to hold their south-easterly course.

He was about to hand the tiller bar over to Drust when Agbal bounded up the steps to the steering platform. 'I think I can see land on the horizon, captain, I mean … Sir. Dead ahead. It's faint, but it must be the coast.'

Sphax smiled to himself, amused that his dual role was causing problems. Translating Agbal's Tassynt for Sabinus, the boy frowned, shaking his head. 'I hope it's not the mainland. Can you ask him to return when he's got a clearer sighting?'

Half an hour later Agbal was back. 'It's a narrow peninsula with a wooded ridge running the length of it. To the south-east there's a small island.'

This time when Sphax translated the boy grinned from ear to ear. 'It's not the mainland, Sir, but the island of Aegilium. I can see it for myself now. It does indeed have a thickly wooded ridge and its southern shores have excellent havens. Captain Tarbo often put in here to load cargoes of wine. The island to the south-east is called Dianium after our goddess of the moon. All we have to do, Sir, is set an easterly course between these two islands. Cosa lies beyond, and will shortly come into view.'

Watching anxiously, Drust hadn't understood a word of these exchanges, but when Sphax translated Sabinus' welcome news into their common Greek it was as if a great burden had been lifted from his shoulders. 'You mean that once clear of these islands we will be in sight of Cosa?'

'If Sabinus is to be believed,' shrugged Sphax, cautiously. 'He seems to know what he's talking about.'

'Even I can steer this lumbering monster between those islands, so it seems the gods have spared us a watery grave once more, my friend.'

'Numidians have a saying,' Sphax frowned, 'don't count on water until you've lowered a bucket down the well.'

'You desert folk are such pessimists,' laughed Drust.

'Just cautious. Besides, even if we reach Cosa safely, the Carthaginian squadron might not be there. Cosa was Malchus' best guess, but nothing is certain. All this might yet be in vain.'

'I'll just be grateful to stretch these legs of mine on dry land!'

'Beneath the walls of a Roman colony?' Sphax teased. 'Is that wise?'

'Then we'll just have to storm it! We captured Pisae, didn't we?'

Smiling at Drust's eternal optimism, Sphax remained silent. In the hazy sunshine he could now clearly see the southern tip of the island of Aegilium. Drust had been right about one thing: a blind man could have steered the vessel between the two islands. Dianium, by far the smaller of the two, was at least ten miles to the south. Noticing its crescent shape, he could see why it had been named after the goddess.

As the vessel swept into the waters between the two islands the seas became rougher and the wind picked up, causing the deck to sway and yaw alarmingly.

When the larboard deck reared up once more, Sphax felt Sabinus tugging anxiously on his tunic. 'Can you ask him to steer a point or two to the south-east? He's sailing much too close to the wind for my liking.'

Sphax passed this on to Drust and immediately the vessel stopped swaying so violently. But his curiosity had been aroused. 'What does sailing too close to the wind mean, Sabinus?' He'd heard the phrase so many times before, but never understood the complicated explanations given. Perhaps a fourteen year old's explanation would be at a level he could understand. He was wrong. After listening to a long, exhaustive discourse on the subject, Sphax was still none the wiser. He would have to be content with it remaining a mystery.

One thing he did understand was the alarming consequences of getting it wrong. 'Do you mean to tell me this vessel could roll over on her side?'

'Yes. If a sudden northerly gust hit us amidships, or if we tried to head north-east. That's what happens when you sail too close to the wind.'

'Have you seen this happen?'

'With my own eyes, Sir. The Venti punish those who do not show them respect.'

'The Venti?' asked a bemused Sphax.

'The winged gods of the four winds, Sir … you *must* know of the Venti?'

Realising the depths of his ignorance had sunk to a new low this morning he asked, 'Forgive me, Sabinus, tell me something of the Venti and their punishments?'

'Captain Tarbo taught us to respect and make offerings to the Venti every morning at dawn. This we do when we come up on deck to begin our work. Today Aquilo, the north wind, and Favonius, the west wind, are working in our favour and we thank them for it.'

His lesson was rudely interrupted by the return of a breathless Agbal. 'There's a new island, dead ahead, Sir. And I don't like the look of its rocky cliffs.'

Sphax quickly translated for Sabinus, who simply smiled. 'That's not an island, Sir, but the mainland. Cosa lies beyond the bay to the south. We should arrive by midday.'

This was the best news he'd heard all morning. Gazing to larboard he could see the island of Aegilium receding into the distance and Dianium was now just a blur on the horizon. Even with his poor eyesight he could see they were entering a broad bay divided by a jutting headland to the east and a lesser one to the south-west.

'We will need to change course soon,' piped Sabinus, pointing to the south-west. 'Do you see that headland, Sir? The harbour of Cosa lies beneath its cliffs.'

Sphax nodded, curious to find out more about the curly-haired lad standing beside him whose only expression seemed to be that of determined concentration. The boy's intelligence and erudition had already impressed him. 'Did Captain Tarbo teach you navigation and to use the tiller bar, Sabinus?'

'Only on short voyages, Sir,' the lad replied without taking his eyes off the headland. 'He said I didn't have the strength yet …' his voice trailed off, eyes filling with tears, realising his captain would never say anything to him ever again.

Placing a comforting hand on the lad's shoulder, Sphax observed, 'I can see you were fond of the … captain.' He almost said old goat, but managed to restrain himself. 'All of you will feel his loss.'

Sabinus almost smiled. 'He cheated everyone he traded with, Sir, merchants and travellers alike. But … I think because he was a freedman himself, he always treated us kindly, as if we were his children.'

Even in death, Tarbo was full of surprises. A thought occurred to Sphax. 'I'll tell you something your captain hadn't noticed, Sabinus. I believe you now have the strength required for the tiller bar. I think you should take over as captain.'

The lad stared at him, searching his face to see if he was being serious. 'Do you mean it, Sir?'

'Absolutely,' assured Sphax, and turning to Drust, added, 'Let the lad take over.'

'You sure?' he queried, an eyebrow raised.

'Certain! Unlike you and me, he really knows what he's doing. I suspect he's forgotten more about sailing than you and I knew in the first place!' Drust let go of the bar and stepped back a pace. 'Take your rightful place, Captain Sabinus,' Sphax gestured towards a young man grinning from ear to ear.

His first act was to shout to Naso on the deck below that he was changing course to the south-east and the mainsail was to be squared. When some of the young crew saw that their friend had taken over the helm they began cheering. Sphax grinned at Drust, sure now he'd made the right decision.

With the full force of the wind now fully behind them, Sphax felt the vessel surge forward towards that southerly headland and the promise of safe haven. His mind was already turning to the prospect of hot food and a good night's sleep when Agbal raced up the steps to the steering platform. 'There are three warships to the south-east, Captain, rowing fast towards us.'

He felt a sudden thrill of excitement. Agbal must have sighted part of the Carthaginian fleet. Malchus had thought they would use Cosa as their base to attack Rome's seaboard trade, but he couldn't be certain. Sphax fingered his ivory pendant of the goddess, grateful for the fact that the Carthaginians had found them, rather than the other way round. With time loaded against them, they might have wasted precious days scouring the coastline or waiting for the fleet to return to harbour.

Curious about the commotion on the steering platform, Idwal had joined them to find out what was going on. After Sphax passed on the good news, all eyes squinted to the south-west, straining to catch the first glimpse of their allies.

'I think we should change course and try to intercept them,' suggested Sphax, 'they may not be heading for Cosa, and I don't want to risk losing them again.'

'I agree,' echoed Idwal. 'We need to clear up the mystery of why they're here and who sent them. Once they see the disc and crescent emblazoned on our supparum, I'm sure they'll be as curious about us as we are about them. When was the last time a Carthaginian merchantman was sighted in these waters?'

'They were *never* welcomed in these waters, Idwal,' and turning to Sabinus he carefully explained the new situation. At first the lad was shocked that they were about to make contact with Rome's sworn enemy; nevertheless, he nodded, shouting to Naso to prepare the mainsail for a southerly heading.

As the ageing timbers of the corbita strained and creaked southwards, all eyes on board were now fixed on the Carthaginian squadron rowing fast towards them.

'I'm sure the two boys working the supparum will recognise those warships, Sphax,' reasoned Idwal. 'They had a week to study them when they were anchored in the lagoon off Pisae. Surely they would recognise figureheads … something that would identify them? If only their sails were raised! Any designs or emblems might tell us whether they're from Carthage or Iberia.'

'You're right,' agreed Sphax. 'Join them on the prow and take Agbal and Drust with you.'

After the three of them hurried off, Sabinus turned to him. 'They've changed course slightly to be sure of intercepting us.'

'Or take a closer look at us.' Sphax sensed the lad was still uneasy about this forthcoming encounter. 'Don't worry, Sabinus, these are our allies, remember.' Even he could see them clearly now: three sleek vessels in line abreast, oars lifting and falling with an easy rhythm, not a mile away and closing fast.

'Do you want us to shorten sail, Sir?' asked Sabinus. 'Otherwise we'll sail straight past them.'

'Yes, but not the supparum, that's displaying our Carthaginian standard.'

'Strange,' mused the lad. 'They're rowing like useless landlubbers!'

'Impossible!' cried Sphax. But now he could see this for himself. No more than four hundred paces away, he recognised them as triremes: one hundred and eighty oarsmen in two banks, straining to deliver their lethal bronze ram to its target, and that spiked ram could split a vessel as effortlessly as a knife slices through cheese.

Something was wrong. Doubts were beginning to fester, further alarmed by the sight of Idwal racing down the deck. Reaching the foot of the steps he yelled, 'They're Roman, Sphax, not Carthaginian! We need to get out of here. Fast!'

But it was already too late for that. Without oars, they were prisoners of the wind.

FIFTEEN

By now the tribune commanding the Roman squadron had almost certainly recognised the Carthaginian standard emblazoned on their supparum as that of the enemy. Merchantman or not, they were now fair game, and judging from the enemy's course changes, it was obvious they were closing in for the kill.

At the prow a scramble was going on to take down the supparum. Sphax knew it was far too late for that. 'Leave it!' he yelled. 'Leave it alone!' They would fight in their true colours or flee, and he would see them in Hades before he sanctioned the latter.

The look of sheer horror on Sabinus' face told him the boy had already guessed what terrors lay in their path. Placing a steadying arm around the lad's trembling shoulders, Sphax willed himself to speak calmly.

'Courage, Sabinus! Hold your nerve. All those ham-handed arsewits have are their oars. We have the wind! The advantage is with us, not them.'

Months ago he'd faced a similar desperate situation in the narrow confines of the harbour at Brundisium. Hopeless as it had first appeared, the Illyrian crew had managed to fight their way out. At the very least he knew what they must do.

'Listen to me carefully, Captain—'

'But I'm not a proper—'

'You are *our* Captain, Sabinus, and your crew have every faith in you. Trust me. Believe in yourself. All you have to do is steer directly for that trireme in the middle. Don't let its bowsprit out of your sight.' Sphax risked a glance forward. Three hundred paces he guessed, and closing.

'Do you see the trireme to the left of it, on our larboard?' The lad nodded. 'Though the vessels are abreast, can you see there's still clear water between them?' Although ashen grey and rigid with fear, the boy still managed to nod.

'That's the clear water I want you to steer into. But *only* when you're almost on top of that trireme. You must hold your nerve until the last possible moment. Leave it until you think you're about to collide before you wrench the tiller bar and steer into that clear water between them. Turning south-east will give us all the wind.' Again, Sphax frantically checked the distance between themselves and their foe. Two hundred paces. This was not the time for speeches. He had to make this quick.

'Don't avoid their oars. Smash them! This sturdy old corbita will make kindling of them.' Sphax forced a grin. 'Have you got all that?' Despite his fear, that look of fierce concentration had returned to the lad's face. 'Do this for Captain Tarbo, Sabinus.'

Turning to the boys on deck he saw they too were frozen with fear, staring up at him. 'Sabinus will abruptly change course to the south-east. You must prepare and be ready for this. We'll need all the power of this north-westerly. Our mainsail must not spill a breath of wind! Have you got that?' Only Naso nodded. 'If we all do our duty we'll get through this.' If only he could be certain … duty might not be enough.

At sixty paces, Sphax could now clearly see the massive curved prow of the trireme bearing down on them. If Sabinus lost his nerve and swung her to the south-east too soon, it would give the Roman helmsman time to respond and alter course to intercept. Even a glancing blow from that ram would slice them open as easily as a knife guts fish. Sabinus had to leave it until the last gasp, that last desperate moment. All their lives were now in the hands of a fourteen year old boy, standing rigid with fear at the helm.

Idwal was standing beside him. 'If we survive this, I have some good news for us all.' So incongruous was this statement that despite Sphax's pounding heart he found himself laughing, but it was laughter born of hysteria.

Then all he heard was the sickening sound of splintering wood as the vessel swayed and juddered under the full force of the wind. His first thought was that the spike of a Roman ram was eviscerating their timbers, but as images of helmeted legionaries flashed past, he realised he was hearing the sound of oars, snapping like twigs. It was over in a heartbeat.

'You've done it!' cried Sphax, grasping the boy's shoulders. 'Captain Tarbo could not have done it better.'

Unfortunately, Sabinus promptly burst into tears. But Sphax could see they were tears of relief, if not joy. 'What now, Sir?' the lad blurted out between sobs.

'Head east, make for Cosa. Let's put as much sea between ourselves and those triremes as our sails will allow,' he ordered, before Idwal placed a hand on his shoulder, urging him to look astern.

One glance was enough to reveal Idwal's good news. Stretched out to the north-west, in a vast arrowhead formation, was the entire Carthaginian fleet: eight triremes gathered around a massive quinquereme at the point of the arrow. This time there could be no mistaking the emblems emblazoned on their sails, and what's more, they were rapidly bearing down on two stricken triremes.

Sabinus' timely swerve into the clear water between the two triremes had done far more damage than Sphax could ever have hoped for, and Rome's ill-trained crew had done the rest.

They should have raised oars when it became obvious the corbita would veer between them. But their captains had issued no such order. As a result, Sabinus had simply smashed into them, exactly as Sphax had intended! Their sturdy little corbita had sheared off a good many of the trireme's starboard oars, leaving her almost dead in the water, whilst the other vessel had suffered the same fate to her larboard oars near the stern. It was one of the oldest tricks in battles at sea, yet it had worked like a charm.

Sphax and Idwal stared in disbelief at the water around the two vessels, strewn with the splintered wreckage of what remained of their oars. Both were floundering, trying to raise sails and come about at the same time; a near impossible manoeuvre in the teeth of a stiff breeze and with ill-trained oarsmen. He could only imagine the panic and terror aboard as they watched the Carthaginian fleet inexorably bearing down on them.

The third trireme, as yet undamaged, had wisely decided to cut and run. With three Carthaginian triremes in hot pursuit, Sphax judged this was a race the Roman vessel wouldn't win.

'Belay that order, Sabinus,' Sphax countermanded. 'The enemy's finished! We'll wait for Carthage to catch up with us. Shorten sail and take down the supparum. Display it amidships where it will be clearly seen. I'm sure we've already demonstrated we're on the same side, but I'm not taking any chances.'

As the drama to the north unfolded, Drust and the Numidians joined them on the steering platform, anxious to witness the final act. For Sphax it was not so much a drama as a foregone conclusion. He knew how this was going to end, and like all tragedies, he hoped it would be mercifully swift.

Idwal had already guessed — rightly in Sphax's opinion — that the Carthaginians were light on marines capable of storming towns or boarding enemy ships with grappling irons and ladders. If the oarsmen on the Roman triremes were inexperienced and untrained, this was not the case with the legionaries now preparing to defend their vessels to the death. But the captain of the quinquereme drawing abreast of the northerly Roman trireme had no intention of risking the lives of his marines by boarding the vessel.

Now in full flight, sails straining to catch every breath of wind, the massive bulk of the quinquereme suddenly swung due south, oars raised with faultless precision before catching the trireme a glancing blow that pierced her amidships, whipping her round like a child's top and eviscerating her timbered bowels. Sphax winced.

In a heartbeat she'd been cleaved in two, reduced to little more than a seething mass of flotsam before disappearing beneath the waves, her crew thrashing around in the water or clinging desperately to spars. The other Roman trireme fared no better.

Like a wake of vultures poised to pick a carcass clean, three triremes circled her, ready to close in for the kill. The first to strike smashed into her larboard bow, but the fatal blow was delivered by a ram to her starboard steering platform, gouging a great rent in her stern. Amidst the crash of falling masts and yards, a bubbling Tyrrhenian sea finally claimed her.

For a few moments, all those gathered on the steering platform simply gaped in stunned silence. None amongst them had ever witnessed death and destruction on such a scale and with such rapidity. On land, battles were decided after endless manoeuvre, charge and counter charge. Death was ground out, man-for-man, often in single combat. At sea, it appeared, hundreds could perish in a thunderbolt, a blink of an eye, with a single blow from a bronze ram. The brutal finality of what they'd witnessed shocked them to the core.

Sphax was the first to break the spell, muttering, 'If only Carthage ruled the seas.'

'It appears she does,' Idwal intoned, 'at least the Tyrrhenian sea.'

'For now,' Sphax reluctantly agreed. 'Sabinus noticed they were rowing like landlubbers. He was right. My guess is this lot were pressed into service yesterday, after they'd removed these ancient hulks from storage sheds. Pressing untrained crews into service is like Maharbal handing a javelin and horse to Libyan footsloggers and ordering them to charge! What is Rome thinking of?'

'I agree. But it tells us a great deal about the alarm and consternation the arrival of this Carthaginian fleet has caused in Rome. They must have sailed in haste from Ostia yesterday.'

Sphax turned his attention to the mainsail and the display of the supparum. Their young crew had worked well. Already the yard had been lowered and the boys were furling and tying off the sail whilst two of them strung a rope from the deck cabin to the bowsprit to display the Carthaginian banner.

Without steerage or forward momentum, the vessel was bobbing and swaying like a cork stopper at the mercy of the waves. Judging from their anxious faces, it was not the rolling deck that was discomforting the crew, but the sight of six Carthaginian warships rapidly bearing down on them.

Only days ago they'd been told this fleet was about to storm their city and slaughter everyone within its walls. Yet here they were, deliberately casting themselves adrift like helpless victims, placing their faith in a hastily scrawled banner with symbols they didn't even recognise. Sphax sympathised.

All six vessels were now lowering sails to slow their momentum. He decided it was high time to make their presence felt. 'Follow me, Numidians, it's time we stood beside our standard.'

After retrieving his sword from the deck cabin he took up position beside Agbal, and raising the blade aloft, began waving it in a gesture he prayed would be interpreted as a greeting, not defiance.

By now it was certain the giant quinquereme was rowing to come alongside them amidships, five triremes having veered off to larboard in line ahead. He could see crewmen gathered on the deck of the quinquereme straining to take a closer look at them.

At first he couldn't believe his ears. But as the towering bulk of the quinquereme raised its larboard oars and drifted slowly towards them, Sphax was certain. The crews were cheering.

A suspicious Naso began tugging at his sleeve. 'Why are they cheering us, Sir?

'Because,' Sphax grinned at the lad, 'you and your crew had the courage to do battle with three Roman triremes, and through excellent seamanship, managed to damage two of them. They are applauding your skill and bravery.'

Naso looked even more bewildered. 'We were only trying to escape—'

'Our Carthaginian friends didn't see it that way, Naso.'

'But ... we are not at war with Rome, Sir.'

'You are now!'

At that moment the graceful curved prow of the Carthaginian vessel towered above them like a great bird of prey, gliding amidships with oars raised as the crew tossed grappling irons like talons, to bind and hold them fast. For a while their vessel swayed and juddered before finally coming under the spell of the giant made fast beside it. Sphax felt like a shrew in a cat's paw.

Above him the deck of the quinquereme was at least twice his height. Gathered on the gunnels, its crew had ceased cheering and were now pointing and staring at them in disbelief. A rope ladder was tossed down and fell at his feet. It was time to introduce himself.

Sheathing his sword, Sphax turned to his men. 'Numidians … you're with me,' and turning to Idwal, added, 'Give us a moment to see how the land lies, then come aboard.'

Idwal laughed. 'They're hardly likely to harm the nephew of Hannibal!'

Sphax placed his boot in a rope rung. 'When I stood before Hannibal and first told him I was his nephew, he threatened to have me crucified. Hasdrubal has yet to discover he has a long-lost nephew. If they have sailed from Iberia, all they will see is four Numidians standing before them. Let's play this safe, Idwal.' With that he began climbing.

The gathering that greeted him on the broad deck of the quinquereme was nothing short of extraordinary. Flanked by his men, Sphax boldly proclaimed, 'I am Sphax, son of Prince Navaras of Numidia. I come from Hannibal and his general of horse, Maharbal, with news of our glorious victories in this war with Rome, and to enquire of your orders and intentions.'

Before him stood a glittering host of soldiers, gathered around a man of middle years, dressed in a simple white tunic bordered in crimson. Beneath his silvered muscled cuirass, pteruges skirts of white leather fell in layers from his waist to his knee-length silver greaves. But the most curious article he was wearing was his cap. In contrast to the rest of his military attire, Sphax recognised it as a lebbade; a conical phrygian cap that curled to a point above his forehead. Made of pure silk and dyed in rich reds and golds, it was the mark of high office in Carthage and could only be worn by a tophet of the council of three hundred. The last time he'd seen such a cap was gracing the head of his dear father.

What little of the man's jaw not hidden by a voluminous forked beard appeared to fall. A buzz of whispered conversation broke out amongst his companions which he silenced with a wave of his hand. 'I was not aware,' he began coldly, expression severe, 'that their son had survived the massacre. Illyrian pirates I believe … the ship was burned … the family butchered—'

'Then I must correct you on several counts, Sir.' Sphax didn't have time for this! 'Illyrians were not responsible for the death of my parents. Roman legionaries boarded our vessel off Corcyra, and by order of tribune Flaminius Nepos, murdered my parents and fired the ship. I was spared for slavery.

'It may interest you to learn that this Flaminius is now a consul of Rome; his legions await us at Arretium, not sixty miles south of our camp. My uncles and I have an appointment with destiny, and I'm impatient to rejoin them.' He cast his eyes over the silvered cuirasses, plumed helmets dripping with gold and silver, all polished like mirrors, and all undented and unused. 'My men and I have not stormed the city of Pisae and risked these dangerous waters to establish my lineage and birthright.'

These last remarks stirred another hornets' nest of conversation which the tophet had difficulty silencing. One glance at the man's thunderous expression told Sphax he was unused to being interrupted, let alone corrected, and being addressed in such a frank and forthright manner he liked even less.

'I am Adherbal, governor of Gades and commander of Carthage's fleets in Iberian waters. I come at the request of Hasdrubal Barca, who instructed me to sail to Pisae, make contact with his brother's army, and offer what assistance we could.'

Sphax sighed, audibly. 'You mean to tell me that you sat in the lagoon off Pisae for a week without sending out parties to search for our camp? A camp that was barely ten miles from where you were anchored!'

Outrage finally got the better of the red-faced governor of Gades. 'It is not our business,' Adherbal erupted, 'to send out scouts like common soldiers!'

No. Sphax smiled to himself. They might scratch all that shiny gold and silver! In the face of this pompous ass, he was struggling to remember the mission and purpose Maharbal had entrusted him with. He had to get a grip of his contempt, otherwise the terrible wounds some of his men had suffered storming that gate in Pisae would be for nothing.

Idwal and Drust appeared, allowing him a breathing space and time to regain his composure. With a flourish of his right hand, Idwal bowed low, exhausting his limited Punic in addressing the tophet. To Sphax's irritation, Agbal also chose that moment to bend a knee and bow, receiving a sharp kick from Sphax for his pains and whispered instruction to get up. What was it about the high-born of Carthage, Sphax wondered for the hundredth time? Numidians and Libyans had ruled their lands for centuries before Queen Dido cheated them with an oxhide!

'May I present Idwal, Sir,' he proclaimed, evenly at last, 'chieftain of the Cavari Gauls, and his lieutenant, Drust.' Lowering his voice, Sphax switched quickly to Greek, 'And this is Adherbal, Idwal, Governor of Gades and chief arsewit of Carthage.'

Idwal nodded, hiding a smile. 'I don't suppose he's got any reinforcements or siege equipment for us?'

'Lord Adherbal,' Sphax enquired, returning his gaze to the tophet, 'my master, Hannibal, is keen to hear if you have brought reinforcements with you from his brother in Iberia. All but one of our elephants perished in the terrible winter following our victory on the Trebia last year, and we're in great want of siege equipment. Without catapults and towers, even the smallest walled town in Italia presents us with insurmountable problems.'

'Alas,' replied the tophet, 'no such reinforcements were supplied to me by Hasdrubal when we sailed from New Carthage. My orders were clear: sail for Pisae and offer assistance. Besides, we are so hard pressed by the legions of the brothers Scipio, nothing can be spared for the adventure your master has undertaken.'

Adventure! Sphax seethed. He translated for Idwal's benefit. 'Then the best he can offer,' Idwal responded, 'is to sit tight and prevent all Roman trade from passing through these waters. At least he can prevent reinforcements reaching the Scipio brothers.'

'Hard pressed my arsehole,' scoffed Sphax, bitterly, 'all the slackhead faces is two legions, not the four we face, not to mention Rome's hordes of alae.'

'You must control your anger, my friend — this isn't helping!' grimaced Idwal.

With a great effort of will, Sphax conjured an obsequious smile. 'Then you can offer us no more than you are already doing, Lord Adherbal, Governor of Gades. Your fleet's presence in the Tyrrhenian sea has already created consternation in Rome and prevents reinforcements reaching Scipio north of the Ebro river. What other assistance had Hasdrubal in mind, Sir?'

'Hasdrubal ordered me … but it's a small matter … a trifle I hardly need mention,' the tophet began, then faltered.

'A small matter of what, Sir?' asked Sphax.

'Of … silver,' Adherbal stuttered between gritted teeth. 'If Hannibal was in dire need … and *only* if he was in dire need of silver to pay his mercenaries, Hasdrubal ordered me to supply you with … a chest of silver.'

So that was it! Silver, the sinew of war. Hasdrubal was indeed sending reinforcements — for Hannibal's war chest. A *small* matter indeed! The man was not only a pompous arsewit, he was a thief! Was this the real reason he'd made such little effort to contact Hannibal?

He translated for Idwal. 'Silver! That's the last thing we need,' the Cavari groaned. 'The Boii looted talents of the stuff last week.'

But Sphax was determined the bastard was not going to get away with this. 'I know of one enterprise deserving of silver,' he said with a wicked smile. Turning to the tophet, Sphax retained the smile. 'This is most generous of you, Lord Adherbal. Only last week our allies the Boii were threatening to desert our cause unless they were paid in silver. Our war chest has emptied at an alarming rate since the campaign began. Hannibal will be truly grateful for your munificence and sing the praises of the Lord Adherbal as saviour of our army!' He was relieved Idwal hadn't understood a word of this.

'Fetch a chest from my quarters,' the tophet muttered to a couple of his lieutenants. How *many* chests were there, wondered Sphax?

Moments later the officers returned, carrying an oaken chest bound with two bronze clasps and iron handles. It looked satisfyingly heavy. Deciding it would be seen as discourteous to open it and check the contents, Sphax continued the flattery. 'My Lord, a thousand cups will be raised in your honour when the Boii are paid with this great gift. You will be the toast of our camp! I cannot thank you enough for your generosity.'

Adherbal managed a desultory grunt before adding, 'And what are your plans, gentlemen, now that we have finally made contact and I have communicated my intentions?'

'We will put into Cosa, Sir, and await the first favourable wind to take us north to Pisae. The sooner Hannibal receives your gift, the sooner our campaign can resume.'

'I would detail a trireme to row you to your destination, but as I understand it, the success of Hannibal's campaign depends on my fleet remaining on station, closing the Tyrrhenian sea to any Roman reinforcements that might outflank you. So you must forgive me if I say I cannot spare a single trireme.'

'Of course, Lord,' Sphax gushed, 'your zeal and sense of duty is commendable, an example to us all. We will make our own way north.'

'Then all that remains is for me to say farewell, young man, and wish Hannibal's army fresh victories.'

'All of you are now freed from slavery. It would have been Tarbo's dying wish to release you from these bonds, but law requires this act is witnessed. Idwal and I will act as your guarantors. On our return to Pisae we will both seal a document that will be given to a magistrate testifying that Captain Tarbo released you from his service and bequeathed to you all a joint share in his corbita.' Sphax searched the boy's faces gathered around the campfire they'd lit on the stone quay.

They'd arrived late in the afternoon to find Cosa's harbour empty and deserted. Fishing nets and small boats lined the quayside, but none of the boats and tackle looked as if they'd been used in days. Jugurtha and Agbal reported that Cosa's walls and gates, built on a steep promontory out of sight of the harbour, were bristling with guards and sentries, dashing Sphax's hopes of a warm bed in a comfortable hospitium. They made the best of it.

'You mean we now *own* our vessel?' cried Naso, thunderstruck by this revelation.

'Unless Tarbo had a wife, sons or close relatives,' Idwal mused, 'you are his natural legal heirs. Does he have such relatives?'

The boys stared at one another, dumbfounded, before chorusing a resounding, 'No!'

'Then you are all the proud owners of a corbita and have an equal share in Tarbo's trading business.' But Sphax's audience seemed unconvinced. A thought occurred. 'Where is the finest wine to be bought in these parts?'

'In Aegilium of course,' a boy piped up.

'And what would be a fair price for this wine?' he asked.

Numbers were bandied around before Naso acted as spokesperson. 'Captain Tarbo would never pay more than forty asses for a jar. Even forty-five would be robbery, Sir.'

'Where would you get the best price for this wine?' asked Sphax, continuing his line of reasoning.

This met with derisory laughter before the boys shouted, 'Massilia.'

Idwal joined in. 'And what would you ask for a jar of fine Aegilium wine in the markets of Massilia?'

There was heated debate before Naso, once again acted as spokesman. 'We would hope to sell an amphora for at least sixty asses, if not nearer seventy.'

'Then by my calculations,' Idwal frowned, 'if you had bought a score of jars of Aegilium's finest wine and sold them in Massilia, you would have turned a tidy profit of at least four hundred asses—'

'But you're wrong, Sir,' chimed in a boy they all called Sciurus, 'Captain Tarbo always bought ingots of copper in Massilia. They fetch a fortune in Arretium. By the time we arrived back home we would've made at least ten times that amount.'

Grinning, Idwal raised his hands in acknowledgment. 'I stand corrected, lad. It seems we have eight extremely shrewd and knowledgeable merchants seated before us. What do you think, Sphax?'

'I couldn't agree more,' he beamed, relieved that his little exercise had gone so well. 'Over the last two days I've watched you closely. As a ship's crew you work well together, have a natural leader in Naso, a helmsman in Sabinus, and all of you seem to know a great deal about markets and trade. I have every confidence you'll make a success of Tarbo's business.'

Sciurus was shaking his head. 'But we haven't a stake, Sir, how could we afford a deposit on our first cargo? How would we pay harbour fees, warehouse dues or taxes on our trade?' The lad they called the squirrel, was obviously destined to be their treasurer. 'All the captain's profits went into that grand house of his.'

Sphax was amazed, he'd never thought of Tarbo as having a domestic life, let alone a grand house, he'd always imagined the captain lived, worked and slept on his vessel. 'Captain Tarbo has a house? In Pisae?'

'Of course,' answered Naso, surprised at Sphax's ignorance. 'It's by the temple of Apollo near the southern gate, though the peristylium and atrium need much work, and there's a great deal of decorating to be done.'

'You should see it, Sir,' Sabinus chipped in, 'it's beautiful.'

'Do you all live there when in Pisae?' Sphax asked, his astonishment growing.

'Of course!' the boys chorused.

'We have our own rooms,' added Naso.

Sphax stared at Idwal. He would never have guessed that deep down the old goat craved a home, perhaps even a family life. Or was it that Tarbo wanted to be seen as a respectable, upstanding citizen of Pisae, a pillar of the community? They would never find out now.

'Then it would appear,' observed Idwal, 'that you are not only proud owners of a trading vessel, but also of a town house. This entitles you all to become citizens of the city, but with citizenship comes the burden of extra taxes I'm afraid. Ah … the responsibilities of coming of age.'

Sciurus was sadly shaking his head. 'But don't you see, Sir, we would have to sell the house to scrape together enough silver to buy a cargo.'

Sphax grinned, 'Ah, but that's exactly where we might be able to help you.' This was the moment he and Idwal had been looking forward to all evening. 'Wait here.'

Rising to their feet, he and Idwal grabbed a torch each and made their way back on board to the deck cabin. Gingerly stepping over the sleeping figures of the Numidians, each found an iron handle and began heaving the chest ashore, placing it carefully beside their campfire.

'One of the last things I said to Captain Tarbo,' Sphax began solemnly, 'was to swear that I would pay him handsomely for the services of his vessel and crew. In view of the danger we placed you in this morning, Idwal and I are deeply in your debt. I hope this will more than repay what we owe you,' and with that he knelt down, unhinged the clasps and opened the chest.

Lowering the torch so all could see, he ploughed his hand through a brimful of silver coins, all struck with the head of an uncle he was yet to meet. For what seemed like an age, the only sound he heard was that of coins slipping through his fingers into the chest.

On the following afternoon a warm gentle breeze arose from the south and they slipped out of the empty harbour of Cosa and headed north. On the uneventful two day journey, the crew were discovering that their newfound wealth brought unexpected responsibilities and choices. After they'd settled on a sarcophagus and sculptured memorial for Tarbo, they couldn't agree where outside the city it was to be placed. Idwal suggested they decide this by ballot. In death as in life, the old goat was still dividing opinion.

But as they tacked into the channel of the Arno on the second morning of their journey, there was little doubt the crew and its passengers were of one mind. One glance at the columns of smoke rising from the rooftops above Pisae told them that something was wrong. Something was very wrong.

SIXTEEN

Sphax had never seen the harbour so crammed with shipping, so much so they had difficulty in finding an empty berth along the quayside. After skilful helmsmanship on Sabinus' part and even sharper work from two of the crew leaping ashore with ropes to tie off on the iron bollards lining the quay, the corbita was at last made fast.

Seeing Naso he yelled, 'The crew are to stay aboard. That's an order! I'll send word when it's safe to come ashore.'

Sphax didn't wait for the boarding ramps. Leaping from the gunnels he began striding down the deserted quayside, forcing Idwal, Drust and the Numidians to run to catch up with him. 'Most of these ships should be at sea. What's going on?'

Idwal finally caught up. 'None of them have crews on board, and this quay is usually thronged with longshoremen.'

His thoughts in turmoil, Sphax was beginning to fear the worst. Had the city risen up against his

Numidians? After all, there were only three hundred of them, in a city of thousands. But his worst fear was that during their absence, Rome had somehow come to Pisae's relief, stormed the city and slaughtered his men.

When they reached the row of shops at the end of the quay his anxiety grew. Every shop, popina or taberna was as eerily empty of customers as it was of bartenders and shopkeepers. Halting outside a barber's, Sphax turned to Agbal carrying their javelins: 'Share them out. Have one threaded at the ready. When we turn the next corner, only Ba 'al Hamūn knows what we may meet.'

Reaching for the pouch containing his leather throwing thong, he balanced the iron saunion in his fist and begun coiling the thin strip of leather. 'Your thoughts, my friends?' he asked anxiously, staring at Idwal and Drust in turn, both of whom had already drawn their blades.

'Gauls should never board ship without their shields,' grumbled Drust.

'If things go against us,' Idwal frowned, 'I suggest we retreat in haste back to our vessel and cast off. We can always return under cover of darkness to find out what has happened to your Numidians.'

'I pray it doesn't come to that, Idwal, but it's sound advice.' Switching to Tassynt he relayed this to his men. Though shocked, they nodded agreement. Sphax was desperately trying to conjure in his mind's eye a street plan of what faced them when they rounded the corner ahead. He seemed to remember a small square marked the entrance to the harbour with a broad avenue leading off left to the forum and a narrower street that wound its way to the city's southern gate.

With javelins raised, he formed his men in line beside him with Idwal and Drust behind them. Whatever happened they would have time to release a volley before retreating behind the Cavari, hoping they could buy them enough time to thread fresh javelins. Shields or not, he knew that Idwal and Drust would defend them to the last.

'Let's get this over with. At the run,' Sphax barked. With that he leapt forward, javelin held aloft. Twenty strides later he raced around the corner only to come to a startled halt, feeling rather foolish, staring at the backsides of thirty mares drawn up in a line across the square.

Astride their mares, thirty Numidians now turned round to see what all the fuss was and promptly burst out laughing. It was Manissa's eshrin.

'And where have you been, you young pup?' grinned the veteran captain. 'Since you left, things have been going from bad to worse. Why did you leave that arsewit Himilco in charge? He hasn't the sense he was born with! Me and Gala told him to his face … but he wouldn't listen.'

Despite the harangue and his embarrassment, Sphax was never more pleased to see one of his captains alive and at the head of an eshrin of Numidian cavalry. To his immense relief he guessed they faced nothing more than civil insurrection, not thousands of marauding legionaries. 'What's going on, Manissa? Tell me everything!'

Ignoring the oaths, curses and told-you-so's, it became clear from Manissa's description that the Roman faction in Pisae had risen up, setting fire to buildings where Numidians were quartered. That at least explained the columns of smoke rising above the city. None of the men had been harmed, Manissa assured him.

In retaliation, Himilco had threatened to close the harbour unless every captain and merchant swore a solemn oath not to trade with Rome. Sphax saw immediately this was a petty, idle threat that could never be enforced. Oath or not, once a vessel left harbour, how could they possibly control its destination or where it traded unless an armed guard was placed aboard every ship? Besides, the harbour and the trade it brought was the life-blood of the city; close the harbour, and you threaten the livelihoods of most of its citizens. It was a spiteful act that almost guaranteed insurrection. What was Himilco thinking?

When the Pisani merchants and captains refused, Himilco had foolishly carried out his threat, blocking off every street that led to the harbour with an eshrin of cavalry. And that, according to Manissa, had resulted in the present mayhem.

Across the square Sphax could see another eshrin

straddling the street that led to the southern gate. 'Is that Gala's eshrin?' he enquired, pointing.

'Yes,' growled Manissa. 'We've sat here like stale farts since daybreak.'

'Has anyone challenged you?'

'Not likely,' the veteran laughed. 'Even last night when those Roman cocksuckers were charging around with torches, none of 'em had the guts to face us man to man.'

'But the place is deserted,' cried Sphax in exasperation, 'where is everybody?'

'In that big square by the temple, Captain, giving Himilco a right tongue-lashing and telling him to his face what they think of him.'

Sphax groaned. Manissa's big square was the forum, and the temple that of Juno, protectress of Rome in times of war. He'd better get there. And fast.

'I need six of your men, Manissa,' and without waiting for volunteers, he leapt onto the nearest mare behind its rider, his Numidians following suit. 'Mount up,' he yelled at Idwal and Drust, who hadn't understood a word of his conversation with Manissa. 'I'll explain later. But we need to get to the forum. Fast!'

The sight that met him reminded him of the simmering crowds outside the Circus in Rome, when against all the odds, the white or red faction had lost a race, and gamblers their wagers. Nothing frays tempers more than losing money. Silver was not only the sinew of war, it was the lifeblood of commerce, and

Himilco's ultimatum threatened more than commerce, it threatened livelihoods.

Other than children, the old and infirm, all Pisae seemed to have gathered that morning in the forum or on the steps of the temple of Juno. In his previous life as a slave, Sphax had learnt to read crowds, and despite the anger, rowdiness and finger pointing, he sensed they were not yet baying for Numidian blood, just a way out. For now it was a finely balanced standoff, but that could change. All it would take was a flashpoint, a careless spark.

Opposite the temple of Juno the javelins of four eshrins of Numidian cavalry held a line in front of the courthouse and what the Pisani erroneously called their senate building, though there were no elected senators, just two magistrates elected annually by a handful of rich oligarchs, and it was they who pulled all the strings in this city. They were the puppeteers. Convince them, Sphax decided, and the good citizens of Pisae would return to their homes like sheep to the flock.

He was beginning to feel sorry for Himilco, surrounded as he was by scores of outraged citizens, shouting and gesticulating in a language he barely understood. Aribal was doing his best to translate; unfortunately, his Latin was not much better than Himilco's. Finger wagging and angry gesticulation, however, needed little translation.

Sliding from the back of the mare, Sphax smiled at Idwal, 'I think I may need your help, my friend.'

'Do you think they'll listen?' Idwal questioned with his habitual frown. 'They don't look particularly receptive to me.'

'We're about to find out. The Pisani speak Latin, so as long as they don't babble on in that strange tongue of theirs, at least we can understand one another.' As far as Sphax was concerned, the Etruscan language was incomprehensible and seemed to bear no resemblance to any language he'd ever heard before.

When Himilco caught sight of him, the relief on his lieutenant's face was palpable. 'Sphax … you're here at last. Thank Ba 'al Hamūn! They won't listen to—'

'—I can see that,' he snapped, testily. 'I'll speak to them.' Handing his javelins to Aribal he raised both arms, 'I am Sphax,' he began confidently, 'nephew of Hannibal and commander of the Numidians that now occupy Pisae …' Faltering, he realised he could hardly hear himself above the cacophony.

Seeing Himilco turning his back on them, three red-faced ladies, standing beside their respectable, tongue-tied husbands, redirected their considerable ire on Sphax. Etruscan women had a reputation for being outspoken and forthright, but even Sphax was shocked by such public behaviour. When the trio of harpies were joined by a jeering gang of youths, clearly enjoying the mayhem and spoiling for a fight, he decided enough was enough.

Raising his arms again he yelled, 'Silence … silence!' If anything, the noise levels of the jeering and laughter increased.

So be it. *Satis verborum*, the saying came to mind, it was time for action, and in the circumstances, to use the only language they would truly understand.

Turning his back on the baying rabble, he began striding down the line of his eshrins repeating a simple command: 'Thread javelins and hold them shoulder high ready to throw. On my signal you will walk your mares forward, javelins raised.' By the time he'd walked in both directions and returned to Idwal who'd been watching with a wry smile, the cacophony had evaporated to an anxious murmur.

'I think they're receptive now,' grinned Idwal.

'Enough talk!' Sphax glared, before raising his right hand and yelling, 'Walk on, Numidians. Walk!' For a heartbeat there was stunned silence. Then the screaming began and a stampede for the rear.

Soon the entire forum was emptied except for those trapped on the temple steps. Fearing the rabble, the priests of Juno had barred the temple doors, so for the unfortunate citizens who'd chosen the best seats to witness the humiliation of the Numidians, there was now no escape. And so it was to a sullen and compliant audience of less than two hundred that Sphax finally delivered his address.

'I am Sphax,' he began again, 'nephew of Hannibal and commander of the Numidians that now occupy Pisae. I am willing to allow you to reopen the harbour on the condition that your magistrates and city council meet me in your senate building within the hour.

If your magistrates and councillors do not comply, I will raze this city to the ground. Do I make myself clear?' Pausing, he glared up at the ashen faces. 'You have one hour! Now go home and tell your friends and neighbours what I have said. And round up those dignitaries!'

When the crowds had warily descended the steps and dispersed, Idwal turned to him. 'It's not wise to make idle threats, my friend. What are you going to do if those oligarchs don't turn up?'

'Let's pray they do,' Sphax replied, fingering his ivory image of the goddess.

'But if they don't, Pisae will be the second city in Italia you've fired in a few months. I must say it's ironic that you were standing on the steps of the temple of Juno when you made that threat.' Idwal was referring to the burning of the harbour in Brundisium and his firing of the temple of Juno Curitis. 'The goddess must really hate you.'

Sphax was mightily relieved when the deputation turned up well within the hour and were ushered into the senate house. He was also surprised to see Malchus amongst their number, but careful not to acknowledge any connection between them.

Without rostra or benches, the senate house was not a debating chamber, just a large, high- ceilinged room filled with a long table with seating for the twelve oligarchs and two high-backed solium chairs for the presiding magistrates.

When they were all seated he got to his feet. 'By now you must all know who I am,' he began, looking around at the grave faces staring at him, 'so introductions are unnecessary. Your presence around this table meets the only condition I laid down, therefore consider your harbour open for business. Already I have ordered my men to withdraw from their positions blocking access to the quays, and I give you my word they will not interfere in any way with lawful trade.

'I consider the restrictions on your trade imposed by my lieutenant to have been ill-advised, if not illegal. The Pisani are at liberty to trade with whomever they wish. There will be no more oath-taking, or receiving. Etruscans are a free people, and the armies of Carthage are not here to impose their will on your citizens. In fact quite the reverse: we are here to uphold your liberties.'

Sphax paused to let his words bite home and give himself time to study the faces around the table. Only a few months ago he would have rushed headlong into the fray with a rousing call to war, exhorting anyone who would listen to take up arms against Rome. The problem was that few listened. But Sphax listened. Firstly to his friend Idwal, who'd taught him something of rhetoric and the art of logical argument, and then to Hannibal, whose silken tongue could have persuaded

Hades to give up his dead. Instead of crowds, he was now learning to read people: their demeanor, expressions and gestures, not to mention their infinite ways of dissembling.

What he could read in the faces seated around the table in the hushed silence that followed his opening remarks, were two conflicting expressions: of surprise and deep suspicion. It was time to confound them even further.

'As my mission to Pisae is now complete, my men will leave this city at first light and return to our Carthaginian camp before Faesulae.'

This news was greeted with a wave of murmuring that circulated around the table. One of the magistrates half got to his feet, 'You're leaving!' Sphax found the man's grubby, purple-bordered toga pretentious, as would any Roman patrician if it was worn by a mere provincial.

'It was never our intention to occupy Pisae, or any other city in Etruria. We have not come to conquer. Hannibal simply requires free passage.'

'Then why did you occupy our city, and disrupt our trade?' growled a darkly bearded merchant, seated at the far end of the table. 'I consider the question not unreasonable, given the unrest you've caused.'

There was no reason to hide the purpose of his mission, Sphax realised. He would be giving nothing away. 'Then I apologise for any civil unrest that has arisen, though I understand that none of it was of our making. Our intention was simply to make contact with the Carthaginian fleet at Pisae. This I have now done. Governor Adherbal of Gades is now anchored off the island of Aegilium opposite Cosa. He's already sunk three Roman triremes. I hope many more suffer a similar fate.'

This resulted in another ripple of muttering. 'No wonder we no longer have to swear oaths!' sneered the toga-clad magistrate. 'This governor is doing your work for you, blocking trade. It would appear we're not at liberty to trade, at least not with Rome.'

It was a fine point. Suppressing a smile, Sphax shrugged, 'I can do no more. Your harbour is open and I've placed no restrictions on your trade. I suggest you take the matter up with Governor Adherbal.'

'This is outrageous! Consul Gaius Flaminius will hear of this!'

Sphax flushed at the name, rounding on the magistrate. 'I had no idea Rome was now appointing magistrates in Etruria. Has Pisae become a colony of Rome? She isn't the first … nor will she be the—'

'Pisae is *not* a Roman colony!' roared the bearded merchant, fist pounding the table. 'Nor will she ever become one. Magistrate Publius Cornelius is an ex-citizen of Rome. That he chooses to parade around in a toga is his business, not ours … or yours.'

'Just for a moment, Sir, try to see it from where I'm standing. Our armies are here in Etruria for one purpose, and one purpose only: to destroy Rome. Yet when I look around, what I see is a city giving succour to my enemies; trading weapons and armour we will face on the battlefield, grain supplies that sustain them in the field and reinforcements that threaten my uncle Hasdrubal in Iberia. If not a colony, Pisae is clearly an ally of Rome.

'After our army slaughtered Longus' legions on the Trebia, Hannibal issued a decree that all Rome's alae were to be spared. In a gesture of goodwill, every Sabine, Campanian *and* Etruscan was released, free to return to their homes. Is this how you repay us? By sending Rome more arms, more grain, and filling up the ranks of the legions we decimated. This feels like a betrayal to me, a treacherous double game. Like the rest of Etruria, sooner or later Pisae will have to decide. Are you with us or against us?'

There was now a hushed silence around the table. Glancing from face to face, Sphax was sure he detected a half-smile flickering on the lips of Malchus. He took it as a sign of approval for what he'd said.

Sphax dearly wanted to meet with the merchant once more to discuss their current campaign, but he would not put the man's life in jeopardy again. As they'd discovered to their cost, the Roman faction in Pisae was too strong. Malchus had already risked too much visiting their hospitium on that first night in Pisae. By a stroke of good fortune, Malchus' membership of the council meant that Sphax had been able to pass on to him the most important nugget of information about

Adherbal and his fleet, openly, without having to resort to subterfuge.

There seemed little more to say. 'Do you have any further questions?' The hush continued. 'Then all that remains is for me to thank you for your time, gentlemen, and wish you good day and farewell.' Muttering began again as the rich and powerful of Pisae rose to their feet and began shuffling towards the door.

Sphax slowly walked over to the high-backed chairs at the head of the table and placed a restraining hand on a toga. 'Not you, magistrate Publius Cornelius, ex-citizen of Rome,' demanded Sphax, 'we have something else in mind for you.'

The man looked terrified. 'What is it?' he muttered. 'I meant no offence—'

'—Of course you didn't. All I require is the small matter of your signature on a document, Sir. Nothing for you to worry about,' he added, with a smile that offered little in the way of reassurance. 'Just official business.'

Idwal brought over two scrolls, an inkstand and pen, placing them carefully on the table in front of the magistrate. Sphax leaned over and flattened the rolls of papyrus so they could be read.

'What's this?' grunted Cornelius.

'It's the signed testimony of the Pisani sea captain, Tarbo, who unfortunately died of natural causes on his last voyage to Cosa. As you see, it's neatly written and copied in Idwal's scholarly hand.'

Sphax began to point out individual passages; 'As you see here, magistrate, Tarbo has listed his worldly goods, including his vessel, a corbita berthed in the harbour here in Pisae and property in the city. Here he lists in red ink his crew. As you see, every name has been testified and witnessed with a mark. Captain Tarbo's dying wish was that his young crew — all poor slaves — should be the sole beneficiaries of his estate and be given their freedom upon his death, elevating them to the happy state of free citizens of Pisae. Praise be to Juno that Idwal and I were able to solemnly witness and verify his last bequest.'

Pointing to a space below the forged signature of Tarbo, Sphax asked innocently, 'Would you care to sign it, Sir?'

'Do I have a choice?' Cornelius sighed. 'Tarbo was nothing more than an uncouth troublemaker, a constant thorn in my side.'

'Then this will close an unpleasant chapter for you, magistrate.' Idwal handed him the pen. 'We've made a fair copy for the city's tabularium. If you wouldn't mind signing that too … it's always wise to keep a second copy, don't you agree?'

Reaching for a candle, Sphax dribbled an equal measure of hot wax onto the edge of each scroll. 'Your ring, magistrate.' Anxious to get this over with, Publius Cornelius pressed his signet ring into the wax, thereby sealing the documents into immutable law.

When the magistrate left, Sphax and Idwal stood there beaming at one another. 'That went better than I expected,' Idwal grinned.

'At least we didn't have to force the arsewit to do the right thing,' Sphax grudgingly acknowledged. 'But he's probably on his way to Arretium to complain to the consul about treacherous Numidians and scholarly Gauls. Seriously though,' he asked, changing tack, 'were you not surprised to see Malchus amongst those oligarchs on the city's council?'

'He's obviously done well for himself,' Idwal agreed, 'but good luck to him. Hannibal needs informants who are in positions of power, and Malchus has clearly wormed his way into such exalted circles. I'm sure he'll prove useful to us.'

Before Sphax had time to consider this the doors of the senate were flung open and Drust and several Numidian captains entered, eager for news and fresh orders. But first, Drust was told to take the precious document, now witnessed, signed and sealed, to the young crew of the late Captain Tarbo, whilst Aribal was entrusted with the copy to deposit in the tabularium in the courthouse next door.

Once this was under way, Sphax turned to his captains. 'We will depart in the order we agreed earlier, one eshrin at a time, beginning with Hanno at the southern gate. Do not draw attention to yourselves and be sure to leave a quarter of an hour between each eshrin's departure. We muster on the hill overlooking the city. Is everything clear?' There was a muttering of assent and relief that they would not have to spend another night in this deeply divided city.

Sphax had determined his Numidians would depart just as unexpectedly as they'd arrived; stealing away quietly, unnoticed, in the afternoon heat. He was not prepared to give the Pisani the satisfaction of a send-off! There would be no jeering crowds or jubilation at their departure. Just surprise and he hoped, consternation.

His eshrin was the last to leave. As his Numidians clattered beneath the arches of the Lucca Gate, where so many had fallen or been wounded, Sphax cried to the heavens: 'If ever I return to this accursed city, I swear I will see it burn.'

SEVENTEEN

'Adherbal, you say,' Maharbal repeated thoughtfully, gesturing to the three of them to make themselves comfortable on a couple of vacant divans.

It was as if time had stood still after Sphax had taken leave of the general almost a week ago. Striking exactly the same pose, propped up by cushions on his favourite divan, it seemed as if Maharbal had not stirred for six days. Pan was still pursuing Syrinx around the panelled walls of the atrium, lit by sunlight flooding in through the impluvium in the roof.

'Have you breakfasted?' enquired the general.

'I thought you'd never ask, Sir,' Sphax grinned, seeing Drust scouring the room for anything edible. 'We rode over at first light to report. We're all famished.'

Maharbal clapped his hands. Something had indeed changed in his absence. Somehow the general had acquired even more servants, a host of them suddenly trooping into the room, mostly giggling young women with a sprinkling of barefooted urchins. Word had got out that the general was a generous employer, especially to the young and comely or any starving urchin he took pity on.

'Bring food and wine,' he boomed in mangled Latin. Soon a table groaned under the weight of everything Etruria had to offer in this season of plenty. Delicacies like smoked ham, oysters and snails were followed by freshly baked bread, pungent goat's cheese and eggs poached on boiled spinach and samphire. Whereas Sphax and Idwal filled a modest plate from the table and returned to their couches, Drust hovered above it like a vulture at a feast, scorning plates or any receptacle other than his mouth. Long ago the general had taken a liking to Drust, and was always happy to indulge him.

'I've been trying to recall what I know of Adherbal, Governor of Gades,' Maharbal began, 'but I'm only acquainted with him through reputation and rumour, much of it scurrilous. What did you two make of him?'

'He obeys orders,' Sphax grudgingly conceded, 'if not in spirit, at least to the letter. Strategically he's well placed to render us great service. Adherbal's stationed off Cosa, so Rome will find it difficult to resupply Scipio in Iberia. But he offers us little in the way of assistance, though I pleaded our cause for siege equipment and elephants.'

'Tell the general about the skill of his captains and squadron, Sphax.' Idwal spoke little Punic, so everything had to be translated.

'Adherbal might not be much of a leader, Sir, but Idwal and I were impressed by his captains and their crews. We watched them sink two Roman triremes in quick succession, and a third was overhauled and sunk trying to escape. They'll be more than a match for any Roman fleet of a similar size.'

'I'm sure that will be a great comfort to us as we head south,' commented Maharbal with barely disguised sarcasm.

It was a constant source of frustration for Sphax that the general, not to mention Hannibal himself, didn't seem to understand the value of sea power, or its implications for war on land. The Illyrians and Macedonians understood. Why couldn't Maharbal? Sphax translated the general's comment for Idwal, who merely shrugged.

'Ah!' chuckled Maharbal. 'I've just remembered what everybody calls the governor of Gades behind his back: he's known as Adherbal the taxman. I believe he's bled the city white. It's rumoured he's the richest man in Iberia.'

'I can well believe it,' agreed Sphax. 'Piracy seems to be his true calling, so he should do well off Cosa.'

'Now tell me how you captured Pisae and found the governor's fleet?' It took Sphax some time to relate the events of the last six days, but Maharbal listened patiently without questions or interruptions. When Sphax described his meeting with Hannibal's informant Malchus, the general seemed particularly attentive.

For some time after Sphax fell silent Maharbal seemed lost in thought before he grumbled, 'We could have done with your ingenuity before the gates of Faesulae, lad.'

'I take it we didn't capture the town then.'

'Against your uncle's better judgment, Hanno persuaded him to attempt to storm it. Unfortunately, the Libyan's mind is not as sharp as his sword. A party did get over the wall and into the place, setting fire to a few buildings. But we never saw them again until the following morning, when the town's militia kindly returned them as headless corpses, flung from the battlements, which unedifying sight ended our futile attempts on Faesulae.'

The general rolled his eyes, 'Meanwhile,' he continued, 'our Boii and Insubres allies have been on the rampage. Somehow we've acquired a baggage train. Not of blacksmiths or armourers, or anything useful, but wagonloads of silver plate and gold trinkets … a plunder train! Ba 'al Hamūn save us from our allies!'

Sphax couldn't help laughing, silenced instantly by an icy glance from his general. 'What are my orders?' he asked, collecting himself.

'Tomorrow at first light we begin prodding and poking Flaminius Nepos, bending the consul to our will. You will take twenty eshrins south and burn every village and field of corn from here to the gates of Arretium. Etruria will burn like a funeral pyre, and Flaminius will be made to watch from the city's walls.'

It was exactly the sort of mission Sphax dreaded. Before the battle of the Trebia, Hannibal had ordered him to burn the villages of their allies, the Insubres, to provoke them into seeking protection from Consul Longus' legions. Even though he and his men had gone to great lengths to avoid needless deaths, it had still ended in bloodshed and the slaughter of women and children.

Maharbal guessed what was going through his lieutenant's mind. 'You must steel yourself, lad, and put aside your scruples. We have to provoke Flaminius into doing something rash. What better way than to burn the province he's been sent to defend?'

'If I know Flaminius, he'll come out and fight, Sir.'

'In which case your actions tomorrow will have served our purpose. We have double his numbers. Seeking battle would mean certain defeat for him. He's not such a fool as to risk that. Every tribune and centurion with any sense will be pleading with him to send messages to Consul Servilius in Ariminum to bring his legions south so they can combine their forces. That's his only hope. But your uncle believes the sight of these rich farmlands going up in flames will push the man over the edge … into madness; then anything can happen, so we must prepare for any eventuality.'

'And what of the villagers, Sir? The farmers, women and children? Do *they* go up in smoke?'

'Hannibal's not ordering you to slaughter innocents,' snapped the general, offended, 'just to drive them out.

They're hardly likely to starve! And someone will take them in. Believe me, lad,' Maharbal sighed, 'it's far better than what the Insubres are clamouring for.'

'Which is?' Sphax queried, curious to know what could be worse!

'That all boys and men of military age be put to the sword.'

Aghast, he stared at the general. 'Then I curse Morrigu! The goddess has no morality or conscience. We are not godless barbarians, Sir. We aspire to principles, justice and honour. Such a despicable act of atrocity would drive the Etruscans into the arms of Rome and set back our cause for a generation. It would light a torch that would brand us as eternal enemies, swelling the ranks of the legions with eager volunteers, bent on vengeance. Such a course of action would be madness, Sir. Brutal, senseless madness!'

Maharbal allowed Sphax's wave of outrage to ebb a little before he answered. 'I agree. Your uncle and I are of one mind on this. But if generations of your family had been butchered by marauding Etruscans backed by Rome's legions, you might feel differently about it. Don't be too quick to condemn them, Sphax, *or* their gods!'

'But why me, Sir? There must be scores of captains who could carry out these orders better than me. Some who might even enjoy it.'

'You know this country better than most. After all, you travelled the road barely a year ago on your way to join us. Secondly, you're the only Numidian who speaks Latin like a native. And lastly, you've proved in the past you can put a stop to looting, which is my gravest concern when we unleash our terror. If you like, you are my conscience. I like this no more than you do, but the men will listen to you. All I ask is you curb their excesses.'

'And what if I refuse, Sir? As *my* conscience demands I should!'

'May Ba 'al Hamūn spare us from such foolishness!' Maharbal erupted. 'You've preached at length how Rome butchered and raped the old and innocent of Mutina. Now is your chance to show them how men of honour and conscience wage war. Even a brutal war such as this. You are the son of Navaras. A Prince of Numidia, born to command Numidians in battle. We are not barbarians. Now is your chance to prove it!'

Sphax groaned. Obey or disobey, he stood condemned. It seemed there was no way out of this particular rat-trap.

'Then I will do as you ask, Sir. Etruria will burn.' Sphax stood, ready to take his leave, aware for the first time that Idwal and Drust were staring at him, fearful, yet ignorant of the exchanges that had taken place.

'Will it be acceptable for Idwal to report alone to Hannibal? In view of the orders the two of you have given me, I have no wish to be interrogated by my uncle. I would not be able to hold my tongue.' Maharbal nodded. 'Then I take my leave, Sir. Look for me before the walls of Arretium.'

He spent what was left of the morning combing the Numidian camp for captains who'd been with him on the raid across the Trebia to fire Insubres villages, summoning them to a council of war at midday. Once they'd gathered outside his humble tent at the appointed hour Sphax outlined the bare bones of their mission without any attempt to explain or justify it.

Aribal was the first to speak. 'Dog's twat! Why is it always Numidians who have to do the dirty work, Sphax? Why can't it be the Gauls for once … or the Libyans?'

'If I told you that in addition to burning every field and village from here to Arretium, the Insubres demanded that we put to the sword every boy and man of military age, would that ease your conscience about taking on this mission instead of them?'

'Surely Maharbal hasn't agreed to that?' cried Aribal, visibly paling.

'No, of course not! But you can see the dilemma we're in. Distasteful as it is, either we do as we're told, or …' Sphax let the word fall into the uneasy silence that followed.

'Then we have no alternative,' said Hiempsal, gravely. 'But will it work? All those legions have to do is sit tight and wait for Servilius, that would double their strength. Surely Flaminius isn't such a fool as to risk everything by offering battle?'

'From everything Sphax and the general have told us about this consul, he's a proud and reckless hothead,' argued Himilco. 'What would you do, Hiempsal, if someone marched through your lands, laying waste to every rick, cot and tree?'

'Chase the bastard and rip out his filthy heart!'

Exactly so, thought Sphax. Consul Flaminius Nepos might be a hothead, but he was no fool. For all their prodding and poking, the best they could hope for was to induce the consul to pursue them. That way he avoided battle, allowed for the possibility of Servilius joining him, and in the event of Hannibal suddenly turning on him, there was always the bolt hole of Arretium to his rear.

Was this Hannibal's intention? To lure him south, out in the open, away from Servilius and the walls of Arretium? To Sphax's mind, a pursuit would be just as foolish as coming out to meet them in battle; sooner or later Hannibal would manoeuvre his opponent into a corner and crush him. But he was certain now. That had to be Hannibal's intention. In which case, it would have implications for their mission.

Instead of halting before the walls of Arretium, they should give the place a wide berth and head south to join the Cassian Way. Rome lay south. He knew this road only too well!

He was jolted from his thoughts by Himilco. 'There's another possibility. Flaminius might send out his cavalry to put a stop to our little game. In which case he may well catch us scattered over a wide area, ill-prepared, and off guard.' Sphax had already considered this carefully, but he allowed his men to voice their opinions.

'If they send out their alae cavalry alongside the legions' equites, they would have twice our number,' Aribal pointed out.

Sphax reasoned this was unlikely. Flaminius would never risk repeating the same mistake Scipio had made on the Ticinus, where a legion's cavalry was routed by a single charge, the consul barely escaping with his life. Sphax bore the scar to prove it. No. Cavalry was Rome's weakest arm. Flaminius would never risk such an encounter. But he wasn't going to tell his men that.

'Have you lost your tongue, Sphax?' puzzled Himilco. 'It's not like you not to have an opinion.' Suddenly all eyes gravitated towards him.

'This is my worst fear,' he lied. 'If our men are weighed down by plunder, or worse, drunk from all the wine they've looted, we will be undone.' Sphax glared back at the faces staring at him.

'I have assurances from Maharbal that he'll ride to our assistance if we're attacked, but if Flaminius' cavalry strike us hard and fast, I fear he will be too late. We will be strung out across fields and villages, some of us on foot, making it impossible to concentrate and fend off attacks. That's why you must control your men tomorrow. At all times they must be in a fit state to fight. That means no drinking or looting. Each of you will hold back a reserve of ten men to keep constant watch.'

He'd neglected to mention that a thousand Numidians would be shadowing their right flank, whilst twice that number would be riding directly behind them. Far more than was needed to see off any attack Flaminius could muster. But he was pleased with himself. They seemed to have swallowed his forebodings.

Only tomorrow would tell if it would put a stop to looting, and meet Maharbal's challenge.

'My men are always ready to fight,' snapped Hiempsal, who'd taken Sphax's remarks as a personal slur on his leadership. 'I always keep my men on a short leash. There will be no looting.'

There was a chorus of agreement around the circle. Sphax raised his eyebrows to the heavens and stared at Hiempsal. 'Then all will be well. All you have to do is ask the good citizens of Etruria to abandon their homes so you can burn them to the ground, along with their worldly goods and the fields they've tilled, sown and toiled over all spring. What could be easier?'

Sphax tore his eyes from Hiempsal and examined the faces gathered around him. 'Not for one moment do I doubt your men will fight like Numidian warriors. You are the chosen few. Your men would follow you into the jaws of Hades. But will your warriors kill innocents?

'Mothers, children, the old and sick, farmers armed with nothing more than scythes, labourers, young hotheads … all desperate to defend their hearths and parents? For my part I would rather face a Roman legion drawn up for battle!' As he'd spoken, Sphax sensed growing unease amongst the gathering.

'You paint a bleak picture, Sphax,' acknowledged Himilco. 'How can we avoid such senseless butchery?'

'Javelins must be your weapon of last resort. Your weapons of choice will be the savage gods of fear and panic. Let Phobos ravage the plains of Etruria and our battlecries strike terror into the hearts of its people. Rant and rave! Threaten and menace! Only fear and dread make people flee for their lives.

'Burn crops and kill livestock first. That way we crush all hope and offer only famine and hunger for those who haven't taken to their heels. Don't enter buildings, simply throw torches at anything that will burn.

'For some today, you will learn your first words of Latin. Say after me,' Sphax pronounced, 'Fugite animas vestras. Galli veniunt!'

He waited until they'd all had a good stab at it. 'In our language it warns, *Flee for your lives. The Gauls are coming!*'

Gazing at the circle of faces he added, 'Tomorrow, this will be your only battlecry.'

The Gauls are coming … was heard amidst the screaming and wailing, amidst the tearing of hair and the cries for mercy, amidst the sheer terror and horror of that morning. As the wall of flame and choking smoke approached, few chose to stand defiantly in its path. Those foolish enough to try were quickly surrounded by the sharp end of javelins and persuaded of their folly. Sphax's fears proved to be ill-founded. His men behaved impeccably: there was no looting, drunkenness or needless killing.

After weeks without rain, the fields of shoulder-high wheat were parched and baked, ripe for a Numidian spark fanned by a stiff breeze from the north. *The Gauls are coming...*! Soon entire villages joined the conflagration as the exodus of Etruscans gathered pace.

That night Sphax slept fitfully, tossing and turning. Sometime in the uneasy grey half-light before dawn he had the dream again. The recurrent nightmare he'd come to dread. Disconcertingly, there were always subtle changes, as if his memory was searching for new evidence or forgotten details, but always, like some irrevocable moment locked into eternity, the events never changed.

Once more he was a helpless seven year old child in the iron grip of two Roman legionaries, one clamping a hand over his mouth to silence his screams. Once more he was forced to look on as his mother was raped, the last brute slitting her throat. All the while her soft green eyes slowly melted into his: 'If I can bear this, so must you.' This wordless refrain was always the same. As was the dream's abrupt ending, with a pool of blood gathering on his mother's breast. This was the moment he braced himself for. Like a silent scream, what followed was always a tempest of pain and grief that no mortal should ever have to bear.

After the pain came the rage. Wave after wave of it, threatening to overwhelm him.

Later he staggered to his feet wailing with grief, vowing never to close his eyes again. Outside in the half-light, he paced around the smoldering embers of a campfire like a caged animal, waiting for dawn and activity to bring relief.

By the third day of the burning of Etruria their work had grown easier, the great pall of smoke marking their progress through the countryside acting as a beacon of despair, a harbinger of the terror to come. Entire villages had emptied and houses were bare, their owners having loaded everything of value onto wagons, carts or whatever they could carry on their backs. Cattle, sheep, goats, and swine, anything on four legs had been herded to safety. In the days to come not a single cockerel would be left to proclaim the new day north of Arretium. Etruria was emptying.

After midday, Sphax, Himilco and Hiempsal sat down to enjoy their second hog-roast of the campaign, prepared earlier that morning by Hannon and others from his eshrin, who seemed to have acquired a sounder of swine.

With fat dripping from his chin on to his immaculately kept beard, Hiempsal proclaimed, 'Even you must admit, Sphax, our men have never eaten so well,' raising the rib he'd been eating as evidence.

Grinning, Sphax agreed. 'And they deserve nothing less! They have behaved well, and my worst fears were ill-founded.' he turned to Himilco. 'Although I'm loth to admit it, sometimes war does call for desperate measures. In the face of a duty that any soldier of conscience would dread, to a man our Numidians have acted with restraint and honour. I'm proud of you all.'

Himilco looked puzzled. 'Then why did you issue such dire warnings, Sphax? Our men

would never take part in senseless slaughter. You must know that.'

Sphax sighed. 'Do you recall the incident before the Trebia when Hannibal ordered Scipio's old camp to be fired?' Himilco nodded. 'At the time we were attacking the rearguard of the consul's retreating legions. The fight was hot that day if you remember, and there came a point when we desperately needed reinforcements, so Maharbal ordered me to ride back to the Roman camp and bring Astegal's eshrins into action.' For a moment he collected his thoughts.

'When I got there I found his men looting and as drunk as Scythians. Astegal was nowhere to be seen. I begged the men to follow me into battle. I pleaded, shamed them by telling them their fellow countrymen were dying on the battlefield on their behalf … but they wouldn't listen. The lure of silver and wine was too great. A drunken Numidian is no better, or worse, than a drunken Gaul. When drink takes a man, he is lost.' Sphax fell silent for a moment before adding, 'With Astegal's twenty eshrins we would have destroyed Scipio that day, and much blood would have been spared.' In his mind's eye the memory of placing the body of Adherbal on the back of his faithful mare came flooding back. It was his dear friend's last journey.

'That bastard, Astegal!' Hiempsal spat. 'I hope he's rotting in Hades.'

Ignoring this, Sphax glanced at Himilco. 'Bitter experience told me to issue those warnings.'

A chorus of raucous laughter burst out from his men seated on benches borrowed from abandoned houses in the village. Hiempsal was right. Their men had never eaten better. Yesterday they'd come upon a granary of the finest wheat, and the mule train they'd formed from abandoned animals was now laden with its contents. That morning he'd agreed with his men that their breakfast flatbreads were the finest he'd ever tasted.

'Share the jest with us, Hannon,' he shouted over to them. 'Your officers are glum and sorely in need of amusement.'

Sphax knew for a fact that Hannon had no time for *officers*. He could count on the fingers of one hand the number of times the veteran had deferred to him as capt'n, let alone, Sir. As far as he could remember, the latter word had never passed the man's lips. And yet … Sphax admired him for it. Over the months of dangers they'd faced together, a deep bond of friendship and trust had grown between them.

Still chuckling to himself, Hannon strode over. 'After eating so much pork I told Agbal his farts are beginning to smell like pigswill and he's grunting like a pig.

'Did you hear him squealing just now? He's wagered the rest of us that in a few days' time he'll be able to sniff out truffles. He's put good silver on it!' Hannon was almost doubled up with laughter now, struggling to continue. 'The lads have taken up his wager, so we're taking him on a truffle hunt! Do you want to wager on him, capt'n?'

Hiempsal laughed. 'I've heard that swine can sniff out truffles—'

'—Oh they can, lad! I've seen it with my own eyes.'

'Agbal's bound to make a pig's ear of it,' quipped Sphax, 'so count me out. I'll wager he'll fail to snuff out a single truffle. I trust his eyes … but not his nose!' Wiping his smile he added, 'Have the men get ready, Hannon. We're moving out soon.'

Himilco shot him a quizzical glance. 'Where are you going?'

Sphax got to his feet, peering to the south. 'To take a look at Arretium,' he said absently. 'It's only six miles down the road. I need to see this legionary encampment for myself.'

Returning his gaze to Himilco he insisted, 'This is where our Numidians change tack. I want you all to change direction and head south-west, giving Arretium a wide berth and burning a broad swathe of the country around the city. Then, with luck and a fair wind, we'll head south again and make for Cortona. Be on your guard at all times.'

At the head of his eshrin he kept the pace to a leisurely trot. There seemed little point in tiring their mares on what was a simple scouting exercise. For the past few days he'd been riding Aethon. Dido hadn't fully recovered from her ordeal in the swamps, and if there was to be a battle in the near future he would need her fit and rested. Willful, and as yet not fully trained, his beautiful golden mare could not be risked in a pitched battle.

As they neared the city along the arrow-straight Cassian, the rich farmlands of standing wheat slowly gave way to olive groves, orchards and endless rows of vines. Orioles called from the tallest branches and occasionally he would catch the turquoise and scarlet flash of a bee-eater darting between the trees. In the hazy afternoon sunshine the distant line of hills to the east took on a bluish hue that spoke to him of a peace and serenity far removed from the world of men and their wars.

That afternoon he was happy to be left alone with his thoughts; the idle chatter and banter of his men riding behind him in double file never troubled him. This road and the city to which it led were rich in memory for him, though he and Fionn had journeyed north, not south.

It was almost a year ago to the day. He'd fallen in love for the first time, yet with every milestone of the Cassian he'd fretted how to tell her, how to reveal his heart, his love. Then there were his vivid memories of Arretium.

They'd entered the city at the culmination of the Cerealia festival, two runaway slaves. He, worried, looking over his shoulder, fearing they would caught by the *fugitivarii* and dragged in chains before a magistrate. She without a care in the world, bent on tasting the joys and pleasures of freedom. As mothers and daughters paraded through the streets garlanded in leaves and spring flowers, Sphax remembered Fionn's excitement at seeing jugglers and fire-eaters for the first time.

Then there was that first vision of her loveliness. If she'd entered the city in the filthy rags of a slave girl, a few silver coins had brought about a miraculous transformation when she'd stood before him in a blue stola and rose pink cape, her golden hair plaited in blue silk and fastened with a copper pin and pheasant's feather.

Somehow, Sphax sensed that a circle was closing around him, that he was returning to a significant moment that would mark the end of a chapter in his life. Would it mark a new beginning? The birth of his son? A life with Corinna? Perhaps.

But when Helios completes his circuit of the earth the world is plunged into night, and Sphax sensed darkness in all of this: the dream of his mother's death, the memory of Fionn's lost loveliness. Rather than being flooded with memory, he seemed to be drowning in it, haunted by the dead.

Sphax was jolted out of his reverie by the sight of his scouts, Jugurtha and Agbal, galloping at high speed towards him. It could mean only one thing. The walls of Arretium had been sighted.

PART THREE

To Kill a Consul

EIGHTEEN

It looked smaller than he remembered. But Arretium's towering walls and gates were unmistakable because of their peculiar look and construction: in the whole of Italia, Sphax had never come upon a city whose walls were made of fired red brick. It gave the place its unique appearance.

Built upon a natural bowl in a hill whose slope faced west, the ground which led to the eastern gate rose sharply, merging with the backdrop of hills beyond its walls. From where they'd halted their mares on the Cassian, Sphax could clearly see the clay-tiled roofs at the eastern edge of the city rising above its northern wall. But there was no sign of a legionary encampment.

'Let's take a look at the western gate,' ordered Sphax, pointing his clutch of javelins to the south west and nudging Aethon forward. After trampling through vineyards and skirting treacherous clay pits they found themselves hidden in the cover of a grove of trees, less than five hundred paces from the western gate. And there it was.

Laid out with Roman precision was the legionary encampment, built in the lee of the city's walls, south of the gate. A perfect grid of tents, pavilions, storehouses and workshops, set out like pieces on a petteia board. They hadn't bothered with a ditch or palisade, Arretium's walls offering a secure refuge from any attack.

As he watched, the massive doors of the western gate began to swing open and a party on foot came out of the shadows. At this distance all Sphax could make out were twelve men clad in scarlet, marching in step and carrying something over their shoulders. As they emerged from the gates they divided and took up position either side of a horseman riding south towards the Roman camp. Even at this distance he could see that the horseman's armour was resplendent in polished bronze and silver, catching the bright sunlight. Behind him, at a respectful distance, six more horsemen emerged riding two abreast.

Sphax suddenly felt icy cold. Something was happening to his breathing. 'Join me, Agbal,' he called, but no words came forth. His throat felt dry, parched, almost incapable of speech. After another attempt he finally managed to summon Agbal to his side.

'What do you see?' Sphax croaked, his heart beginning to race.

'All they're up to,' shrugged Agbal nonchalantly, 'is a spot of drilling—'

'— No! No!' He yelled, finding his full voice at last. 'Not in the camp … look to the western gate! Tell me what you see. Describe it!'

Taken aback by the intensity in the captain's voice and manner, Agbal stared at Sphax's ashen face before doing what was asked of him.

'There are twelve guards,' Agbal began, 'carrying wooden rods and axes escorting two men on big stallions, capt'n. One of them's wearing the fanciest armour I've ever seen … quite a peacock by the looks of him!'

'Describe this peacock,' demanded Sphax.

'Well … he's wearing the biggest gold helmet I've ever set eyes on. It's got a crest with crimson tassels, and his poor old stallion's draped in a tiger skin.'

Sphax had heard enough. 'Those are not guards,' he snarled, 'but lictors, carrying their badge of office. And that peacock's a Roman consul! None other than Gaius Flaminius Nepos.' Sphax almost spat the words.

A white-hot rage descended on him like no other he'd ever experienced. Sweat broke on his brow, his blood coursed his veins like molten iron and his breath came in great gasps, causing his entire body to convulse. But somewhere, deep in the pit of his stomach, a chasm of hatred had opened that was colder than the grave. Caught between the agony of fire and ice he couldn't bear it … it was consuming him. He could not bear it!

'The bastard's mine!' Sphax screamed, digging his knees into Aethon's flanks so hard she rose up on her hind legs, almost unhorsing him before leaping into a gallop.

Thundering forward, the world closed in around him. All he saw now was the back of a bronze helmet, its crimson tassels swaying in the breeze. But that was all he needed to see.

Aethon had covered a hundred paces before he realised he needed something to kill the bastard with: his bare hands would do, but his saunion would make certain. Frantically fumbling for his leather throwing thong, Sphax selected the weapon, swapped it to his right hand and began threading it. He could do this in his sleep, so in a few strides he had the slender iron javelin raised and levelled.

Spotting him racing towards them, the lictors hurriedly began ushering their charge towards the safety of the Roman camp. At the same time, the six tribunes trailing behind their consul also caught sight of him, and seeing the imminent danger, formed line to block his passage. To make matters worse for him — if this was possible — equites began pouring out of the western gate.

Sphax had come to kill, and nothing would deflect him from that purpose. Nudging Aethon's flanks, he veered to the south, skirting the line of horsemen blocking his path. He would overtake Flaminius, circle around and charge him from the front. All he needed was one throw, and speed was on his side — Aethon was thundering faster than he'd ever ridden her.

But the tribunes had other ideas. Seeing the danger, they were trying to head him off. On their big stallions they'd soon overtaken the consul and once more formed a wall of spears between Sphax and his quarry. He'd won the race for the camp, but faced the same enemy.

Behind him the air suddenly erupted with a cacophony of trumpet calls as legionaries were summoned to arms. All around the alarms of war reverberated. To stand still was to die.

Now beyond thought or reason, only blind rage spoke to him, and it urged him forwards.

Levelling his saunion he raced for the centre of the line of tribunes, selecting a target. If the six horsemen had charged him at the same time, the issue would have been decided instantly. The only way to meet a Numidian charge was to fight fire with fire, to stand still was to invite death.

Twenty paces from the enemy line Sphax flung his saunion at the throat of a mail-clad tribune. As the leather thong released its deadly burden and the saunion began spinning towards its mark he thrust himself backwards on the mare, nudging her to the left. But Aethon was not Dido.

Within two strides Dido would have come to a standstill and completely changed direction, keeping her safe from thrusting spears. But Aethon hadn't had the years of training he'd devoted to Dido, and now the poor creature was going to pay for Sphax's utter recklessness with her life.

In an agony of horror, he realised her turn would bring her much too close to the enemy. Spears flew by, missing him, but one lodged deep in the mare's neck. Staggering, she let out a cry that could only be described as a scream, a fountain of blood pouring from the wound. Bravely she managed two more strides before her forelegs gave way and she collapsed, flinging Sphax from her back.

For a heartbeat he was too dazed to move. With a last effort of will he forced himself to his feet and reaching over his shoulder, drew his sword, prepared to meet his own death.

But something strange was happening, instead of closing in for the kill, the tribunes were backing their stallions away. Hearing the thunder of hooves behind him, Sphax half turned to see a volley of Numidian javelins whistling over his head. Amidst shrieks of pain four tribunes slumped in their saddles before crashing to the ground; the other fled with a javelin still lodged in his arm.

His last sight of that bronze helmet with its golden crest and crimson tassels was of it disappearing behind ranks of hastati, drawn up as in battle.

'Quick lad!' In a daze he recognised Jugurtha's voice. 'We have to get out of here. Now!'

But all Sphax could see was the body of his beautiful golden mare, his beloved Aethon, twitching with pain in her death throes. He couldn't bear her suffering. With a heart-wrenching cry of despair he plunged his dragon sword into her heart to speed her passing.

Agbal handed him the reins of one of the tribunes' stallions. 'We must go *now*, capt'n. Otherwise you'll get us all killed!'

Somehow he managed to get into the saddle, allowing Agbal to lead him like a child across the empty plain towards the grove of trees they'd hidden in before the onset of his madness. Jugurtha and the rest of his rescuers seemed to head off in a different direction.

There in the safety of the trees they waited: he, like a lifeless corpse whose soul had taken flight, whilst Agbal paced and fretted. At last the rest of his eshrin returned.

'Hannon is slain,' cried Jugurtha, tears unashamedly coursing down his cheeks, 'along with Juba and Vermina. They died as Numidians should, honourably in battle. In memory they will live forever, and I will tell their stories so long as I have breath in my body.'

As the light slowly drained from the world and they entered the shadowlands, they rode wearily back to camp. Sphax had no recollection of the journey.

When campfires were lit later that evening he slumped onto the nearest bench and stared at the flames. Food and drink were offered. He refused. Sleep was out of the question, but at some stage during the night he remembered someone placing a blanket around his shoulders.

That's how Maharbal found him, shortly after dawn.

'Jugurtha came to see me last night and told me what had happened.' The general's handsome face looked particularly careworn that morning, but his piercing grey eyes had lost none of their sharpness. 'What were you thinking?'

All around them the sound and smells of corn being ground and baked on iron paddles over campfires filled the pungent air. It was a time of day he always relished. But not this morning. His men were deliberately giving the two of them a wide berth.

'I wasn't thinking,' were the first words Sphax had uttered since he'd plunged his sword into Aethon's flank.

'No,' observed Maharbal, flatly, not intending the word as a reproof. 'None of your men knew the part Flaminius Nepo played in the deaths of your parents. They do now.'

Sphax avoided the general's gaze. *He* was responsible for the deaths of three of his men, not Flaminius. Nothing he could ever say or do could possibly redeem his actions yesterday. He knew that now.

'Tannith pene ba 'al hamūn,' Maharbal intoned.

'Our flaming goddess with the face of Baal,' Sphax translated from the Tassynt. He'd once stared into the goddess' blood-soaked eyes and lived to tell the tale, though such a sight was usually a harbinger of one's own death. 'I was not possessed by the goddess, Sir, just the mortal evils of madness and revenge. And if proof were needed, I still live.'

'You owe your life to Hannon, not the goddess,' the general said gently. 'You need to honour his sacrifice, and the two that fell by his side, not sink into some black despair of your own making. They should be feasted, their lives treasured in memory … stories told of brave deeds and acts of courage … toasts drunk and fair speeches made. Not this! Not this … pit of despond, lad.'

Maharbal glared at him. 'Just look at the state of you! Hannon would be ashamed, and you give his soul no rest. His death was for a purpose. Honour that purpose.'

'I don't even know what happened,' whispered Sphax. 'My men haven't told me.'

Sighing, the general shook his head, but eventually took pity on the lad. 'According to Jugurtha, Hannon flew after you, shaming the rest into following him. Whereas you only had eyes for that bastard of a consul, he could see your greatest threat was pouring out of the western gate. Whilst Jugurtha and a few others rode to your rescue, Hannon himself led what was left of your eshrin against three times their number drawn up in battle before the gate. Only your eshrin would dare to take on such odds.'

Rising from the stool Sphax's men had found for him, the general felt the need to take a turn around it before resuming his seat and continuing. 'It was with pride that Jugurtha told me that after their second charge the field was strewn with Roman dead. Hannon and the others are heroes, not victims of your undoubted folly! Can't you see that?'

This offered not a crumb of comfort to Sphax. In his eyes, Hannon was a martyr for an unworthy cause. And it grieved him to the point of despair that his body, along with those of Juba and Vermina, would be stripped and tossed idly into some common pit without their due rites of passing, a ceremony sacred to all Numidians.

Maharbal could see he was wasting his breath. 'I will not indulge your self-pity by relieving you of command. Your eshrins will continue south as ordered,' and before turning on his heels, added, 'In the name of Ba 'al Hamūn, you will hold a feast for your eshrin to honour your fallen comrades. I don't suppose you've noticed, but amongst your many failings you're also gaining a reputation for miserliness!'

Even in his present state this last remark stung. After their exploits in Pharos and Epidamnos this winter, Sphax had become rich beyond measure. But he'd been generous with his wealth, sharing it with his companions, Hannon, Jugurtha and Agbal. All three had acquired the means to buy the richest farmland in Numidia and live out the rest of their lives at ease, far from the tribulations of war. Yet all three had chosen to stay and follow him.

There was no denying the fact that his dire warnings had prevented his men from plundering villages. The theft of a few trinkets had never worried him, but as night follows day, drink follows plunder, and they were passing through an area where wine flowed more freely that water.

Was he being unfair? Had his orders amount to *miserliness*?

The day after taking up Maharbal's challenge to wage war with honour, he remembered staring at burning fields of wheat when a new thought had occurred; one so dark and insidious he had difficulty contemplating its implications, let alone facing the bitter truth it held.

Unlike all those around him, Sphax was not inured to the savagery of war. He hadn't been present during the butchery that marked the storming of Saguntum, or witnessed the mass crucifixions his uncle sometimes inflicted on his enemies. Remembering the sea of moaning wounded and dead at the end of the battle of the Trebia was enough to turn his stomach. What had Maharbal said? 'For the sake of your soul, remember this sight.'

Could one ever become accustomed to such sights, inured to them, indifferent? For the sake of his soul he hoped not, if only to hang on to that last vestige of hope for honour and justice. But he'd seen for himself how in times of war these qualities hung by a slender thread.

So long as there was war, the burning would continue, and with the burning would come the slaughter of innocents. This was the pitiless face of Ares.

In his current state, racked by guilt and remorse, he'd become easy prey to such dark thoughts. They haunted him as mercilessly as the image of his quivering sword poised above Aethon's flank, or the thought that Hannon's pierced and bloody body would be tossed into some abandoned cesspit.

He wasn't fit company. Staying aloof from his own men and the rest of his captains, in the day he issued the few orders required of him, and through the lonely watches of the night sat alone before his campfire until sheer exhaustion delivered him into the arms of sleep. He yearned for Corinna, ached for her, but Sphax would have to confront his demons alone.

Luckily, his Numidians had other things on their mind. By now they'd burned a smouldering swathe of land south of the city of Cortona, leaving Arretium miles beyond, yet Flaminius and his legions still hadn't left the sanctuary of its walls. The question was on everyone's lips: what would he do? Sit tight and await the arrival of Consul Servilius, or come out and fight? The men could talk of little else.

On the fourth morning after Maharbal's visit, he came upon a sight that stirred even deeper memories. In the middle of a mean street of storehouses and humble wooden dwellings stood the charred remains of what in its heyday had been a grand stabulum, boasting a paved courtyard, well-appointed stables and rooms for twenty guests. Sphax was all too aware of its history, because almost a year ago to the day, he'd burnt it to the ground.

Sliding from Dido's flank to poke around in the ashes, he idly wondered what had become of mistress

Clodia, wife of Marcus, a vicious ex-legionary, horse-thief and proprietor of the establishment. Sphax had spent the night there, stabling Dido and Arion, the magnificent stallion he was taking to Hannibal as a gift, but when he went to saddle up Arion next morning, he was greeted by a leering Marcus wielding his old legionary blade. The stallion wasn't going anywhere, Marcus had told him. Sphax was no match for the ex-legionary. Somehow he'd managed to escape.

What happened next had proved to be a fateful moment, his first real test of courage.

As he stood amongst the charred remains, Sphax was assailed by vivid memories of the night he'd returned and not only rescued Arion, but a waif of a slave girl into the bargain. He'd intended firing a few rooms in the stabulum as a diversion to get Marcus out of the stables where he was guarding Arion. But the slave girl who caught him red-handed in the act, had other ideas. After years of beatings at the hands of her brutal master and mistress, she would settle for nothing less than burning the place to the ground. Only later did he discover the girl's name was Fionn.

'I have need of a guide. Ride with me, Nephew,' commanded a voice, distant, almost disembodied.

Startled out of his reverie, Sphax turned and found himself staring up into the limpid brown eyes of Arion. As if a raw nerve had been plucked like the string of a lyre, a shiver ran down the length of his spine.

NINETEEN

'Memories?' Hannibal guessed.

'Ones I would prefer not to recollect, Sir,' sighed Sphax.

'I wish we could be selective about such things, Nephew, but alas, our memories have a life of their own. Coming to terms with a troubled past is one thing, but clinging to regrets we have no power to change is quite another.'

'I fear you're right, Sir, nevertheless …' whistling for Dido. Instantly his faithful mare stopped grazing and cantered up to him, hooves now fully recovered from her ordeal in the swamp.

'Your memories are what I'm relying on today, Sphax. You are the only person in my army who's recently journeyed to where my geographers tell me is a vast inland lake.' Sphax guessed that Maharbal had also had a hand in this.

At a discreet distance behind them, a score of companion cavalry followed, flying the crescent-and-sun standards of Carthage. To his immense relief, Hannibal hadn't mentioned Sphax's tirade in the swamp. He hoped the incident had been forgotten.

Mounting Dido he shouted over to Jugurtha to take command of his eshrin until he returned, then turning to his uncle explained, 'The lake you refer to is called Trasimene, Sir, and the road we are about to take through the hills leads to its shores. Beyond lies the city of Perusia, and beyond that the Via Flaminia … and Rome itself.' Intrigued, Sphax added, 'Is this your intention, Uncle?'

Hannibal almost smiled, 'I like to keep my enemies guessing, that's all. Describe in detail the route we are to follow.'

For the best part of half an hour Sphax described from memory the route they were to follow, answering a battery of questions as to the state of the roadway, its elevation, twists and turns.

When last he'd ridden this stretch of road between the lake and the Appian he recalled the heavens had opened and torrential rain had soaked every stitch he had on, drenching him to the bone. This morning the day was set fair and he found the thickly wooded valley they were following easy on the eye. After the acrid smell of smoke and charred wood, even the air smelled sweet and renewed. He decided this was just what he needed; a pleasant diversion from the dark thoughts that had haunted him of late.

His uncle had the most remarkable mind Sphax had ever encountered. Widely read and knowledgeable on subjects as diverse as geography and natural philosophy, his conversation was never dull, and often full of insight and wisdom.

He knew that Hannibal sorely missed his scholarly companions, Sosylos and Silenos. Both of whom were too frail and elderly to have risked the Arnus marshes, so he'd had to leave them behind in Bona until it was safe for them to cross in high summer. Besides their long friendship, Silenos was also his uncle's tutor, and Sosylos was meticulously recording their campaign for posterity. It was a rare mind that would take a tutor and a historian on campaign. It spoke volumes for his uncle's reverence for learning and knowledge, unlike the barbarians they were at war with.

Whenever the opportunity arose, Hannibal preferred to practise his Greek. So other than a few commands to his escort in Punic, Greek was the language they spoke all day. At midday they sat briefly beside the bubbling stream they'd been following to eat a frugal meal of bread and soft goat's cheese.

From here Sphax knew the road rose steadily to the summit of a pass that would give them their first sight of the waters of Trasimene. When they reached that point some two hours later his uncle raised a hand to bring everyone to a halt. Gazing to the south his uncle slipped back into his more familiar Punic. 'It's truly a formidable body of water, Nephew. Are the hills to the north and west of its shores as steep as they appear from here?'

Switching to Punic, Sphax replied, 'Especially to the southwest, where the road narrows to a corridor between the lakeshore and the hills that rise immediately above it. Only goats can live amongst the thorns and scrub on those steep slopes.'

'Let's see for ourselves.' From the head of the pass the road dropped steeply until the sides of the valley broadened and the going became easier. Narrow and in poor repair, at times the roadway was no better than a rutted cart track and they had to ride in single file. At last they reached the flat water meadows beside the lakeshore where his uncle halted and gazed west, following the course of the shoreline.

'Where is that narrow section you mentioned?' asked his uncle, returning to Greek.

'About five miles to the south-west, Sir,' he replied, pointing.

'Then let us exercise our horses,' and with that Hannibal dug his knees into Arion's flanks and the stallion bounded into a canter.

Dido struggled to keep up and began to drift behind, but the going was flat and easy, and Sphax knew his mare could keep up this pace far longer than the stallion. Half a mile ahead a spur from the mountains swept down to the lake and the road began to ascend to clear the ridge.

Smiling to himself, Sphax belatedly realised his uncle had thrown down a challenge. It was now a race for the ridge. Nudging Dido into a gallop he began gaining on the stallion, but Arion was the victor, if only by a length. Hannibal was smiling, flushed and exhilarated from the exercise.

Reining in the stallion once more his uncle asked, 'Is this the stretch you pointed out from the pass?'

'Yes, Uncle. Once you cross that stream down there, the road follows the shoreline for about four miles before it turns east, away from the lake and climbs that low lying ridge you see in the distance. Beyond that lies Perusia, less than two hours on horseback.'

Side by side they rode down the gentle grassy slope and splashed across the shallow river. A mile beyond, Hannibal again reined in Arion, but this time he dismounted and began unstrapping his helmet, sword and breastplate.

'Wait here,' he grunted, and without another word began climbing up the steep slope, quickly disappearing into the scrubby bushes and thick undergrowth that covered the hillside.

'Where are you going? Sir … wait!' But it was too late, there was no sign of him. Sphax was left wondering what to do. Should he follow? Even if he tried it would be almost impossible to find him amongst the tangle of thickets and scrub. Hannibal's companion guard caught up with him.

'Where's he gone now?' grumbled Annaeus, his uncle's standard bearer.

'Probably for a shit,' laughed one of the men.

'I wouldn't bare my arse in that tangle of thorns,' another pointed out.

'I think he's gone to climb the ridge, Annaeus,' said Sphax, at a loss what to do. 'Do you think I should follow him?'

For a moment the standard bearer squinted upwards, taking in the steepness of the climb and the impenetrable undergrowth. 'No, lad,' he sighed. 'Leave him to it. Your uncle never does anything without a sound purpose. Beyond a few scratches, he can't come to much harm. We'll wait here for him.'

But there wasn't much room to wait anywhere, other than a narrow strip of land between the water's edge and where the hill rose abruptly in a tangle of scrub. Sphax dismounted and paced it out. He counted fifteen strides, barely space for four Numidians to charge abreast. Staring to the south he could see that in places the strip was even narrower.

Sliding back on to Dido he nudged her cautiously into the lake, relieved to see the bottom shelved into deep water very gradually. When the waters reached her hocks he halted and nudged her around. They were now some thirty paces from the shoreline and Sphax had a much better view of the hillside.

At times like this he envied Agbal's sharp eyesight. But even he could see that the scrub and bushes were not as extensive as they were on the lower slopes. Higher up he could clearly see barren patches of bracken and rough grass as the hill rose steeply to the ridgeline. Though he peered into the distance until his eyes began to water with the strain, there was no sign of his uncle. Giving up, he nudged Dido to wade back to the shoreline.

As the afternoon dragged on, ribald laughter slowly turned to genuine concern as the men searched around them for a sight of their general. Only Annaeus seemed unconcerned.

During his second scouting mission along the lakeshore, Sphax suddenly heard a distant cheer. Guessing what had happened he urged Dido to the gallop and returned to find Annaeus helping his uncle on with his gilded breastplate and helmet. Other than his disheveled appearance and a couple of scratches on his cheeks, Hannibal looked none the worse for his adventure.

Without a word of explanation for his absence, Hannibal simply glanced at Annaeus and commanded, 'I've seen enough. We shall return to camp. If we're to keep the light we must ride with all speed.'

As a body they set off immediately, stepping out briskly. Sphax rode beside Hannibal, but found his uncle distracted, absorbed in a world of his own and barely taking in his surroundings. He'd seen that look on Hannibal's face before; what he could only describe as rapt concentration, like someone working out a complex geometrical problem in their mind's eye. He tried on a couple of occasions to start a conversation, but all he got by way of reply was a desultory grunt, so he gave up and left his uncle to his thoughts.

Shadows were lengthening as they began the long descent from the pass. They'd been riding at a swift canter when Hannibal abruptly slowed Arion to a walk and turned towards him. 'When you crossed the Trebia with your eshrins that night and attacked the Roman camp, how did you find your way? I recall there wasn't much of a moon that night. It must have been pitch black.'

Sphax was taken aback, not so much by the question, but the earnest intensity in Hannibal's tone. For a moment he simply stared blankly at his uncle before gathering his wits and recollecting the events that evening.

'To cross the river we were aided by Gala's cylinders,' he began. 'Gala's an eshrin captain who owns two bronze cylinders that contain oil lamps. These devices are ingenious … and were invaluable that evening. The concentric sides of the cylinders can be slid open to reveal more light, or closed to allow the merest sliver to be seen. This way the light can be directed to where an enemy would never see it. They have simple carrying handles and are about a foot tall by six inches in diameter. Even on a windy night the oil lamps inside are shielded, so will never blow out.

'I've pondered these lamps many times since then, Sir. They would be most useful for operations at night. Gala's cylinders could easily be simplified and replicated using a simple lidded clay pot, drilled with holes that could be covered or uncovered as necessary. All you would need to do is attach carrying handles and place an oil lamp inside. This way it would be possible to set up a series of beacons to guide men in complete darkness. They could be positioned to warn of obstacles or where a path became difficult … I truly believe their uses are legion!'

Sphax was excited now. For months he'd longed to talk about these ideas, and now he had the ear of Hannibal himself, hanging on his every word.

'Will you bring one of these cylindrical devices to me first thing tomorrow? I would like to examine it. Engineer Bostar should also be present.'

'Certainly, Sir. Gala will consider it an honour that you've shown an interest in his instruments.'

'Then that's settled.' Hannibal seemed more than satisfied. 'And you're quite right, Sphax, generals like myself balk at night operations because of the difficulty of leading men in darkness. Usually such operations descend into chaos and confusion. But if such devices could be used to guide men into position, it would change the face of war. I believe darkness is a weapon as powerful as the javelin. We should harness it!'

At that moment they both froze. Somewhere ahead they could hear the unmistakable sound of hoofbeats.

'To me, Annaeus!' yelled Hannibal. 'Draw swords and form line.'

Sphax fumbled for his throwing thong and selected a javelin, all the while listening to the sound of hoofbeats growing ever closer. Whoever they were they were galloping flat out. Because the roadway curved gradually to the north, the densely forested valley prevented them seeing any further than three hundred paces ahead.

At last they came within sight. All thirty of them. 'They're Numidians,' Sphax shouted, and as they drew closer he recognised Himilco. Turning to his uncle. 'It's Himilco, one of my captains. Something must be afoot for him to be leading his entire eshrin at such a pace.'

Sliding from his mare in one sinuous movement, Himilco strode over and stood before Hannibal. 'I come directly from Maharbal, Sir. At midday Consul Flaminius left Arretium with his army. Our scouts counted two Roman legions and two of alae. He's coming after us, general.'

Hannibal laughed. Not a pleasant sound, and one that conveyed triumph rather than humour. Raising his voice so all could hear he declared, 'The game has begun. We will lead Flaminius by the nose like a pig before we turn around and destroy him. Utterly!'

Cheers broke out amongst the Numidians as well as the companion cavalry. His uncle never wasted an opportunity for theatre! Turning to Himilco he thanked him for the good news and the speed with which he'd been informed of it. To Annaeus he said, 'Ride on with these Numidians. I need a moment alone with my nephew. We will catch up shortly.'

Sphax felt suddenly anxious. He'd been alone with his uncle for much of the day. Why choose now, of all times?

When the sounds of hooves had retreated into the distance, Hannibal turned gravely towards him and held his gaze. 'Maharbal told me what happened outside the walls of Arretium a few days ago.' Sphax's heart sank. 'I will say this only once, Nephew, then it will never be spoken of again. If I lead Consul Flaminius by the nose like a pig, he leads you by the scruff of your neck! You are not in control of your actions. *He* is! You must break this hold he has over you. Otherwise Maharbal and I will never be able to trust you again. Do you understand?'

Drained of colour and utterly shaken, Sphax barely managed a nod.

* * *

'Remarkable,' muttered Hannibal for the fourth time, sliding the bronze bars of Gala's cylinders open again to reveal a broad beam of lamplight from the Greek lamp burning inside. 'What is the purpose of the perforations in the lid, Bostar?'

His uncle's chief engineer frowned. Asked to determine the strength of a bridge or specify the number of trees to be felled to construct a watchtower, he would be ready with an answer. But explaining away the peculiar properties of this delicate mechanism was quite beyond him.

Sphax intervened. 'There is a long-standing theory by Aristotle, Uncle, stating that if a flame is denied the sub-element of phlogiston from the air, it will be extinguished. I believe that's the reason for the perforations in the lid; so that even when the cylinder is sealed, the flame will not be starved of air.'

'Have we not been given the perfect opportunity to test Aristotle's theory, Sphax?'

Equally curious of the outcome, Sphax reached for his cloak, packing it tightly over and around one of the cylinders. After counting out loud to fifty, he removed the cloak and lid from the cylinder: the flame had been extinguished.

Hannibal was smiling. 'It would appear we have proved Aristotle correct, and at the same time found a way to douse a flame as effective as water. Like you, Nephew, I have always found natural philosophy a fascinating study.' To Bostar he continued, 'Returning to more pressing matters, do you think this instrument could be replicated using simple clay pots with holes drilled on three sides that could be covered or uncovered … by a cloth, or something similar, perhaps? It would need a lid and handle, of course.'

'I don't see why not, Sir,' agreed Bostar, now on much firmer ground. 'Such items are readily available, and quite capable of holding a small lamp, if not a candle. And clay is an easy material to cut or drill. How many of these lanterns might you require?'

'There's the rub, Bostar. I will need at least sixty. One hundred would be better.'

For an instant the chief engineer's jaw dropped, but he soon recovered. 'I'll get my men working on a solution immediately.'

'You have my full authority to go round the camps and requisition whatever you need, Bostar.'

'Then with your permission, Sir, I will take my leave and begin work.' Bowing low he opened the double doors of the vestibule, suddenly flooding the room where they'd conducted the investigation with light.

Sphax doused the flame in Gala's remaining cylinder and followed his uncle and Maharbal into the atrium of the former estate where Hannibal had taken up residence. His uncle needed little in terms of comfort and despised ostentation, so he and Maharbal found themselves sharing a hard wooden bench in a room that had almost certainly been furnished with comfortable divans.

'I had no idea you had an interest in Gala's *toys*, Hannibal. Are you planning a night operation?' Maharbal enquired.

'I'm just considering every contingency, my friend, that's all.'

Sphax was intrigued. Manufacturing up to a hundred of those lanterns was quite an undertaking! What contingency had his uncle in mind?

'With our compliant consul now in tow,' Hannibal continued, 'we have the initiative, and I intend to lead him on a merry dance. He will now be thinking this is a race for Rome. Flaminius will drive his men by forced marches, hoping to catch us up or even overtake us. That way he can block our path to that city.

'Rome is due south, so I intend to strike out westwards towards the lake we scouted yesterday. That will keep Flaminius guessing. Beyond the lake lies the city of Perusia, and beyond that the Flaminian Way. I'm convinced that by now Consul Servilius will have received news of our army. If he is to join forces with Flaminius, his legions will have to march south along the Flaminian. There is no other road from Ariminum! If we position ourselves in the vicinity of Perusia, we'll be within striking distance of both consular armies, and can pick them like ripe fruit, one at a time.'

Hannibal had taken to wearing a leather patch over his sightless eye, held in place by a thin cord tied behind his head. If anything, it seemed to exaggerate his gaunt and severe appearance, focusing all attention on his one good eye, blazing forth more brightly than ever.

Maharbal had been nodding attentively as Hannibal outlined his intentions. Now he asked, 'Where do you want me and the cavalry?'

'In the rear, keeping a close watch on Flaminius and his legions.'

Nodding, Maharbal rose to take his leave and Sphax followed suit.

'Not so fast, Nephew!' snapped Hannibal, still with his eye fixed on Maharbal. 'I want this young hothead kept as far away from Flaminius as possible.'

Turning towards him with that thin smile of his — Sphax had grown wary of that smile — 'I want you to ride at speed with your ten eshrins and set up camp where the road leaves the lakeshore for Perusia; the area you described to me yesterday. From there you will send eshrins west to the Via Flaminia. I want that road watched night and day. Captains will report to you every day. Is that clear?' Sphax nodded.

'And make sure your men stay well clear of Perusia. There's little point in alerting them of our presence until it's strictly necessary.'

So, thought Sphax, he was only to be trusted if kept at arm's length from his sworn enemy. He could hardly blame them. All this was of his own making.

They set out immediately after Sphax had gathered his captains together and passed on Hannibal's orders. Relieved to be free from the all-pervasive stench of smoke and ash, his men were soon breathing pure forest air.

The day could not have been more perfect, with a gentle cooling breeze offsetting the heat of the sun blazing down from a cloudless sky. He rode in the company of Himilco and Hiempsal at the head of his eshrin. Reaching the head of the pass the three of them gazed down at the lake bathed in low-lying mist.

The heat of the day had burned off most of the mist swirling above the surface of the water, but where it still lingered by the shore it made progress cold, damp and unpleasant. A few miles beyond the spot where Hannibal had climbed the ridge they were all relieved when Sphax led them away from the shore to a low-lying hill overlooking the lake and its dispiriting mist. The effect was like climbing out of a damp cellar into warm sunshine, and once above the mist, the views around the lake were magnificent.

Once the brow of the hill was reached the ground dipped to form a natural grassy amphitheatre, dotted here and there with stands of birch and willow. An entire army could camp here with room to spare, and fresh water would never be a problem.

Except for positioning a rope-line for the scores of pack-horses carrying their tents and baggage, Sphax never supervised encampments. Numidians despised the Roman obsession with straight lines and rigid uniformity. Eshrins generally pitched their tents close together, but there were no rules to this, and sometimes two or three eshrins clustered together to share campfires.

As for their mares, they were simply turned out to graze at their leisure or trot down to the lake to drink. They never strayed far, and a simple call or whistle would be enough to return them to their masters.

The duty roster for eshrins watching the Via Flaminia had been decided by drawing lots at the captain's meeting that morning. Manissa had drawn the short straw, but as he and Gala were virtually inseparable, Gala cheerily volunteered to share this odious duty with his friend. Two days had been agreed as a fair stretch for such a tedious task, so Manissa and Gala would be away for four. This was unknown territory for Numidians, so Sphax would have to go along as guide.

Anxious not to be seen from the gates and roads emanating from the city he gave Perusia a wide berth, sticking to woods and little-known tracks as they headed south-west. Luckily he knew the area well. Returning alone, it was the sight of the great temple of Juno crowning Perusia's hilltop that first put the idea into his head. By the time he arrived back at camp, he'd made up his mind.

Saying nothing to his eshrin, he simply asked them to call their mares. Only Agbal gave him a quizzical glance, the rest of his men accepted their delinquent captain was up to his old tricks.

Seeing his men mount up, Himilco strode over, an anxious frown playing about his lips. Sphax grinned down at him. 'You're in charge tonight. We'll be back tomorrow morning,' but seeing the man's sour expression deepen, he added. 'Don't look so worried, Himilco, the rest of the army won't arrive until tomorrow afternoon at the earliest.'

'But where are you going, Sphax?' griped an exasperated Himilco.

'To a feast.' That did raise eyebrows amongst his own men.

TWENTY

It was just as he remembered. Marked by porticoed columns, the grand entrance to the villa Myrteta opened to a vestibule, beyond which a paved walkway led to a similar entrance at the rear, dividing the inner courtyard into two carefully tended peristyle gardens. Around this square were arranged the living quarters, bedrooms and library, besides opulent dining and reception rooms. Only now could Sphax truly appreciate that no expense had been spared in the design and construction of this country estate.

As the sun began to set in the west, its golden glow was reflected in the polished columns of marble, their capitals finished in Corinthian flourishes. Above this a triangular pediment, painted in deep blue, carried a white stucco emblem of the hearth, symbolising Vesta, goddess of the home and family life.

Some way from the villa he recognised a familiar sight: the stable block! This backed onto a huge granary and storehouses, and beyond that an extensive fish pond. Sphax could count on the fingers of one hand the number of times he'd entered the villa. Filthy slaves like him were fit only for the stables or the farm labourers' huts, where they were chained like animals at night after toiling in the fields from dawn.

It had been two years since he'd last set eyes on his former owner's estate. Staring at the place in the twilight, it felt to Sphax a lifetime ago.

To escape the stink and unbearable summer heat of Rome, every year Gaius Lucilus and his entire family would decamp to his Umbrian estate until the cool of autumn stirred, or the lack of gossip or rumour of an election in the senate got the better of him. At least here there were no chariot races to lose, ergo fewer beatings.

Lamps were being lit in the villa, but the rolling vineyards and fields of corn that stretched endlessly to the horizon were empty and deserted. It would be different in a week or so when the corn was ready to harvest.

His men had fallen into an uneasy silence, confused as to why their captain had brought them to such a place. Jugurtha, the elderly statesman of the eshrin, confronted him. 'In the name of Ba 'al Hamūn, Captain, what are we doing here?'

Despite the turmoil of half-remembered memories swirling in his head, Sphax managed to laugh. 'This is the Myrteta estate, and before you stands the grand villa of my former master, Gaius Lucilus. By my reckoning he owes me recompense for ten years of injury, beatings and misery.' Sphax rolled down his sleeve to remind them of the fugitus sign branded on his forearm. 'Tonight he will begin repayment of this debt! This evening Lucilus will host the most splendid feast you've ever attended. A feast to honour Hannon, Juba and Vermina. Tonight you will toast their memory with his wines, sit in his magnificent couches, and from his best silver, eat the finest food his cooks have ever prepared. Lucilus never paid a servant or freed a slave in his life. So remember, every person you meet, from the chief steward to the lowliest kitchen maid is a slave. Do them no harm and treat them with courtesy, for tomorrow I will set them free.'

'What if this Gaius Lucilus and his family are there, Captain?' smirked Agbal. 'What will you do then?'

'Invite them to the feast, of course!' This met with a great deal of laughter. 'It would be rude not to … and we have so much to talk about.' With their army burning Etruria and marching south, deep into Italia, it was highly unlikely the family were in residence. Lucilus would be with his equites in one of the consular armies.

Sphax drew his blade. 'I'm not expecting trouble, but at least try to *look* like soldiers, not a bunch of Scythian door slaves!'

Even in his wildest daydreams, Sphax could never have imagined he would have the satisfaction of leading an eshrin of Numidian cavalry into the courtyard of Lucilus' villa. For the first time since that dark day before the walls of Arretium, he smiled to himself as he nudged Dido up the steps and into the high-ceilinged vestibule.

As more of his men clattered into the room on horseback, the walls echoed to the sound of hoofbeats on polished marble. Then all was confusion as doors were suddenly flung open and a dozen men and women burst into the room before freezing like statues to stare and gawp.

'Who are you?' asked an elderly man dressed in a grubby toga.

Still mounted on Dido, Sphax glared at the man. 'I am Sphax, Prince of Numidia and nephew of my commander, Hannibal Barca.' At this a wave of horror gripped the crowd as if a judge had passed a sentence of execution on them all. Instinctively, he knew they were all about to make a run for it.

Quickly he slid from Dido and sheathed his sword. 'I swear that none of you will be harmed if you do what I ask. We are not here to loot or pillage, or do you any injury. You are quite safe. And will remain so until we leave in the morning.' Turning to Grubby Toga he asked, 'And who might you be?'

'I … I am, Servius … Sir,' stammered the man. 'Assistant to the chief steward, Titus Calvus.'

'And what in your opinion, good Servius, is the largest and grandest room in the villa?'

'Why … the Trojan room, Sir,' he replied tartly, surprised Sphax hadn't heard of it. 'It can seat up to fifty guests and has magnificent murals and furnishings.'

'Then be so good as to conduct me and my men to the Trojan room, so we can view its splendour.' Smiling broadly, Sphax gestured for Servius to lead the way, then turned to his men. 'Dismount and follow me.' Two of the mares had already despoiled the beautiful marble floor. 'Gauda, Adherbal … lead our ladies into the courtyard gardens. There'll be something there for them to graze on.'

By now the crowd that had gathered seemed to have overcome their worst fears and were chattering away like door slaves. Sphax could hear the word *Numidian* being bandied about, so possibly they were questioning the fearsome reputation his people had gained in the eyes of Rome!

Following Servius down a broad corridor lit by stands of candles, the assistant to the chief steward paused momentarily before painted double doors before flinging them open with a dramatic flourish. 'The Trojan room, Sir.'

Unfortunately, his theatricality misfired. Opening the doors revealed nothing more than gloom and darkness. Grabbing candles, Servius and the villa's staff trooped into the room and began lighting candles and Greek lamps, proud to show the place off in its true glory.

Sphax blinked. This was no dining room. It was a banqueting hall. And 'magnificent' hardly did the Trojan room justice. It was a shrine, a homage to Helen of Troy.

He would never have guessed that beyond a passion for chariot racing, Gaius Lucilus was obsessed with Helen and the Iliad. From floor to ceiling every wall was adorned with painted murals, exquisitely done and so life-like they took his breath away. Wherever his eyes rested, Helen's seductive smile stared back. Those lovely eyes seemed to follow him round the room. A love-struck Paris holding her hand. Standing naked beside Aphrodite. Staring from the prow of a trireme bound for Troy. The hall was nothing less than a love poem to Helen … *the most beautiful thing on this dark earth.*

And on the mosaic floor, to be trodden underfoot, depictions of her would-be rescuers: Menelaus, Achilles and Odysseus. There was little doubt which side Gaius Lucilus was on.

Overall, there was something unnerving, almost uncomfortable about the room's exquisite beauty. Something he couldn't quite understand. Then it struck him. For the first time in his life he'd caught a glimpse of his ex-master's inner life, his imagination, perhaps even his humanity. But to Sphax he'd always been a monster. It was this that he couldn't come to terms with.

Clapping his hands to gain everyone's attention, Sphax raised his voice. 'Servius, would you summon all the villa's staff to gather in this hall so I may address you all? That means everyone! From the humblest door slave to Titus Calvus. And bring the estate manager, Crassus. I'm eager to talk with him.'

It didn't take long. After the clatter of hooves and all the commotion in the vestibule, most of the household had already wandered into the Trojan room to find out what was going on. Now they stood around in small groups, chattering to each other. Sphax vaguely recognised a few faces, but the stables and household hardly mixed and their duties rarely overlapped, so none of them knew who he was. Except one, who was the last to enter along with Servius and the chief steward.

'Sphax!' exclaimed Crassus, staring at him in astonishment.

'You know this boy?' sneered Titus Calvus, whose toga was not much cleaner than his assistant's. Sphax was amazed that Lucilus allowed his slaves to wear togas. Only freed slaves could become Roman citizens with entitlement to the wearing of a toga. But then the steward would have need of something to keep his bald head warm in winter.

Sphax drew his sword again to silence the muttering that had begun. 'He does, steward. But for the rest of you I'll repeat what I've already said to Servius. I am Sphax, Prince of Numidia and nephew of Hannibal. We are not here to loot or pillage, or do you any injury.'

The muttering began again. 'Silence!' Sphax yelled, fiercely this time. 'My Numidians might not harm you, but thirty miles from here are twenty thousand Insubres and Boii who would take great pleasure in ransacking this place, raping every woman and then selling the lot of you to new masters. And after they'd stripped this villa bare, they would burn it to the ground. Gauls have little use for Roman villas!'

'Then my master and Consul Servilius' legions will wreak a terrible revenge on you and your kind!' screamed Titus.

'Shut this pompous arsehole, up,' Sphax yelled at his men. 'Bind him and lock him in a room. I want him out of my sight.' Roughly manhandling the steward, three Numidians dragged him from the room still mouthing obscenities.

'Then how might we avoid this terrible fate you've predicted for us all?' asked Crassus.

'By fulfilling a simple request. If this is done to my satisfaction, in the morning you will no longer be slaves, but free to go wherever you please. Perhaps to a new life in the south of Italia, far from Rome. Or across the seas, back to the homelands you were taken from. You will be free to choose your own path, your own destiny.'

'But we will not be free,' sighed Crassus, 'we will be fugitives, hunted down by the fugitivari like animals, and if caught, dragged back in chains and branded like you were, Sphax.'

Crassus looked much older than he remembered, his grey hair thinner and his stoop more pronounced. But those grey eyes seemed just as troubled and sorrowful as when Sphax had last gazed into them.

'In normal times that would be true,' agreed Sphax, gazing around at the hushed, grave faces now staring at him. 'But these are *not* normal times, Sir. In weeks, or perhaps even days, Hannibal's army of sixty thousand men will descend on Umbria and destroy anyone foolish enough to stand in our path. Consular armies will be crushed and slaughtered, just as we did at the Ticinus and the Trebia.'

Sphax shook his head. 'This is not an idle boast. I speak from experience. In a week or so Rome will fighting for its life, its very existence. I can assure you that it will not be the fugitivari scouring the countryside, it will be marauding Numidian and Iberian cavalry, and they will not be looking for runaway slaves to brand!'

'And what is your simple request? And how might we fulfil it to your satisfaction?' asked Crassus.

'By providing the most sumptuous feast your household has ever prepared for guests. This is all I ask. I want my men to eat off your best plate, drink Lucilus' finest wines, and eat to their hearts' content. It's been a year since my men faced the Volcae across the Rhodanus, crossed the Alps and routed the legions at the Ticinus and the Trebia. I owe them a feast! Is it too much to ask in return for setting you all free?'

'No,' agreed Crassus, with a faint smile, 'it is a generous bargain.'

Looking around, Sphax was relieved to see that many from the household were grinning at one another. 'Once the feast is prepared, I invite you all to join us to celebrate your freedom. What say you?'

The room suddenly echoed to joyous cheering. Crassus smiled broadly at him. 'I think you have an answer, Sphax.'

'Then fetch tables and benches,' he shouted excitedly, 'Numidians can't abide couches. Light ovens, chop vegetables and roast meat, but above all, bring wine. My men are thirsty!'

'I give you a toast to our fallen comrades,' Sphax proclaimed, rising unsteadily to his feet and mildly slurring his speech. 'To Hannon, Juba and Vermina.'

The words echoed around the hall as they were repeated by twenty-six Numidians with raised silver goblets. True to their word, the household slaves had brought tables and benches to form a board long enough to seat his entire eshrin. Having wolfed their way through oysters, turbot and eggs with spinach, they were now on their fourth course, the pork, and all of them were looking forward to the peacock, which Servius informed them was a rare delicacy. His men had shown as much interested in the solid silver tableware as the food itself. Sphax hadn't told them yet that every dish would be theirs by morning. As for the wines? It would be safe to say they'd drunk none finer and the jug had flowed liberally! He'd lost count of the number of toasts they'd drunk. Even the slaves serving them were weaving around with cups in their hands.

Sphax remained on his feet as the men sunk back

on their benches. 'I'm now going to tell the tale of how I witnessed Hannon run faster than any Olympian athlete has ever achieved in the history of the games. It also concerns Jugurtha, Agbal and the strangest beast I've ever encountered: a black monster twice the height of a man with horns as sharp as a razor and as long as my arms, a demon they call an aurochs—'

'Oh no, Captain!' groaned, Agbal, blushing. 'Not that story …'

'He protests, gentlemen, because this is the only time — and by the gods I hope it's the last — that I witnessed the heroic young Agbal actually shit himself!' Sphax soon had his men roaring with laughter as he described — with colourful invention — the encounter between Hannon, Agbal and Jugurtha, and a fearsome aurochs in the watery wilderness where the river Podanus meets the Adria. It was indeed true that at one point in the proceedings they'd watched in horror as the beast chased Agbal around the trunk of a giant oak. And Hannon *had* sprinted faster than he'd ever seen him run before. But then his life depended on it!

Well after the peacocks had been devoured the stories and toasts continued. One after another his men stood and took the stage. Numidians were consummate storytellers who could hold their audience in the palms of their hands, spellbound, causing them to weep or cheer, laugh or jeer. Most of the tales were comic, and seemed to involve Hannon, Juba or Vermina getting into the most hair-raising scrapes, but as Sphax laughed or jeered along with his men, he sensed his self-inflicted wounds beginning to mend and the bitter anguish drain away. Maharbal had been right all along. His eshrin needed such a night to mourn their loss.

Sphax was pleased to see the household had taken him up on his offer. More than a score of them were reclining on couches pushed to the edge of the hall, cups in hands, finishing off what was left of the banquet. Some were deep in conversation whilst others were watching the antics of his Numidians with amusement. Seeing Crassus sitting by himself in a corner of the hall he wandered over. 'What will you do, Sir?' he asked, sinking into the couch opposite.

Closing his weary eyes the man gravely shook his head. 'If what you say comes to pass—'

'It will, Sir! I must assure you of that,' interjected Sphax, desperately trying to clear his head of the fog of wine.

'Then I will take ship to Corinth. I have friends there. And from Corinth it will be easy to find passage to my home in Lilybaeum.'

'You are Sicilian!' gasped Sphax. If he was taken aback by this, what Crassus said next came as a complete revelation.

'From a noble Carthaginian family who'd lived there for generations,' he revealed, speaking in perfect Punic. 'When the truce was negotiated by your grandfather, Hamilcar, and the legions marched into Lilybaeum, they took hostages, mostly children or young men from noble families. That's how I ended up in Rome, and Crassus seemed a more convenient name than Cathalo. In theory I am not a slave, but a hostage of Rome.'

Sphax was reeling from all this. 'You speak of my grandfather, Hamilcar. Then you have known all along who I was? How?'

'Gaius Lucilus told me.'

Sphax gasped. 'But I was sold as a common slave at a market. I remember it.'

'That's why he bought you. All slaves are identified before their sale.'

In truth, Sphax remembered little of that day. He'd been seven years old, understood not a word of Latin let alone what was happening to him. 'Then his hatred of Numidians and the Barcas must run deep. He used every opportunity to beat me! He made my life unbearable! You saved me from many a beating … you know what he was like. He had me branded a fugitus!'

'It's true that he possesses a cruel streak, and a temper he's never learned to control. But in many ways he was torn between vicious jealousy and admiration. You are of noble blood, a prince, whilst he will always be a lowly plebeian. The highest office he could ever aspire to is that of tribune. And you had skills with horses that he could only dream of.'

This was becoming too much for Sphax. Falling silent he stared at the mosaic depiction of Agamemnon by his feet, a man who was willing to sacrifice his own daughter to summon the wind.

'And he couldn't help comparing you with that worthless son of his,' Crassus quietly explained. 'You and Marcellus were of an age, but whereas you came back with a bloody nose from battles with the crossroad gangs, he slunk home from trips to whorehouses. You were a scholar, studying Greek—'

'He knew about Elpis and Airla?'

'Not only knew, he allowed it.'

'But they never told me, Crassus!'

'They were sworn not to.'

Sphax suddenly felt nauseous. The combination of too much wine and Crassus' revelations were beginning to turn more than his life upside down.

'Lucilus hated the fact that you were everything his son was not. And when Marcellus disappeared with that whore and chest of coin and silver—'

'Which whore?' cried Sphax, wondering if this could get any worse.

'The whore he'd slept with at the popina. She went missing the following day. Lucilus knew that you would make a run for it given half a chance. He talked to Elpis and found out you had discussed the whereabouts of Hannibal's army only a week before your journey to Perusia. He knew you would follow your destiny. And he was right. But as for his son … that Marcellus would run off with a whore. It was more than he could bear!'

Sphax knew he was going to throw up. Staggering to his feet he ran from the hall, along the corridor and into the courtyard gardens where he knelt and vomited. When at last his belly stopped heaving, he got unsteadily to his feet. The night air felt refreshing, but did nothing for his racing thoughts, caught up in a maelstrom of speculation.

Sphax had killed Lucilus' son, Marcellus, and made off with his chest. He'd dumped the body in a swamp in the middle of nowhere, so it had come as no surprise that his corpse had never been discovered. That the whore he'd slept with had also disappeared was just pure coincidence.

What troubled him was his recollection of the events before the Roman camp on the eve of the battle beside the Trebia. Sphax had spotted Gaius Lucilus outside the camp. The man had fled and Sphax had given chase, wounding Gaius' stallion to prevent his escape through the western gate. However, several equites had rushed out to save him. Sphax had killed some of them, but Lucilus had managed to escape. The last sight he'd had of Gaius Lucilus was of him crawling on his belly towards the gate.

Later, Sphax had stood before the same gate and issued a challenge for Lucilus to come out and avenge his son's killing. No one had taken up the challenge.

Now he wasn't sure. About anything.

It had been a dark night. The little he'd seen of the confusing running battles was by torchlight, and Sphax had caught the fleetest of glimpses of Gaius Lucilus. Driven by his deep hatred, perhaps Sphax had wanted it to be Lucilus, had a desperate *need* for it to be Lucilus. No one had answered his challenge, which in itself was shameful. And Crassus had not mentioned any of these events.

The only certainty Sphax felt at that moment was that hatred was blind. Blind hatred twisted and corrupted, preventing you from seeing the truth.

In the centre of the garden he found a pool of water lined with clay tiles, one of his eshrin's mares drinking from it. Kneeling down beside it he cupped his hands and threw water over his face. It felt cool and refreshing, and at last he felt ready to face the world again.

Despite their sore heads, his men were in excellent spirits next morning, sharing out silver plates and goblets, and finding sacks with which to load up their mares. None of the household objected, or even seemed surprised. Silver plates were but a small fraction of the wealth contained within its walls, and Sphax was certain that once they'd left, the rest would be methodically looted.

When he said his farewells to Crassus the sun was high in a clear sky. An hour later an anxious Himilco was waiting for him in camp.

'Has anyone reported in from Gala's or Manissa's eshrins?' asked Sphax.

Himilco shrugged, 'No. Not a word so far.'

'Why is it those two are incapable of following the simplest of orders?'

'They wouldn't be Gala and Manissa if they did,' laughed Himilco, with a forbearance that Sphax didn't share when it came to those two.

'I may have to ride over there myself if no one turns up.'

Himilco nodded, before staring into the distance at something that had caught his eye on the northern shore of the lake. Mist had covered the lake again that morning, but the hot sun was just beginning to burn it off.

'What can you see?' Sphax asked.

'Cavalry. Riding fast. Hundreds of them.'

'Ours or the enemy's?'

'Can't say,' frowned Himilco.

'Then we'd better find out,' snapped Sphax. Striding around their little camp he began yelling, 'Mount up, Numidians. Mount up!'

TWENTY-ONE

When he and Himilco reached a grassy knoll on the ridge where the shoreline began to broaden out they both recognised Maharbal's standard at the head of a long column of Iberian cavalry, snaking its way around the lake's shore. Even though it was well past midday, patches of mist still lingered at the water's edge. As the column drew closer, Sphax saw that Maharbal was riding in company with the Iberian chieftain, Gárgoris.

'This accursed damp mist is not good for my old bones,' grumbled Maharbal, by way of greeting. 'Is it always like this, lad?'

'Most mornings, Sir,' observed Sphax, stifling a grin.

'Old bones my arse,' laughed Gárgoris, 'my bones are a good deal older than yours. You've just grown soft in your dotage, master of horse.' Grinning at Sphax he enquired, 'Have you found us a pretty camp, master Sphax? My men have ridden hard today.'

Since first meeting the chief, Sphax had loved and feared Gárgoris in equal measure. His face alone had more scars and chunks taken out of it than a butcher's block. 'I'm sure your men will find it pleasant enough, Sir.' Nodding towards the lake, 'There's no shortage of fresh water.'

For a while the two veteran cavalrymen gazed over the broad valley that narrowed to where the shallow stream bubbled into the lake. Ahead lay the ridge that Hannibal had climbed, sweeping steeply down to the water's edge, and some five miles to the south, Sphax could just make out the tents of their camp. He pointed them out to Gárgoris.

'Interesting ground,' was all Maharbal would say.

'Dog's twat, general! Cavalry are as much use here as a eunuch in a brothel.'

Maharbal grinned, 'Then we'll have an easy time of it, my friend.'

By mid-afternoon their camp had grown from a few tents to the size of a small town. Pioneers were digging out latrines, hauling dead wood for campfires and hammering posts to carry the miles of rope lines needed for the Iberians' stallions and pack trains. These creatures couldn't be turned out to graze like Numidian jennets.

Sphax smiled at the sight of Maharbal's old pavilion being erected. After the comfort and splendour of the grand villas he'd been quartered in over the last few weeks, his cold and draughty tent would provide an endless source of displeasure for him to grumble about.

At least there had been one piece of good news. Belatedly, a man from Gala's eshrin had reported that nothing of consequence had been seen on the Via Flaminia. When Hannibal arrived he would pass this on.

Sphax didn't have long to wait. In the late afternoon Hannibal thundered into camp at the head of his companion cavalry, their stallions sweating from being ridden hard. His uncle had the appearance of a man in a hurry. The moment he dismounted he began an earnest discussion with Maharbal.

When Sphax strode over his uncle immediately caught his eye. 'Any movement on the Flaminia?'

'None, Sir,' assured Sphax. 'I have two eshrins watching it.'

'Good.' His uncle seemed to make up his mind about something. 'Before we lose the light, Maharbal and I are going to scout the ridge I climbed. I would like you to join us, Nephew. Call your mare.'

Judging from Maharbal's sour expression, this had also come as news to him. By the time he mounted Dido, the two of them were already halfway down the hill where the road to Perusia intersected the ridges.

Once across the paved road the ground rose steeply to the crest of the ridge. They were following nothing better than goat tracks, but the going was easy, only gorse and low growing shrubs hindering their progress.

Riding in single file they soon reached the ridge line where Hannibal dismounted to take a closer look.

With the entire lake revealed, the view was spectacular. Looking north, the ridge seemed to maintain a uniform height, its appearance unbroken save for an occasional rocky outcrop dotted here and there. Its western slopes fell away gradually before plunging steeply into the tangle of stunted trees and scrubby undergrowth at the lake's shoreline. To the east a broad shallow valley ran parallel to the ridge, densely forested in the valley bottom with stone pine and juniper.

All the goat and animal tracks were on the eastern slopes, so Sphax guessed the prevailing winds in these parts came from the west. Animals were not stupid, preferring sheltered paths out of cold winds. Without a word to either of them his uncle remounted Arion, following tracks that led north in the lee of the ridgeline.

Maintaining a resolute silence, neither he nor Maharbal had commented or questioned Hannibal about the purpose of this scouting exercise. After long years of friendship and campaigning together, Maharbal knew Hannibal's mind better than most, so following the general's lead, Sphax kept his mouth shut, feeling he'd been included to observe, not make lame comments, but his patience was growing rather thin.

Two miles later Hannibal repeated the procedure. Dismounting from Arion he strode up to the crest of the ridge and began gazing around, eyes darting from lake to ridge, landmark to landmark, locked in some impenetrable, unfathomable world of his own. He seemed to be more interested in the eastern slopes and the valley it formed rather than the view to the west.

When his uncle wasn't looking, Maharbal glared at Sphax and placed a warning finger across his lips. Sphax got the message.

'Good ground is often thought to be essential for victory on the battlefield,' Hannibal declared, without prompting or preamble, as if reporting out loud the silent conversation he'd been having in his head. 'In my experience,' he continued, 'though it plays a part, good ground is never essential for victory. However, in the case of the forthcoming battle between ourselves and the legions of Flaminius Nepos, the choice of ground will play a vital role. To turn my reasoning on its head, the nature of the ground is the only compelling reason for this battle to be fought at all.'

Riddles within riddles, was Sphax's only thought. It came as a complete surprise that his uncle was even considering a battle, let alone that the nature of the ground was compelling him to fight one. This made no sense to Sphax. He stared quizzically at Maharbal, but he was no help, returning his look with a broad smile.

Sphax couldn't contain himself any longer. 'Are we to fight a battle, Uncle?'

'Almost certainly. When nature offers you a perfect gift, it would be churlish to refuse it,' and turning to

Maharbal, 'I've seen enough. We will return and leave the rest to my nephew.' More riddles, thought Sphax.

'You, Sphax, will continue this scouting mission alone. Do you see how this valley falls away to join that broader valley to the north of us?' Sphax nodded. 'The river in that northern valley flows due west, but as it nears the lake it narrows, pinched by the ridge we're standing on and that spur running down from the hill over yonder.' As he'd spoken his uncle pointed to each feature in turn.

'From here I want you to ride due east through that woodland until you find the stream. Follow it north to where it enters the river that flows west into the lake below that knoll over there.' Hannibal pointed. 'Do you see the knoll?'

'Yes, Uncle.' It was where he and Himilco had waited for Maharbal and Gárgoris earlier that afternoon.

'Once you reach the knoll return to camp. I will speak to you later this evening about your impressions of the ground and its principal features.'

Sphax had already done that once today and struggled to see the sense in doing it again. In fact, he was now totally bemused about what he was being asked to do, and more to the point: why?

'And what do you require me to report on, Sir?' sighed Sphax in exasperation. 'The vegetation? Tree types … animals I come upon?'

His uncle almost smiled. 'I'm simply asking you to cast your cavalryman's eye over the ground, Nephew, not conduct a survey in natural philosophy. I want you to imagine the enemy were defending that valley and you had to drive them back with a thousand Numidians. What positions would you take up? Where would you attack? What feature of the ground would give you the most advantage? Where would you expect counterattacks?'

All hints of a smile had now disappeared from his uncle's expression. 'In short, I expect you to ask a thousand questions and come up with a few answers. Which is little more than I've been doing for the last two hours. Are you equal to such a task, Nephew? Or do I need to revise my opinion of you?'

'Make no mistake,' insisted Idwal, 'Flaminius will have caught up with us tomorrow. He's driving his legions on like beasts, eager to get his claws into us.'

Returning from the gruelling interrogation his uncle had given him on the ground in those distant valleys, it had come as a pleasant surprise to find Idwal sitting beside his campfire. But the news was not good.

'My uncle has decided there is to be a battle.'

'Where?' asked Idwal, in some alarm.

Sphax shrugged. 'Here, I suppose … on the rising ground in front of our camp.'

'I've seen better ground. But now we've allowed Flaminius to catch up, I don't suppose we have much choice in the matter.' His friend stared into the firelight.

'We had four days' march over the legions, why has your uncle let it slip? I'm sure we could find a better position to fight in than this.'

'He doesn't seem at all concerned,' shrugged Sphax. 'Remember, we have nearly sixty thousand men, and at best the consul can only muster half that, so as long as we prevent him from joining forces with Gnaeus Servilius, the gods will favour us'

'The gods teach us to rely on ourselves, Sphax, to be self-sufficient, not depend on their favour. Take our cavalry; this is where we have our biggest advantage over the legions. We outnumber them by four to one. But in these hills around the lake,' Idwal deliberately caught his eye, 'cavalry are almost useless. This is hardly the flat plain we had at the Trebia or the Ticinus, where our cavalry was decisive. It seems to me your uncle is deliberately squandering every advantage we possess!'

Sphax considered this for a moment. 'I was with him for a couple of hours this afternoon, Idwal. He didn't strike me as being indecisive, like a man searching for a plan. In fact quite the opposite, he struck me as someone who'd already made up his mind and was simply confirming his instincts.

'Before the Trebia he said something I've never forgotten and thought about a great deal since. "As you prepare to strike the enemy," 'he told me,' "show him only weakness." 'And this afternoon he said something equally puzzling, a riddle I've been trying to untangle ever since. He said, "the nature of the ground is the only compelling reason for this battle to be fought at all."

'What you describe as squandering advantages, he would see as *showing weakness.* But what he's seen in this ground that compels him to fight here is something of a mystery to me, another of his riddles.'

'We'll find out soon enough,' sighed Idwal.

* * *

Shortly after dawn a lad arrived from Manissa's eshrin to report there had been no military movements on the Via Flaminia yesterday. Immediately striding over to Hannibal's pavilion to report this welcome news, Sphax found his uncle preoccupied in discussions with Bostar, his chief engineer. Hannibal's only reaction to the news was a cursory nod.

By midday their camp had grown to the size of a large city. The last to emerge from the mist beside the lakeshore was his uncle Mago and the rearguard; thirty eshrins of Numidians and hundreds of weary Gauls who'd lagged behind the pace of the march. Hannibal, Maharbal and a score of senior officers were there to greet them. Sphax found himself standing beside Idwal.

'Flaminius and his legions will be with us by late afternoon,' announced Mago. 'They've made up half a day on us since dawn. By the gods he's keen to get to grips with us!'

'Then he will soon have his heart's desire,' was all his elder brother said.

'What of the equites?' asked Maharbal, his eyes darting between Mago and Aribal, one of his senior eshrin captains. 'Are they sending out cavalry scouts ahead of their columns?'

It was Aribal who replied. 'No, general. Those cocky bastards don't believe in scouting! Hastati are leading out their columns. From what I saw the equites are in the middle of the column — much good they will do there, the imbeciles!'

'Rest your mares, take your ease and fill your bellies, Numidians,' instructed Hannibal, raising his voice so all could hear. 'You have done well.'

Two hours later the cry went up. On the grassy knoll, five miles to the north of them, Sphax caught his first sight of glinting bronze helmets, raised standards and blood-red cloaks. Rome had arrived.

Something was afoot. It was almost palpable. Sphax could sense it, feel it in the air, like the oppressive heaviness before a thunderstorm. He saw it in the faces of Libyans and Iberians, Gauls and Numidians, standing idly around in small groups, talking with lowered voices. It wasn't exactly anxiety or unease he sensed, but a nervousness, a listless tension.

Before he had time to dwell on it, Sphax was summoned to Maharbal's modest pavilion. The general was seated on his favourite stool and waved Sphax towards a bench. Looking around, he could see that most of Maharbal's possessions still lay unpacked in their chests; even his prized Seleucid carpet lay rolled up in a corner, and the only things neatly laid out on the floor were his collection of shields and javelins.

'Not planning a long visit, Sir?' observed Sphax.

'I think we'll both have our hands full for the foreseeable future, lad, and there certainly won't be time for creature comforts. I hear you feasted your men and treated them to a little silverware.'

It never ceased to amaze him how Maharbal kept his ear to the ground. He seemed to know what was going on *before* it happened. 'You were right, Sir. It did my men a power of good. They haven't laughed like that since … it happened. I think you would have enjoyed the stories, general.'

Maharbal smiled, 'I'm sure I would. But remember, your men don't blame you. They understand. Jugurtha also knew and loved your parents.'

'I hope I've learned my lesson—'

'Of course you haven't!' the general roared with laughter. 'I've managed to beat out most of the recklessness and drill some sense and discipline into that empty head of yours, but you will always be your father's son. The stories I could tell of your father would make your hair stand on end!'

'I've heard some of them. And they did.'

'Listen, lad. I didn't send for you to reminisce about your father,' Maharbal began with an uncharacteristic awkwardness. 'I know you wasted the last saunion I gave you, so I wanted you to have this.' Getting to his feet he began rummaging around at the back of the pavilion.

Sphax frowned ruefully. 'It wasn't wasted, Sir. It just met the wrong mark.'

Returning to his stool, the general placed in his hands the most fearsome saunion Sphax had ever set eyes on. Wrought from the finest Iberian iron the leaf-barbed blade was a hand's length, socketed and riveted to a shaft no thicker than his thumb. Raising it aloft he felt its rigid strength and balance. He suddenly felt overwhelmed.

'I cannot accept this as a gift,' stammered Sphax. 'It's far too precious!'

'Why not? It's mine to give. And I choose to give it to you.'

They were both spared further embarrassment by the sudden blast of a horn, summoning everyone to arms.

Assembling on the gentle slopes leading down to the road to Perusia was one of the strangest sights Sphax had ever beheld. A collection of the most incongruous warriors he could ever have imagined. Except they were not really warriors but long-barrelled trumpeters, Libyan horn players, standard bearers of every tribe and chieftain from Iberia to Cisalpine Gaul, and standing proudly amongst them all, scores of Gauls wielding carnyxes, the wailing sirens of Morrigu.

Maharbal looked anxiously at the sun: shadows were already lengthening. 'Call your mare and bring two from your eshrin with you.'

When Sphax returned with Jugurtha and Agbal, the general was already mounted on his Egyptian mare beside his standard bearer, Bartho. Maharbal lead the way down the slope to where a small group of mounted officers were gathering around Hannibal.

As they drew closer, Sphax realised the last time he'd been in such exalted company was at Hannibal's council of war in Mago's pavilion, months ago. Besides Hanno, Magol and Orison, he could now put a name to several more faces. Once he and Maharbal had fallen in at the rear of the mounted party his uncle raised his hand and they all set out.

Once across the Perusia road they began the steep climb to the crest of the ridge, riding slowly at a walk to allow the standard bearers and musicians, many of whom were no more than boys, to keep pace.

Instead of riding to the crest of the ridge and dismounting as he'd done yesterday, Hannibal followed the track north for a further five hundred paces before leaping from Arion and striding up to the crest to gaze around. At the back of the party they couldn't hear a word of what was said, but judging from his actions, he guessed his uncle was simply checking his bearings.

What happened next only deepened Sphax's sense of incomprehension. Hanno and three of his lieutenants shouted for standard bearers and horn players. Three hundred paces apart, crescent-and-sun standards were planted to which three boys were allotted, armed with circular Libyan horns.

It was only when Bostar directed one of his own men to each standard that Sphax began to understand what might be going on, and it was what they were carrying with rope handles that provided a clue. Each had a cylindrical clay pot the size of a small storage jar. Had Hannibal's engineers succeeded in making a simplified version of Gala's lamp cylinders? With growing excitement he watched carefully.

Turning to the general, Sphax asked, 'Are you going to put me out of my misery, Sir, and tell me what's going on?'

Maharbal chuckled. 'As you played a small part in this and selected the ground, I thought it would be far more entertaining to let you guess our plan. After all, you're always telling me about Greek philosophers' powers of deductive reasoning. I thought this would be a fine test, lad. Don't you agree?'

'It's inductive reasoning, Sir. Making observations to form a theory. And I played no part in choosing this ground. I would rather fight anywhere but here.'

'Aren't you overlooking something?' the general crowed with a knowing smile, clearly enjoying himself. When he was in such a mood, Sphax had learned to bear Maharbal's irritating entertainments with stoicism.

Luckily the column was moving on, avoiding further conversation. But Sphax was surprised to see Hanno and his three lieutenants turn their stallions and head back to camp, accompanied by another meaningful look from his general.

Half a mile later the procedure was repeated. His uncle dismounted, peered over the ridge, and Orison and four of his lieutenants were ordered to plant Iberian standards and summon trumpeters.

This time Sphax was taking no chances. Leaping from Dido he accosted one of the men about to place a storage jar beside a standard and examined it carefully. Lifting a lid that had been drilled with small holes, he saw that inside the jar sat a candle. Two large holes had been punched in the sides of the vessel that would only emit candlelight from two directions. In this case to the south and east, he surmised.

When Orison and his lieutenants trotted past him with broad grins, he guessed that Maharbal had shared his insufferable little jest with a few others. Sphax felt as if he was being put on trial. Now he was absolutely determined to figure this out for himself.

It dawned on him as Magol and the Insubres and Boii chieftains began dismounting to plant their strange assortment of standards and carnyx players at intervals below the ridgeline. How could he have been so blind? Hannibal's plan was so obvious he was kicking himself for being so stupid! Now Maharbal's taunt that he'd been *overlooking something* made perfect sense.

What they were overlooking was a narrow strip of roadway for the most part no more than fifteen paces wide. Flaminius had no alternative but to take that road. His entire army of twenty-five thousand would be strung out for four miles along its path. Could there be an easier target?

Looking for chiefs and generals who were *not* present helped him guess some of the finer details of his uncle's plan. Idwal and Gárgoris were absent, neither could he see any of the captains who commanded contingents of velites and slingers, the light troops of their army. But he could see how lightly armed men could be dangled as tempting bait.

As for Idwal's Cavari, Hannibal was obviously going to place them in some prominent position on the slope beside their camp. From there they would be clearly seen from the Roman encampment on the knoll, five miles to the north. More bait, Sphax guessed. And Gárgoris?

Iberian heavy cavalry would be totally unsuited to the broken, wooded valleys where Sphax had scouted yesterday, but it was ideal ground for his nimble Numidian mares. Gárgoris, he decided, would be held in reserve. But if Hannibal's daring and meticulously organised onslaught succeeded, Flaminius and his legions would be utterly annihilated. There would be no need for reserves, or even a pursuit.

Magol and his chieftains were beginning to mount their stallions and return to camp when Bostar, carrying Gala's two light cylinders, walked over to Sphax and handed them over. 'I believe these are yours, young man. How useful they've proved to be.'

Managing a polite nod, Sphax gazed over the ridgeline at a blood-red sun beginning to sink behind the western hills bordering the lake. He felt suddenly alone, lost in this alien wilderness, miles from Corinna and everything he'd ever loved and sometimes lost. In this strange twilight zone between light and darkness, he realised how the fates of an entire people, perhaps even of mighty empires, could be decided by the character of one man.

Tomorrow morning, on a narrow strip of road beside the lakeshore, thousands, perhaps even tens of thousands would die because of the arrogant, hotheaded foolishness of one single man. Gaius Flaminius Nepos would be the one to tip the scales. Neither the stars in their courses nor the song of the Moirai had the power to deflect the fatal path that Flaminius would choose at first light.

And what of his people, of Rome? With half her legions destroyed and the rest blocked by a vast army sitting on the only road back to the city, Rome's fate would be sealed.

With a sudden jolt he felt a hand on his shoulder. It was his uncle.

'Will it succeed?' Hannibal enquired. The question was idle rhetoric. His uncle already knew the answer.

'Your ambuscade …' Sphax sighed, gathering his thoughts, 'will be devastating, Sir. Flaminius will wake up to the sight of a few Gauls lining the slopes of our encampment and only slingers and lightly armed Iberian velites barring his path. Without a single thought in that empty head of his, he'll march his men to their deaths.'

Maharbal had joined them. 'We still have to get over fifty thousand men into position on this godforsaken hillside in the dark. And everything has to be done in perfect silence.'

'At least we have the means to do it, Maharbal. Those lamps will guide us, and our men have the discipline.'

'Where do you want my eight eshrins, Sir?' Sphax asked.

'In those woods you described to me yesterday,' explained Hannibal, 'where this valley meets that broader one. You assured me it is out of sight of the knoll on the spur.'

'It is, Sir, and the trees will deaden any sound.'

'Good. Then that's where you will muster.' With a rare smile his uncle continued, 'Which leaves one last thing to be settled. Maharbal and I have decided that tomorrow you will command all our Numidian cavalry in battle. Over a hundred eshrins. Do not disappoint us.'

TWENTY-TWO

There was so much to do and so little time in which to do it. Sphax's thoughts had been racing since posting Agbal and Jugurtha in positions where their cylinder lamps would be clearly visible. On the journey back to camp in the fading light he took several fateful decisions, praying to the goddess they would be the right ones when they faced the enemy at dawn.

With unerring logic, his uncle had determined the best way to avoid confusion was to position the most northerly forces first, then work methodically southwards. Which meant that Sphax's Numidians would be the first to lead out the army. This way no group would have to weave its way in the pitch black through hordes of men already assembled, and the unit at the head of a column had the simple task of marching towards the most northerly lamp. Once assembled, Hannibal had ordered that the lamps be extinguished.

The lamps themselves were no better than a line of signposts, beacons emitting little more than pinpricks of light. They wouldn't cast a shred of light on the path the army was to follow, and the moon, being in the first quarter that evening, would be of little help. It was inevitable that men would fall and stumble, curse and grumble, but this evening the swearing would have to be done under their breath. Hannibal had prohibited talking, and restricted commands to a whisper.

Sliding from Dido he ordered his men to fetch Himilco, Aribal and Hiempsal. Even on a flat grassland plain it was difficult to command three thousand cavalry effectively. In the narrow forested valleys where they would be fighting the task would be impossible. He needed lieutenants.

Sphax had decided to divide his forces into three groups, each with thirty eshrins. This would leave him with a reserve of about fifteen eshrins, commanded by Hiempsal, one of the ablest, but most hotheaded, of all his captains. If anyone needed desperate assistance, Sphax knew that Hiempsal wouldn't hesitate, and holding him back in the reserve might just keep him alive tomorrow. Himilco and Aribal were the obvious choices for the other groups.

By the light of a campfire he watched the growing amazement as he revealed Hannibal's astonishing plan in all its fine detail and the prominent role Numidians would play in its execution.

'It's nothing short of an ambuscade!' exclaimed Hiempsal, hardly able to contain his excitement.

'Will it work, Sphax?' frowned Himilco. 'Won't Flaminius send out scouts … cavalry? Surely they wouldn't just walk into a trap?'

'Oh yes,' assured Sphax, 'it will work. Since he left Arretium, Flaminius hasn't sent out a single scouting party. Why would he change his bad habits tomorrow?' Sphax pointed to the Roman camp five miles north of them, illuminated by scores of campfires. 'Just as we are certain the sun will rise in the east at dawn tomorrow, Flaminius will call his legions to arms and march for our camp as fast as their hobnails will carry them. And just as certainly, before the sun sets, his army will be utterly annihilated.'

For a moment the three of them simply gaped at him, struggling to take in this last statement. Aribal's disbelief finally got the better of him, breaking the spell. 'In the name of Ba 'al Hamūn, how's your uncle going to get our entire army into position on a mountainside in the dark? Dog's twat, Sphax, it's not possible!'

'Ah, but it is,' Sphax laughed. 'Do you remember Gala's cylinder lamps we used when we attacked Longus' camp the night before the Trebia?' Nods all round. 'Useful, were they not?' More nods. 'Well, Hannibal's engineers have managed to reproduce them using simple clay storage jars. And they've manufactured scores of them! One for every unit in our army, marking the position they will take up this evening. Be they Gauls, Iberians or Libyans, every man will know his place. Battle lines have already been decided. From our noblest generals to the lowliest captain, everyone will be guided to the beacon they've been allotted. Lamps are already in place along the length of the ridgeline and waiting to be lit. That's how it will be done, Aribal.

'All we have to do this evening is ride a few paces below these lamps, keeping them always to our left. They will be our beacons, marking our path. Two of my men are already positioned with Gala's original lamps. They will guide us to our final destination.'

Again there was a stunned silence as his captains began to comprehend the meticulous planning and organisation Hannibal and, Sphax suspected, Maharbal, had put into this operation. Would that they had applied themselves in the same way before attempting the Arnus swamps, Sphax reflected ruefully.

To make the most of the moonlight, his uncle had decided the Numidians must begin their march at the second watch. Time was pressing. 'We need to decide which eshrins each of us will command. Any thoughts?' Sphax was relieved when everything was quickly agreed, and he could move on to talk about more basic things such as food, flasks of water and weapons. Breakfast would have to be bread, cheese and cold meats, carried in sacks, but Sphax insisted every man ate a hot meal that evening before they set out.

His lieutenants were about to leave when an angry camp steward confronted him to grumble that Numidians were allowing their campfires to die down. Hannibal had insisted campfires be kept blazing throughout the night to conceal the fact that the camp was emptying.

Sphax had no time for this. 'Then you do it!' he blazed. 'In two hours we'll be miles away, and none of my men will be coming back to put a log on a fire!'

'May Melqart guide you safely in darkness,' exclaimed Hannibal in full voice. 'Fear nothing, for tomorrow victory is certain. Rome will be crushed and trodden beneath your mares' hooves. You are the finest horsemen the world has ever seen. Your reputation alone strikes terror in the ranks of every legion. You are the scourge of Rome, their nemesis, and tomorrow will see your greatest victory. Tomorrow you will add to the glorious roll call of Numidian victories that will be remembered down the ages. Go forth! To victory!'

For everyone who understood Punic, this met with jubilant cheers and the beating of javelins on hide shields. Those who hadn't understood a word of it cheered anyway. Sphax winked at Maharbal, seated on his mare beside Hannibal. Neither he nor Maharbal put much store in rousing speeches, but the men seemed to expect it.

'I never got to thank you for your most generous gift,' Sphax reminded the general. 'I do so now, Sir, and swear not to waste it next time.'

'Good luck, lad,' was all Maharbal said, with a gravity that touched Sphax.

'Forward Numidians!' he yelled, raising his shiny new saunion and savouring the last time he would be able to shout such a command until he looked his enemies squarely in the eyes.

He'd already decided not to risk riding more than three abreast, so as he nudged Dido up the steep slope to the ridge he calculated their column would stretch back for more than two miles. Sphax hadn't ridden in darkness for months, so it took him a little while to settle into the mare's easy swaying rhythm. At least the skies were clear and bristling with stars, so what little moonlight guided them would not be obscured by cloud that night.

On horseback, being unable to see more than a few strides ahead was always unnerving to begin with. If anything, moonlight exaggerated the size and shape of things; bushes loomed as trees and rocks grew alarmingly in size. The secret to peace of mind was to become a compliant passenger, allowing Dido to tread her own path, trusting in her surefootedness and superior night-time vision.

By the time the column reached the ridgeline and he'd spotted the first lamp, Sphax had become so lulled by Dido's gentle swaying he had to remind himself to stay awake. If that wretched swamp had taught him anything, it was that it was all too easy to doze off on the back of a horse.

It felt eerie to pass so close to fellow comrades in the dead of night without a greeting, but counting lamps had been his salvation, the only thing that had kept him awake. As the count rose, so did his weariness. He'd been awake before dawn, ridden countless miles and his emotions and intellect had been tested beyond their limits. With each weary mile and passing hour every bone in his body yearned for sleep, his mind numb, incapable of thought.

After recording the seventy-sixth lamp he cast around for the next, suddenly disorientated. Nothing. The moon had set and they were alone in the darkness with nothing more than starlight to guide their way.

For a moment Sphax had to stifle rising panic. For the last few hours, he now realised, his entire being had been focused on searching out the next glimmer of light and guiding Dido gently towards it. Now there was nothing; just a sea of darkness. He could barely make out the saunion he was holding in his right hand.

'Halt,' he whispered, and turning around to the trio behind him, 'Pass the word down the column we're halting until we've sighted the next beacon.'

In his mind's eye he tried desperately to remember what had happened yesterday afternoon after the last lamp on the ridge had been positioned. But he was dog tired, and his mind objected to such labours. All he could recall was the discussion he'd had with his uncle and Maharbal. Sphax remembered Bostar handing over Gala's lamps, but where he was standing at the time, and the direction in which he'd headed with Jugurtha and Agbal remained a disturbing blank. Presumably it must have been in a north-easterly direction, but engulfed in this disorienting pitch-black sea, north-east could be anywhere.

Sphax almost jumped out of his skin when he felt a hand grip his thigh. It was Aribal, on foot, though he could barely recognise his features in the darkness. 'I can see a beacon to the north-east from my position in the column, but I lost sight of it as I walked forward,' he whispered.

This made perfect sense. Agbal had only partially opened the cylinder to allow a narrow beam of light to be seen. Sphax had been so absorbed in following the beacons north that he'd forgotten to look to his right, to the east. With enormous relief he whispered, 'Thank the gods, Aribal. If you walk back to your mare I'll follow and get the column to double back on itself,' and turning to the men behind, 'Pass the word down the column we're changing direction and doubling back.'

Allowing a little time for the word to filter down the line, he raised his saunion, nudged Dido around and followed Aribal. He'd not just missed the beacon, he'd sailed past it for over half a mile, judging from the time it took for Aribal to locate his eshrin and mount his mare. By this time Sphax was cursing himself. The beam of light was much clearer — and brighter — from one of Gala's cylinder lamps. How could he have missed it?

The column was now twisted snake-like around the valley, but as he led them north-east, the line slowly uncoiled and they made good progress. As the beam of light grew brighter and more distinct he began to hear the sound of bubbling water and remembered that Jugurtha had suggested they make camp beside a stream; water for their mares would be essential.

And there it was. Gala's lamp, resting on a tree stump with Agbal fast asleep beside it, snoring so loudly that Sphax was surprised Flaminius' legions hadn't come to investigate.

With the blunt end of a javelin Sphax tickled the lad's braided hair and Agbal immediately jumped to his feet with a look of sheepish embarrassment. 'Sorry, Sir,' he said out loud, before Sphax had time to put a hand over his mouth. Agbal tried again, this time in a whisper, 'Sorry, Sir, it's been such a long night.'

'Believe me, you bastard,' hissed Cirta, who'd been riding beside Sphax all evening, 'it's been longer for us! All of us are done in, and here you are … snoring!'

At least Sphax knew who would be the first volunteer for sentry duty. 'Where's Jugurtha's lamp?' asked Sphax. 'I can't see it from here.'

'You can't from here, Sir, too many trees in the way, but I can find it easily enough. Shall I lead the way?'

Half a mile further on they could see Jugurtha's lamp burning brightly in the middle of the grassy clearing Sphax had selected for their camp. Although he couldn't see it, he knew they were surrounded by thick woodland. It turned out that Jugurtha had slept more than Agbal, and was happy to take on sentry duty with him.

Sphax's first duty was to lead Dido to the little stream where the mare gratefully bent her head and slaked her thirst, along with hundreds of others. Placing the lamps a few paces apart, he stood between them, knowing that Himilco, Aribal and Hiempsal would join him shortly.

'That was a nightmare!' hissed Himilco. 'I never want to do that again!'

'Let's hope we never have to,' Sphax replied, 'and if Aribal hadn't spotted that lamp, it would have been far worse than a nightmare.'

'Do you want me to post sentries, Sphax?' whispered Hiempsal.

'I've already done it, thanks. Our men are dog tired, so let's get some sleep. But tell your men not to let their mares wander off. Agbal and Jugurtha will wake us at dawn.'

Before he curled up to sleep, Sphax blew out the candles in Gala's lamps. The instant his cheek met the soft grass in the meadow, he was sound asleep.

* * *

At the second blast of the trumpet Sphax struggled to his feet in alarm, every nerve in his body tingling. Was this Hannibal's signal to attack? But it was pitch black! Rubbing sleep from his eyes he heard it again; a longer phrase this time, harsh and strident. If it was the signal, a score of other instruments should have joined in by now to create a blazing cacophony that would've been heard in far-off Perusia. No. This was a single trumpet. And he'd heard the sound once before.

What he was hearing was the morning call to arms in a legionary marching camp. Sphax had last heard the call hiding in bushes, crouched beside his uncle, outside Longus' camp near Placentia. Despite the darkness, somewhere beyond the hills to the east the sun was rising, and inside the Roman camp men were yawning, tossing off blankets and looking forward to breakfast.

For Sphax, sleep was now impossible, and judging from the amount of coughing and hawking all around him, he sensed that scores of his men had also been woken by the trumpet. He would let the rest sleep on. Sunrise was his favourite time of the day, so he was determined to view it from somewhere, and he was also keen to make contact with Agbal and Jugurtha.

Waiting patiently for the pre-dawn greyness to percolate the wooded valley where he stood, Sphax began to think about the coming battle. Hannibal would not spring the trap until the Roman vanguard reached the point where the road left the shoreline and began the gentle ascent of the hill on which the Carthaginian camp was pitched. Judging the distance between the two camps to be about five miles, Sphax guessed it would take Flaminius' legions well over an hour to reach the Carthaginian camp. Allowing two hours for roll call, breakfast and the tedious preparations necessary for a day's march, it would be at least three hours before their own trumpets and horns blazed in fanfare.

At last, in the grey dimness of the gathering dawn he could see a few paces ahead. It was enough. Staying within earshot of the bubbling waters of the stream he gingerly stepped over sleeping men, javelins and all manner of equipment before reaching the trees bordering their encampment. All he had to do now was follow the stream's course until the woodland ended; there he knew from memory he would be gazing down on a broad grassy valley with a shallow river running in its bed.

By the time he reached the edge of the wood the light had improved to the extent that he could indeed gaze down into the valley. But what he saw was not the meandering river and lush water meadows he was expecting, but a vast sea of white mist that extended across the length and breadth of the valley. This morning the mist was thicker than he'd ever seen it before. A sudden movement to his left caught his attention. It was Jugurtha. Sphax waved to attract his attention.

'I wasn't expecting a sight like this,' whispered Sphax.

Jugurtha pointed to the east, where the valley bottom finally emerged from the mist and Sphax could make out the glittering waters of the little river. Higher still and he saw the first shafts of red and gold light spearing across the sky. 'In an hour or so I reckon the sun will burn a lot of this off. We might be able to see what we're doing then.'

'Where's Agbal?'

'I placed him about five hundred paces down the valley, closer to the Roman camp. The lad's got the eyes of a hawk and would've spotted any movement sooner than me.'

'Did you hear the legion's trumpet?'

Jugurtha nodded. 'By now the bastards will be eating their breakfast.'

'For many it will be their last,' hissed Sphax.

Eating a cold breakfast was not something Numidians ever looked forward to. With the smell of barley being ground, and dough being rolled, shaped then roasted on paddles over campfires, breakfast was Sphax's favourite meal of the day. Eating stale bread and cheese from a sack fell well short of this, but as campfires were out of the question, they made the best of it. At least their ladies were content, grazing on the fresh pasture beside the stream.

Hannibal's order to maintain absolute silence proved to be a curse, something they'd never faced before. Sphax needed to discuss his plans with his three lieutenants and they had to pass these orders on to their eshrin captains, who in turn had to explain it to their men. For Sphax it was easy to whisper detailed instructions to three men bunched closely around him, but to whisper complicated orders to a group of thirty proved impossible. In the end they had to do it in relays, ten men at a time, which ate up time and patience.

On the other hand, as far as Sphax was concerned, anything that ate up time was to be welcomed. In the pit of his own stomach he could feel the knot tightening. It would be the same for every Numidian under his command. Waiting for a battle to start was infinitely worse than the first order to charge. Fear was like that. It sapped the spirit. Fear of the unknown was a greater enemy than any legion they'd faced, and it fed on idleness: a man with nothing to do had time to imagine the worst.

His men's incessant banter and humour, even their grumbling — and Numidians were inveterate grumblers — helped them endure the anxiety of waiting. Having to communicate in hushed whispers offered little relief from dark thoughts.

Once Sphax was satisfied that all his orders had been relayed to the men, he and his appointed lieutenants joined the new sentries that had replaced Agbal and Jugurtha at the edge of the woodland. Juba had taken over from Agbal, and from where Juba was crouched beside a gorse bush, they all had a fine view of the valley and the road that descended the spur and followed the lakeshore. But it was a strange sight.

By now the sun had climbed above the eastern hills to reveal a cloudless azure sky. Without a breath of wind the day was already hot. Jugurtha's prediction that the sun would burn off the mist was only partially true. The mist had indeed retreated down the valley, but where it met the cool waters of the lake it remained, ephemeral, yet impenetrable, a vast sea of white. Not much more than a mile away they could clearly see men and horses disappearing into its depths, as if being swallowed by it.

Gesturing for everyone to follow him under the canopy of the woodland, for the first time Sphax simply spoke in a low voice, without feeling the need to whisper: the hobnails and grinding wagons of an army on the march made quite a racket.

'That mist is a gift from the gods,' Sphax began, 'If we can't see them, they can't see us. Which means that once their rearguard marches down that hill and disappears into it, we will be free to move into this valley and form up.'

Himilco frowned, 'Won't that be a bit risky, Sphax?'

'I think you have to weigh that risk against the time it will take us to get into position once we hear the signal to attack. It would be pointless to form up in the clearing where we spent the night; by the time we'd ridden through this woodland our ranks would be in chaos and we would have to start again. All that takes time. Time we don't have. Remember, even here we're still a mile from where we need to be.'

'I've ridden through that mist,' agreed Aribal. 'You can't even see the horse in front of you, Himilco, let alone horsemen in a valley a mile away.'

'You're right,' Himilco conceded. 'It's a small risk.'

'I also sense our men are growing anxious and restive, so the sooner we get them on their mares the better. Do you agree?' asked Sphax. Everyone nodded. 'Then it's decided. We ride to the edge of this woodland and once we're sure the Roman rearguard has cleared that spur, we break cover and form up in the valley.'

At first the sound was faint, like a thin distant wheezing, but as it was taken up by more instruments along the length of the ridgeline, it grew to become a cacophonous roar. The last to take up the call were the wailing carnyx of the Gauls, transposing what had been a roar into a cry from some monstrous beast.

Sphax raised his saunion and over three thousand Numidians nudged their mares into a trot, moving forward in four great columns, ten men abreast. After a few strides he raised it again and they began thundering down the valley at the canter towards the mist shrouding the lake and its shoreline.

Hannibal's orders could not have been simpler: attack where you can, but prevent any of Flaminius' legions escaping the trap. The Numidians' task was to close the northern gate and bar the door. For any in Flaminius' army lucky enough to flee or retreat, only three escape routes were available to them; the valley down which the Numidians were now thundering; back the way they'd come along the lakeshore road, or to swim for it.

As the latter option meant certain death, all his Numidians had to do was block this valley at its narrowest point, which was where it met the long ridgeline Hannibal's infantry were now charging down, and place eshrins along the spur to cover the road. Both positions would have the advantages of high ground, above the blanket of mist.

When they reached the place where the valley funneled to its narrowest point between the ridge and spur, he signaled Himilco to continue the advance and rode over to Aribal, who was already barking orders to his captains.

In short order Aribal had six eshrins stretched across the width of the valley in loose formation. Leaving enough space for each rider to turn around their mares and retreat was essential for a charge; a Numidian eshrin delivered its lethal volley of javelins at the gallop, twenty paces from the enemy, which left three strides to turn around their mares and retreat, a feat of horsemanship no other cavalry in the world would even attempt. It also called for smaller, more agile horses. That's why they rode mares like Dido. Big stallions could never be trained in such arts.

It took superb judgement and skill to execute such a manoeuvre, qualities Numidians possessed in abundance. But as Numidians were taught to ride as soon as they could walk, it came naturally. That's why they had no equal on the battlefield.

When all five lines were positioned to Aribal's satisfaction, he turned to Sphax. 'Shouldn't we send scouts into that mist to investigate?'

'We will shortly,' agreed Sphax, 'but I would like to get all our men in an attacking formation before we do that. Then we can give Flaminius a truly nasty surprise.'

Aribal laughed. 'You wouldn't think it to look at you, Sphax, but you've got a really cruel streak, do you know that?'

'Only where Rome's concerned,' replied Sphax, without a trace of a smile. 'Once we're in a position to bar that road, look to my signal. Bring your own eshrin forward and I'll be waiting with mine. Together we'll see what carnage Hannibal has brought down on Flaminius' thick skull.'

Nudging Dido into a trot he continued down the valley. Plunging into the dank shroud was like entering winter. Instantly the cold and damp suffused his skin and he could see no further than twenty paces in any direction. It was hardly a place for cavalry. Crossing the shallow river he was relieved to ride up the slope and out of the mist's clammy grip.

Himilco and Hiempsal had done well. Lining the length of the spur, four hundred paces beyond the white shroud, Sphax counted ten eshrins drawn up in loose formation, and behind this Hiempsal was organising his reserves. The gateway to the north was barred.

As he rode towards Himilco a sudden roar erupted along the length of the ribbon of mist shrouding the shoreline.

Only now did he hear the blacksmiths' song; the clash of iron on iron, the unmistakable ring of metal being wielded against metal. In their rapid movement down the valley, it seemed his Numidians had won the race to the shoreline and only now were Gauls, Iberians and Libyans hacking and slashing at their enemies.

Sphax could barely imagine the terror and consternation amongst Flaminius' legions when Hannibal's infantry suddenly appeared out of nowhere and tore into their ranks. Shrouded in mist, they couldn't possibly have seen what was about to descend on them — until it was too late.

To begin with every Roman was facing the wrong way. Caught unawares, forming a defensive line when under attack would be almost impossible. It would be a case of every man for himself.

With their long blades scything through the air and great oval shields used as battering rams, the Gauls would be hurling themselves at men totally unprepared for the onslaught. Naked above their plaid braccae, hair slaked in ash to resemble the manes of wild stallions, Gauls knew only frenzied fearlessness, for Morrigu would only spare the brave.

Sphax and his Numidians didn't have to wait long for the results of this unseen battle now raging below them. Out of the mist staggered hundreds of men with only one thing on their mind: to save their skin.

And they were such a strange, ragged assortment: Lucanians and Samnites, equites on foot, velites without their javelins, triari, hastati, even a standard bearer wearing the head of a lion; a rabble of beaten men, fleeing for their lives.

Most took one look at the fearsome lines of Numidians ranged against them and sunk to their knees, casting aside what weapons they still carried. But some did not.

Sphax watched uneasily as a centurion exhorted the men gathered around him to make a last stand. None of them seemed to be armed with pila, spears with a soft iron spike that posed a threat to charging Numidians; nevertheless, many still retained shields and long spears.

This would have to be nipped in the bud, he decided. 'Gulussa, Gauda,' Sphax yelled to the eshrin captains either side of his men, 'have your men thread javelins. Our three eshrins will charge that rabble before they set an example to the rest.'

By now the centurion had managed to get his motley collection into some sort of order, with some kneeling on one knee, shields resting against a bronze greave, whilst a ragged second line wielded an assortment of swords and spears. Sphax guessed there were no more than fifty.

Pointing the tip of his saunion at the centurion's

gaudy red-tasseled helmet, Sphax shouted, 'Forward!'

That familiar thrill, tinged with fear, surged through his body as he nudged Dido into a trot. After a few strides he picked up the pace, nudging her into a canter — he would save the gallop for the last few strides. Already he could see Gulussa and Gauda peeling off to the left and right to outflank the desultory little army they faced. Sixty paces from the wall of shields, Sphax dug both knees into Dido's flanks and she bounded into a gallop. Raising his saunion and tightening the thong, he selected a crouching triarius, held his breath then hurled the spinning weapon towards its victim.

Numidians never saw their javelins strike home, for in that heart-stopping moment they were frantically leaning back on their mares to get them to turn a half circle and head off in the opposite direction, all in three strides and at the gallop. It meant certain death for any Numidian who misjudged or got this wrong, for they would find themselves tangling with spears. It was only when they'd reformed their line could they turn around and judge the effect of their handiwork.

The centurion's rag-bag army had been reduced to a handful of wounded; the rest were littering the blood-soaked ground where they'd fallen. A volley of ninety javelins against a mere fifty men made for healthy odds.

Now that the lesson had been driven home, Sphax decided it was time to end this senseless bloodshed. There was no honour in this. For Numidians this was little more than target practice. On the gentle grassy slope leading down through the mist to the river, hundreds were now on their knees, heads bowed low in surrender.

Looking to the south east, to the valley where Aribal's men were posted, he could see his lieutenant was dealing with even greater numbers. Hordes of legionaries were cowering behind a thick carpet of dead and dying, desperately seeking a way out. But the door to the east had been slammed shut.

It was time to make up their minds for them. Nudging Dido forward he walked her to where they could at least hear him. Unknown to Sphax, behind him Jugurtha and Agbal exchanged meaningful glances. Fearful their captain was about to do something *brave*, they led the eshrin forward, three strides behind their captain, javelins readied for trouble.

All Sphax heard were pleas for mercy. A chorus of *misericordia* resounded around the field. 'I swear you'll not be harmed,' he began to yell in Latin. 'Lay down your arms and throw away your helmets and armour. You will not be harmed.' He caught sight of a wounded Samnite, his white tunic splattered with blood, spear and bronze breastplate tossed aside. He was silently weeping. Sprawled on the ground with a javelin lodged in his throat, he saw that the centurion had paid for his misplaced courage with his life. Wherever Sphax looked he saw broken, beaten men.

Hearing a sharp noise, Sphax turned around,

smiling when he saw the entire eshrin had followed him. 'I see you don't trust your captain anymore,' he said wryly.

By way of reply it was answered by shaking heads, but at least they were grinning. 'Then make yourselves useful. Jugurtha, ride back to Hiempsal and tell him to bring some eshrins forward to escort these prisoners to the rear. And you, Cirta, tell Himilco to join me here.' Switching to Latin he began repeating his pleas to lay down arms.

Hiempsal and Himilco arrived at the same time. 'Escort these men to the rear and post guards,' Sphax ordered. 'Leave the weapons and armour, we'll collect it later. See to their wounds and give them something to drink.' Turning to Himilco he continued, 'Aribal's facing even greater numbers. Take ten eshrins and sweep that valley, either side of the river. A few javelins up their arses might persuade them to surrender like this lot.'

Himilco nodded. 'What do you think's going on down there, Sphax?' he asked, staring down into the impenetrable mist.

Sphax sighed, 'A slaughter, most likely. I think all these men are from their rearguard. They took one look at what was happening ahead and simply turned on their heels and fled. I can't say I blame them.'

TWENTY-THREE

Glancing at the position of the sun, Sphax came to a decision. 'I'm going to take my eshrin down there, on foot.'

'I'll come,' chorused Aribal and Himilco, who were mounted beside him, staring into the abyss that was the mist, still enveloping the lakeshore like a white shroud. Below them the battle had been raging for well over an hour, though the clamour of war appeared to be retreating to the south. The Numidians were now struggling to deal with over a thousand prisoners.

'No,' he said firmly. 'You both know how narrow that road is. I certainly wouldn't take our mares into such a confined space, but my eshrin has some experience fighting on foot.'

'I beg you, Sphax, take another eshrin with you, if only as a reserve … something to fall back on should the need arise.' Today, Himilco's frown seemed to be permanently attached.

'Very well,' Sphax shrugged, 'I'll take Gauda's eshrin with me. But remember, you two must remain in position here and in the valley. Our first duty is to bar all escape to the north. Only the gods know what I'll find when I cross that river down there, but it may be that Flaminius decides to retreat the way he came, down this road. In which case, Numidians will be the only thing standing in his way. He must be stopped!'

It took some time to inform Gauda and hand over their mares to the safekeeping of Gulussa's eshrin, but flanked by Agbal and Jugurtha, he finally strode down the hill and plunged into the mist. By the time they'd crossed the shallow river at the foot of the valley they were all shivering and feeling wet and miserable. At least it explained one thing that had puzzled them all morning: why had the sounds of battle seemed so muffled and distant? It was the mist. It seemed to deaden all sound.

Despite the burning heat of the day, visibility had hardly improved; at best it was only possible to see thirty paces in front of their noses. When they came upon their first corpses — mostly Lucanian velites, many not much older than boys — Sphax halted them. 'Thread javelins,' he ordered. 'Have one ready at all times.'

Where the road finally met the lake's shoreline he suddenly froze and stiffened, revolted by the horror of what he saw. As far as the eye could see, the lake was choked with Roman corpses, floating on the surface as thick as water lilies smothering a pond. The sight was so terrible it would haunt his dreams for months to come.

As they trudged on they came upon places where vicious fights had taken place, leaving the roadway so carpeted with dead and dying they had to step gingerly. Amongst the dead they now came upon Insubres. Wounded men were everywhere, many having crawled into the thick undergrowth beside the road. His men offered water and what comfort they could to the Gauls, but there was little they could do. And everywhere the detritus of battle was strewn on the ground: pack animals pierced and skewered, overturned wagons, shields, helmets and weapons of every description. It was a vision from Hades.

Judging from the evidence of his own eyes, the legions had been taken completely by surprise. In places they came upon entire files of legionaries who'd simply been hacked to death where they'd stood. In other places they must have rallied for a while and fought back, until sheer numbers had overwhelmed them. Perhaps the presence of a decurion, tribune or centurion had given them heart and the courage to make a stand for a while. But from what he'd seen, it had all been in vain, and many had been cut down trying to flee.

Despite the mist, the sounds of battle were drawing ever closer, more distinct. Now he could hear battle cries, shouts of triumph and anguish, and something he never expected to hear: horses' hooves.

They were entering one of the few sections on the causeway where it broadened out a little, the dense scrub retreating up the hillside. Halting his men again, Sphax yelled, 'Cirta, Manissa, Juba. Join my line at the front. Form ranks of six behind me. All of you, be alert and raise javelins!' Six men could easily march abreast in this section, and six javelins hurled as a volley was better than three.

Out of nowhere and without warning Sphax suddenly heard hooves beating towards them. 'Javelins!' he screamed.

Three horsemen loomed out of the mist. He saw they were Gauls. 'Lower shields and javelins,' he cried, immensely relieved to be able to give the order.

'Sphax!' shouted one of the men, mounted on a magnificent grey stallion. 'In the name of Morrigu, can it really be you?'

A moment later Sphax found himself staring up into the winter-blue eyes of the Insubres chieftain, Ducarius, who promptly burst into laughter. When his mirth subsided he gestured to his companions; 'Gentlemen,' he boomed, 'I have the honour to present Hannibal's nephew, Sphax, Prince of Numidia.'

Unlike the last time they'd met in the glade beside Artula's funeral pyre, Ducarius was wearing his finest war gear. Beneath his horned helmet, his long fair hair spilled onto the shoulders of a magnificent mail coat.

Despite the sombre surroundings and his dark mood, Sphax managed a smile. 'Unfortunately, Sir, I only bring sixty men with me. But they are at your service. We have already taken a thousand prisoners which the rest of my Numidians are guarding.'

'See what I mean, Lenu!' exclaimed Ducarius. 'These warriors have already accounted for a thousand of the devils.'

'But what of the battle, Sir?' questioned Sphax, desperate for news. 'Magol and the Boii … the Iberians and Libyans? Do we have victory?'

'I know nothing of the Iberians and Libyans, but the Insubres and Boii have slaughtered many. Magol lives, but the Boii have suffered grievously. I myself was riding to summon reinforcements. Flaminius has rallied his legions and is threatening to break through—'

'—Flaminius must not be allowed to escape,' Sphax hissed with venom, 'I've come here to kill him.'

Ducarius was taken aback, smile evaporating in an instant. 'Mine is the greater claim, Numidian. He's butchered and enslaved so many of my people. Long have I sworn his head will adorn my hall.'

Sphax erupted, 'What greater claim could there be than a son's duty to avenge the deaths of his mother and father!'

For a heartbeat Ducarius stared at him, speechless. 'Is this true?' he asked finally, almost in a whisper.

'Legionaries butchered them on Flaminius' orders. I myself was forced to watch as they slit my mother's throat. I was spared for slavery.'

A hushed silence now hung around the gathering. His own men hadn't understood a word of the Latin, but they'd recognised the name, Flaminius, and its significance for their captain.

'Now I understand the meaning of the dream Morrigu sent me,' said Ducarius at last. 'Did I not tell you we would meet again? In my dream you appeared as an avenging demon wielding a flaming spear, just like that iron javelin you hold in your right hand.' Sphax realised he was referring to his saunion, which was a forearm longer than a wooden javelin. 'Until now,' continued Ducarius, 'I've never seen such a weapon.'

Ducarius fell silent for a moment, lost in thought. 'It would appear that Morrigu has yet to reveal our true destiny.' Slowly he drew his sword from the sheath belted at his waist, a long Gaulish blade with gold-ribbed hilt and silver pommel. 'There was another flaming weapon in my dream. I'm holding it in my hand.'

Riddles within riddles, thought Sphax. Time was being wasted on this nonsense. 'Then let us strike a bargain, Ducarius: Flaminius' life is mine, but his head is yours.'

'Agreed!' roared the chief, 'It's a fair exchange.'

Out of curiosity to discover what was going on, Gauda's eshrin had already joined them. Now Sphax turned to him, raising his voice so all could hear. 'Flaminius is trying to rally his legions and break through the Insubres' ranks. We'll follow Ducarius and do what we can.'

At last the mist seemed to be lifting a little as they followed in the wake of the three riders. They didn't have to walk far. Ahead, Sphax could now see the Insubres, most of them naked above the waist, bunched together in groups of a score or more. As they drew closer he saw that many had been wounded, not grievous wounds that forced men from the field, but deep cuts and slashes, sorely in need of stitching and binding. But for proud Gauls, these were mere trophies to be displayed as a testament to their courage. The other thing he noticed was that many looked utterly exhausted.

Of the hundreds he could see, few had helmets, let alone fine mail coats like Ducarius. For Gauls, battle was decided by sword and shield. As he rode amongst his men the chief raised his voice and began what Sphax guessed was a rallying speech. Other than the word Numidia, the Gallic was lost on his ears, but it did seem to rouse the men.

'Let's take a closer look,' he said to Gauda. Together they began to weave their way through to the front line. It was an unnerving sight. Fifty paces away stood the ranks of Rome, brazen, defiant and as yet, undefeated.

It reminded him of the sight they'd met earlier when facing the centurion's little army. But this line stretched into the mist and was four ranks deep in places. Despite its appearance of strength and solidity, the closer Sphax looked, the more he realised this was simply another ragged collection of desperate men, rounded up to make a last stand. In the front rank velites stood beside hastati, Lucanians next to equites.

It was a perfect standoff: the Insubres were exhausted, and the ramshackle ranks they faced lacked the leadership to decide on anything other than to stand. Long ago, Rome had decided the citizens of its legions must never be taught to think for themselves. After all, they were merely peasants and plebeians, fodder, incapable of thought. Only consuls, tribunes and centurions made decisions.

Legions fought in maniples, three ranks deep, a hundred and fifty strong, each line supported by a similar line, fifty paces to their rear. They never fought like this. And to their rear lay a deep lake. If this single fragile line was fractured, there could be no hope of escape.

However, as testimony to their courage, scattered on the road before them lay a good many Insubres, none of whom would be leaving the field as wounded.

'Do you see how many pila they've wasted, lad?' Jugurtha observed. 'There's scores of 'em lying on the ground.' Sphax hadn't noticed his veteran scout and Agbal joining him at the front. He might have known. At the mention of the name Flaminius, these two became his shadows.

'We can take them, captain!' Agbal chimed in. 'Between us and Captain Gauda's eshrin we have almost three hundred javelins. That should thin them out.'

Sphax's mind was racing. 'What do you think, Gauda?'

'Jugurtha's right, Sphax, they don't seem to have many pila left, so all they could fling at us are spears, and for most of them that's the only weapon they've got left. We should be able to risk throwing from close range.'

Numidians practised hurling javelins on foot as often as they did on horseback. With a throwing thong and a short run, they could easily throw sixty paces.

But in that instant something else caught Sphax's attention. To the south four horsemen emerged from the mist and brazenly began to walk their stallions along the length of the legion's line. One of them seemed to be addressing the men. Whenever he stopped, cheering broke out. Sphax stared, transfixed. As the four drew closer his blood ran cold with a sight he'd dreaded yet longed for all day. One of the horsemen was Gaius Flaminius Nepos.

Agbal had been wrong. His helmet was not made of gold but burnished bronze, topped by the figure of Scylla, from which three dyed horsehair tassels flowed onto the shoulders of his finely woven mail coat. But he'd been right about one thing. Flaminius' dun-coloured stallion was draped in the skin of a tiger, an encumbrance the poor creature must surely resent.

Flaminius addressed his men no more than sixty paces from where Sphax was standing, before turning around and disappearing once more into the mist.

To prove he was master of his demons, Sphax met Jugurtha's and Agbal's expressions of concern with a sour smile, knowing they'd been watching him like hawks.

Now on foot, Ducarius barged his way towards them. 'Did you see that arrogant bastard?' growling through gritted teeth. 'I'll give him this: he's got some nerve!'

All Sphax had seen was a man acting with leadership and considerable courage. Ignoring the chief's comments, he carefully explained the plan he'd worked out. When he'd finished Ducarius nodded. 'So, you're going to fight like velites, eh?'

'Exactly so,' Sphax agreed. 'If it works — and I can't guarantee it will — at some point they will either break ranks and run for it, or they'll charge forward to kill their tormentors. In other words — *us*! There will only be one such moment, one opportunity. Your men must be ready to seize it. Once our javelins are gone, my Numidians will be defenceless.'

'I understand,' Ducarius solemnly acknowledged, 'I swear we will not let you down. I will go and prepare my warriors for one last charge.'

His first thoughts were that the eshrins should charge forward together to deliver their volleys. But they would have had to retreat, thread fresh javelins then run forward again. It would be slow and spread their efforts over too wide a front. There had to be a better way.

When Gauda returned with both eshrins, Sphax began organising them into three lines, one behind the other with wide gaps between the men in each line. Lines extended to about forty paces. If this was to work, he'd decided, speed was of the essence, and for maximum effect they had to concentrate their efforts on a small section of the Roman line. He'd used the same tactic at the Trebia, but that had been on horseback. Still, Sphax reckoned, the principle was the same.

Laughter broke out in the enemies' ranks when Sphax began to organise, followed by taunting and insults questioning their gender. Latin was wasted on his men, but it was beginning to get under his skin. Evidently Rome didn't have a high opinion of Numidians.

His men were ready. With a glance to check that Ducarius was marshalling his warriors, Sphax placed himself in the middle of the first line and threaded a javelin. 'Aim high,' he yelled. 'Throats and faces. Ready … charge.'

Charge seemed an inappropriate order for a few running strides forward, but he couldn't bring himself to shout *run*! At fifteen paces from the enemy line they couldn't miss. A few desultory spears were thrown as they jogged back through the open gaps in the next two lines, but none found their mark, and the jeering had ceased.

Gauda's line were delivering their volley by the time Sphax had threaded his next javelin. Striding forward to keep in step with Jugurtha's line, all he could hear now were cries of agony. When Gauda's men returned through the gaps, Jugurtha's line sprang forward. Levelling his weapon and tightening the thong, Sphax strode forward to where Jugurtha's men had stood. It would be his turn next.

Orders were now unnecessary: the cue for each successive charge was men returning through their ranks and clearing the field. Every dash forward was followed by a sickening chorus of searing pain as javelins found the gaps between bronze, iron and wood, chinks revealing flesh and bone to be pierced and shattered. It took no more effort than their morning javelin exercise. Except this wasn't target practice, it was cold-blooded murder.

As Sphax's second javelin pierced the cheek of an unfortunate Lucanian, he could see from their expressions of terror the enemy couldn't take much more of this. Desperately they were trying to replace the fallen with men from either flank, but they couldn't fill the gaps fast enough. As he began to run back to his mark, several broke ranks to chase their tormentors. Sphax had prepared his men for this eventuality. Gauda's line simply moved forward early to pick them off.

It was Jugurtha's charge that decided it. Before his men had time to launch another murderous volley, the enemy's decimated ranks simply turned on their heels and fled for their lives. With less than a hundred javelins, his Numidians had torn a forty yard gap in the enemy's line.

But Sphax knew it was far from over.

'Attack the flanks!' he yelled. 'Gauda's eshrin to the right, mine to …' But he never finished the order. Even if he had, no one would have heard it.

In that instant carnyx wailed and the frenzied battle cries of three hundred Insubres rent the air as they leapt forward in a last savage charge. Sphax's only concern was that his men might be trampled to death by the eagerness of the Insubres to close with the enemy. He need not have worried.

Before a single Insubres blade came anywhere near the enemy, the rest of the legions' ranks simply disintegrated and melted away in a stampede to the south.

Sphax had witnessed such sights before on the field of battle. Fear could spread like a contagion, a wildfire, until it brought about a complete moral collapse. In one moment men appeared to be standing firm with courage and determination, and, in the space of a heartbeat they were running for their lives, casting aside shields and armour, anything that would impede their flight.

Looking over his shoulder he saw the Insubres were astonished at this turn of events and had halted, unsure what to do next. Sphax could see Ducarius, mounted on his grey stallion, frantically waving his sword and bellowing at his men to continue the advance.

'Gauda,' he shouted over to the captain, 'retrieve our javelins then lead both our eshrins in the Insubres' advance.' Eyeing Jugurtha and Agbal wearily he added, 'You two may as well come along. You'll follow me anyway.'

Stepping gingerly over the detritus of battle, Sphax led the way to the lakeshore. The mist was lifting quickly now, revealing such sickening sights Sphax had to look away. Reaching the lakeshore, they continued south. With a sinking heart, somewhere ahead still wreathed in mist, Sphax heard again the sounds of raging battle. Would this day never end? he thought. How long could men go on killing one another?

Fighting back his mounting despair he trudged on to where lakeshore and mountainside were only separated by the width of the road. As the mist cleared and swirled in wraiths over the waters of the lake it revealed a chilling sight.

Mounted on his tiger-clad stallion and surrounded by a score or more desperate fugitives, Flaminius appeared to be trying to rally them one last time.

For a fleeting moment Sphax felt again the unbearable torment of fire and ice. But something had changed. Fire had condemned his dear friend Hannon and two others to a martyr's death. If ice could be melted, would it quench the fire? For years his cup had overflowed with the bile of bitterness and hatred; it had become part of him, embodied, like a second skin, as inescapable as his shadow.

Would the hurling of a javelin make it go away? Disappear like this mist? Was vengeance a mere conjuring trick? Sphax was jolted from his thoughts by a firm hand on his shoulder.

It was Jugurtha. 'Only the death of that bastard will end the slaughter,' he said gravely. 'After Hannon was slain, me and Agbal want him to pay. But no one has a greater claim than you. It's justice, lad … not vengeance.'

This might end a battle, thought Sphax, but would it end the war within himself? Jugurtha and Agbal were staring at him as he threaded his saunion. They too threaded javelins.

As the three of them stalked forward Agbal said, 'We'll soon have company. Ducarius and his two lieutenants.'

Sphax could hear the hoofbeats, but now he only had eyes for one man. Thirty paces away, all Sphax could see of the consul was his back. The men he was addressing looked so utterly broken and defeated, they no longer posed a threat to anyone.

Sphax had a sudden overwhelming urge to hear Flaminius' voice. Drawing closer he came within earshot. 'Have you no discipline? Pride?' the consul was bellowing. 'Sons of Rome, have you no honour?'

'Why should they listen to you, Gaius Flaminius,' Sphax screamed, 'when you yourself have none? Come forward and face my challenge.'

Viciously yanking on his reins, the consul managed to turn his snorting stallion around to face his challenger. No more than twenty paces apart, their eyes locked on one another.

'And who are you, boy?' Flaminius sneered with utter contempt, 'I like to know the names of those I kill.'

'I am the son of Navaras, Prince of Numidia, and Similce Barca. I'm here to avenge them. It is fitting their names will be the last you hear before I cast you into Hades.'

For a heartbeat the consul hesitated. Had he remembered the names? Recalled the events? Sphax would never know, for in that instant Flaminius levelled his spear and dug his knees into the tiger skin. Sphax allowed the creature two strides before hurling his saunion with a strength he never knew he possessed.

His saunion pierced the consul's neck, sailing clean through. This was followed by two more wooden javelins, flung with such force they sent him sprawling from his mount. Trotting harmlessly past Sphax, the stallion left its master gurgling on the ground, choking on his own blood.

Staring into the consul's lifeless dark eyes, Sphax realised this was just another Roman corpse, one amongst thousands. As Agbal strode forward to wrench two javelins and a precious saunion from the body, Sphax felt a familiar hand on his shoulder.

'Let us leave this place, Jugurtha,' he said.

As Sphax turned away a horseman swept past, reining in his stallion beside Flaminius' body he leapt from the saddle. Placing a sandaled boot unceremoniously on the corpse's chest, he began unstrapping the tasseled helmet before flinging it aside. Unsheathing a long slim blade with glinting silver pommel he reached down, grabbed Flaminius by his thick black curls and raised the head to expose a bloodied neck. With a deft, scything stroke he cleaved Flaminius' head from his wretched body.

Ducarius raised his grizzly trophy aloft, still dripping blood. 'Flaminius is slain!' he yelled in triumph. 'Flaminius is slain! Victory is ours!'

But Sphax and his two companions saw none of this. For them, Ducarius' cries of victory signified nothing more than empty words. It was over. Not one of them cast a backwards glance as they trudged wearily back along the shoreline, through the limp dead and moans of the dying, wrapped in a deep silence.

HISTORICAL NOTES

Though it may seem like a novelist's flight of fancy, the written evidence for Hannibal's elaborate disguises is undeniable. All the historical sources mention it, invariably as evidence of Carthage's capacity for subterfuge and deception. Polybius, somewhat disparagingly, describes Hannibal's wigs and outfits as a 'truly Punic artifice.' As a stark reminder, Hannibal's brother-in-law, Hasdrubal the Fair, was murdered by a slave as a result of a Keltoi conspiracy.

As that terrible winter of winters turned to spring in the Po valley (Gallic: Podanus) and the campaigning season loomed, Hannibal was faced with a dilemma. He knew through his extensive network of informants that the consuls elect that year (217 BC) were Gnaeus Servilius and Gaius Flaminius Nepos. He also learned (again, probably through informants rather than his Numidian scouts) that Servilius had been assigned to guard the eastern flank of the Apennines, based at Ariminum (modern day Rimini), whilst Flaminius was encamped outside Arretium (modern day Arezzo) watching the western flank. Each was in command of a consular army consisting of two Roman legions and two allied legions (roughly 25,000 men).

Where to strike? That was Hannibal's dilemma. Both routes offered geographical advantages and stubborn obstacles. The eastern route offered easy passage down the Adriatic coastal plain, but if Hannibal was to threaten Rome, at some stage he would have to find a pass over the Apennines. If he took the shorter western route, crossing the Apennines would place him in the heartlands of Etruria, bountiful in everything from olives to wheat. Only one thing stood in his way: the Arno marshes (Latin: Arnus).

Encompassing hundreds of square miles, the annual flooding of the Arno river would present an almost impenetrable barrier for any army attempting to march south. According to classical sources, the winter of 218-217 BC was one of the worst in living memory. Therefore I feel it safe to assume the extent of the flooding would be unprecedented in the spring of 217 BC.

Probably what decided it for Hannibal was not geography, but personality. We know that he studied his opponents carefully: their strengths, flaws and foibles were just as important as the number of legions they commanded, and whereas Servilius was a steady, level-headed patrician, Flaminius was anything but. The consul charged with guarding the western approaches to Rome had acquired the reputation of an arrogant hothead, who would not listen to reason, let alone advice. Furthermore, the Insubres and Boii loathed him.

Both Polybius and Livy (the most reliable classical sources) are somewhat lacking in their descriptions of the remarkable passage of the Carthaginian army through the Arno marshes. Polybius describes in detail the order of march, which is in itself revealing, if not slightly sinister.

Hannibal knew the Gauls would straggle and fall behind, perhaps even turn back when the going got tough. So why place all the Numidian cavalry in the rear unless they were there to spur on the Gauls and deter them from retreating by the threat of javelins? Why Hannibal, or his guides for that matter, hadn't considered the catastrophic effect upwards of fifty thousand boots would have had on the state of the ground beneath their feet, completely defeats me. In the rear of the column, the Gauls and Numidians must have been squelching through churned up mud that reached to their calves!

What we do know is that the army endured three nights without sleep (foot soldiers snatched some sleep by lying on the carcasses of dead pack horses), that the Gauls suffered grievously, and that Hannibal, riding the only surviving elephant, suffered a severe attack of ophthalmia and lost the sight in one of his eyes.

It seems scant description for what must have been a supreme test of endurance on such an epic scale it can be compared with the crossing of the high Alps.

One of the most intriguing references in the classical sources is the mysterious appearance of a Carthaginian naval squadron sighted off Pisa (Latin: Pisae). Livy mentions them again, some weeks later, intercepting Roman merchant vessels off Cosa. Whether the vessels were there by prior arrangement with Hannibal's brother Hasdrubal, in Iberia, or the squadron was sent directly from Carthage, history remains silent. From the extant texts it would appear that Hannibal ignored them, making no attempt at contact. I don't believe this for a moment. Hannibal would be just as intrigued to know what they were doing there as I am, over two thousand years later!

The maritime episode in *To Kill a Consul* explores these possibilities and re-acquaints readers with Tarbo, an irascible character from *The Walls of Rome*. Adherbal was governor of Gades (Cadiz). His only claim to notoriety is leading a fleet to its total destruction at the hands of a Roman squadron in the naval battle of Carteia in 206 BC.

Consul Flaminius watched the burning of Etruria from the walls of Arretium. He was said to be incandescent with rage, and against all the advice of his military tribunes and staff pleading for him to wait for Servilius' legions, he broke camp and chased after the Carthaginians. This sealed his fate, along with his army. Hannibal selected his opponents carefully; he seemed to possess the uncanny ability to judge character and temperament to the extent that he could second guess their every move.

South of the town of Cortona, Hannibal changed the direction of the march, striking out south east towards Lake Trasimene and the city of Perusia. There has been much conjecture about this change of direction. Rome lay due south, not to the south-east. If indeed it was ever his intention to threaten Rome, this route was taking him away from the city. On the other hand, this road led through rugged, mountainous terrain, ideally suited to trap or ambush an army bent on headlong pursuit. Perusia (modern day Perugia) would also put him in striking distance of the Via Flaminia, the main Roman artery linking Ariminum on the northern Adriatic coast with Rome. If Servilius was to join forces with his fellow consul, he would have to march south on the Flaminia.

Putting the question of Rome aside for a moment, I think Hannibal's intentions are self- evident: find a strong position along the line of march where Flaminius' army could be brought to battle and crushed (bearing in mind the Carthaginians had twice the numbers of the consul's army), then straddle the Flaminia so as to block Servilius' path south to Rome.

Hannibal found such a position beside the shores of Lake Trasimene. In the novel I've tried to describe the terrain in as much detail as possible, but the truth of the matter is that the lake's shoreline has changed so much over two millennia, military historians are still unsure of the exact location of the battlefield. However, this much is clear; the consul's army was strung out for at least four miles along a narrow strip of land between the lake and a steep ridge down which the Gauls, Iberians and Libyans launched their devastating charges.

What is not clear is how Hannibal managed to marshal over fifty thousand men into position on a rugged hillside in the dead of night and in perfect silence. Even for a modern army using satellite navigational aids and electronic communication, a night march such as this would present considerable challenges. For a mercenary army that spoke no less than five different languages, it's nothing short of miraculous!

My account of this night march is pure speculation. But without the use of lanterns or some form of lighted beacons to guide men and horses in the darkness, I just don't see how this was possible.

Even today Lake Trasimene is prone to mists that shroud the lakeshore. On that fateful June morning all accounts describe an impenetrable mist descending: 'in that enveloping mist ears were a better guide than eyes: it was sounds, not sights, they turned to face — the groans of wounded men, the thud or ring of blows on body or shield, the shout of onslaught, the cry of fear' (Livy).

As for the battle itself; it wasn't so much a battle as a slaughter. Entire swathes of Flaminius' army were hacked to pieces where they stood in marching order. The bloodbath continued for three weary hours. Both

Polybius and Livy estimate Rome's losses at fifteen thousand men, but there is some confusion as to whether this refers to the dead, or includes wounded or those who'd surrendered. Either way, Flaminius' army had ceased to exist.

Legend has it that the Insubres chieftain Ducarius killed Gaius Flaminius Nepos. Polybius lays the entire Trasimene disaster squarely on the shoulders of Gaius Flaminius, whereas Livy is more generous, maintaining the consul was always in the thick of the fight. After the battle, Hannibal initiated a thorough search for the consul's body so he could be buried with full honours, but he was never found. My description of Flaminius' extraordinary appearance is taken from Silius Italicus' epic poem *Punica*.

Somehow, six thousand men at the head of the consul's army, perhaps hidden by the mist, managed to break through the ranks of Carthaginians barring their way. Once clear above the mist they saw the slaughter taking place beside the lakeshore and realised it would be futile to attempt to rescue their comrades. Seeking out sanctuary was their only hope. Then there was the earthquake. But that's a story for next time …

Dear Reader!

Thank you so much for reading *To Kill a Consul.* If you have enjoyed the story, I would really appreciate it if you took the trouble to write a review on the site where you purchased the novel. Just a simple sentence is always helpful! If, like me, your favourite place to buy books is from a bookshop on the high street, you can still write a review on Goodreads or any site where you enjoy sharing your passion for books. Please contact me on my website if you have any questions about Sphax and his adventures. I'd love to hear from you!

www.robertmkidd.com

goodreads

I'm also on

Facebook & Twitter

If you would like to read more about Sphax's adventures, why not try the first book in The Histories of Sphax Series — *The Walls of Rome.*

The Walls of Rome

THE HISTORIES OF SPHAX SERIES

BOOK 1

218 BC. Sphax is seventeen and haunted by the brutal murder of his parents at the hands of Rome. After ten years of miserable slavery he will make his last bid for freedom and go in search of Hannibal's army and his birthright. He will have his revenge on the stinking cesspit that is Rome!

Destiny will see him taken under the wing of Maharbal, Hannibal's brilliant general, and groomed to lead the finest horsemen in the world – the feared Numidian cavalry that would become the scourge of Rome.

From the crossing of the great Rhodanus River, Sphax's epic journey takes him through the lands of the Gaul to the highest pass in the Alps. This is the story of the most famous march in history. A march against impossible odds, against savage mountain Gauls, a brutal winter and Sphax's own demons.

Reviews from book bloggers

Robert's writing is so impressive that it's hard to believe it was his debut novel. Wonderfully rich in historic detail, the plot is grounded around actual historical settings and characters. The fast pacing narration, great action-packed scenes, and the description of the locations, weaponry, tribes of Gaul, and the different battle techniques of the Numidian cavalry immersed me in the story. I was drawn in and didn't want to put this down.

Sumit

The writing is wonderful. The descriptive nature of this book just let me get lost in the story. Not only is this story descriptive, it's also fast-paced and riveting. I didn't want to put this down.

Jessica Belmont

The Winter of Winters

THE HISTORIES OF SPHAX SERIES

BOOK 2

218 BC. Hannibal's exhausted army staggers down from the last Alpine pass like a rabble of half-starved savages, the remnants of a once magnificent army that had set out from the Rhodanus with such hope. Now there is no way back. With the legions of Consul Publius Scipio closing fast, Carthage needs its Gaulish allies like never before. But where are the Insubres? Where are the Boii? Where are the thousands of warriors pledged by solemn oath?

In the maelstrom of battle, Sphax, nephew of Hannibal, forges a reputation as the scourge of Rome. But will his ingrained recklessness and quest for honour set him at odds with the forbidding genius of his uncle? Only one thing is certain in this winter of winters, a great battle is coming that will decide the fates of Rome and Carthage.

Reviews from book bloggers

If you are someone who enjoys historical fiction I would definitely recommend this book, everything about it is amazing!

Sophie — bookreviewaholic.blog

I love this book. I typically enjoy historical fiction like this, but this one really stood out to me.

The pacing is phenomenal, and really kept me glued to the pages from start to finish. The suspense and action picks up and slows down nicely in a way which kept me interested, but not overwhelmed.

This is one of my favourite reads so far this year, and I can't wait to read more of the series.

Veronica — babybackbooks

The first book was so good I was hoping Robert M Kidd had continued on his A-game for this one, well, for me he had. The story is as immersive and compelling as the first.

Everything about this book had me glued to it. The battle is an epic one and had me speeding through the pages faster than I was before that.

Will be waiting for Robert's next one and hoping it is soon. He has a love for this historical period and it shines through every word in the book.

Sharon Rimmelzwaan — sharonbeyondthebooks

Hostage of Rome

THE HISTORIES OF SPHAX SERIES

BOOK 3

217 BC. Rome has been savaged, beaten and is in retreat. Yet, in that winter of winters, her garrisons cling on behind the walls of Placentia and Cremona, thanks to her sea-born supplies. If he could be freed, a hostage of Rome may yet hold the key to launching a fleet of pirates that could sweep Rome from the seas. For that hostage is none other than Corinna's son Cleon, rival heir to the throne of Illyria, held in Brundisium, four hundred miles south of the Rubicon.

But Hannibal is set on a greater prize! Macedon is the great power in Greece, feared even by Rome. Its young king, Philip, is being compared with his illustrious ancestor, Alexander the Great. An alliance with Macedon would surely sound the death knell for Rome.

Given Hannibal's blessing, Sphax, Idwal and Corinna face an epic journey against impossible odds. Navigating the length of the Padus, past legionary garrisons and hostile Gauls, they must then risk the perils of the storm-torn Adria in the depths of the winter. If the gods favour them and they reach the lands of the pirate queen, only then will their real trials begin.

Reviews from book bloggers

The Hostage of Rome is a thrilling ride you'll love to be part of … a tremendous tale packed full of energy and excitement. Fans of the genre will love this one.

Davidsbookblurg.co.uk

The author's a wonderful story teller; his ability to weave historical detail into the very fabric of his writing, seamlessly mixing fact and fiction, his attention to detail, his world building, all truly exceptional ... and what a tremendous cast of characters.

Felicity Grace Terry

Printed in Dunstable, United Kingdom

65928388R00241